THE PLAYGROUND

Michelle Frances has worked in television drama as a producer and script editor for several years, both for the independent sector and the BBC. *The Playground* is her sixth novel, following *The Boyfriend*, *The Girlfriend*, *The Temp*, *The Daughter* and *Sisters*.

THE PLAYGROUND

MICHELLE FRANCES

PAN BOOKS

First published 2023 by Pan Books
an imprint of Pan Macmillan
The Smithson, 6 Briset Street, London EC1M 5NR
EU representative: Macmillan Publishers Ireland Ltd, 1st Floor,
The Liffey Trust Centre, 117–126 Sheriff Street Upper,
Dublin 1, D01 YC43
Associated companies throughout the world
www.panmacmillan.com

ISBN 978-1-5290-4968-8

1 3 5 7 9 8 6 4 2

A CIP catalogue record for this book is available from the British Library.

Typeset in Sabon by Palimpsest Book Production Ltd, Falkirk, Stirlingshire
Printed and bound by CPI Group (UK) Ltd, Croydon, CR0 4YY

Visit **www.panmacmillan.com** to read more about all our books
and to buy them. You will also find features, author interviews and
news of any author events, and you can sign up for e-newsletters
so that you're always first to hear about our new releases.

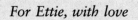

For Ettie, with love

Sticks and stones will break my bones
But words will never hurt me.

Nineteenth-century rhyme

I would rather be a little nobody, than to be an
evil somebody.

Abraham Lincoln

ONE

Thursday 3 September

Nancy had always wanted a circular driveway. Ever since she was a little girl. She had seen a Disney movie where a carriage had pulled up, led by snow-white horses and a girl in a floaty gown had stepped out. Or something. She couldn't quite remember but it was the sense of arrival that had stuck with her. Of owning the home you'd always dreamed of.

She drove her car slowly around the gravel circle, then after her mammoth drive, she finally stopped. Switched off her new electric Tesla and tentatively patted it, as if to say: *thank you for getting me here*. She'd only had it a couple of weeks and was still getting used to it. She then turned and gazed at her new house.

It was all hers. One hundred per cent owned outright.

And it was the first house she'd ever bought in her life.

Willow Barn was nothing like a barn in the traditional sense. It had made her laugh when she'd first heard its name, sitting despondently at the kitchen table in a poky two-bedroomed flat in London, where the very air they breathed was polluted by the poisonous fumes floating up from the traffic-packed South Circular road below them. As far as Nancy knew, barns were buildings that were cold and draughty where farmers stored hay. But Gemma the estate agent was on the phone, telling her that she might have found 'the one'. And the pictures that arrived in her inbox were breathtaking.

Gleaming black-framed windows that reached from the slate roof right down to the ground, stretching the length of the building. Airy vaulted ceilings. Solid oak staircases that led up to sizeable bedrooms with balcony views over the largest reservoir in Derbyshire: Heron Water, a nature's paradise. Three acres of gardens that included woods and even an orchard. Nancy had clicked through, her jaw dropping more with every photo. Some of the rooms admittedly weren't to her taste. The previous owners had had a tendency to go for decor that was apparently the latest trend; in this case walls that were painted a mix of dark grey or deep blue with a hint of grey, or crimson with a grey hue. All colours that in Nancy's unsophisticated opinion resembled the water in the paint pot once the kids in the children's ward where she used to work had rinsed their brushes. But she could change all that and the potential – my God, the potential! . . . It was magnificent.

The absolute best thing about the barn was its position. Heron Water formed the shape of a swift in flight: a head, forked tail and two wings spread wide, the feathers marked by dozens of inlets lined with reeds and trees. Nancy's house-to-be lay under the bird's right wing. In the photo that she'd stared at, Nancy could see the eponymous herons wading along the banks, the willow trees draping their branches into the water. It was this proximity to nature and the house's air of peace that made Nancy say yes. She was desperate for a change from London, a new start after a devastating eleven months. She thought that a move to the countryside, where the air was clean, where it was friendly, where there would be a strong sense of community, this would be the best thing for both her and her ten-year-old daughter. Nancy had wanted a quick purchase, no chain. She'd wanted to get out of London the second the money was in her bank account. Willow Barn had a repossession order on it, so Nancy, being a cash buyer, had been able to pick it up at a bargain price and she'd pushed for the sale to go through as fast as possible so that Lara could make the start of the new term.

'Mum, look!' squealed Lara from the back seat.

Nancy turned her head in the direction her daughter was pointing. A V-formation of birds was flying low towards them. Were they ducks? Geese? Nancy had no idea. She had a lot to learn about the country. The birds, honking loudly, flew above the car then disappeared over the barn, presumably heading for the reservoir.

Lara was already opening her door in excitement and Nancy smiled as she followed. Lara ran down the side of the house, through the gate and into the back garden. Nancy saw trees that would be climbed, borders that were still full of the late summer gold of grasses and some rather lovely, but to her untrained eye, unidentifiable tall orange and pink flowers. In the orchard that was on the south side of the barn, she could see trees laden with apples, pears and plums. Ahead of them was a vast expanse of green lawn. Faced with such an inviting wide-open space, Nancy was suddenly filled with a child-like compulsion. She looked questioningly at Lara, unsure of whether it was a good idea, but Lara grabbed her hand. They held tight, laughing as they ran to the far end of the garden. For a brief moment, all Nancy's troubles fell away and she was liberated, carefree and full of joy.

They stopped at another gate and Nancy looked hawk-eyed at Lara.

'Are you OK?'

'I'm *fine*, Mum. The air tastes different here.'

Nancy looked again, just to reassure herself that her daughter had no problems breathing. 'It does,' she said. 'But that doesn't mean you can forget about your asthma pump.'

'I know, Mum,' said Lara impatiently. She looked through the gate down towards some steps: their own private access to the water itself. 'Can we go to the lake? Please?' she begged.

Nancy smiled but shook her head. 'Later. The removal vans will be here soon. We'll need to let the guys in with our boxes.'

'I want the holidays to last forever so I can explore and play in the garden.'

'School starts tomorrow. Nervous?'

'A bit. But excited to meet new friends.'

'*Loads* of new friends!'

They headed back up to the house and Nancy dug in her jacket pocket for the keys. She opened up the oversized grey front door and the large light hallway welcomed them.

'Can I explore, Mum?'

'Go ahead.'

Lara ran off, opening doors out of sight and Nancy heard squeals of 'It's so big!' and 'This is amazing!' from all over the house.

'I'm going upstairs,' called Nancy and headed for what was going to be her bedroom. She ignored the indigo-blue walls and dark grey carpet and made her way to the back of the room. She pulled open the long bi-fold doors and stepped out onto the balcony. *A balcony!* Never in her wildest dreams . . .

The warm breeze blew her auburn curls across her eyes and she tucked them behind her ear. Willow Barn was positioned high on the bank and she could see over the trees at the bottom of the garden out at her first proper sighting of Heron Water. It gleamed with a blue that was more akin to the sea in southern European climates, the sun glinting off its surface. The trees were still green and glossy, thick with foliage, but it wouldn't be long before they began to turn into a palette of red and gold.

It was utterly beautiful. Tranquil. More than that. Nancy searched for the word. Healing. That was what it was. For the first time in months she had a sense of hope.

TWO

Thursday 3 September

It was the horns that Imogen heard first. Frustrated drivers weren't unusual in the narrow village high street but by the cacophony she could hear out of the window, these car owners were clearly multiple and on a scale that was tipping into apoplectic.

Curious, Imogen wiped her hands on a cloth to clean off the pastry flour. Bruno's Cafe faced the high street and she headed for the window and looked out.

She reeled in surprise. There were one, two, three, she counted, massive removal vans in the road outside, each trying to get past the line of parked cars. They had blocked the road in each direction. Imogen watched as they moved forward determinedly, set on their task of getting to their destination, unable to reverse, having *no intention* of reversing.

A weight, solid as a stone, fell into the pit of her stomach. She was inexplicably reminded of old Second World War footage, enemy tanks rolling into French villages, conquering, flags aloft, taking everything that wasn't theirs. The tribal drumbeat of the soldiers' marching boots menacing as they advanced.

Imogen had a sudden urge to run out of the kitchen and stand in the middle of the road. Stop the advancement with her bare hands. As she watched, she caught her reflection in the glass of the windowpane. Her cool blonde hair was tied up, her chef's whites a reminder of what she was being paid to do. She was powerless, trapped in this kitchen with no prospect of leaving.

The procession continued outside. Imogen shook the earlier image from her head. There were no soldiers, no military tanks. Just removal vans.

She knew where they were going.

What she didn't know yet was who they belonged to.

THREE

Thursday 3 September

The sound of an engine broke her from her reverie. Nancy hurried in from the balcony and made her way back downstairs where she found Lara kneeling at the window seat in the hallway.

'Our stuff is here,' said Lara.

Nancy opened the front door as the three vans, their tyres crunching on the gravel, came around the circular driveway. The first driver hopped out, eating a sausage roll out of a paper bag.

'Nice place,' he said, looking up at the gleaming barn with undisguised admiration in his eyes. '*Really* nice.'

'Thanks,' said Nancy.

'You ready for us to get started?'

'Sure. Can I get you guys a tea? Coffee?'

'Three teas, three sugars.'

Nancy was confused. 'You mean three sugars *each*?'

'Yes please.' The driver returned to the van, where his colleagues were already opening up the back doors, ready to unload.

Nancy went to her car where she'd kept back a few essentials: a kettle, mugs, teabags. A sharp, sudden crack made her look up at the barn.

'Mum, it's a bird,' cried Lara. 'On the ground.'

Nancy went over to where her daughter was standing outside one of the huge windows. Lara was staring at a small bird that lay on its side on the earth. The eye facing upwards was open and to Nancy's mind it was staring into the middle distance, seemingly unable to understand what had happened. The bird was light brown and white with gold feathers at the base of its tail and a red patch on its head. It twitched pitifully, tiny movements that seemed to fade and grow less frequent. There was a mark on the window where it had struck it.

'Is it dead?' asked Lara, holding her breath.

God, she hoped not. Death had dealt too harsh a blow to her family of late. Nancy looked at her daughter's stricken face and prayed for a miracle. She went closer to the bird and, bending down, she carefully picked it up. It was lighter than she'd imagined, its tiny bones and feathers barely registering in her hands. She felt it twitch further and then it cocked its head, regaining awareness. She opened up her palms and to her immense relief the bird flew off up into the blue sky.

3 September
RIPTON PRIMARY, YEAR 6

Erin Mackie, Tilly's mum
Another traffic nightmare in Ripton.
Couldn't believe it when one of the three
removal vans even stopped right in the
middle of the high street to get a sausage
roll from Bruno's! Blocked the road entirely.
I was late for my high-impact class.
Grrr! 16:51

> **Lorna Fielding, Phoenix's mum**
> Did you get their company details off the
> side of the van? Email their boss! 16:52

Sarah Ramsay, Noah's mum
Oh that's not good. What if an ambulance
needed to get through? 16:54

> **Erin Mackie, Tilly's mum**
> I'm guessing they were going to Willow
> Barn. You OK, Imogen? 16:54

Imogen Wood, Rosie's mum
Yes, why wouldn't I be? 16:55

> **Lorna Fielding, Phoenix's mum**
> Has everyone got their uniform ready for
> tomorrow? Phoenix has grown out of his
> school shoes! Argh! 16:59

Erin Mackie, Tilly's mum
I have some news . . . can't hold it in as
I've just heard. You guys are looking at the
new editor and owner of the Ripton
Gazette! 17:00

> **Lorna Fielding, Phoenix's mum**
> OMG congrats! I can't believe you're going
> to be in charge of our local paper. We'd all
> better be on best behaviour in case you
> run a scoop on us 😩 17:01

Sarah Ramsay, Noah's mum
Could I get some church events advertised?
Mates rates? 17:02

> **Erin Mackie, Tilly's mum**
> Am happy to help where I can but even
> God needs to understand I have to make a
> profit. 17:02

Imogen Wood, Rosie's mum
Huge congratulations, my friend. At least
we know the news around here will be
covered fairly and in an unbiased way. 17:03

FOUR

Friday 4 September

The first day back at school was always nerve-racking but even more so when it was your first day at a brand-new school. Nancy glanced at Lara. Her daughter had always been confident at school. She'd thrived in lessons and had lots of friends, being gentler than some of the other more outgoing children. She was a normal kid with normal interests and normal friends. Then tragedy had struck and Lara had retreated into herself for months. Her teacher would pull Nancy aside at the end of the day saying Lara had spent the breaks wandering listlessly around the playground by herself. Her friends had tried to get her to join in the games, but Lara had shaken her head so many times, they'd drifted off. She'd been the same at home, spending hours gazing out of the window of their second-floor flat. It was only when they were making plans to move to a new house and get out of the city that Lara started to show tentative hints of her old spark.

Nancy squeezed Lara's hand. Lara smiled nervously then extracted her hand from her mother's as they crossed the road into Ripton Primary. Nancy hid a smile. This was a good sign. Lara was embarrassed to have her mum hold her hand. It meant she wanted to make a good impression on the other kids and get to know them quickly.

Nancy gazed across the playground. It was like a reunion of long-lost friends. Squeals of recognition as parents and children were reacquainted with those they hadn't seen for weeks. Nancy watched as women threw their arms around each other, faces aglow with the remnants of summer holiday suntans. Conversations were held at rapid speed, news was exchanged, all against the glossy backdrop of the first day of term. The kids in their brand-new uniforms, their shoes shiny and unscuffed; refreshed mums having made an effort with their clothes and make-up. There was an energy that Nancy could feel in waves but which she wasn't a part of. So engrossed was everyone in each other that she couldn't even catch anyone's eye and give a friendly smile.

She watched as the head teacher, James Whitman, toured the grounds in his suave suit, being welcomed like a revered leader as he approached each group of parents. The tight circles of mums would break open to let him join them, and they would stop talking and listen, basking in his charm. Nancy had had a Zoom call with James when she was applying to Ripton Primary back in the early summer. He'd had an impressive energy for a man in his late fifties and had made the school sound like a progressive establishment full of enthusiasm and opportunity. He'd let slip during the conversation that he advised government on education policies, had the ear of the Education Secretary herself. Nancy admired his achievements but also had an underlying sense he thought a lot of himself. She got an image of him in her mind, in an expensive suit, his sandy hair combed back, accepting an MBE from the King for services to education, and she stifled a laugh. She looked over at him again – he was deep in conversation with a cool blonde woman. Then he glanced up and she was caught in the full beam of his smile and – more cheeringly – his look of recognition. It only lasted a moment before his attention was taken by the cool blonde again and Nancy was returned to the role of Billy No-Mates.

Nancy suddenly pitched forward, open-mouthed with shock. A football had hit her on the head.

'Are you OK, Mum?' asked Lara, alarmed, as the ball, launched by Nancy's skull, bounced across the playground.

'Phoenix!' admonished a short woman but half-heartedly. 'I'm so sorry,' continued the woman, coming up to Nancy. 'He's mad on football, absolutely obsessed with it, and I do try and tell him to be careful. Are you all right?'

Nancy mustered up a smile. 'Yes,' she lied. Her head felt as if it was still vibrating.

'Phoenix!' called the woman. 'Come and apologize!'

But Phoenix either couldn't or didn't want to hear her and the woman let out a semi-exasperated sigh.

'I'm Lorna,' she said, holding out a hand but still keeping it close to her body, a bit like a T-Rex. 'Chair of the PTA.'

'Nancy,' she said, shaking Lorna's hand. 'Brand-new parent.'

'Welcome to Ripton,' said Lorna warmly. 'Once you're here, you'll never leave.'

Nancy turned to her daughter. 'This is Lara.'

'Nice to meet you, Lara. Whose class are you in?'

'Miss Young.'

'Oh, you're with Phoenix!' said Lorna. 'And Miss Young's lovely. Everyone here is lovely.'

That was statistically impossible, thought Nancy, but nevertheless nice to hear. It was good to know she'd moved somewhere friendly.

'I met her earlier in the week when I was in for a PTA catch-up. We're really lucky to have her. She's only young – twenty-five – but was one of the best teachers at her previous school. It was a real coup to get her – she had three other offers locally!'

Phoenix was busy kicking his football against a wall. Lorna rolled her eyes in a faux-vexed fashion. 'Practise. That's all he does. We've got our eye on Kingsgate for secondary. You know, the private school. It's the best educational establishment for miles. Their results are *incredible*.' She lay her hand briefly on Nancy's arm and lowered her voice. 'We're hoping . . . well, I shouldn't really say, but we're secretly hoping he'll get a sports scholarship. But keep it to yourself.'

Nancy gave a perplexed nod at this premature intimacy and made a mental note never to tell Lorna anything remotely confidential.

'Anyway, let me introduce you to some of the other mums.' Lorna coasted around. 'Oh, there's Erin. Erin!'

A woman dressed in expensive running gear nonchalantly walked over with a girl in tow.

'Put me to shame, you do,' said Lorna, looking at Erin's outfit.

'It's only 10K. Sets me up before I get to my desk,' said Erin.

'10K! I couldn't even run for the bus. Let me introduce you to my new friend, Nancy. Nancy, Erin used to play netball for England.'

'Wow,' said Nancy.

'World Championships. 2008.'

'Did you win?'

'No,' said Erin abruptly, her gaze suddenly elsewhere.

Sore subject, mouthed Lorna. 'They were robbed,' she said out loud, her voice loaded with sympathy. 'Erin has also just bought the local paper, the *Ripton Gazette*. One of the few still with a proper print run.'

The girl standing beside Erin looked at Lara. 'Which school are you going to next year?' she demanded.

Lara was taken aback. 'I don't know.'

'This is Tilly,' said Erin. 'She's in Year 6.'

'How far can you swim?' asked Tilly. 'I can swim three kilometres. No one believes me – well, except for Rosie because my mum told her it was true.'

God, she wasn't backwards in coming forwards, Nancy found herself thinking. She expected Erin to rein her daughter in from the boasting, but she said nothing.

'Oh, there's Hannah,' exclaimed Lorna, waving at another mum in the playground. 'Hannah's a farmer. She has six hundred acres, mostly sheep and arable. Her son is Jakob, he's in the same class as ours.'

Nancy saw a woman in scruffy jeans and a long-sleeved pink striped shirt walk over. She had dark curly hair that was tied up roughly on the top of her head and the bluest eyes Nancy had ever seen.

'Nancy's new,' announced Lorna.

'Welcome,' said Hannah. 'Been filling Nancy in with all the gossip, Lorna?'

Lorna flushed. 'Not gossip. Friendly chat. Hey, is anyone doing extra tutoring before the Kingsgate entrance exams?'

'Tilly's doubled to two evenings plus a Saturday morning,' said Erin. 'Although I'm pretty sure she's going to be OK. The tutor says she's already at Year 8 level in many subjects.' Erin bent down to speak to her daughter. 'Remember to make sure you mention this morning about eco schools. It'll get you more votes. You need to get this, you deserve it.'

'Votes?' asked Nancy.

'Head of School,' said Lorna. 'Traditionally, first day back the Year 6 kids get to vote for who they want. I'd put Phoenix forward but he's more sporty than an all-rounder.' She laughed, a little desperately, thought Nancy.

'The kids who want to stand are set a summer project to write their speech. Did no one tell you?'

'No,' said Nancy.

'Don't worry. We all know it's going to be Rosie anyway,' Lorna added under her breath.

'Rosie?'

Lorna nodded over to the blonde woman. 'Imogen's daughter.'

Nancy saw a girl with the sort of angelic blonde look that featured in upmarket clothing catalogues. It was obvious she took after her mother. Imogen was elegantly tall, with effortlessly dewy skin. Her long hair fell forwards over one shoulder, contrasting beautifully with the silver-grey blouse she was wearing with her impeccable white trousers. She looked faintly recognizable to Nancy, but she couldn't quite place her. She felt she'd seen her on TV or something, years ago. Maybe Imogen used to be on one of those plethora of lifestyle shows, but Nancy couldn't remember which one.

Imogen had stopped talking to the head and was looking over at them, a slight frown on her face. She started to approach and one by one the other women clocked her and turned towards her like flowers radiating towards the sun. Nancy was faintly aware of a nervous hush as they waited for Imogen to arrive.

'Imogen!' beamed Lorna quickly, in a one-woman race to be the first to welcome her.

'Hi, ladies,' said Imogen. 'Glad to be back?'

Lorna and Erin voiced their delight enthusiastically.

Then Nancy felt Imogen cast her gaze towards her.

'Hi,' said Nancy.

'Hello,' said Imogen.

'Nancy's new,' said Lorna.

'We've just moved here,' said Nancy.

'To Willow Barn,' said Lara.

Nancy looked down at her daughter and smiled. She was suddenly aware that it had gone deathly quiet. She looked up and none of the women were meeting her eye and Imogen had seemed to go rigid.

A bell rang from inside the school.

'Right,' said Hannah quickly. 'First day of the last year of primary school has officially started.' She waved to Jakob as he headed into the building.

'Remember, I'm going to drop your inhaler in the office so it's there if you need it,' Nancy said to Lara. She threw her arms around her and enveloped her in a hug that Lara tried to wriggle out of.

As Lara walked off, Nancy turned back to speak to the other mums but they had all drifted across the playground, away from her.

FIVE

Friday 4 September

'It's all got to be green. I'm ditching chemicals,' said Nancy, as she led the builder into the kitchen. He padded in in his socks and she'd been cheered that he had taken his shoes off at the front door. She liked that, liked the fact he was respectful. She also liked that he had his company logo on his polo shirt: Dean Chapman Builders. He had a kind face that was weathered permanently brown from at least two decades of working outside. 'I want to change this floor too,' she added, pointing. 'I know it looks new but it's laminate.'

'Oh?' said Dean.

'It gives off toxic fumes for the first ten years at least. Could I have natural limestone?'

'You can have anything you like,' said Dean.

'I want to replace the front door as well. It's drab. Much of this house is drab,' she mused, looking around at the pewter-coloured walls. They sucked the life out of the room. Nancy liked colour. Colour gave everything a sunny levity. Her own furniture was helping a little. Most of it she'd never seen in situ before. Moving from a tiny two-bedroomed flat to this large, airy, four-bedroomed barn meant she'd had to go shopping and she'd spent a few days wandering around sustainable furniture shops, picking out eight-seater dining tables with a beautiful oak grain and soft sofas the colour of cornflowers. She'd had a sense of guilt at first. Never before in her life had she been able to spend such sums. It was all for Lara, she'd reminded herself. It was what she and Sam, Lara's dad, had always dreamed of for her. Once purchased, all the furniture had gone into storage, only brought to life now, once she'd finally moved.

She switched on the kettle. 'Tea?'

'Yes, please,' said Dean, pulling a notebook from the back pocket of his shorts. 'So are you planning to redecorate?'

'God, yeah. This place needs cheering up. But the paint needs to be non-VOC. My daughter, she's got asthma. It gets aggravated easily.' Nancy had spent hours researching what was best and for the first time in her life she had some control over what Lara breathed in. The persistent mould on the walls and the formaldehyde from laminate in a rented flat was not something she had to suck up any more. She had the money to be able to provide a safe home for her child. 'And I mentioned the garden on the phone to you as well,' she continued. 'Do you have any experience of natural pools? You know, the ones you can swim in that are kept clear without any chlorine. Like wild swimming.' Nancy had come across a picture of one in a magazine in the hospital waiting room a few months ago. It was one of the most beautiful things she'd ever seen. A large pond – a pool, really – with crystal-clear water and bulrushes and purple irises growing around the edge. Giant rocks on one side formed both a jetty and diving-off point. It was idyllic, a picture that seemed as if it was from a more simple and innocent time. There was the reservoir, of course, but a natural pool would be private, warmer and somewhere Lara could play where she could keep an eye on her.

'That's a specialist job, but I know someone who could help you out,' said Dean. 'Did you say you only moved in yesterday?'

Nancy shrugged. 'I want to get it changed as soon as possible. And I quite fancy chickens. A coop or whatever it is you need for them.'

Dean laughed. 'Now that I can help you with. My wife is a farmer. Hannah.'

Nancy's eyes lit up in recognition. 'I think I met her this morning. At the school. With Jakob?'

'Yes, that's right. Village life. It's small. You'll get to know everyone and everyone will get to know you. And your business.'

Nancy smiled. 'Got nothing to hide.'

'Just as well. What made you choose Ripton?'

'I used to go to university in Derby, years ago. With a friend. She still lives in the city.'

'That's a way away.'

'Only thirty miles.'

'Might as well be three hundred. Chalk and cheese.'

She handed Dean the tea she'd made. 'Do you want to see the rooms that need decorating?'

'Sure.'

'Let's start upstairs.' She led him up to the bedrooms, opening the door of hers first. 'I was thinking of a light blue in here,' she said, walking over to the bi-fold doors, which she'd opened earlier. A soft breeze came into the room, lifting the curtains. The reservoir shone in the sunshine. 'Something to echo the colour of the water,' said Nancy, 'although I'm sure it can go every which shade depending on the weather.'

'It certainly can.'

'Have you swum in it?'

He laughed. 'Swimming's not my thing. But loads of people do. Some nutters go in all year round but there's also a start-of-season swim in March. To coincide with the Straw Bear Festival.'

'What's that?'

Dean pointed out of the bi-fold doors. 'See that yew tree?'

Nancy stepped onto the balcony. She wasn't sure what a yew was but further along the water's edge, towards the reservoir cafe, there was one particular tree that stood alone. It was huge, majestic. The trunk looked as if it was made of a collection of wooden stalagmites, all packed tightly together, out of which grew gnarled, crooked limbs.

'That's where I was standing in my straw bear outfit the night of the spring solstice, before being slain,' said Dean.

'Slain?'

'It's a village tradition. Every year someone from the village gets the joy of dressing from head to toe in a straw costume – you can't even see their face – and they parade through the village with the Spring Queen. When the bear reaches the two-thousand-year-old tree, it's "slain" by the Queen and the spirit of spring is released. Yeah, it's pretty nuts. But you know these centuries-old traditions, no one really wants to give them up.'

Nancy nodded, even though she personally thought the Straw Bear Festival sounded a little disturbing. 'Who's next year's bear?'

'Dylan Wood. Married to Imogen. You might have met her this morning too.'

Nancy thought of the beautiful blonde. 'I did.'

Then something caught her eye out in the water. She gasped and stepped forward, unable to truly make sense of what she was seeing.

'Is that a . . . *spire*?' she asked.

Way out in the centre of the reservoir, a tall, pyramidal stone point broke through the surface of the water, a black cross at its tip.

'Old church,' said Dean. 'The site of the reservoir used to be a hamlet – Wakeley Green. When they decided to flood it they moved some of the buildings but about eleven remain. At this time of year, when the water levels have dropped, you can see the roofs of some. Sometimes you'll have a view of the chimney pots too.'

The spire was darkened by decades of being submerged in the cold of the reservoir. No doubt it was slippery with algae. There was something ghostly about it and Nancy tried to imagine the rest of the church sunken beneath the surface. People's homes too. She shivered.

'You want to show me the rest of the house?' asked Dean. 'Then I can work up a quote for everything.'

'Sure,' said Nancy. She pulled her gaze from the water and led him out of the room.

SIX

Unpacking boxes was hungry work and Nancy had looked up from the mountain of protective paper she'd accumulated to see that it was lunchtime – and she was starving.

She walked into the village – her first proper exploration of the high street. Ripton was several hundred years old and the buildings were of the original warm grey stone with slate roofs. There was everything she could possibly need: a chemist, a local grocery that also housed a post office, a bookshop with all the latest titles displayed in its bay windows, a butcher's, a gift shop, a pub. She found herself wandering into them all, buying bits and pieces before remembering she had nothing in for dinner and her friend from university, Beth, was coming to visit for the weekend. She spotted a deli and it was when she came out, clutching a bag full of fresh pasta, a jar of homemade tomato sauce and three large slices of pecan pie, her stomach by now screeching with hunger, that she found herself jostling for space on the narrow pavement with an elderly lady.

'You're the new girl,' declared the lady, smiling. 'Moved into Willow Barn.'

Nancy, who had been about to cross over the road to a cafe to get some lunch, turned in surprise. So this was what Dean had warned her about . . . *everyone will get to know you. And your business.*

She looked at the elderly lady in her knee-length green mac and soft, wide-fitting shoes, the kind that allowed for bunions. A floral scarf set off the cheerful expression on her face as she waited for Nancy to answer.

'I am,' said Nancy, a touch distracted as she wondered how this woman could possibly know. Perhaps a new face stuck out a mile in this village, perhaps the woman had seen her going to her new house – or perhaps word had got about and she had been thoroughly discussed. But this lady was looking at her with a wide, friendly smile.

She put out her hand. 'Nancy,' she said. 'Pleased to meet you.'

'Hazel,' said the woman. 'I've lived in Ripton my whole life. All seventy-two years. Never had any reason to go anywhere else. You've definitely picked a good 'un.'

'Oh, excuse me,' she said, suddenly seeing something behind Nancy and she dug into her coat pocket, where she extracted an old metal tin that had once held travel sweets. Nancy saw Lorna approaching with a dog on a lead.

'Would Cooper like one?' asked Hazel and, barely waiting for Lorna's nod of approval, she fed the cocker spaniel a treat.

'Thanks, Hazel,' said Lorna. 'How's the exercise plan going?'

'I'm out here every day. Doctor's orders. "Got to get the blood sugar levels down." It's exhausting to tell you the truth. And not the same since I lost Sukey,' she added, her eyes welling up.

Lorna patted her arm. 'She was a lovely dog. And she did get to fourteen, you know. That's a ripe old age.'

'Thanks, love. Anyway, I've given up all my biscuits and I only have sweetener in my tea now. Hopefully that'll shut the doc up. Diabetes, my backside.'

Lorna turned to Nancy. 'Hazel's our resident dog whisperer. Been shopping?' she asked, looking at Nancy's bags.

'A few things for dinner.' Nancy nodded across the road. 'And I think I need a coffee.'

'You're going to Bruno's?' said Lorna.

Nancy thought she detected a note of alarm in her voice. 'Yes. Unless . . . it's a bad idea?'

'Not at all,' said Lorna hastily. 'In fact, mind if I join you?'

They settled themselves at a table, Cooper taking up residence underneath, resting his head on his paws and falling asleep.

'The food here's amazing,' said Lorna. 'Ah, there's the chef!'

Nancy looked up. A woman in chef whites, her blonde hair up in a bun, had just come out of the door that led to the kitchen.

'Imogen!' called out Lorna, waving.

Nancy could swear Imogen stiffened when she saw them, but she had no choice but to come over.

'Nancy dragged me in here for a coffee,' said Lorna.

It hadn't been like that at all, but Nancy didn't know how to correct her, and anyway, it shouldn't matter, should it?

'I needed a break from emptying boxes,' she said. 'You never realize how much stuff you can accumulate. And I only moved from a tiny two-bedroomed flat.'

'Well, enjoy,' said Imogen stiffly. 'I'd better get back into the kitchen.'

'She's a fantastic chef,' said Lorna, as Imogen turned away. 'With friends in high places!'

When Nancy didn't ask who, Lorna added in lowered tones: 'Nigel Slater. They've even worked together.'

Nancy smiled politely.

'So . . .' said Lorna, once they'd placed their order with the waiter, 'where in London have you moved from?'

Nancy didn't remember telling Lorna that she'd come from London and wondered how she knew.

'Lewisham.'

'Oh right.'

'You know it?'

'No.' Lorna paused. 'Does it have posh parts?'

Nancy let out a bark of laughter. 'What do you mean?'

'I thought the whole of London was posh . . . or at least cost a fortune to live in. Don't sheds go for a million quid or something?'

'Not exactly.'

'But property's worth a lot more than here, right? I mean, your old flat, for example . . . it would be more expensive to buy down there than up here.'

Lorna looked at Nancy quizzically and Nancy suddenly realized that she was trying to work out how someone who came from non-posh London could afford a million-pound house on the edge of a reservoir.

'My husband and I rented,' said Nancy. 'So I wouldn't know.'

Lorna was floored and Nancy was saved from further interrogation by the arrival of the coffees.

'Do you live in the village?' asked Nancy.

'In one of the lanes opposite the school,' said Lorna. 'There's myself, my husband Simon, and Phoenix you met this morning. My youngest is Pepper. She's six and currently mad about mermaids.'

'Cute,' said Nancy. 'Lara went through a mermaid phase too. I had to get her a costume, which she insisted on wearing in the bath.'

'Aww,' said Lorna. 'Pepper would love that. Do you work?'

'No.'

Lorna's eyes widened. 'Nice.'

'I used to be a children's nurse but gave it up a few months ago.'

'Are you looking for something new?'

'I'm not sure yet. My old job . . . I loved it but by the end I was exhausted. The pressures on the NHS are well documented. I might go back to nursing at some point, but I might try something completely new.'

'Like what?'

Nancy threw up her hands. 'No idea. I used to have a

childhood dream of running a shop. Or a gallery.' She laughed at her pretensions. 'There's an empty premises in the high street. Used to be a restaurant? Maybe I'll make some enquiries.'

'What, for *there*?'

'Have I said something wrong?'

Lorna glanced over at the kitchen. 'No.' She looked down at Nancy's hand, at the wedding ring on her finger. 'Is it just you? Or will Mr Miller be joining us?'

Nancy baulked.

'Sorry,' said Lorna. 'I'm asking too many questions. My Simon says I should work for the secret service. Divorce, is it? There's loads of single mums here. I'll introduce you to some in the playground.'

Nancy nodded mutely.

A strange noise was coming from under the table.

'Cooper!' exclaimed Lorna as she peered underneath.

The dog had thrown up.

'I'm so sorry,' said Lorna. 'We tried him on some new food this morning. It obviously hasn't agreed with him.'

Nancy seized the chance to make her excuses and leave.

SEVEN

Friday 4 September

Nancy pulled up in the yard of Hilldale Farm, being careful not to run over the chickens that seemed to have a death wish and kept strutting in front of her car.

As she got out, she immediately noticed the quiet. Nothing but the sound of birds. The sun lit up the round bales of hay, scattered through a field like giant golden playing pieces on a board game. The ground beneath them was now stubble. A large farmhouse was on her left, with pale grey stone walls and a green front door. Two outbuildings were opposite – essentially big wooden sheds. Nancy jumped at the sound of a loud whinnying and looked behind her to see a black horse staring at her over the fence. Behind it were more fields, stretching as far as the eye could see.

She went up to the house and knocked on the door but it was silent inside. Of course, she thought, farmers don't sit around drinking tea. They're out, working the land. She was starting to think she'd made a wasted journey when she saw a figure crouching down, a distance away in the fields. Nancy screwed up her eyes against the sun to see better. The person seemed to be dragging something along the ground. She thought it was Hannah up there so climbed the stile and walked the footpath that crossed the field.

As she approached, Nancy saw she was right. It *was* Hannah. She was bent over, dragging something heavy, and then, in a sudden shock, Nancy saw what. A sheep lay dead on the grass, its limbs stiff and comically aloft, while Hannah pulled on two of those limbs.

'Everything OK?' asked Nancy, the words no sooner out of her mouth than she realized what a stupid thing it was to say.

Hannah looked up and her face was contorted with effort and anger. 'No. A dog attacked my flock this morning, killed a ewe.'

Nancy looked down at the mangled creature, its coat matted with blood. Its neck was on show and she suddenly saw the inside of its neck was on show too. She gagged, then turned away, unable to stomach the sight of ravaged flesh and sinew.

'A dog did that?'

'I've seen worse. Some left without faces once.'

'Where's the owner?'

'At the time of the attack, who knows? Shouting ineffectively at their dog? Failing to put it on a lead? Witnessing the destruction then scarpering like a shameless coward?'

Hannah seethed and Nancy felt uncomfortable. 'I've come at a bad time,' she said.

Hannah stood up straight and exhaled. 'It's fine. Can I help with something?'

'I wanted to see if you had any chickens for sale,' said Nancy. 'Dean mentioned you might. When he came over to quote for the house.'

'You ever looked after chickens before?'

'Never,' said Nancy, thinking she was about to be told it was no business of hers, a townsperson going around trying to acquire living creatures.

'It's pretty simple,' said Hannah. 'I'll show you the ropes.'

An hour later, Nancy shut the boot of her car on four plump Derbyshire Redcaps, a coop and all the necessary food and bedding to get her started. She headed down the road, driving with extreme care, nervous about her cargo. She could hear them clucking to each other, perhaps terrified of what this utter novice was going to do to them.

'Only eggs, ladies,' Nancy called from the front. 'No roast dinners, so you've got nothing to worry about.'

As she returned home, Nancy turned into her driveway and let out a delighted laugh when she saw a blue car parked outside her barn, a woman leaning against it, her face tilted to the sun. The woman looked up as Nancy leapt out of the car and ran over to envelop her in a tight hug. 'You're early!' She pulled away and looked at her friend. 'It's so nice to see a friendly face.'

'Are people around here not friendly?' asked the woman.

Nancy drew back, as if surprised that the question had arisen. 'No, they are. It's just, you know, everything's new. Honestly', she reiterated in response to the look on her best friend, Beth's, face.

Satisfied, Beth looked up at the barn. 'Well, haven't you gone up in the world? A country house. You, a lady of the manor.'

'It's nice, eh?'

'Nice? That's like saying Buckingham Palace is nice. Or a pink diamond is nice. It's better than nice. It's positively amazing.' Beth moved over to the Tesla, ran her hand over it. 'And check this out.'

'Well, you know . . . after where we used to live. All those car fumes. It was really important to me to go electric . . .'

'I hope you're not apologizing for doing the right thing by your daughter,' said Beth. 'Now, you gonna show me around?'

'In a minute. There's just one thing . . .'

Beth was looking at the car, puzzled. There was a distinct sound of clucking.

'Are those chickens I can hear?' she asked.

Nancy beamed and went to open the boot, revealing her new purchases.

The chickens seemed content enough once they'd been removed from the car and they'd been pecking happily at the grass in their run when Nancy and Beth had left to pick up Lara from school.

The two women stood in the playground as the crowds of parents grew, friendship groups clustering together.

Beth watched with interest. 'It's quite tribal, isn't it? All these clans preparing for battle.'

Nancy laughed. 'There's no battle. Well, not usually on day one.'

'I know I don't have my own and I work in a secondary where the kids are older and get themselves to school but, trust me, as a receiver of dozens of parent emails, there's *always* an issue of some sort.' Beth grimaced. 'God, I've only been back a week. You should have seen my inbox, groaning with complaints, pleas, passive-aggressive missives about how their darling child should be in receipt of a scholarship or a bursary.' Beth looked around. 'Might even be from some of the mums here,' she mused.

Nancy put on a polite smile as Lorna bounded up to them.

'So lovely to have coffee with you today,' Lorna said, linking arms with Nancy as if they were best friends. Her eyes slid to Beth and she raised an expectant eyebrow.

'This is my friend, Beth,' said Nancy.

'Oh, are you a new mum too?' asked Lorna.

'Good God, no,' said Beth. 'I just enjoy the little darlings at work instead.'

'Are you a teacher?' asked Lorna.

'Bursar. At Kingsgate School.'

You could practically see Lorna blossom. 'Oh wow. Bursar.' She quickly checked herself. 'What a coincidence! We've applied to Kingsgate. My son, Phoenix, is a sporting fiend. We're hoping he's lucky enough to get a scholarship?' She did a small, self-effacing laugh. 'Don't know if you remember our application?'

Beth thought, a concentrated frown on her face. 'Phoenix . . . Hmm, no, don't think I do.'

Lorna's face fell. She was about to say something else

36

but the doors of the school had opened and Lara, newly released by the teacher, ran across the playground.

'Auntie Beth!' she cried, throwing her arms around her. 'You came!'

'Of course I did,' said Beth, twirling Lara around. 'And you've grown again. I know children do but it always seems to take me by surprise.'

'How was your first day?' asked Nancy, leaning in for a hug.

'I met loads of new friends. This morning I sat next to Rosie and she invited me to her birthday party.'

'Oh wow,' said Nancy, pleased her daughter was already being included. 'What else?'

'This afternoon we had a vote,' said Lara.

'Ah, yes, Head of School,' said Nancy. 'Was Rosie the winner?'

Lara smiled shyly and pulled her cardigan aside to reveal a blue badge pinned to her polo shirt. 'No. It was me.'

Nancy's jaw dropped. Then she became aware of numerous gazes turned their way. She looked up to see Erin, Imogen and several of the other mothers staring at them with a mixture of disbelief and thinly veiled hostility.

Beth threw her arms up in delight. 'Congratulations!' she said. 'They picked the best candidate.'

'But,' said Nancy, 'you hadn't even written a speech.'

'Miss Young, she's really nice by the way, Mum, she's got pink hair and a pierced nose!'

Nancy looked over at Miss Young, who was making sure the rest of the children were being reunited with their parents. She immediately liked her, felt herself warm to her non-conformist attitude.

'Anyway,' continued Lara, 'Miss Young said I could write something in class. Then we all had to stand at the front and tell the other kids what we stood for.'

'And what do you stand for?'

'Being kind and supportive and encouraging everyone not to drop litter but mostly campaigning for the teacher to give kids sweets if they get three smiley faces on their work in a row.'

Nancy was still a little stunned. 'Smiley faces?'

'Yeah, you get one for good effort. And when I read my speech out, one of the other kids, Jakob, he asked Miss Young if she would actually do it, give out the sweets, and she said yes and I got voted in.'

Beth laughed. 'Nice work, kid.'

'You need to speak to Rosie's mum about the party,' Lara said to Nancy.

Nancy looked up at Imogen and saw her resting her arm around Rosie's shoulders, quietly talking in her ear, no doubt commiserating with her about her failure to be voted Head of School.

'Sure. No rush though.'

'No, there is. It's tomorrow,' said Lara.

'Oh right.'

'I'm your wing woman,' whispered Beth in Nancy's ear.

Nancy put on what she hoped was a warm smile and walked over to where Imogen was surrounded by Erin and several other friends. The conversation died as she approached.

'Lara says she's been invited to Rosie's party.'

'Yes,' said Imogen.

'She thought it was tomorrow?' prompted Nancy.

'That's right. Heron Water. Two o'clock at the activity centre.'

'OK, great.' Nancy looked at Rosie, saw her red eyes. Felt she should say something. 'Sorry it didn't work out, Rosie.'

'It was a close call,' said Imogen. 'Only one vote in it.'

'Oh right,' said Nancy, taken aback at her quietly aggressive tone.

'Rosie's friend Bella was off today. Wasn't really fair to go ahead without all the kids having a say.'

'Can't really wait though, can you?' said Beth. 'Always someone off sick.'

'Maybe she should have been allowed a proxy vote. You know, like proper politics,' said Imogen.

'It's important school reflects real life,' said Erin. 'Teaches the kids about the world.'

'Maybe Bella wouldn't have voted for Rosie anyway,' said Beth breezily. She looked down at the aggrieved girl. 'No offence, Rosie.'

Nancy's stomach tightened at the collective sharp intake of breath from the gathered mums.

'Right, well, we'd better get home,' she said and, with a quick nod to the others, guided Beth away.

'Thanks, Beth,' she hissed with affectionate exasperation, as they walked out of the playground.

'Sorry, but the woman's clearly some sort of tinpot

dictator. It's only a kids' school vote. She needs to get some perspective.'

'That's as may be but we're trying to fit in here.'

'It'll all blow over by tomorrow, just you see,' said Beth. She stepped forward and took Lara's hand. 'Now come on, your mum and I have got a little surprise for you.'

'Ferdinand, Harriet, Henry and the one with the black neck is called Bow-tie,' said Lara.

'You like them?' asked Nancy.

'I love them! Can I give them some food?'

Nancy nodded and as Lara began chucking corn in their run, a champagne cork popped. Nancy turned to see Beth step out of the bi-fold doors with a bottle and two glasses. She set them on the patio table and poured them both a drink.

'Congratulations,' said Beth, raising a toast. 'You have the most amazing new home. Although I have to say that the drowned buildings are a little spooky.'

'I'm telling myself it's just atmosphere,' said Nancy. 'Anyway, they'll be covered up again in a few weeks. Once the weather turns.'

The two women settled themselves at the table and watched Lara as she played with the chickens.

'I can't believe she's in her last year of primary,' said Beth. 'I remember when she was born. And now look: running her own chicken farm!'

'She's always adored animals,' said Nancy. 'Ever since she was little, but we've never been able to have any before.'

They hadn't had the room, the money or the time, even though Nancy was acutely conscious that her daughter was obsessed with them. Lara had yearned for a pet but had to make do with the woodlice she'd collected outside and brought in the flat, keeping them in a shoebox under her bed.

'I've had a request for a puppy, some sheep and, of course, a pony,' said Nancy.

'Wow. Which are you giving in on?'

'Not sure yet. The sheep could keep down the grass. The pony too, I suppose . . .'

'And it's not like you don't have the space.' Beth took a sip of her champagne. 'Look at her. She looks so . . .'

'Happy?'

'Yes. A bit like the old Lara.'

Nancy smiled. 'I think she's a country girl at heart. I know we'd do anything to change what happened, but moving here . . . it's been one good thing to come out of so much awfulness.'

'How's the asthma?'

'Good. No attacks so far. Although that pump is never far away. The doctors have said it will make all the difference being here. When I think of the years we spent in that flat . . .'

'You had no choice,' said Beth firmly. 'Stop beating yourself up.'

She'd probably always beat herself up. Nancy would never forget the day Lara came home from school, two summers ago. It was hot and the air was thick and still.

Nancy had closed the window against the stink of the traffic outside. Lara had looked pale and had sat on the sofa, not in the mood to do much, struggling even to watch the TV. Her breath had been wheezy and Nancy had watched as she'd taken puffs on her inhaler. A dozen in the end but it still didn't seem to ease her breathing. And then suddenly, Lara was struggling, a panicked look on her face as she realized she couldn't get enough air in. It had been so quick, that was what had terrified Nancy. In less than a minute she'd been calling 999 and then had clutched Lara's hand in the ambulance as they'd sped to the hospital. As a nurse, she had understood the serious looks on the paramedics' faces, the intervention the doctors were taking to save her daughter's life. When Lara had lain in bed, surrounded by machines but over the worst, she and Sam had looked at their child and thanked their lucky stars. But it was the flat, they both knew, the continuous, malevolent vapour of nitrogen oxide winding its way into their home that they couldn't get rid of, even with all the windows closed.

Later, she and Sam had curled up together, talking through their options, knowing that on their combined modest salaries they couldn't afford to move for months, if not years, not with the several thousand pounds they were trying to save for a hefty deposit and three months' rent up front. They'd fantasized about winning the lottery, a desperate, futile attempt at trying to find a solution. 'Imagine,' they'd said, 'imagine winning millions. Think about where we could go, the house we could buy.' It had seemed impossible, a dream that was far out of reach.

'Have I told you yet how happy I am you've moved back up here?' said Beth.

Nancy smiled. 'Only about a hundred times.'

'So . . . no more nursing.'

'Not for the moment. I've got enough to keep going for a while. Maybe in a year or so I'll look for something new.'

'What are you going to do with your days?'

'Settle Lara in. Get to know the area. Take up hobbies.'

Beth sat up, interested. 'Like what?'

Nancy looked embarrassed. 'Don't laugh.'

Beth pointed to her serious face. 'Not laughing.'

'Pottery.'

Beth smiled.

'You promised!' said Nancy.

'Honest, that's a smile of approval. Lara isn't the only one who needs to heal, you know.'

Nancy nodded. 'I've always wanted to do something creative. Never had the time before. How's Martin?'

'Good. Still working at the Royal Derby. They're short on anaesthetists so he's doing extra shifts. Hey, we can see so much more of each other. Whenever Martin's on a weekend shift, I'll let you know.' She took a sip of her champagne and gazed around the huge garden, the view down to the reservoir. 'Derbyshire. It's our spiritual home. Ever since university.'

'Yes. Although I don't remember venturing out into the countryside much. Most of our spare time we spent in Derby's bars and clubs.'

'Keeping the local economy alive,' said Beth. 'Where's Lara going to school next year?'

'Thought I'd apply to Kingsgate.'

Beth clapped her hands in delight. 'I was hoping you'd say that. I'll be able to see her from my office window on her way to maths.'

'Well, I have all this money. Lara should benefit as much as possible. It's a great school and now I can afford the fees.' A year ago, she'd never have been able to say that; the very notion of it would have been laughable.

'You need to promise me something,' said Beth.

'What?'

'You call me if you need anything. And I mean anything. I'm only thirty miles away now.'

Nancy looked up at her friend. She knew what she meant. When Nancy had been living in London, the calls had been few and far between. Life had caught her up in its whirlwind: the nursing shifts, Lara's illness, and more recently, Sam.

'I can't hear you,' said Beth, cupping her ear.

Nancy smiled. 'Course. I promise.'

4 September

RIPTON PRIMARY, YEAR 6

Lorna Fielding, Phoenix's mum
Don't mean to stir but does anyone think the Head of School vote was a bit unexpected? I mean, she seems lovely, but they've only just moved here! 😒 I had to volunteer two years at the school before I was voted PTA Chair. 😒😒 15:21

Nicole Wilson, Bella's mum
It's a novelty vote. Not to mention the brazen use of bribery. Someone should have intervened. The teacher or someone. 15:22

Erin Mackie, Tilly's mum
It was the teacher who agreed to the sweets. I'm still gutted we didn't get Miss Brookes. Tilly's already bored in Miss Young's class. I don't think the teacher's bothered with her. It's always the same with the bright ones. Miss Young knows Tilly's going to get a high SAT mark so spends her time with the less able. It's not fair, Tilly needs stretching too.

Re vote. Imogen, you should have said something to James. What's the point of being besties with the head if you can't exercise some influence? How is Rosie, btw? 15:22

Imogen Wood, Rosie's mum
Devastated. Inconsolable. I just feel it's so unfair. She didn't deserve this. 15:23

Nicole Wilson, Bella's mum
Bella's SO sorry she was off sick. She would have voted for Rosie defo. 15:24

Erin Mackie, Tilly's mum
That new kid, Lara, shouldn't have been
allowed to run. 15:25

Hannah Chapman, Jakob's mum
She's as much a part of the class as
anyone. It doesn't seem right to criticize
Lara for this. 15:27

Erin Mackie, Tilly's mum
It's all right for you to say, Jakob wasn't
even interested! 15:27

Lorna Fielding, Phoenix's mum
Did you see what the mother drove up in?
A brand-new Tesla. Probably worth more
than my house 😂. 15:29

Sarah Ramsay, Noah's mum
Sorry to hear about your sheep,
Hannah. It's such an un-Christian thing,
leaving an animal like that. People
should take more responsibility for
their dogs. 15:32

Hannah Chapman, Jakob's mum
They should. If anyone hears anything,
please let me know. BTW, Lorna, I think
you're admin on this group. Do you want to
invite Nancy to join? 15:32

Nicole Wilson, Bella's mum
Bit early, isn't it? 15:33

Hannah Chapman, Jakob's mum
Early for what? Term's started. 15:34

Erin Mackie, Tilly's mum
Actually, I don't think any of us have her
number. 15:34

Lorna Fielding, Phoenix's mum
Just reminding you ladies, the open day for
Ripton High is only a week away. 15:36

Erin Mackie, Tilly's mum
It's so bad. I saw a kid in uniform the other
day smoking. And not cigarettes. No
wonder so many of us are forced to pay for
Kingsgate. 15:37

Lorna Fielding, Phoenix's mum
Maybe Lara's mum could sell her Tesla and
pay all our fees! LOL 15:38

EIGHT

Saturday 5 September

When Imogen had booked Rosie's birthday party, she'd come up against strong resistance from her husband. It was costing a bit, considering what they'd gone through the last eighteen months. But despite Dylan saying Rosie should settle for having a couple of friends over to the house, Imogen had insisted. Yes, they needed to save for a deposit so they could actually buy somewhere, not just rent the poxy little cottage they all now had to manage in, but she couldn't bear the idea.

She didn't want to feel destitute. She didn't want the shame of it, the misery. She was Imogen Wood – one of the village's most notable residents. She'd been on prime-time TV, for God's sake! Two series co-presenting *Maestro Chef*.

She also wanted her daughter to have something nice to look forward to. God knows they'd hardly got her a present – some flowery stationery – which was a far cry from what Rosie had received in previous years. With a pang, Imogen remembered Rosie's gift from a couple of years ago – a new pony. Lupin had had to be sold, along with everything else.

So no, they would not be getting out some popcorn and putting on a movie in the too-small house, they would be allowing Rosie to do some paddleboarding with her friends on the water.

Only one child was missing. Lara. That new kid. And her awful mother. When that woman – Nancy – had come over saying that Rosie had invited her child, for a moment, Imogen had been unable to speak. Later, Rosie had said she hadn't known who Lara was at the time. And now she wished she *hadn't* invited her. She wanted to uninvite her but, as much as Imogen wished it too, it was impossible.

She looked over towards the activity centre, where Dylan was talking to the rep and the kids were all getting into wetsuits. It was only two minutes until the party started. Maybe they wouldn't turn up. She allowed herself a brief glimmer of hope and then she saw a brand-new car pull up in the car park. A Tesla.

Imogen tried not to watch as the car doors opened – in that way that looked like a bird of prey, lifting up towards the sky. The other mums were staring in a mixture of admiration and envy. It wasn't just Nancy and Lara getting out but that other woman too – the one who had been so mean to Rosie in the playground the day before.

Then they were at the picnic table, all smiles. Imogen plastered her own on.

'Sorry we're a bit late,' said Nancy.

'It's my fault,' said Beth. 'I couldn't tear myself away from Nancy's garden.'

Imogen gritted her teeth. 'It's not a problem.' She nodded

over to the activity centre building. 'It's about to start.' Lara ran over to the other kids to get changed.

'Would you like a coffee?' asked Imogen.

They both accepted – of course they did – and Imogen went in to the cafe, feeling the cuts of spending money she didn't really have on someone who had already robbed her. She took a deep breath and looked out of the window, back towards the picnic table where all the mums were gathered, chatting. Nancy seemed to be as much a part of the group as anyone.

Imogen suddenly had an urge to go back over. As she arrived back at the picnic table, the mums were all turned towards the reservoir, watching as the children clambered onto their paddleboards.

Imogen whispered in Erin's ear. 'What did Nancy have to say for herself then?'

Erin looked confused. 'What do you mean?'

'You two were having a very cosy chat.'

Erin gave her a reassuring squeeze on her arm. 'Darling, you have nothing to worry about. Just exchanging pleasantries.' She smiled. 'You know what they say, keep your friends close and your enemies closer.'

It was reassuring to hear, although it did nothing to repair the gaping hole in her heart. She was suddenly aware of Nancy speaking.

'. . . Dean was great,' she was saying to Hannah. 'He's quoting for pretty much everything except for the pool.'

Imogen instantly froze. Pool? What pool?

'You're having a pool?' blurted Lorna, surprised.

'Oh, not anything fancy,' said Nancy. 'Not a traditional tiled one. I was thinking of a natural swimming pond.'

She had made it sound as if that was the less ostentatious choice, thought Imogen, incensed, but she herself knew a natural swimming pond would cost tens of thousands of pounds. Fucking hell, how much money did Nancy *have*?

Nobody had said anything.

'That's nice,' piped up Lorna, trying to fill the awkward silence. 'I guess everyone wants to make their own stamp. The house is beautiful though, isn't it?'

Imogen seethed. God, Lorna was so excruciating. She didn't need comments like that. Didn't need to be patronized.

She waited for Nancy to reply. The house was exceptional, Imogen knew. Farrow and Ball paints throughout, a handmade kitchen, luxurious wallpaper. She could see Nancy was aware of a tension but was unsure of what was going on.

'Beautiful,' agreed Nancy.

'But you're still decorating?' said Erin.

'Yes. Well, it's maybe a bit dark . . .' said Nancy.

What?

'Dark?' repeated Erin, with an edge to her voice.

'Um . . . just a bit.'

'What Nancy is trying to say is that it's dismal,' said Beth. 'The paint colours. As if the previous owners wanted to live in a dungeon.'

Imogen felt her face go flame red.

'I don't think Imogen ever thought she was living in a dungeon,' said Erin coldly.

Nancy looked at Imogen, then the penny dropped. 'I didn't realize . . .' she started, flustered.

'Yep. Imogen's old house,' said Erin.

Imogen could see Nancy mentally trying to work out her personal story, the fact the house was a repossession order, realizing there had obviously been major financial troubles, and her face burned. She was vaguely aware of some of the other mothers looking at her with pity on their faces.

She raised her head and cast her eyes along the shoreline at what she'd been avoiding the whole morning. Her beloved house, the place she'd bought as a rundown project, where she'd sunk hundreds of thousands of pounds, all her love, sweat and tears, the home she'd brought Rosie back to as a baby. The place that had been wrested away from her, despite her trying everything to save it. A sense of panic was rising up from the pit of her stomach. Imogen felt light-headed and was desperate to get away from them all.

A scream came from the water, loud, guttural, steeped in terror.

It took a moment for Imogen to register what was going on. She frowned as she turned her head towards the reservoir and saw the instructor urgently paddling out. Then the screams amplified, more kids panicking and the mothers on the bank were now agitated. Everyone was moving towards the water, speeding up as they went. Imogen searched for Rosie in the distance but couldn't see her and her legs moved faster as a growing fear hooked itself into her and then she was running full pelt, all the mothers also running to the bank in a protective herd. Imogen was close enough now to see the frightened look on the activity instructor's face as he went from desperately gazing into the depths to diving right in. She became vaguely aware of Erin's relief as her friend spotted her own daughter, Tilly; of Lorna's as she saw Phoenix and she knew, she *knew* and she started to wade into the water herself, shoes on, and the instructor came up empty-handed and Imogen screamed, a primal, blood-curdling sound. The instructor went back under and Imogen tried to run towards where he was diving but the pressure of the water was holding her back and her sodden skirt trapped her legs and she wailed but then he came back up and this time he had Rosie clutched to him, her head flung back as she gasped in air, her hair splattered across her face, and Imogen moaned with relief.

NINE

Saturday 5 September

'Rosie said Lara pushed her in deliberately,' said Imogen, her face set hard as she passed the dish of fondant potatoes across the table to James. As head teacher of the primary school, he should know about these sorts of incidents. OK, so it hadn't happened in school hours, but he needed to be aware of who he had just accepted into Ripton Primary.

'What a little cow,' said Erin. She refused the potatoes as they came around. Imogen knew the carbs and butter wouldn't be to her best friend's taste.

It was the first dinner party Imogen had thrown since she'd moved into the tiny rental several months ago. It had taken a while for her to face the idea. There was no grand kitchen any more, no twelve-seater dining table in a beautiful dusky blue dining room. Not a dungeon at all, thought Imogen angrily. There was no large patio to serve pre-dinner drinks in the late evening sunshine. She'd lost it all, brought down by crippling debt on her restaurant. It had been so promising at the start. A fanfare opening at the end of 2019, glowing reviews from her dear friend Nigel – but also from

Jay Rayner too – and every other national restaurant critic. It had cost a small fortune to set up, but she'd managed to borrow against the house, which already had a substantial mortgage on it, but all the signs were there for a successful restaurant business. And it had been a success for the first five months and then Covid had come along and everything had stopped. There had been a death-like silence every time she'd gone into her beautiful, empty restaurant and nearly cried at the terrible waste of opportunity, and the money she could virtually see flushing at a continuous rate down the bone-dry sinks. It had become untenable in the end, and the debts were too big for Dylan's teacher salary. She'd been stubborn, had refused to sell her precious house that she'd spent years doing up exactly how she'd wanted it. God, she'd even had a feature article in a national home decorating magazine. How proud she'd been to see her home on show, see the photo of herself at her Lacanche range cooker. No, there was no way she could have sold. She would have been a laughing stock. Instead, the decision had been taken out of her hands and the bank took it all. It had broken her heart.

'Is Rosie all right?' asked James.

'Still traumatized,' said Imogen.

'I'm not surprised,' said Erin. 'That kid tried to drown her.'

'We don't know it was like that,' said Dylan.

Imogen shot her eyes up at her husband. They'd been disagreeing on a lot lately and sometimes she felt as if he said black to her white just because he could. Surely he was going to side with his own daughter on this?

'Lara pushed Rosie in,' said Erin. 'Then while no one was looking, she held her head under, right where there was a tangle of underwater reeds. If that instructor hadn't pulled her out, then . . .'

Imogen shuddered.

Dylan stopped eating, his knife and fork held in mid-air. 'Thank God for him,' he said. 'But what I mean is, Rosie has had a terrible experience but we haven't got to the bottom of what exactly happened. Remember, Lara had a different version of the story.'

'Now hold on a second . . .' started Imogen.

Dylan looked at her. 'I didn't see it. Did you?'

She hadn't, but it aggrieved her that he should be airing this . . . *notion* that their daughter might not be telling the truth in front of their friends.

'I believe her,' she said firmly.

'You should set out some sort of punishment,' said Erin, looking at James. 'Strip her of her Head of School status, for starters.'

'He can't do that,' said Carol, spooning potatoes onto her plate as they came to her. 'This incident didn't even happen at school.

'My wife is correct,' said James.

'She shouldn't even be Head of School,' said Erin. 'She's only just started there. And anyway, who's going to take any notice of her after she's done this?'

'It was a democratic vote,' said Carol firmly. 'Fair's fair.'

Imogen hid her irritation. It was nothing to do with Carol. She seemed to think that because she was married to the head teacher and her daughter, Lorna, was Chair of the PTA she could wade in with her opinion. Well, it was unwanted.

'So what is Lara's side of the story?' asked Carol.

'She said Rosie had fallen in herself,' said Imogen. 'And swore blind she hadn't held her head down.'

'Lied through her teeth, in other words,' said Erin. 'She's a menace.'

'This wouldn't get by in a court of law,' said Marcus drily, as he waved a hand around the table. Erin's husband was a criminal barrister who worked on extremely high-profile cases in London and thought local village 'spats' mildly amusing.

'It's a character assassination,' he continued, 'and this Lara kid's got no defence counsel.'

'What, are you offering?' said Erin sharply.

'Hang on a moment, hasn't Rosie got form?' said Marcus, seemingly remembering something.

Erin nudged his arm – an instruction to shut up.

'What do you mean?' Imogen asked.

'For fibbing. At Tilly's party, remember? Didn't Rosie say she hadn't opened the hamster cage and let Claude escape? Next thing we know he's hanging limply from the jaws of next door's cat.' He smiled mischievously. 'And we know it was her because it was on the nanny cam.'

'Good God, Marcus, she was *five*,' said Erin, before mouthing a 'sorry' to Imogen.

'That's all right,' said Imogen graciously.

'All kids lie at five,' added Erin. 'And that was *years* ago.'

Imogen was beginning to tire of the conversation, was irritated that her husband was staying so quiet and not sticking up for Rosie more. The fact was, Rosie had been caught in reeds under the reservoir and had she not been pulled out, she would have drowned. She had come out of that lake near hysterical. And yes, Lara had denied everything, hot tears running down her cheeks, but Imogen had seen the terror in Rosie's eyes.

'Everyone else was wobbling except for me,' Rosie had explained, as she'd sat hunched on a bench, wrapped in a towel. 'Because I'd done it before. When we lived at our old house.'

It was true, they'd all had their own paddleboard – she and Dylan too – and they'd often gone out onto the water at the weekend. They'd been sold along with everything else.

'Lara didn't like it – that I could stand up. She kept trying herself but it was too difficult for her and she got really angry, and so she tipped the edge of my board so I fell in.'

When Imogen had asked if the instructor had seen, Rosie had replied: 'No, she made sure he wasn't looking. He was helping Tilly when she did it, so he was distracted. Then when I tried to get back out of the water, she held my head down.'

Imogen's blood had run cold. 'She what?'

'She put her hand on my head, kept pushing me under the water and I was kicking so much, my feet got caught in the reeds.'

Imogen had seethed when she'd heard it all, furious that

58

another girl's petty nastiness had led to near-tragic consequences. Was her own daughter supposed to diminish her
achievements merely to satisfy some jealous child?

'More wine?' asked Dylan, picking up the bottle.

James held out his glass. 'Thanks,' he said, as Dylan filled
it. 'How's school? Sorry to hear about the Ofsted inspection.'

Dylan bristled. 'It was unjust. As you know.'

'Don't know why you stick it out there anyway. You
know there's going to be a job coming up at Kingsgate?
Good teacher like you, you'd walk it.'

'The kids at Ripton High deserve good teachers too.'

'Dylan wants to make a difference,' said Imogen drily.

'And what's wrong with that?' said Dylan.

'Nothing. But if you worked at Kingsgate, we'd get a
sixty per cent reduction in fees for Rosie.'

'We'd still have to find the other forty per cent,' said
Dylan. 'She'll be fine at Ripton High.'

'No. She won't,' said Imogen.

'How do you know?'

Her mouth had dropped open. 'What . . . are you serious?
The drugs, the class disruption, the . . . *underage sex*.'
Sometimes it frightened her how far apart she and her
husband seemed to have grown with their thinking. It wasn't
like that when they'd first met, almost fifteen years ago now
in London. He'd been a new-ish teacher, recently awarded
gold for 'Teacher of the Year in a Secondary School' at the
National Teacher Awards. She'd just been promoted to chef
de partie at a restaurant owned by a French culinary genius.

She'd been impressed with what she'd seen as Dylan's ambition, his future starry rise to the top. They'd fallen in love and everything had seemed to slot into place, especially when she was offered a sous chef position by her boss, who was opening a new restaurant in one of the most affluent villages in Derbyshire. Dylan had been ready for a change too – he had grown up in the Northern countryside and wanted to return. She'd thrown herself into her job, always with an eye on opening her own place one day. Dylan, however, seemed to stall. He was content remaining as a teacher in a secondary school, and Imogen began to realize they had different ideas of what 'ambition' meant. For her it was money and status, something she didn't feel the need to apologize for. For her husband it was all about serving the community and grassroots teaching.

Dylan sighed. 'They're not all like that. Stop being such a snob.'

Imogen was stung. 'I'm not,' she said. 'I just want the best for my daughter.'

'Of course I want that too. It'll teach her a bit of resilience. She's had a lot handed to her on a plate – ponies, clothes, the latest tech.'

'I'm sure Rosie will keep on the straight and narrow,' said Carol diplomatically.

'You know I'm Chair of Governors at Kingsgate,' said James to Dylan. 'And a close friend of the head. Why don't you let me put in a good word for you about that position?'

Imogen looked at Dylan in hope.

'Thanks, but that won't be necessary,' said Dylan.

'Gotta say, Ripton High sounds like more fun,' said Marcus, then let out an 'Ow!' as Erin kicked him under the table.

Imogen lowered her eyes, unable to hide the anger and upset that coursed through her. Erin's daughter, Tilly, would be going to Kingsgate, Marcus's salary would ensure it. So would Nicole's daughter, Bella, Rosie's other friend. Nicole's parents had offered to pay. For a brief moment she let the question enter her mind about Lara. She didn't need to think about it; with the money Nancy appeared to have it was a given she would go too. She would take Rosie's place, just as she seemed to take everything else.

Later, when Imogen and Dylan were clearing up, he took the cloth from her hands and gave her a hug.

'Sorry, I didn't mean to go off on one earlier. It's that man. I know he's a friend of yours but sometimes he really winds me up. So bloody pompous and condescending.'

'He was only trying to help.'

'Thought I was incapable, more like. What, a word from him and the head of Kingsgate is going to be on the phone, offering me a job?'

'That's not what he said.'

'It's what he implied. I get the feeling he looks down his nose at me. Thinks I need a leg-up, and an education on what's good for me and my family.'

'He doesn't,' said Imogen. 'He thinks a lot of you.'

Dylan gave a wry smile. 'Is that what he says when you guys go on your weekend runs together?'

'Not exactly . . .'

'No. So what do you talk about?'

'Not much. Usually too out of breath.' Imogen paused. 'Why won't you even consider Kingsgate for Rosie?'

'It's not an option,' said Dylan gently. 'We can't afford it. Even if I did go and work at the posh school.'

Deflated, Imogen looked at the clock – it was after midnight. 'Let's finish up. I want to go to bed.'

As James and Carol walked home through the village, Carol tucked her arm into that of her husband's.

'You'll have to keep an eye on the kid,' she said. 'At school.'

'Yes. I'll mention it to her teacher. Don't want Rosie falling behind after her ordeal.'

Carol stopped. 'I meant Lara – this new child. It seems perfectly clear that Imogen and Erin have got it in for her and her mother.'

'You think? Surely this will all blow over.'

'The woman's bought Imogen's house, James.'

'I know. But Imogen will get back on her feet. She's that type of person. It's all new at the moment. Time has a great way of healing things. Trust me, I've been teaching for thirty-five years.' He smiled at her indulgently. 'You might like to think I know what I'm doing.'

Carol inwardly rolled her eyes.

'These spats come and go and everything settles down in the end. By Halloween, they'll be best friends and their kids will be out trick-or-treating together.'

Carol looked up at her husband. Sometimes, for such a smart man, with his wealth of experience, she couldn't understand how he could be so short-sighted. She thought about pressing the point but knew there was no getting through to him when he was in this mood, so she let it drop.

TEN

Saturday 5 September

'I can't sleep,' said Lara, standing barefoot in the doorway of the living room. Nancy glanced over at Beth, then, pausing the movie, she untucked her legs and got off the sofa.

'What's up?' she asked, giving Lara a hug.

'I keep having these scary images,' said Lara. 'Of dead straw bears. The straw's all soaking wet and it's dripping on my carpet.'

'Except it's not real,' said Nancy.

'No, but that's what Rosie said. There are ghosts in the reservoir. Drowned straw bears. She says she knows this because she used to live here. And she says they come up through the garden gate and into our house. I feel like they're in my bedroom.'

Nancy composed herself. She could kill that Rosie for telling Lara such a stupid story, for being so mean to her at the birthday party. When Rosie had been dragged from the lake, Nancy couldn't believe it when she'd started telling everyone that Lara had pushed her in – worse, had held her head under the water. Lara was beside herself with upset and had desperately tried to say what had really happened – that Rosie had made nasty comments about Lara being voted Head of School, saying she shouldn't have been allowed because she hadn't been there since Reception class. Lara had tried to shrug it off, but Rosie had moved onto scare tactics, stories about straw bears. When Lara tried to paddle away, Rosie put an oar out to stop her – which was how she'd lost her balance and fallen in.

Rosie had pointed the finger of blame at Lara and even said Lara had pushed her head under the water. It was unbelievable really. Nancy had tried to reason with Imogen, but the other mother was too angry. The party had ended prematurely as Rosie was so upset, leaving several boxes of burgers and chips uneaten at the cafe, not to mention a large, uncut cake. Nancy, under the weight of all the curious and condemning glances from the other mothers, had been desperate to go, and she and Beth had quickly helped Lara change and been the first away.

And now Lara was having trouble sleeping. It had only been a few weeks since she'd stopped having night terrors – something that Nancy had been immensely relieved about. Except now this other girl seemed to have single-handedly started them off again.

Beth moved over to Lara and put an arm around her. 'Now you listen to your Auntie Beth. No one's in this house except you, me and your mum, and no one can *get* in.'

Lara still looked dubious.

'You want me to kip on your floor? Just to be certain?'

Lara smiled. 'I snore. Mum said so.'

'Like a thunderstorm,' said Nancy.

'Well, I snore like a tornado,' said Beth. 'So we make a good team.'

'I don't think we'd get much sleep,' said Lara.

'No, but we could sneak in some chocolate and eat it at midnight.'

'Not a chance,' said Nancy.

Lara sighed. 'What if she's still mean to me on Monday?'

Nancy felt her heart tighten. 'Then you tell me.'

'No one else saw what happened. They're all going to believe Rosie. I won't have any friends.'

'They won't all believe Rosie,' said Beth. 'Lots of those kids are smart and they'll know she's lying.'

'And anyway, this will all be forgotten about soon,' said Nancy, hoping she was right. Lara needed to settle, needed some stability. This was meant to be a fresh start.

'Your mum's right,' said Beth. 'Now go on, back to bed before I come and snore on your floor.'

Lara, a little more pacified, turned and went back upstairs.

Nancy sank back down onto the sofa, took a sip of her wine. She exhaled with worry.

'She deserves it, you know,' said Beth. 'Everything. The house you've got for her, the fact she can breathe fresh air. She deserves the school accolade.'

'I know. I just have a horrible feeling I've made an enemy of the most popular woman in the village.'

'Define popular.'

'What?'

'Go on.'

'Well,' said Nancy. 'It's someone who's liked.'

'Bullshit,' said Beth. 'It's not about being liked, it's about being dominant. Don't let this woman, or anyone else, get you down. They're going to have to put on their big girl pants and get over it.'

Nancy smiled. Beth was right.

5 September

RIPTON PRIMARY, YEAR 6

Lorna Fielding, Phoenix's mum
Hey Imogen, just reaching out to see if Rosie is feeling OK 😊😊😊 20:17

> **Nicole Wilson, Bella's mum**
> Yeah, poor Rosie. And poor you! Just goes to show, you can't turn your back for a minute. Can't believe that Lara actually pushed Rosie in. And held her head down! Awful. 20:18

Erin Mackie, Tilly's mum
It's terrifying. I think we all need to keep a close eye on our kids. I'm certainly not leaving Tilly alone with her. 20:18

> **Hannah Chapman, Jakob's mum**
> Seems a bit strange to me. To do something like that just because Rosie was better at paddleboarding? And anyway, I thought that Lara said Rosie had fallen in. 20:19

Erin Mackie, Tilly's mum
Of course she said that, she doesn't want
to get into trouble. And some kids can do
really evil stuff for the pettiest of reasons,
you know. Just look at the news. Didn't that
kid in America shoot up his school because
his teacher gave him a D minus in English?
20:19

> **Sarah Ramsay, Noah's mum**
> I'll pray for her tonight. 20:20

Erin Mackie, Tilly's mum
Good, cos she needs someone to exorcise
the devil out of her. 20:20

> **Sarah Ramsay, Noah's mum**
> No, actually I meant Rosie ☺ 20:21

Imogen Wood, Rosie's mum
Thanks, most of you, for your support. I
know when Rosie is fibbing and this isn't
one of those times. And Lara didn't just lie,
she hardly blinked an eye when Rosie got
dragged from the reservoir, half drowned. It
could have gone horribly wrong and there
would have been a tragedy in this village. I,
for one, am not going to stand back and
watch anything else happen. So I WILL be
keeping an eye on that Lara. 20:22

ELEVEN

Sunday 6 September

'I'm off for a run,' said Imogen as she came into the kitchen.

Dylan was making pancakes. It was his and Rosie's weekend treat while Imogen went to get some exercise. It had started when she'd needed to get out to run off her dark moods, the pain and devastation of losing the house and the restaurant. As life had settled into a new normality, she'd kept on running and her husband and daughter still relished their sugar-filled breakfasts.

'Enjoy,' he said, as he flipped a pancake.

She left the house and once she was away from the windows, she checked her phone. The message she'd been expecting was there.

Imogen ran out of the village then continued three miles down Cuckoo Lane. It was the road that had some of the largest houses in the area. Six-bedroomed detached places with long driveways. She slowed as she neared one of the houses, an Edwardian red-brick with tall windows, then, checking no one was around, she turned into the driveway. She ran uphill to the house itself, feeling her muscles ache as she passed the stone lion, the neat, tiered fountain. Then at the top of the hill, just before the front door, she stopped. Resting her hands on her thighs, she leaned forward and caught her breath.

A hand landed on her backside. 'Glad you could get away,' said James, grinning at her. He too was out of breath, dressed in running gear.

Imogen smiled. She followed him into his house and he got her a glass of water. 'Carol at yoga?' she asked, still needing to check, even knowing that the very fact of her being inside meant Carol was out.

'She is,' said James. He came over and kissed her, then she followed him upstairs. There were five spare bedrooms in the house but 'theirs' was the green one, as it faced over the front driveway. Just in case. It was possible to hear if a car drove up. Within minutes they were naked.

Afterwards, they lay entangled in the sheets, Imogen enjoying James stroking her skin.

'Nice dinner last night,' said James. 'You must give that potato recipe to Carol.'

Imogen rolled her eyes. 'I'm sure Carol has her own recipes,' she said drily. When he was like this, she understood why Dylan said he was so egotistical. But he was kind too, that she knew. In fact, it was his kindness that had brought them together. Soon after everything had come crashing down for her, Imogen had been on one of her runs, her mood bleak. She'd stumbled in the lane near his house, twisted her ankle badly and been unable to walk. Fortunately, James had been on his way home and he'd picked her up and helped her limp into his house, where he'd strapped the ankle and found an icepack. She'd been so taken aback by the act of kindness after everything that had happened, she'd burst into tears.

He had put his arm around her and in his nice, large house, which was a warm, familiar environment after having her own nice, large house taken from her, she had felt safe, as if she was back where she belonged. They had ended up having sex on the living room rug. Then he'd driven her home.

She'd felt guilty for days afterwards and had initially vowed not to cheat on Dylan again. In any case, she'd been more or less housebound being on crutches for a couple of weeks, going stir-crazy in the tiny cottage she'd been reduced to. Then James had got in touch and suggested they go running together next time. Just in case she should fall again. She thought of being in his house, of the balm it gave to her broken ambitions, the losses that still felt so raw, and she had agreed. Only to run, she told herself, even while knowing she was deluding herself. Of course they had slept together and now they 'ran' together most weekends while Carol was at her exercise classes.

They both enjoyed it but for James it meant more, Imogen knew. An ego stroke. She was only forty, eighteen years his junior. And she held a certain status in the village that was attractive to him. One weekend she'd texted to say she couldn't make a run and was surprised by how much this disappointed him. He had practically begged her to change her mind, but she'd made him wait another week. It had been worth it to see how much he wanted her. She had felt appreciated. Recognized for her value. Not that Dylan didn't do that, but it was frustrating when he didn't get her point of view. Like last night, failing to grasp how important it was to get the right school for Rosie. She sighed deeply.

'What's up?' said James.

'This whole Kingsgate thing. Dylan not wanting to go for the job.'

'He's stubborn, isn't he?'

She shrugged. 'He's got strong opinions.'

'That's fine as long as you don't use your child as a social experiment in order to prove them.'

Imogen couldn't agree more. And she had lain awake last night trying to think of a way round it. It wasn't the only thing that had kept her awake. Before all the agony in the water, Lorna had mentioned something to her at the party that had really rankled. Something about Nancy musing about looking into the lease on what used to be her beautiful restaurant. It had gone round and round in her head. That woman taking her house, her child trying to drown Rosie and, not satisfied with those two despicable acts, also wanting to take over her old business premises.

At about three in the morning, Imogen had had an idea.

She rested her hand on James's bare chest. Leaned up on her elbow and gave him her most attractive smile.

'James?' she said, caressing his skin. 'I have a proposal for you.'

TWELVE

Monday 7 September

'There she is,' said Erin, nudging Imogen's shoulder and indicating over to the entrance gate where Nancy was walking in with Lara. 'As brazen as you like.'

'She still has to go to school, Erin,' said Hannah. 'What do you want her to do, come in in sackcloth and ashes?'

Imogen cut Nancy and Lara an icy glare. 'I've already let the school know what happened so they will be keeping an extra close eye on her.'

'Imagine being her mother,' said Nicole, shuddering. 'You'd be horrified.'

'Unless it's her parenting,' said Erin. 'We don't know what it's like in their home, remember.'

On the other side of the playground, Nancy could feel the animosity coming over towards her in waves. Those who weren't giving her cold stares had their backs turned. She sighed.

A child walked past her, turned her head. It was Tilly, Erin's kid.

'I speak to my mum not in sentences but in spelling out. I-M-G-O-O-D-A-T-I-T,' said Tilly. Then she sauntered off.

'Tilly regaling you with her latest achievements?' said Lorna, approaching.

Nancy turned, grateful for a friendly face. 'She's quite the achiever.'

'Yes. I'm not really keen on the boasting approach though. Better to keep things under your hat,' said Lorna without a hint of irony. 'You still OK for the PTA meeting later?'

Nancy wasn't sure she would be welcome after the weekend. Although maybe it would be a chance to clear the air and, she reminded herself, neither she nor Lara had done anything wrong. She'd come here planning to be a part of the school community and so that was what she was going to do. She smiled. 'Yes.'

'I'd like to start today's meeting with a warm welcome to our newest member of the PTA . . . Nancy!' Lorna beamed at the group gathered and added a round of applause. There was a smattering of hand-clapping in return. Lorna's smile dipped slightly. She glanced at Nancy but she either hadn't noticed the muted reception or was pretending not to.

'Some of you will have already met Nancy . . .' Lorna tailed off, realizing her choice of words weren't the most tactful. Imogen was sitting at the back of their group, having chosen a seat at a table with Erin and Nicole. As Chair, Lorna had decided to have this meeting at the Heron Water Cafe before the awful incident on Saturday but was suddenly conscious they were in full view of the exact section of water where Rosie had been dragged out, coughing and spluttering.

She quickly moved on. 'First on today's agenda is the Christmas fair. I know it's only September, but it comes around quickly and there's always loads to organize. Shall we take a stall each again? Sarah, you were very good on decorating biscuits last year.'

'I'm happy to do that,' said Sarah. 'But I would like to add more of a nativity theme this time. I think the kids would like that. Perhaps they could ice some baby Jesus shaped cookies?'

'You could use silver balls for eyes,' said Erin.

'Then he'd look like an alien,' said another mother.

'God, the kids will be wanting to join a cult,' said a woman called Cheryl.

'I'm sure we can iron out the details closer to the time,' said Lorna quickly, seeing Sarah was becoming affronted. She cast her eyes over the group. 'Is there anyone who'd like to volunteer taking charge of the whole event this year?'

'I thought that was what you always did,' said Erin.

Lorna smiled, felt herself puff up a bit. 'Well, usually I do, but now I'm Chair . . . I have a lot more responsibility – and less time. So if there was anyone who fancied taking it on?' She looked around at the blank faces. 'It's a fun one, you know how everyone loves Christmas. And even the teachers help out. They're not too jaded as it's still early in the school year.'

'I'll do it,' said Nancy.

Lorna stopped, surprised. She flicked a glance over to Imogen. Her face was blank but Lorna knew she was seething.

'It's quite time-consuming . . . ' said Lorna, a touch nervously.

'That's OK. I have plenty of spare time,' said Nancy.

'Thank you, Nancy. That would be wonderful,' said Lorna. She swiftly moved on to the next item on the agenda – the second-hand uniform sale – and other than the low-lying hostility from Imogen, the rest of the meeting went without a hitch. They finished at the scheduled time of eleven. Lorna was pleased – she'd brought her dog Cooper with her with the intention of taking him for a walk around the reservoir before heading back home. In fact, he was her decoy. There was something else she wanted to do. She waited while the mums gathered themselves, most of them dashing off to jobs or errands, and then Lorna saw Nancy start to head away from the cafe down to the reservoir path.

'Nancy!' she called out, untying Cooper from the table leg and letting him off the lead. 'Are you heading along the water?'

Nancy turned. 'It's only a short walk home. Easier to come this way rather than go back via the roads.'

Lorna looked over in the distance to where Nancy's house stood proudly on the banks above the reservoir, the sun glinting off its windows. She really did have the most beautiful home in the most amazing location. 'Fancy some company?' she asked. 'I need to walk Cooper.'

Nancy agreed and the two women walked down to the water. Its surface was mirror-like, broken only by a pair of ducks swimming across to the other side. They left a gentle 'V' of rippling water in their trail as they moved effortlessly along.

'Thanks again for taking on the Christmas fair,' said Lorna. 'It's so great you're able to get involved.'

'I'm very happy to. It'll be fun,' said Nancy, but Lorna thought she detected a note of doubt in her voice.

Lorna had watched the fallout from the accident with interest. It was obvious Rosie was lying – Lara was so distraught – but Rosie had still had a nasty scare. Lorna had felt the pain of both mothers – one convinced her child had been deliberately harmed, the other upset her daughter had been unfairly accused of something serious – but she had been careful not to take sides. Imogen was not the sort of person you wanted to get on the wrong side of and Nancy . . . well, Lorna was hoping to get to know her a whole lot better.

'I was wondering . . .' she said, 'would you and Lara like to come over to ours for a barbecue? Perhaps weekend after next?'

'That sounds nice,' said Nancy, 'but my friend Beth is coming to visit again.'

Lorna felt her heart do a little leap to the jackpot. This couldn't have worked out better, her plans suddenly fast-tracked. 'Bring Beth along too,' she said. 'One o'clock, Saturday week— Cooper!' she suddenly shouted at the top of her voice. Her dog had seen a gaggle of geese down by the water's edge and was running full pelt at them, determined to get one in his mouth as they all honked and hissed and tried to get away, a chaotic mix of feathers rising into the air.

'Cooper!' Lorna shouted again, chasing after her disobedient dog, cursing the fact it had interrupted her conversation. She caught the dog and clipped him back onto the lead, bringing him back up to the path.

'Sorry about that,' she said. 'This dog's always chasing something. It's a bloody nightmare actually . . .' She gathered herself, then saw they were at the gate that led up to Nancy's garden.

'Well, this is me,' said Nancy.

'Have a great day,' said Lorna. 'I'll text you my address.'

She waved as Nancy went up her path and watched, enthralled by the size of the garden, the balcony she could see that was the length of the house until she suddenly realized she was probably spending too long looking and turned away.

When Lorna got home it was lunchtime. Her husband, hearing her come in, ventured out of the office and as soon as she saw his face she knew she was in for a lecture.

'I've had the credit-card bill,' said Simon, holding up a piece of paper.

She tried to look innocent. 'Oh?'

'There's an item on here for thirty pounds. From a phone shop.'

Lorna pretended to think. 'Oh yes, I remember. It was the phone case. For Rosie's birthday present.'

Simon's mouth dropped open. 'You spent thirty pounds on a phone case?'

'It's the one all the kids want these days.'

'So?'

'So it was her birthday.'

'It doesn't mean we have to spend thirty quid!' Simon took a breath, tried to compose himself. 'Do you not think that's too much money to spend on a gift for an eleven-year-old child who isn't even ours?'

It was, she knew it was, but it wasn't about that, it was the fact it needed to be the right *brand*. That was what counted. Rosie's face had been a picture when she'd opened her gift. And even Imogen had looked surprised – and Lorna had enjoyed the feeling of being able to demonstrate to Imogen that she could keep up with her, was as good as her. Better even.

'It's important,' she said. 'It's all about positioning.'

'Positioning?' repeated Simon, baffled. 'Positioning is being at the right angle when you're taking a penalty.'

Football, always football. That was what her husband was passionate about. She sighed inwardly. It was a heavy burden being the only one looking out for their family, their children, wanting them to have the right opportunities, the best start in life. She remembered the battles she'd had to persuade him to name their children Phoenix and Pepper. She'd tried to explain how an unusual name gave someone a head start in life – made people notice them when faced with a pile of CVs. All Simon thought was that they'd get bullied. Well, neither of them had and she knew she'd made the right decision.

'Sorry,' she said to Simon, knowing it was wise to be contrite. It would save an argument.

'We don't need to follow the latest fashions,' said Simon. 'It's just a bit of plastic that goes on a phone.'

Lorna hid a smile. He was so sweet sometimes. Didn't have a clue.

'Or you're going to have to go back to work,' added Simon.

Lorna felt a stab of panic. Not that. She'd promised herself she would be the one to bring up her children, take them to school, pick them up at the end of the day, do their homework with them. 'What?'

'Lorna, you're only thirty. You've got years ahead of you. Good earning potential.'

'I'm doing a very important job bringing up the kids.'

'I don't dispute that. But at some point . . .'

She refused to bite.

He held his hand out.

'What?' asked Lorna, looking at it, confused.

'The card.'

'Seriously?'

'Lorna, we're nearly a grand in debt. I can't afford to pay all that off this month. I'm a data analyst, not a striker for Leicester City.'

'But I wanted to get something for Pepper.'

'What?'

'A toy. A pretend pet dog. Her friend has got one, Pepper's feeling left out.'

'Are you kidding me?'

Lorna grimaced, got the card out of her purse and handed it over. Simon got a pair of scissors out of the kitchen drawer. Each cut felt as if it was slicing right through her.

THIRTEEN

Monday 7 September

When the double doors opened at the end of the school day and it was Lara's turn to point out her mother so she could go, it was obvious to Nancy that something was wrong. Lara's body was rigid with tension and as she walked over, Nancy could tell she was doing her best not to cry.

She rested her hand gently on her daughter's shoulder. 'Everything OK?' she asked quietly.

Lara quickly shook her head.

'What's happened?'

Lara paused. 'Today, in break, Rosie wasn't very nice.'

Nancy kept her voice level. 'Go on.'

'Everyone was sitting in a circle playing Duck, Duck, Goose. I was watching and then Rosie said I could join in. So they made room for me. Then Rosie said . . .' She tailed off, upset.

'What? Come on, you can tell me.'

'"Anyone who actually likes Lara, put your hand up."'

Nancy's breath caught in her throat. 'Then what happened?'

'No one did.' A tear rolled down Lara's cheek.

'The little . . . !' Nancy put her arm around her daughter, held her close.

'So I got up and tried to get away,' continued Lara, 'but I was hurrying and accidentally stood on Rosie's hand and she started crying like I'd broken it or something and then I got into trouble with Miss Young.'

'Did you explain to Miss Young what Rosie had done?'

'No . . . I didn't want to tell on her. And by the way, Miss Young wants to have a word with you.'

Nancy looked up and, sure enough, the last of the children had been released to their parents and Miss Young was looking over expectantly.

Good, thought Nancy. She could clear this up. She approached the teacher, Lara trailing behind her.

'Hello,' said Miss Young. 'We've had a bit of an incident today.' She looked down at Lara. 'Maybe Lara's already told you about it?'

'Yes, she mentioned.'

'I'm afraid, as this is the second time Lara's used inappropriate behaviour towards Rosie, we had to take it to the head.'

'Second time?' asked Nancy, confused.

'Yes . . . I understand there was an incident at the weekend? I appreciate it didn't take place at the school and ordinarily Mr Whitman wouldn't take anything out of school into account, but I understand it was quite a serious altercation?'

Nancy was struggling to take it all in. 'I'm not sure what

Mr Whitman has told you but I can assure you, Lara is completely innocent of any wrong doing,' said Nancy, her voice growing in emotion as she spoke. She went on to explain how Rosie had been teasing Lara on the water and how she had fallen in, fabricating a story about being pushed in. She also explained how Rosie had humiliated Lara in the playground earlier that day. As she spoke, she saw Miss Young's face shift, and her eyes harden, as if some suspected notion had been reinforced in her mind.

'I didn't know that,' Miss Young said levelly and then she turned to Lara. 'I'm sorry to hear about what happened earlier but please feel you can talk to me at any time.

'Thank you for telling me,' said Miss Young, and Nancy heard a steely note in her voice. 'I shall be keeping an eye on the situation.'

As Nancy came away, she saw Rosie running around the playground, screaming with laughter with Tilly as they waited for their mothers to finish talking. She felt a sudden smoking rage. She turned away and led Lara out of the gates towards home.

FOURTEEN

Monday 7 September

'Did you see her hand?' said Imogen to Dylan as she chopped vegetables at the kitchen counter. Her husband had just come in from work and had been greeting Rosie in the living room where she was watching TV.

'She showed me. It's a bit of a nasty scrape but it'll heal,' said Dylan. He put his bag of books down on the floor, right by the fridge, where Imogen knew it would be in the way. Like he always did. Even though she always asked him to move it. She resisted the urge to ask him to move it yet again.

'But did she tell you how it happened?' she asked instead.

'Something about Lara treading on it.'

Imogen waited for a sense of outrage, but none came.

'On purpose,' she added forcefully.

'It was probably an accident.'

'Did she tell you it was an accident?'

'No. But it's easy to misconstrue things.'

Imogen couldn't quite believe how calm her husband was being. 'Lara deliberately walked up to Rosie, looked at her meanly, trod on her hand and then sauntered off.'

'What?' Dylan screwed up his face.

'Exactly,' said Imogen.

'No, I mean, is that what she told you?'

'Yes!'

'Hmm.'

'What does that mean?'

'Nothing. I just think Rosie is upset. Maybe she's being a little dramatic.'

'I think she's telling us what happened. And the point is this other child has hurt Rosie. Again.' Imogen stirred the soup then put down the spoon, wiped her hands on her apron. 'I'm going to call James.'

'It's half seven at night. He's not going to want to be bothered with it now.'

'Bothered? This is our daughter.'

Dylan took her hands gently. 'I know. And I don't like seeing her upset any more than you do. But let the man have his evening. You can call tomorrow.'

Imogen thought. James would be at home with Carol. It might be difficult to talk. 'OK.'

'And . . .' continued Dylan, 'I think we have to be careful.'

Imogen removed her hands from his. 'What do you mean?'

'Rosie's upset about leaving the house, her room, her pony. We know this. She's not going to be that enamoured with the child who's taken over her old home. Especially when they're in the same class. I think we need to factor that in when she tells us about these run-ins with this other girl.'

'Are you suggesting she's making it up? Treading on her own hand?'

'Of course not.' Dylan paused. 'But she does know how to play you.' Imogen went to speak – she hated it when Dylan patronized her like this – but he put his hands on the tops of her arms. 'She knows you'd do anything for her,' he said softly.

Imogen sniffed, mollified a little. 'Miss Young did say she was going to speak to Nancy.'

'There you go, then. I'm sure this is all being sorted out.'

'Glass of wine?' asked Imogen, pulling a bottle of red out of the cupboard.

'It's Monday night.'

'I know, but a small one can't hurt.' She got the corkscrew, popped the cork and poured them both a glass. She took a mouthful, swallowed then smiled at Dylan.

'I've had an idea.'

He returned her smile, a touch nervously. She knew he was sometimes intimidated by her 'ideas' but this was a good one. 'Oh yeah?' he ventured.

Imogen moved closer to him, put her hand on his chest. Dylan was tall – over six foot – it was one of the things that had made her fall in love with him when they first met. She looked up into his eyes.

'We want to save up for a deposit, right? Get our own place again?'

'Yes . . .'

'Now please hear me out. I know you love your job but there will always be teaching jobs at state secondary schools.'

She paused. 'They've published the ad for the job at Kingsgate—'

'You know how I feel abou—'

'It pays twenty thousand a year more.'

A tiny bud of satisfaction bloomed quietly as she saw the look of surprise on his face. 'You'd walk it, Dylan. I know you would. You're the best teacher at Ripton High – Kingsgate would be mad not to hire you.'

Dylan gave a half grimace. 'Not sure about that.'

'Just think about it. Please?' Imogen gave her best earnest look. 'And I want to help out too.'

'Oh?'

'The restaurant premises are still empty.'

'I don't understand . . .'

'You know no one ever gets rich working for someone else. I want to set up another company—'

'Imogen—'

She shook her head. 'Not like before. Not with tons of upfront investment to create the most high-end restaurant and be saddled with loads of debt. No, this time, I was thinking of a pizzeria.'

Dylan looked doubtful. 'But who's going to fund it? Our credit's stuffed for some time.'

'I have an offer from a private investor.'

He was surprised. 'Who?'

She paused. 'James.'

'*James?* Since when has he been into funding restaurants?'

'It's not restaurants that interest him, it's viable businesses. He and I have talked it all through. He's fronting the capital, my part is my expertise in running a restaurant – and of course the cooking. Profits fifty-fifty.'

Dylan laughed nervously. Ran his hand through his hair. She could tell he was on the verge of telling her it was too soon, too risky.

She jumped in quickly. 'You know we need a hefty deposit on a house to be considered by a lender . . . with the new business – and your help too, of course – we should be able to achieve that in a year.'

Dylan was surprised. 'Really? A year? As soon as that?' The carrot she was dangling was having an effect. He was allowing himself to think of the impossible – their own place again.

'What's he charging on the funding?'

Imogen smiled. This was the sensitive part. 'Nothing. He wants to help. Get us back on our feet.'

'Why?'

'Why not? He's our friend.' She rested her hand on his, leaned in to kiss him. 'It's an opportunity that only comes along once in a blue moon. We're lucky. It's our chance to change things.' She moved over to the hob, stirred the soup. 'We plan to open in December,' she added casually.

'*This* December?'

'Yes.'

'But . . . the lease . . . setting everything up . . .' He was looking at her and the penny dropped. 'You've already done it.'

'I saw the estate agent today. Haven't signed anything yet. I'm so excited about it,' she pleaded. 'It's all for us, you know. Me, you and Rosie. Think about it. This time next year. Our own front door again.'

She stopped, let that sink in. She knew what he was wrestling with in his mind, knew he was feeling under pressure.

'So what do you think?' she asked tentatively.

He looked at her and in his eyes she saw admiration, but also exhaustion. And deeply hidden, a flash of resentment. She held her breath.

'I think I'd better apply for the job at Kingsgate,' he said, 'seeing as we're in this together.'

Her heart leapt with joy. She threw her arms around his neck.

'On one condition,' said Dylan, his voice muffled by her hair.

'Yes?'

'I do it on my own. I don't want you talking to James, asking him to help.'

'But—'

'I mean it, Imogen. It's on my own or nothing. You promise?'

She looked at him, realized his mind was set. 'Promise.'

Imogen closed her eyes with relief. Another victory. Step by step she was going to reclaim her rightful place in this village.

FIFTEEN

Monday 7 September

It was a warm evening, what Imogen knew would be one of the last warm evenings of the year. She was restless, full of burning ambition. She needed to walk. She needed space like she used to have, where she'd either stroll around her three-acre garden, lost in its meditative enchantment, or if she needed to let off more steam, she'd head across the lawn then down the steps and out onto the reservoir path where she could walk for fourteen miles if she so wanted, right around the perimeter of the water, through the nature reserve, past the woods, until she arrived back at her house. *Had* arrived back at her house. It was no longer her house. But the path was bloody well open to all and Imogen got a sudden urge to claim it.

She snapped on Arthur's lead and calling out to Dylan, who was marking books in the kitchen, and to Rosie, who was colouring in the living room, she left the house.

The minute the door shut behind her she felt less suffocated. She breathed in the night-scented air – someone's dinner being cooked, a honeysuckle at a neighbour's gate –

and headed down the high street towards the water. Dusk had already claimed the sky in the east but over the reservoir, sitting above the horizon, the sun was still a golden orb. Imogen headed for the water's edge and stopped for a moment. It was quiet; everyone else had gone home for the day. The cafe was shut and the fishermen and water sports enthusiasts had long ago put away their boats and kayaks and the water was still.

In the far distance, away from the sunset, the edges of the reservoir were nearly black. When Imogen stared at them the line between water and bank blurred together. Ahead of her, the sun lit a golden path across the reservoir. Bats flitted amongst the trees and a fish leapt out of the water, once, twice, a third time and it was as if it were welcoming her back. She smiled, remembering the times she would come down here, just she and Dylan at first, when they'd bring a bottle of wine and takeaway pizzas and sit on the bank, once making out behind some trees. Then later, with Rosie in a baby pouch strapped to her chest, Dylan holding her hand as they strolled around to get their daughter to sleep. All the while knowing their home was only a short distance away.

Arthur was eager to get walking and Imogen knew she didn't have long before it would get dark. She could take the dog to the grassy bank around the cafe, let him have a run around or . . . She looked to her right. High up on the bank, the barn's lights were on. She knew exactly how many minutes it would take to reach it. Twelve and a half. Bit too far really, seeing as she had to get back again and, judging by the sun, in fifteen minutes it would be dark.

The pull was too strong. Imogen turned and headed down the path and as the light faded she got a sense of excitement, a feeling the night was covering up her approach. It made her feel hidden, clandestine, as if she had special powers, the darkness offering her a cloak of invisibility from which she could observe unnoticed. Before long she was at the gate. The sign saying 'Private Land' was still nailed firmly to the wood. She opened the catch and slipped through, making her way past the trees and then up the steps into the garden itself.

Imogen's breath caught in her throat. There was her house. She glanced up quickly to make sure no one was on the patio; the bi-fold doors were shut. It was the same upstairs on the balcony – no one was there. She breathed out, feeling safe enough to go closer. Keeping to the edge of the lawn, she smiled in recognition at the heleniums she'd planted three years ago with Rosie on a day when she was off sick from school, an attempt to cheer her from her cold. Their deep orange blooms glowed softly in the last of the light. Arthur was pulling her onwards, recognizing his home, Imogen knew, and she shortened the lead to keep him close. It wouldn't do for Nancy to spot the movement of a dog in her back garden. And Arthur was straining at the lead as he had smelt the chickens that Imogen could hear clucking in a pen across the other side of the garden. He'd chase them, given half the chance. Imogen went further still, emboldened by the knowledge she hadn't been seen, until she was within spitting distance of the house itself. She stopped for a moment, looking across at the windows, which had their curtains drawn. Imogen could see tantalizing glimpses of lights burning in rooms she used to own. But try as she might, she couldn't see properly into any of the rooms. The cracks in the curtains were too small. She suddenly, desperately, wanted to see something, anything and so she would go a little further, she thought, just around to the front and then she would head home again.

She walked past the four-hundred-year-old oak tree where the swing still hung from one of the low branches and around the north side of the house to the front driveway. As she turned the corner of the building, she stopped. There, on the driveway, was a large skip. And in the darkness, various jagged, haphazard shapes protruded and suddenly Imogen recognized her beautiful grey front door on the top. Ripped off its hinges and discarded.

Thrown away. Devalued. Tossed aside.

It shouldn't affect her the way it did – it was only a door, for God's sake – but it was like a slap in the face. A reminder that it was no longer her house, it belonged to someone else and they could do whatever they liked to it. She looked back up at it, at its new front door – a bright yellow one – and it looked good, goddammit, but she hated it. Hated the fact it no longer looked like her home. Then, it was as if once she could see one thing, she could see many. The solar panels on the roof, the start of what looked like the installation of a heat pump. And in the skip itself, some carpets.

For the first time she felt as if she was trespassing – as if she'd been called out and made a fool of. Stealing up to an ex-lover only to find someone else in his arms. She couldn't bear to look any more – and the dark was beginning to feel menacing instead of adventurous, and suddenly Imogen just wanted to get out of there. She was about to turn and hurry away when something else caught her eye. A movement in the kitchen. The main lights were off so it was semi-dark, only the under-counter lights cast a glow in the room. At a table, she saw Nancy, a glass of wine by her side. But she wasn't drinking it, she was sobbing, her head resting on her arms, her shoulders heaving.

Imogen stopped and watched. The crying went on for a good minute or so and then Nancy pulled her head up, wiped her eyes. She looked utterly miserable.

Imogen was intrigued. Surely this upset was not a result of their earlier meeting. No, this seemed much more serious, much more . . . entrenched. She wondered what it could be. She continued to wonder all the way home.

SIXTEEN

Thursday 10 September

It was better to nip this situation in the bud before it festered and got out of hand. That was the sensible thing to do, the grown-up thing, Nancy had thought when she'd sent a message to Imogen, her cover being that they meet to go over the detail for the Christmas fair.

Imogen had replied saying: Thursday. Heron Water Cafe. 2 p.m. 30 minutes. Nancy had been a little taken aback by the abruptness of the message, but that was what she was here to hopefully resolve.

She looked into her coffee cup. Near empty because Imogen was already twenty minutes late. Maybe she wouldn't turn up, thought Nancy. Maybe she'd said she would just to make Nancy sit here like an idiot, waiting. *No,* she thought, *you don't even know the woman, stop assuming the worst.*

She gazed around and her eye caught on the ancient yew tree down near the water. Up close, she could see how twisted its limbs were. There was something malevolent about it, something spellbinding.

She checked her phone again but there was no message. Nancy was about to give up when she heard a car pull into the car park. She looked up to see Imogen getting out and walking across to the cafe. She was wearing a pair of dark sunglasses, cropped chinos and a T-shirt. Nancy watched as she approached, then pulled out a chair opposite her and sat down. She crossed her legs and waited.

Nancy knew she was a fool if she thought she was going to get an apology for Imogen's lateness.

'What can I get you?' asked the waitress who'd approached their table.

'A flat white, please,' said Imogen.

Nancy ordered the same. She was pretty certain Imogen was looking at her but she couldn't see her eyes through the glasses.

Then Imogen raised them onto the top of her head. 'Bottle stall, pound a go, tickets that end with a five or zero win prizes. What else is there to discuss?'

Nancy thought she was laughing at her, baiting her, and it rankled for a moment before she reminded herself why she'd suggested this meeting. But if Imogen wanted to play it direct, then so be it.

'I know we haven't got off to the best of starts,' she said, 'but Lara and I, we just want to fit in. It's a small village, our girls are in the same class and . . . I think it might be a good idea to draw a line under what's happened and start afresh.'

The waitress arrived with the drinks. Imogen took a long, slow sip of her drink, and said nothing.

Nancy bit her tongue.

'Is that why you asked me for a coffee?' asked Imogen, as she replaced her cup. 'To brush everything that's happened under the carpet so you can go on your merry way without feeling any guilt at all?'

Nancy was taken aback. 'Guilt?' she repeated. 'For what?'

Imogen let out a little laugh. 'Oh, come on. Your daughter appears to be on a campaign to hurt mine. Rosie has the scratches to prove it.'

'Actually, I don't think that's quite right,' said Nancy carefully. 'Rosie was belittling Lara in the playground and Lara accidentally scraped Rosie's hand in her hurry to get away. It wasn't a "campaign" and what Rosie said was quite hurtful.'

Imogen was looking at her coolly and Nancy tried again. She laid her hands on the table. 'I appreciate that we're each getting two different sides to the story, but I think if we can sort things out now, before they escalate, it might be best for everyone involved,' she said. She attempted a smile. 'We've only just got here. I certainly don't want to fall out with anyone.'

'No, I'm sure you don't,' said Imogen.

Nancy's smile slipped. 'What do you mean by that?'

A tear was rolling down Imogen's face. This woman sitting in front of her was beyond contempt. She had no feeling at all, no sensitivity. Did she know what it was like to lose everything you've worked for? All your plans, money, your whole dream gone up in smoke? Did she bother to think whose feet walked across those floors before hers did?

Did she even stop *for one damn second,* and think about what it was like to watch the locks getting changed on your house and then the bailiffs hand the key over to a total stranger?

Of course she didn't.

And now, because life had finally got a little inconvenient for her, she wanted to smooth it all over, so she could carry on in whatever way she pleased.

'I have never been so scared in all my life as when my daughter was pulled out of the water barely breathing,' said Imogen. 'Until you actually think there is a chance your child is going to die, you cannot begin to understand.'

Nancy went to open her mouth but Imogen wasn't finished.

'If you don't want to fall out with anyone, then tell your daughter to stop bullying innocent kids.'

'*Lara* bullying?'

But Imogen had got up from the table. She pushed her glasses onto her face and walked back to her car.

SEVENTEEN

Friday 18 September

RIPTON GAZETTE

APPEAL FOLLOWING SHEEP SLAUGHTER ON LOCAL FARM

By Erin Mackie, Editor-In-Chief

WARNING: This article contains content some may find distressing.

Police are appealing for information after a number of sheep have been found attacked at Hilldale Farm in Ripton. The incident happened on the evening of Wednesday 16 September. At around 8 p.m., the farmer, Hannah Chapman, found two sheep dead in the field, both with injuries that were consistent with being attacked by a dog.

When asked what happened, Hannah said she assumed 'a dog had got into the field and chased the sheep, attacking two'.

The dog that carried out the attack is yet to be found. 'Somebody will have seen this,' said Hannah, 'or know about it. Please get in touch, whether it is a dog being walked or one that has escaped.'

The police have asked people to 'check their property to make sure there are no holes in fences where dogs could get out'. They added: 'If your dog's got any blood on it, please contact the local police so we can sort this matter and bring some peace of mind to the farmer.'

Sad news for local pet owner

A pet dog has been found dead in a local meadow near farmland. The vet's post-mortem found that the dog had died of kidney failure and had possibly ingested something poisonous.

EIGHTEEN

Friday 18 September

'We can keep all the original booths and tables, just paint the walls and I was thinking more plants, all green, not flowers,' said Imogen to the top of James's head. He was currently positioned between her legs, doing exquisite things to her with his tongue.

They were lying on the floor of what used to be Luna's – soon to become her new pizza restaurant. Imogen now had the keys, and this visit was supposed to be a recce to ascertain the changes needed to the decor. She shifted the cushion under her head.

'Sounds very Italian,' said James, raising his head briefly. 'Romantic.'

She caressed his shoulder. 'Thanks again. It's only because of your investment that I'm able to set up busine—'

'Enough thanks,' said James. 'I'm getting my return, aren't I?' He grinned. 'In more ways than one.'

'Ha ha, very funny,' started Imogen, but then was unable to speak as he brought her to orgasm.

Afterwards, she lay next to him. They were both naked

from the waist down, a sort of necessity fuck, not exactly romantic but practical. She pulled her discarded skirt towards her, slipped it on.

'So what are you going to call it?' asked James. 'Whitman and Wood?'

Imogen baulked. 'Not sure what Dylan would make of that.'

James rolled towards her. 'As your business partner, not your lover,' he said. 'What does he think about it all, anyway?'

'He couldn't be happier,' she said. 'And about the name – your suggestion doesn't exactly roll off the tongue.' She looked at him. 'When do you have to get back to school?'

James glanced at his watch – one of his more expensive ones, Imogen noted. She knew he liked to collect them.

He groaned. 'I've got a senior leadership meeting in twenty minutes.'

'That's a shame,' said Imogen.

He kissed her. 'Dead right it is. We'll have to organize an investors' meeting again soon. There's lots to discuss, I'm sure.'

She smiled. 'There is. In fact . . . I was wondering about Dylan . . .'

He was starting to get dressed. 'He's not joining us, is he? Only I don't fancy that kind of threesome.'

'Course not. It's about the job. At Kingsgate. Will you put in a good word? Seeing as you have the head's ear.'

'Dylan made it very clear he didn't want my help,' said James sniffily. 'I'm not entirely sure why my offer was so distasteful.'

'You know what he's like. Proud.'

'I don't know. What if he found out? It'll piss him off no end. Your revolutionary husband.'

'Why would he? In fact, you're on strict instructions to keep it quiet.' Imogen placed her hand into his pants. 'Please?' she asked. 'It would mean a lot to me.'

He resisted for a few moments but she knew what she was doing and before long he was agreeing.

James left first. Despite his comments about an investors' meeting, it wouldn't do for them to be seen together – especially during school hours. Once he'd gone, Imogen tidied up the cushions and looked around the room. The remnants of her last endeavour didn't depress her as much as she'd thought they would. It was all water under the bridge now. This new pizza restaurant was going to be a success, she knew it. She would be open in two months. Just in time for the Christmas party season. In fact, the contractors were already booked to start the refit.

As Imogen locked the door behind her she thought she'd take Arthur out for a quick walk. She went home to get him and then headed towards the reservoir. Almost immediately Arthur started pulling on his lead.

Hazel was walking towards them. Imogen smiled. Arthur knew exactly which locals were dog lovers. He planted himself at Hazel's feet, sitting immediately and obediently, and waited for his reward.

'Oh, you're such a good boy,' said Hazel, reaching into her coat pocket.

'You've got him better trained than we have,' said Imogen. 'How's the exercise regime going?'

'I've lost four pounds!' said Hazel. 'The doctor is very pleased with me.'

Imogen decided to get a takeaway coffee from Heron Water Cafe to celebrate her new venture. She tied Arthur up and went inside. When she came back out again, she noticed he'd been sick. A half-eaten hot dog was lying on the ground.

She sighed. 'Serves you right for scavenging,' she reprimanded, and then untied him so they could walk down by the water.

She strolled along the reservoir path, taking in the explosion of red and gold leaves that covered the acres of trees all along the banks. A few fishermen were out in their boats, the on-board motors sending a gentle rumble across the water. Then they stopped and the ripples from the boats' movement lapped all the way to the shore, down by her feet. There were a couple of people out on pleasure craft too – a windsurfer who was confidently streaming across the water, the sun catching on the plastic sail. Its bright red colour and the sunlight on the water made Imogen think of holidays abroad. Maybe next year they might even be able to afford one. Behind the windsurfer was a more sedate paddleboarder, the person on the board wobbling as they attempted to stand up. Imogen watched, wondering if they were going to fall in, and then as they stood, she realized who it was: Nancy.

Imogen watched for a moment, then smiled. She wondered if Nancy had found out yet that the shop premises she'd had her eye on had been taken by someone else.

It tasted sweet. Revenge. Or comeback. Whatever you wanted to call it. And now Imogen had a taste for it, she wasn't going to stop there.

NINETEEN

Nancy pressed 'Send' on her email to Miss Young and got up from her desk. Things hadn't improved – in fact, they had got worse – and she wanted a meeting with the teacher to talk it over.

Lara had come home from school several times over the last week upset about things that Rosie had said to her. Lara had struck up an early friendship with another girl in the class, Mia, but Rosie seemed intent on destroying it. Having ignored Mia for months, Rosie now suddenly seemed to want to claim her. She had gone over to where Mia and Lara were talking and, tucking her arm into Mia's, insisted they needed a 'private conversation' and had dragged her away, leaving Lara alone in the playground. When Lara had asked to join a group game, Rosie had played up the drama, deliberating whether she was going to let her in – then humiliatingly said the group was full. Then, to Nancy's growing fury, Rosie had declared she and Mia were going to sunbathe one breaktime and told Lara she could be their 'sunshade' and instructed her to stand so that she cast a shadow over them.

Dean was in the kitchen working and Nancy went to make him a drink. She opened up the *Ripton Gazette* she'd got from the village earlier.

Both their eyes went to the headline.

'I'm sorry about the sheep,' said Nancy.

Dean shook his head. 'That's three this month. Hannah's devastated.'

'It must be difficult to keep an eye on them. I mean, people can walk the footpath at any time.'

'Hannah's spending a bit more time up there – checking every hour. I've told her to take the gun.'

Nancy started. 'What?'

'Shoot any dog that's worrying the sheep. It's her legal right.' He saw her face. 'It's a last resort. But we've put up the signs, advertised the fact we've now had three dead. It's still happening. Thanks for the tea,' he said cheerfully as he put down the empty mug, then went back to work.

The sound of a drill starting up in another room made her jump. She sighed and put the mugs in the dishwasher. Still feeing unsettled, she decided she needed to get out of the house.

Nancy changed into her wetsuit and took her paddleboard down to the reservoir. The minute she got onto the water, kneeling to get her balance, she felt a little better. She drifted along, meandering her way across the water to the opposite bank in the far distance. She lowered her hand, letting the water flow over her fingers, enjoying the cool, rippling sensation. A small patch of algae floated on the water's surface just ahead of her and she retracted her hand. It

looked like the blue-green algae she'd seen on the notice-
boards near Heron Water cafe. The algae was toxic and
dog owners were warned not to let their pets drink from
the water. It could be harmful to humans too.

The board drifted to a stop and Nancy sighed. She looked
at her legs, motionless, dangling in the water and decided
it was time to get moving. She was going to attempt to
stand up. Slowly, carefully, she shifted into a kneeling position and then put her feet flat on the board and raised up
from a squat until, amazingly, she was standing. She laughed
to herself, then tentatively raised her head. She was doing
it! She lowered the paddle into the water and pulled, moving
gently forwards. High on the sense of achievement, Nancy
looked around, thinking about where she would go. It was
then she spotted the half-submerged church spire and the
chimney pots.

She turned her board, then paddled over. It was exciting.
An adventure! She thought of the number of times she'd
gazed out at these relics from her balcony, wondering about
them. Well, now she could explore properly. Energized by
her progress, it was only a short time until she was upon
the spire. She slowed, letting the board come against the
stone. Up close, she could see it was covered with algae,
the once grey stone now a pillar of dark green. Tendrils of
algae and river weeds hung from the two arms of the cross
on the top. Nancy reached out a hand, touching the top of
the spire. It was cold and slippery. She withdrew her hand,
wiping it on her wetsuit. She lowered herself down on the
board, wanting to peer into the depths.

She got onto her knees and, hands on the edge of the board, she looked down into the water. It was dark, visibility only going about half a metre and then the spire seemed to disappear from view. She thought of how far down it went, the church it was attached to. Thought of the windows, their stained glass never again lighting up in the sun – or maybe they had broken under the pressure of the water. She imagined what had happened when they'd flooded the valley. Had the church doors been closed? How long before the water had crept under the cracks, inching along the stone floor, pooling amongst the pews, the altar? Places where people had sat and sung. Where they had gathered for weddings and funerals. The water would have started slowly at first and then the pressure pushing against the doors would have burst through, smashing everything in its path, turning it over, crushing it with its force.

The sound of a boat broke Nancy from her reverie. She frowned – it seemed loud – and then she caught a glimpse of it passing her, seconds before the waves barrelled their way across the water. She tried to right herself but it was too late and before she really knew what was happening, she'd plunged in head first.

She gasped, shocked by the sudden change of temperature. Sucking in a mouthful, the water rushed past her ears, adding to her disorientation. She was facing down, looking at the church roof. Many of the slate tiles were missing; the dark wooden skeleton of the rafters visible. It felt as if the sunken building was pulling her downwards and, in a panic, she fought to reverse her trajectory. She kicked her legs hard and flapped her arms until she rose above the surface again. Swimming to her board, she threw her arms over the edge and held on, her cheek resting on the fibreglass.

It's just the shock, she told herself, *of falling in. There's nothing sinister about what lies under the water, nothing threatening.* But even thinking about it made her chilled again so she climbed back onto the board, her movements ungainly as she seemed to be drained of energy, and then she started to paddle back to the bank, this time staying kneeling all the way.

TWENTY

Saturday 19 September

Lorna could hear voices coming through the open patio doors, people walking through the house heading for the back garden, and she quickly nodded to Phoenix, who was kicking a football against the wall of the house.

'Now,' she said, 'and remember what we talked about.'

She checked her son had begun his performance and then turned swiftly to see Simon lead Nancy, Lara and Beth into the back garden. Carol had also arrived and was bringing up the rear.

'You made it!' she said. 'Have you all been introduced? This is Carol, my mum, also married to James Whitman, your head teacher.' As Simon went over to check the barbecue, Lorna introduced Pepper, who promptly dragged Lara off to the outdoor playhouse. 'Can I get anyone a drink?'

Beth accepted a glass of the Marlborough Sauvignon Lorna had purchased especially from the village wine shop but, to her disappointment, Nancy stuck with sparkling water. Instead, Lorna tried to tempt her guest with some of the French charcuterie she'd got from the deli, and was pleased when Nancy accepted.

'Does it still count as supporting local shopkeepers when it's imported from Alsace?'

'Why wouldn't it?' replied Beth.

She was so abrupt, thought Lorna, somewhat crushed. Perhaps Beth thought she was showing off, she thought, burying the faint nagging feeling that maybe she was. She glanced up at Phoenix, who had been passing the ball from knee to knee for what seemed like an impressively long time.

'You're right,' she said. 'It's still putting money into our local economy. Talking of which, I'm so excited for you, Nancy, on your home improvements. Have the builders started yet?'

'I was lucky in that Dean had a cancellation, so he's been able to begin work.'

'And the pool?'

'Well, it's out of season so they're able to start too. Next week.'

'It's going to be lovely,' said Lorna. 'Imagine! Swimming in your own back garden. All that clear water. No chlorine in sight.'

Carol turned to Beth. 'Did you know Ripton much before Nancy moved here?'

'Not really,' said Beth. 'I came to a restaurant in the high street once with my husband. Food was amazing but I noticed on our walk down that it's closed now.'

'Ah. Yes. That's Imogen's old place,' said Lorna. 'Luna's.

It was such a shame for her, she put everything into it, financed the renovations herself. Then Covid came and it lost so much money.' Lorna held her hands out in sympathy. 'The bank took the house. Even though Imogen did everything she could to save it.'

Lorna was vaguely aware of her mum's discomfort at the way the conversation was going but it wasn't as if this wasn't public knowledge.

'Oh right,' said Nancy, taken aback. 'I didn't realize.'

'It was quite a shock,' said Lorna. 'For everyone around here. She was our local success story.'

'Do you work, Lorna?' asked Beth.

Lorna bristled. Beth's question felt like a test. She lifted her head. 'No, but I've decided to start looking for something now that Pepper's established in school.'

'You have?' asked Carol, surprised and pleased.

'Since when?' said Simon.

'I've been thinking about it the last few days,' said Lorna haughtily.

'Good for you,' said Carol. 'And I'm here to help. With anything.'

'Ladies, rare, medium or well done?' Simon called over from the barbecue.

Lorna pulled the Sauvignon out of the upright wine cooler she'd placed on the patio – and as Nancy and Beth placed their burger orders, she held up the bottle.

'Sure I can't tempt you, Nancy?'

'Oh, OK. A small one.'

Lorna smiled, pleased. As she poured, she was suddenly

aware the football had fallen silent. Phoenix was looking at her, the ball in his hands, a furrowed frown across his forehead.

'Mum, is that enough now? Can I stop?'

Colour rushed into Lorna's cheeks. 'Of course!' she said, with forced surprise. 'Why are you asking me?'

'Because you said—'

'Why don't you go and play on your Xbox?'

Unused to being allowed such a privilege so early on a Saturday, Phoenix's eyes widened and then he scarpered.

Lorna took a deep breath, looked up and thought she caught the tiniest glimpse of a smile on Beth's face.

'I think it's nice Imogen's old house is being lived in again,' said Lorna. 'Although it must feel big with just the two of you. Even if it had been your ex-husband moving in as well it would still be a large house. Lovely and spacious.'

'Lorna . . .' said Carol.

'Mum, there's no shame in being divorced. Right, Nancy?' said Lorna with a generous smile.

'I should imagine not. But I'm not divorced. My husband died. Eleven months ago.'

'I'm so sorry,' said Carol.

'How?' asked Lorna.

Nancy was surprised at the audaciousness of the question. A hush rang out over the group. Nancy paused for a moment before answering. 'It was an accident. A lorry went into the side of the car. Killed him outright.'

'Oh. That's awful.'

'Yes, it was. And I got a payout from the haulage firm – two million pounds.'

'I don't think we need talk about that,' said Carol awkwardly.

Lorna's jaw had dropped. 'That's some payout.'

'Sam was insured for a sum too.'

'Good God.'

'That's how I was able to buy Willow Barn. Is there anything else you need to know?' Nancy looked Lorna straight in the eye.

'I didn't mean . . .'

'Course you didn't,' said Beth, her nose in her wine glass.

'I'm so terribly sorry. Must have been awful. Well, of course it was . . . I mean, I feel for you so much, such a terrible—'

'Burgers are ready, ladies,' said Simon, coming over with a plate piled high with chargrilled meat.

Despite the unbelievable nosiness of Lorna's questioning, it had felt good for Nancy to say what she had. Cathartic. Though she loved her new home there had been guilt that it had come off the back of Sam's death. But the way they were living now – that was what he would have wanted. Admitting it had given her a new strength. And boy, did she need it. She had lost Sam and, once, had almost lost Lara. It made her feel quite vulnerable. And protective. Very, very protective.

As the others selected their food, Lorna was swept away by what she'd learned. All Nancy's worries had been taken away in one fell swoop – well, the financial ones anyway, she hastily corrected. Nancy had been able to buy a beautiful house and could send her child to the best fee-paying school if she so wanted.

Imagine.

19 September

RIPTON PRIMARY, YEAR 6

Hannah Chapman, Jakob's mum
I've had another two sheep die on the farm.
Another dog attack. It's devastating, as you
can see in the pic. Please, if any of you hear
anything, can you let me know? 18:22

> **Lorna Fielding, Phoenix's mum**
> Sorry for your loss, Hannah, but in future,
> please could you not post the picture? It's
> quite graphic and I wouldn't want Pepper
> to get hold of my phone and see that.
> 18:23

Hannah Chapman, Jakob's mum
Well keep your phone away from her then.
18:23

> **Lorna Fielding, Phoenix's mum**
> I can understand you're upset but no need
> to take it out on me. I obvs do keep my
> phone away but she's so bright and curious
> it's impossible to stop her inquisitive mind
> 100% 18:24

Erin Mackie, Tilly's mum
Has Nancy got a dog? 18:25

> **Imogen Wood, Rosie's mum**
> Not as far as I know. Why? 18:26

Erin Mackie, Tilly's mum
These attacks have only started since she's
moved here. 18:26

> **Sarah Ramsay, Noah's mum**
> I don't think we should be accusing anyone
> of anything. Not without any proof. 18:27

Erin Mackie, Tilly's mum
I'm not. I'm just working as an investigative
journalist – process of elimination. 18:27

> **Hannah Chapman, Jakob's mum**
> Let's be careful. Nancy hasn't done
> anything wrong. 18:28

Lorna Fielding, Phoenix's mum
I feel sorry for her actually. What with her
husband dying recently. 18:28

> **Erin Mackie, Tilly's mum**
> WHAT? 18:28

Lorna Fielding, Phoenix's mum
Yes. It was a car accident. Tragic. 18:29

Imogen Wood, Rosie's mum
How do you know all this? 18:30

Lorna Fielding, Phoenix's mum
She really opened up to me earlier. I felt
like she needed a friend actually. It's all so
sad. But fortunately there was a payout. A
large one. Seven figures. Plus he had an
insurance policy. So at least she's safe,
financially. 18:30

Nicole Wilson, Bella's mum
Bloody hell. Terrible. But that's some insurance policy. Willow Barn cost a mill! 18:32

Lorna Fielding, Phoenix's mum
It's nice she doesn't have to worry about
the mortgage. Even though it's very sad of
course. 18:34

Erin Mackie, Tilly's mum
Wow, maybe I should off my husband! 18:34

Lorna Fielding, Phoenix's mum
No one is suggesting that she killed her
husband. 18:35

TWENTY-ONE

October, the previous year

It was night. Dark. She rested her head on the window and looked up at the motorway lights, flashing past in a regular rhythm. It was comforting, added to the content, fulfilled feeling she had after a week's half-term holiday. They'd been to Cornwall and even though it was October, it had been unseasonably warm; the sun had shone every day.

It was quiet because it was so late. Only a few other cars passed them. And lorries, there were quite a few lorries, getting their goods to their final destination. She liked to look at the number plate country codes. Think of holidays in European lands: Holland, Spain, France. She remembered a trip to Brittany on the ferry a couple of years ago. They had eaten lots of crepes. Played as a family on the beach.

When she saw the lorry move across the lane, she thought it was overtaking at first. But it kept on coming. Closer and closer.

She always asked herself the same questions. What had gone through his mind when the lorry hit them? Was he scared? Did he feel the impact? What was it like for him when he died?

TWENTY-TWO

Nancy stood on the edge of a very large hole. It was twice her height at the end where she looked down, tapering to a few inches deep way down at the other end of the teardrop shape it made in her back garden.

It was magnificent. Or at least it would be in another few weeks once the gravel and plant filtering system was in place and it was filled with water. The natural pool company had made up a CGI image of the final article and where Nancy was standing there would be a cluster of natural boulders, designed to sunbathe against, or jump off into the clear water below.

'Big enough?' asked Dean, with a smile. He'd come outside to see the pool in its partially built state.

It was ten metres long and six metres wide. Plenty of room to swim. Nancy still couldn't quite believe that it was hers, in her own garden. It didn't feel real.

'Just imagine,' said Dean, indicating with his hand. 'A dragonfly darts across the surface, its wings iridescent green.

Purple irises framing the bank. Crystal-clear warm water to dip your toes in.'

She laughed, embarrassed. 'It feels so decadent.'

'Hey, you paid for it, you enjoy it,' said Dean.

He was right, she knew, she just wasn't used to being able to do things like this. It felt weird. But the rich did things like this all the time without a thought, she reminded herself. Nancy looked down at her pocket. Her phone was ringing. The number had come up as the school.

'Excuse me,' she said to Dean and moved away.

'Hello?'

'Mrs Miller? It's Esther here from the office at Ripton Primary. I'm afraid there's been an accident. Nothing serious,' she quickly added, 'but I think you should come and pick Lara up.'

TWENTY-THREE

Tuesday 29 September

Nancy was aware of the entrance CCTV camera pointing at her and wondered why those at the other end, looking at the screen, were taking so long to answer her call. What were they saying? Were they talking about her? She wanted to get to Lara. Then she was buzzed in at the gate and it automatically opened at what felt like one millimetre an hour. Her frustration building, she waited for the smallest possible gap and then slipped through and hurried across the playground. She passed several classrooms, set back from the play area, but through the windows she could see glimpses of children sitting at desks, facing towards the teachers. She realized she didn't know which was Lara's class. Did she spend most of her day in one of these rooms she was passing now?

Esther had told her very little on the phone: something about a game that had gone wrong and Lara had received a bump to the head, and then Esther had layered it on thick about how they'd followed protocol, got the icepack, made sure Lara was in a 'comfortable' and 'safe' environment where she could rest. She was checked regularly. They didn't usually call out the parents if a child got a minor injury but a bump to the head was occasionally an exception. They liked to 'notify Mum just to be on the safe side'.

Nancy got to the entrance door of the school and had to buzz again. She was let in and a woman got up from a desk and pulled aside a glass panel that separated the office from the visitors.

'I'm Nancy, Lara's mum.'

The woman smiled. 'Esther, office manager. We spoke on the phone.' Esther came out from the office and, using her staff pass, buzzed another door at the end of the reception area. 'She's in here. Our sick bay.' Nancy was led past a couple of closed doors, noting that one was marked 'Head teacher', and then further down the corridor into a small room adorned with cheerful pictures and bright yellow plastic chairs. Lara was seated on one of the chairs, clutching an icepack to the side of her head. She looked up as Nancy came in and then lowered her eyes again.

'I'll give you five minutes,' said Esther, backing out.

Nancy went to sit next to Lara and gave her a hug. 'Let's have a look at you,' she said, pulling the icepack away from Lara's head.

Underneath, just visible through her hair, was a large lump. *Jesus*, thought Nancy.

'Ouch,' she said out loud. 'That's quite a bump.'

Lara was uncharacteristically quiet.

Nancy smiled at her. 'Did you trip?'

Her daughter shook her head.

'So what happened? The lady in the office said a game had got out of hand or something.'

'It was Rosie,' said Lara. 'She hit me on the head with her lunchbox. Full,' she added, for emphasis.

A surge of anger and shock welled up in Nancy. She swallowed it back down before it could erupt. 'She did what?'

'We were in the playground, next class to go in for lunch, and she came over to the quiet zone where I was standing with Mia. Rosie came up to us and took Mia's arm and said she was going to sit next to Mia at lunch today. I said that wasn't fair, Mia and me had already decided to sit together, and she said, "Tough", and when I tried to take Mia's other hand, Rosie spun around and hit me on the head with her lunchbox. On purpose,' said Lara, upset. 'Then she ran off. So did Mia. Except she went to get one of the lunch teachers because I was crying.'

'But why do the teachers think you got hurt from a game that went wrong?'

'Because Rosie told them that.'

'But you told them the truth, right?'

'Yes. But they don't believe me.'

Nancy was incensed. 'But what about this Mia? Didn't she back you up?'

'She said it was an accident too.'

'*What?*'

Lara flinched. Nancy checked herself. She had to keep calm or she'd frighten Lara into silence.

'Sorry. Why did Mia say it was an accident?'

'Because she's scared. Rosie said she'll kill her mum if Mia tells anyone it was on purpose.'

Inside, Nancy was seething. Who the hell did Rosie think she was, going around hitting Lara and lying and threatening other kids so she could get away with it? She was probably sitting in the classroom right now, all smug and carrying on with her day as normal, while poor Lara was isolated in this room with a lump on her head, waiting to go home.

What was going on with this school anyway? It was over a week since Nancy had asked for a meeting with Miss Young. They'd ended up having a conversation on the phone where Miss Young had promised to have a chat with Rosie. But it seemed to have made no difference.

With tremendous effort, Nancy kept her anger in check and stood up. 'Darling, I'm just going to use the bathroom and then we'll take you home, OK?'

Lara nodded. 'You won't be long?' she pleaded.

Nancy assured her she wouldn't, then left the room. She walked a little way down the corridor and stopped outside the door with the 'Head teacher' sign emblazoned on the front.

She knocked, once, but didn't wait for an answer and let herself in.

James Whitman was sitting at his desk, typing something into his laptop. He looked up, surprised at the intrusion. Then he stood, smoothed a hand down his pale blue tie and offered up a charming smile.

'Sorry, do you have an appointment?' He gestured towards his laptop. 'Only there's nothing in my diary.'

'No, I don't,' said Nancy.

'It's Mrs Miller, isn't it? Lara's mum? How are you?'

He remembered. It surprised her. Worked to disarm her slightly. She dug in firm. 'I'm pretty pissed off.' She walked across the room and sat herself down in his armchair.

He waited a moment then came from around the desk and took the armchair opposite her. Opened up his hands. 'Go for it.'

She'd been expecting more resistance. It threw her.

'I have just been called into school to pick up my child who has been hit on the head by another child.'

'I'm so sorry, Mrs Miller. Sometimes the children's games get out of hand.'

'Out of hand?' Nancy could feel her blood pressure rising again. She took a deep breath. 'It wasn't a game. It was a deliberate attack on my daughter.'

'I understand that's what Lara also told the teachers.'

'Yes, because it's true.'

'Except the other two children involved both said it was an accident.'

'They're lying. Mia is under duress.'

'And Rosie has been nothing but contrite,' said James.

'I'll bet she has.'

Mr Whitman paused. 'Mrs Miller, I am aware that children can – and do – lie. All children. And I'm also aware that there have been other incidents here at the school where Lara has reported unkind acts – although not physical – by Rosie. Today's incident is a difficult one,' he continued. 'No member of staff witnessed it. I've asked all the lunch teachers to keep a close eye on them. Miss Young is also going to keep a distance between them in the classroom.' He leaned forward, his arms resting on the tops of his thighs, his hands clasped together. He looked younger up close, Nancy realized, more good-looking. He had a sort of George Clooney thing going on: eyes alive with intelligence, flecks of grey in his hair. Good for him. But she wasn't done yet.

'Rosie has done nothing but pick on Lara since she started at this school.' She looked him in the eye. 'It's bullying.'

'That's a very strong word.'

'But appropriate in this case.'

He didn't answer at first. Nancy knew he didn't want to admit to the accusation. It made it official, something that he had to take more seriously.

'We all here – especially myself – take any sort of unkindness, whether it's bullying or not, extremely seriously. There's no place for it in this school and I won't have children made to feel unhappy.'

Nancy considered him. He sounded genuine but it was the sort of stuff every head teacher across the land would say. *Had* to say. And he still hadn't admitted *bullying* was what was going on in his school. Right now. She had a sudden overwhelming longing for Sam, so acute it felt like a heavy weight had landed on her chest. God, it was hard doing this alone.

'Have you spoken to Rosie's mother?' she asked.

'Imogen?' Mr Whitman indicated his desk, presumably referencing a notepad or something. 'I was actually just about to before you popped in.' He smiled, to soften what could be construed as a criticism.

Nancy nodded. She believed him but there was something about the way he'd said it that sat a bit strangely with her. She couldn't put her finger on it.

'Please reassure Lara it's not that we don't believe her. We just have to be sure. And I know Miss Young has spoken to Rosie about the previous incidents and Rosie has recognized that what she did was wrong. So I hope Lara knows we do act when we have all the evidence.' He sat back in his chair again. 'And hopefully, to reassure you, my door is always open.' He smiled. 'Even when it's closed.'

Was she supposed to be amused at that? She suddenly felt awfully tired. Maybe she was too uptight. She looked at him and his expression was warm and genuine. She knew he would be accommodating should she barge into his office any time she wanted. He also appeared to have the situation in hand, so why did she feel dissatisfied?

Maybe it was simply because it was her child with the bruise on her head, she thought. *Lara.* Poor thing, she'd be wondering where her mother had got to. Nancy stood up. They shook hands and said their goodbyes.

She stepped out of the room and closed the door behind her. In the corridor she could see Miss Young talking to Lorna. They both looked up.

'Oh, hi, Nancy,' said Lorna, her eyes flickering to the head's door.

God, does the woman never stop poking her nose in other people's business? thought Nancy.

'I'm sorting out the second-hand uniform sale, ready for Friday,' said Lorna. She indicated a cupboard behind her, full of bags spilling over with blue and grey clothing.

'Is Lara OK?' asked Miss Young quietly.

'Oh, is she ill?' asked Lorna. 'Poor thing.'

Nancy didn't confirm or deny. She looked at Miss Young. 'She's been better.'

Miss Young seemed uncomfortable, as if there was something else niggling her, something she wanted to say, but couldn't. Nancy wanted to get to Lara, take her home. She said as much and left them to it.

As she walked back across the playground, Lara beside her, Nancy realized what it was that Mr Whitman had said which had seemed so off to her. Teachers always, *always* referenced other parents as 'Mrs So-and-So' or 'So-and-So's mum'. Particularly in a situation like this.

But Mr Whitman had said 'Imogen'. Without a second thought.

Nancy wondered why.

29 September
RIPTON PRIMARY, YEAR 6

Lorna Fielding, Phoenix's mum
Poor Lara's ill. Went home from school early today. Hope ours don't all go down with it!
16:03

Erin Mackie, Tilly's mum
It wasn't illness. It was high jinks in the
playground. Got a small bump on the head
apparently. Although I hear she was trying
to stop Rosie from hanging out with Mia.
Bit controlling if you ask me. 16:04

TWENTY-FOUR

Friday 2 October

She had originally wanted to take her mum somewhere special for coffee, somewhere where you could get home-made biscotti to go with your freshly ground single-origin beans, but she couldn't afford it. The only place that served that sort of thing was the posh hotel and spa on the outskirts of the village. And anyway, as much as it was a nice idea, it sent the wrong message for the purposes of the meet.

Instead Lorna had settled on Heron Water Cafe, down by the reservoir. She thought they could go for a walk afterwards – mother and daughter – perhaps discuss Carol's grandchildren's future in more detail.

For early October it was still warm and, as Lorna arrived, she saw there was only one table still free outside. She bagged it, putting her jacket on the opposite chair, ignoring the two women who came out of the cafe clutching coffees, looking pointedly around for seats. Fortunately, Carol arrived, which averted any confrontation.

'There you are,' said Lorna.

'Am I late?' asked Carol.

Lorna looked at her watch. She wasn't actually. And she didn't want this meeting to get off on the wrong foot. 'Not at all.'

'I'll get us a coffee, shall I?' said Carol.

Lorna jumped up. 'No, my treat.' She hurried into the cafe before Carol could protest and came back with two drinks and two slices of cake. Carrot, her mum's favourite. Lorna hadn't been sure whether to get one for herself. Why was it that both she and her mum were short but Carol managed to be petite and feisty, whereas Lorna just felt small and dumpy? How could her mother carry off a small stature when she couldn't?

'What have I done to deserve this?' asked Carol as Lorna placed the cake in front of her.

'Just treating my mum.'

'Well, thank you. It's nice to see you too – you don't usually have time for a coffee in the middle of the day.'

'Well, like I said the other day, now Pepper's at school I do have a bit more time on my hands.'

'Lots, I should imagine.'

Lorna bristled but kept it covered. 'You'll be pleased to hear I've started my job hunt,' she announced.

Carol sat back. 'You have? That's fantastic.'

'No interviews yet, but it's early days.' The truth was she hadn't actually applied for anything but she had been thinking about it.

'What kind of job?' asked Carol.

'I want to work with children.' Lorna had decided this was probably the easiest number – better than being chained

133

to a desk all day. If she worked with kids, it would be an extension of what she'd been doing for the last few years. And she'd enjoyed bringing up her two, felt she understood young minds and that she could contribute. That notion in itself made her feel important. As if she might change a child's future and in years to come, when the next CEO, prime minister, Nobel Peace Prize winner made a speech they would cite her as the turning point in their journey to greatness. She felt herself getting proud and teary just thinking about it.

Carol nodded. 'In a nursery? School?'

'A teaching assistant. It'll work around the school hours. With the kids, you know?'

'Well, I wish you all the luck in the world. Well done, Lorna.'

Lorna smiled.

'How are Phoenix and Pepper?'

'Good. The deadline for the secondary applications is coming up.'

'Can't believe Phoenix is growing up so fast. High school! Ripton High won't know what's hit them.'

'Yes . . . well, we're still hoping he might get a scholarship. You know, for Kingsgate.'

'But that wouldn't cover all the fees, would it?'

'No . . . actually there was something I wanted to ask you.'

'Go on.'

Lorna had seen the hesitant look in her mother's eye, but she'd started now so she had to finish, and anyway didn't her mum say at the barbecue that she wanted to help more?

'It's so important to give the children the best start in life and well, I was wondering if there was any chance . . .'

Carol's face was sinking in disappointment and Lorna felt herself flare up. She knew what was coming and what the response was going to be.

'James has so much *money*,' she said.

'That's James's money, not mine.'

'But you're married. Surely, I don't know, a loan or something? Would he even miss it?'

'Lorna, I think he might miss several thousand pounds.'

Lorna doubted it. And what about her mum? When she'd met James and moved in with him, she'd been able to rent out her own house – a place just outside Derby that had been left to her when Lorna's father had died twelve years ago. Her mother had hit the jackpot really. The house brought in a nice income every month – Lorna had looked it up. It always aggrieved Lorna that someone else was living in the place where she grew up, but it was more than that. Her mother's generation – the baby boomers – had had the best of everything. Final salary pensions, jobs for life, affordable property. Whereas her own generation had meagre contributions from their employers, hardly any job security and house prices that were through the roof.

'You said you would help more.'

'When?'

'At the barbecue.'

'Did I?' Carol seemed genuinely puzzled. 'Oh!'

Finally, thought Lorna. She felt a flare of hope.

'I meant with childcare,' said Carol. 'Picking the children up from school, looking after them until you got back from work.'

What? Was that it? Why had her mother allowed her to think it was something else? 'But . . . Mum, I know there's the rental money. That could make a huge difference.'

Carol took a careful breath. 'I know you feel a particular affiliation with the place, having grown up there—'

'It was my childhood home!'

'—but that rental money is going into a pot for the future. None of us know where we're going to end up.' She put her cake fork down. 'Lorna, why are you so set on this school anyway?'

'Because . . .' Lorna tried to formulate her answer. Because it was the best one around? Because she wanted her children to be considered a certain type? Able to keep up with the more privileged and well-to-do? Because she didn't want to miss out? Because she wanted to feel as if she'd made it, had done something for her children, if not for herself?

'The local academy is perfectly fine,' Carol said gently. 'Lots of children at state schools come out with good grades, go on to get good jobs.'

Now she was getting palmed off. Lorna could feel herself getting angry.

'Except me,' she said.

'Pardon?'

'Well, I went to one and it's not exactly like I've hit the dizzying heights.'

'It's not the—' Her mother stopped abruptly.

'What?' prompted Lorna.

'Nothing.'

But she knew what Carol had been about to say. It wasn't the school, it was *her*. She hadn't had the brains or the ambition. She was a disappointment. The shame of it burned in two pink dots on her cheeks.

Her mother looked awkward and, worse, sympathetic.

Lorna was furious. Her children would be going to Kingsgate. She would make it happen somehow. Her eyes blazed. *Just you watch me, Mother.*

TWENTY-FIVE

Friday 2 October

RIPTON GAZETTE

SECOND DOG DEATH

By Erin Mackie, Editor-in-Chief

In a shocking discovery, a second dog in as many weeks has been found dead in the pretty, desirable village of Ripton. The dog was found by local Caroline Smith, who was enjoying a run across the footpaths that cross Hilldale Farm to the west of the village. 'It was horrible,' said Mrs Smith. 'I was out training for my marathon when I stumbled upon the poor creature.'

Mrs Smith reported the dog immediately to local vet Stephanie Prosser. Mrs Prosser came up to the farm to retrieve the animal. It had no collar but the pooch's microchip identified it as belonging to a local Ripton family, who are devastated by their loss. Mrs Prosser, who performed a post-mortem, said all indications pointed to the dog having 'died from poisoning'. Conker, as the dog was called, had been missing for two days and the owners had been frantic with worry. It's the worst possible news for them.

With two animals now dead in what appear to be suspicious circumstances, this reporter asks: Do we have a Canine Killer on our hands?

3 October

RIPTON PRIMARY, YEAR 6

Lorna Fielding, Phoenix's mum
Did you see the news? Sad about the dog.
11:12

> **Nicole Wilson, Bella's mum**
> What, another one? Where was it found?
> 11:12

Lorna Fielding, Phoenix's mum
Near the farm. Like the first one. 11:13

> **Nicole Wilson, Bella's mum**
> Maybe one of them was responsible for the sheep deaths. Have you been taking your revenge, Hannah? 😂 11:13

Hannah Chapman, Jakob's mum
Is that supposed to be funny? 11:14

> **Imogen Wood, Rosie's mum**
> I wonder what the poison is? 11:14

Lorna Fielding, Phoenix's mum
You know there's loads of blue-green algae
down at Heron Water this year. It's really
poisonous to dogs. 11:16

>**Sarah Ramsay, Noah's mum**
>Yeah, I'd seen it's really bad. Especially near
>Willow Barn where Nancy lives. 11:17

Imogen Wood, Rosie's mum
It's only got bad since she's moved in. 11:19

>**Erin Mackie, Tilly's mum**
>What if the dog drank some of Nancy's
>water and wandered up to the farm? 11:20

Hannah Chapman, Jakob's mum
Nancy's water? Are you mad? 11:21

>**Erin Mackie, Tilly's mum**
>Just a turn of phrase. 11:21

TWENTY-SIX

Thursday 15 October

A cluster of girls from Miss Young's class gathered together in the playground, excitedly chatting about something. Their backs were turned, barring anyone else from their exclusive conversation.

It was impossible to miss. Especially if you weren't a part of it. Nancy felt Lara slow beside her and she scrambled around for something to say, to take her daughter's mind off it.

'Fish and chips tonight,' she said, but it landed flat. Of course it did, Lara was too old to be palmed off with such distractions. Tilly was running towards them and Nancy's heart sank – what world record-breaking feat did this girl have to boast about now? But to her surprise, Tilly kept on running until she'd passed them and joined the group of girls. Nancy and Lara watched as a gap was made to let her in. Then Rosie, who appeared to be holding court, handed her a green envelope. Tilly threw her arms around Rosie then ripped open the envelope and pulled out a brightly coloured card – a party invitation.

The girls were still squealing and fragments of their conversation floated on the air:

'—I'm going to be a witch—'

'—my mum's getting me a proper bucket for the sweets—'

'—I swear I was sick last year—'

All the while Nancy felt Lara shrink with humiliation, and yet when she glanced at her daughter's face, she saw a longing to be a part of the group.

Rosie looked up then and caught Lara's eye. She gave a small, triumphant smile, then turned back to the other girls, thoroughly enjoying their attention.

Nancy glowered. 'Whatever it is,' she said to Lara, 'don't let it get to you.'

'It's pretty hard, Mum,' said Lara.

Nancy's heart cracked. She looked back at the girls. It seemed quite a large group – there was Rosie, Tilly, Bella, that girl with the glasses, the one who was almost as tall as her mother . . . and then something dawned on her. It was *all* the girls in Miss Young's class. All of them except for Lara. And each one was clutching a green envelope.

Anger erupted deep inside her. *What a shitty thing to do.*

'How are the chickens getting on?'

Nancy turned to see Hannah dropping off Jakob. 'What? Oh, fine.'

'Laying well?'

'Yes. In fact, we have more than we need. I'm selling a few in boxes at the front gate.'

Hannah suddenly noticed the squealing girls clutching their envelopes. 'Someone having a party?' she said, then her gaze fell to Lara, standing alone, pushing a piece of gravel around with her shoe.

'I take it . . . ?' she said quietly.

Nancy lifted her head. 'No, Lara has not been invited. Although it would appear every other girl in the class has.'

'Wow,' said Hannah. 'Pretty low blow. Sorry,' she added.

'It's not that I mind Lara being missed out – they're hardly best friends, after all – but it's that Imogen has let Rosie do this so publicly.' She kept her voice low so Lara didn't hear.

'Yeah, well, it's kinda the way she operates. Lara could do without friends like Rosie, to be honest.' Hannah leaned in closer. 'Don't pay any attention to the petition either.'

Nancy's head jerked up but then the bell rang and Hannah was already turning to go and Lara was collecting her bag from Nancy's feet.

'Bye, Mum,' she said.

She looked so forlorn Nancy got an agonized lump in her throat. Somehow she had to gee her up. As a mother, it was her job.

She leaned down, put on her biggest smile. 'Don't let it get to you.'

'But I don't have any friends.'

Slice. Another part of her heart shaved off.

'You do. Not all the girls are like Rosie. I'll pick you up later, OK?' She gave Lara a hug, part of her never wanting to let go, to take her home again and look after her and not release her to make her own way amongst the class of hyenas she would have to encounter.

She watched until Lara had disappeared into the school, her bag huge on her tiny back, then she turned and sighed.

Oh yes. What was that Hannah had said about a petition?

15 October

RIPTON PRIMARY, YEAR 6

Imogen Wood, Rosie's mum
I think it's time we made a stand on the
Head of School. 07:45

> **Erin Mackie, Tilly's mum**
> Yh, it's not like we haven't given it a
> chance. 07:45

Imogen Wood, Rosie's mum
It's almost the school's fault, not Lara's. Too
much for her when she's only just joined.
07:45

> **Erin Mackie, Tilly's mum**
> None of the kids really respect her. 07:46

Hannah Chapman, Jakob's mum
FFS ever thought it's because your kids
haven't exactly made her feel welcome?
07:46

> **Cheryl, Aisha's mum**
> I object. Aisha's been friendly. 07:46

144

Imogen Wood, Rosie's mum
Let's not forget she tried to drown one of those kids. Mine. No wonder she's not exactly flavour of the month. I think we need a petition. I'm happy to collate votes and hand them in to Mr Whitman. A show of thumbs, please. Up to keep Lara, down to request another vote. I'll kick off. 👎 07:46

        Cheryl, Aisha's mum
        👎 07:46

Stacey, Fred's mum
👎 07:46

        Erin Mackie, Tilly's mum
        👎 07:46

Helen, Lottie's mum
👎 07:47

        Nicole Wilson, Bella's mum
        👎 07:47

Hannah Chapman, Jakob's mum
👍 07:47

        Lorna Fielding, Phoenix's mum
        👍👎 07:47

Erin Mackie, Tilly's mum
You can't have both. 07:47

Lorna Fielding, Phoenix's mum
OK, I abstain. I do think it's unfair she got it when she only just joined the school but it doesn't seem right to kick her out. She's only ten. 07:48

Imogen Wood, Rosie's mum
Those CVs start ever earlier. Do you know what 'Head of School' can do to your prospects? 07:49

Sarah Ramsay, Noah's mum
Come on, guys! It's anti-bullying week! 07:50

Hannah Chapman, Jakob's mum
You know Mr Whitman will completely ignore this. It's totally unfair. 07:52

Imogen Wood, Rosie's mum
Doesn't matter. The important thing is that we know we're all on the same page. 07:53

Hannah Chapman, Jakob's mum
Not all. 07:53

Imogen Wood, Rosie's mum
Almost all. 07:54

'The complete and utter bitch!' exploded Beth down the phone. 'Just because you bought her house. Who the *fuck* does she think she is?'

'Well, I don't know it was Imogen who started it—' said Nancy.

'I bet it was.'

'Yes, but I don't *know* that.' Nancy was sitting at her breakfast bar, absentmindedly stirring her coffee.

'How did you find out?'

'Another mum told me. Hannah. She's pretty cool. Sold me the chickens.'

After drop-off, Nancy had gone home and brooded on Hannah's last words so much she'd called her. Hannah had been embarrassed, explained how it was insecure mums with too much spare time on their hands, just venting behind the safety of their screens. They did it with loads of stuff and it always blew over. It was the same with the school changing the team house names; Nancy should have seen the uproar when they changed from the world's highest mountain peaks to more local landmarks. She should give it a 'damn good ignoring'. As Hannah was speaking, Nancy had become acutely aware that whatever group it was, she hadn't been invited to be a part of it.

'What do the school say about all this?' asked Beth on the phone.

'I haven't spoken to them about the petition – I've only just found out myself. But they are aware of Rosie's general behaviour.'

'What are they doing about it?'

Nancy sighed. 'They say they're addressing it . . .'

'. . . but bugger all seems to be happening?' finished Beth. 'You need to get on to the Chair of Governors. Put it in writing. You'll find his or her email on the school website.'

'I already looked,' said Nancy.

'Something tells me this isn't good news,' said Beth.

'The Chair of Governors is Erin Mackie. Best friend of the mother of the bully.'

'For God's sake!'

Nancy took a sip of her coffee. 'The most important thing is that Lara doesn't hear about this petition.'

Both she and Beth lapsed into silence. Neither had to say anything to know they were thinking the same thing. There was a very good chance Rosie would make sure Lara did hear about it.

TWENTY-SEVEN

Thursday 15 October

Lorna enjoyed being the boss of something. It didn't happen very often in her life, and as she put the finishing touches to the second-hand uniform sale that was happening in the playground in exactly – she glanced at her watch – five minutes, when the kids were released, she realized she particularly liked being a boss amongst her peers. Cheryl and Sarah were behind the boys' clothes stall and Erin and Imogen were behind the girls'. The clothes were all folded neatly on the trestle tables or hanging on the rails. Many of the mums who'd arrived to pick up their kids were already clutching items and starting to hand over money, which was going into the cash boxes that Lorna had carefully prepared with ample change.

She surveyed the scene, temporarily queen of the playground. Erin and Imogen had insisted on going together and they were gossiping as much as selling. Lorna wondered what they were talking about. Nancy and Lara, probably. And that petition. Lorna couldn't quite believe it when she'd seen it on the WhatsApp group. It had both thrilled and shocked her in equal measure. Talking of Nancy, there she was, over by the fence, waiting for the kids to come out. Lorna made her way over.

'I just want you to know . . . the vote . . . about the Head of School petition. I made it very clear that I wasn't going to be a part of it.' Lorna smiled sympathetically. That was *pretty* much what she'd said.

Nancy merely nodded. Maybe she didn't believe her. Lorna felt the need to reinforce her point.

'I think it's outrageous, actually. And that's what I told them.'

Hmm, definitely going outside the boundaries of the exact way it had happened now. The bell went and the children began streaming out. Carol was picking up her two and Lorna waved to them all, Phoenix and Pepper excited to be met by Grandma for a change. Over by the sale, mums were holding up dresses and trousers against their offspring, checking for size. Lorna felt she might be needed.

'Duty calls,' she said with a smile and headed towards the tables. It looked as if they would raise a significant amount for the school den area they wanted to build. Since she'd become Chair of the PTA it had surprised Lorna how much work it took. Even something as small as a second-hand uniform sale. She milled about, enjoying the bustle of the sale, talking to mums, soaking up the energy of what she had created. She walked between the two tables, seeing uniforms going to new homes, seeing cash going into the boxes.

*

Nancy watched Lara as she came out of the school, looking for evidence of the outcome of her daughter's day etched on her face.

'How was it?' asked Nancy as Lara came up to her.

Lara shrugged. 'It was OK.'

'Did you hang out with Mia today?'

'Yeah. A bit. And some of the Year 5s.'

It was Lara's way of saying the Year 6s still wouldn't let her in. 'Can we go home now, Mum?' she asked.

Nancy put an arm around her daughter's shoulders and guided her away.

Lorna watched as Nancy left. She must catch up with her on how the Christmas fair arrangements were coming along. The crowds were dwindling now and the PTA mums were starting to pack away the unsold uniforms. Lorna waited while a Reception mum paid for two cardigans, and then went to close and lock the two cashboxes. She carried them into the school and headed for the staffroom. It was empty.

Lorna opened both boxes and tipped the money onto the table. A large pile of coins mixed with several notes – some blue, some brown, and there were even a couple of purple twenties too. It surprised Lorna how much money could be generated in such a short space of time. She set about counting it, placing the notes and coins in neat piles on the table in front of her.

The total came to just over two hundred pounds. All for some second-hand clothes. It was quite a significant amount for one of the smaller fund-raising schemes. As a PTA member for several years, she knew the big generators, the Christmas fair for example, could raise in excess of several thousand pounds.

She looked at the money. It was only her who added it up, then it would go into the office safe until the treasurer picked it up to bank it.

The clock ticked on the wall. Lorna looked up at the door, which remained firmly shut. She quickly took out a couple of tens, three fives and a few coins and opened up her bag. Inside was a small daisy print purse that she used for her shop loyalty cards. She slipped the money into it. She was careful to make sure she left the two twenties untouched – someone might remember them and query if they'd gone.

As soon as she'd done it, she felt bad. Only a little bit bad. Because hadn't she put hours into organizing this? Weren't there several more hours' work ahead of her for all the other events that, as Chair, she would be overall responsible for? Hours that if used for the PTA, she couldn't give to a paid job.

She picked up the rest of the takings and went to hand them into the office.

They'd still raised one hundred and fifty pounds. It was a good figure.

TWENTY-EIGHT

Saturday 31 October

Imogen was aware it was cruel to miss only one child out but she couldn't invite her – the girl had tried to drown her daughter. What kind of a mother would she be if she overlooked something so big, allowed this kid to do something else to Rosie – maybe something even worse? Purely for the sake of sticking to playground protocol. Imogen shuddered. No, much better to keep it to the children she could trust.

She looked at the group of girls that had been invited. They were all completely absorbed by putting on their costumes, painting each other's faces. Even that slightly odd child, who Rosie had only recently befriended – Mia. Imogen knew the family didn't have much money and previously that would have brought her out in an allergic reaction, but she understood it a little now. Although heaven knows the mother could've made sure her daughter washed regularly and used deodorant, she thought, catching a faint whiff as she came further into Rosie's bedroom brandishing a tray of Halloween-decorated cupcakes. She thought she saw

Rosie quickly stuff something into the pocket of her costume. *Sweets already*, she thought, inwardly rolling her eyes. From Nicole, no doubt. Nicole's daughter Bella was always a little on the round side. She'd pretend she hadn't seen, just this once.

'Anyone hungry?' she called out.

The girls squealed with excitement and their eyes lit up with wonder at the pumpkins, tombstones and ghouls Imogen had iced into the cake toppings. Imogen noticed Mia took two. She was always so skinny. It suddenly occurred to her that there might not be much to eat in her house.

'Are you nearly ready?' she asked the girls. 'Only it's almost dark. I think we should start heading out.'

The girls cheered and the excitement levels moved up another notch.

'First: group photo,' said Imogen, 'to record your amazing costumes.'

They all gathered together, Rosie in the middle, of course, grabbing Tilly's hand to make sure her bestie was by her side. The rest filled in the gaps around them, with Mia right on the edge. Imogen could only get half of her in the picture.

'Say spiders!' she called, and they all chorused back as she took the shot on her phone.

Imogen checked the image. Rosie looked amazing front and centre in her ghost costume with a Scream face mask. Tilly was pretty good too – a creepy clown – and you couldn't recognize either of them now they had their masks on. The rest of the girls were also masked with the exception of Mia. Her costume was handmade and was already looking the worse for wear. She'd wrapped several sheets of toilet roll around herself and it wasn't robust enough to withstand much movement. Her leggings and T-shirt were clearly on view. She was meant to be a mummy, Imogen supposed.

'Ready to go trick-or-treating?' she asked.

The exhilaration almost went off the scale. The kids left the room, a primeval energy surging through them as they bounced off each other, jostling for space in the hallway.

'Good luck,' said Dylan, coming into the hallway. Imogen went to kiss him. He hated these kinds of events and she'd forgiven him for not coming with her as a reward. That morning he'd had an email inviting him for an interview for the teaching position at Kingsgate. Imogen had been delighted and made a mental note to ask James what the other candidates were like.

'Thanks,' she said, pulling a face.

'You sure you don't want me to come?'

Imogen knew there was a cold beer in the fridge and football on the TV. 'No, you relax. I'll see you later.'

The noise and impatience levels were rising and Imogen went to open the front door. 'Remember, no tricks, please!' she called out as the kids yelled what sounded like a war cry as they surged out onto the street.

Imogen watched them go. Maybe she shouldn't have loaded them up with sugar before they'd even started.

TWENTY-NINE

Saturday 31 October

'I don't think I want to go,' said Lara.

She was standing in the hallway, dressed as a vampire, bag clutched in her hand. It had been hard to persuade her to still enjoy the Halloween fun – after all, she was the only one not invited to Rosie's party.

Nancy looked at Beth, who had come over for the evening as her husband Martin was on shift. She'd turned up on the doorstep earlier that afternoon fully dressed in a tight bat costume and Nancy and Lara had giggled as she'd regaled them with the looks she got from other drivers on the journey over. Nancy had hugged her friend – she'd told Beth in advance of Lara's disappointment and loved Beth for her attempt to cheer Lara up.

Beth crouched a little so she was at Lara's level, her bat wings draping on the floor. 'Because this other girl left you out and you don't want to see them all out there?'

Lara nodded. 'I'm on my own.'

'Now that, my darling, is untrue. Have you any idea how long it took me to get into this lycra outfit?'

Lara gave a small smile. 'A hundred years?'

'You cheeky little . . .' laughed Beth.

'Yeah, but you're not going to be knocking on the doors with me, are you?'

'No, but then that's probably a good thing as I'd take all the sweets before you got a look in.' Beth stood. 'Come on, half an hour. What do you say?'

Lara thought. 'OK.'

Thank God, thought Nancy and flashed Beth a grateful smile.

THIRTY

Saturday 31 October

It was a cold, clear night and Imogen watched as the kids hurried along, blowing out cold breaths in the air and laughing at the clouds of vapour, pretending they were smoking. The streets were busy, children spilling into the road, parents keeping them from being run over, trying to work out in the dark which were their charges for the night from the assortment of mini ghosts and ghouls that covered the ground like worker ants. Many of the houses were decorated and the younger children stopped wide-eyed at the skeletons hanging from gate posts, the giant spiders in gardens, unsure of whether to approach. But the lure of the lit pumpkin won out in the end; the promise of sweets was enough to persuade even the most timid child to brave the gauntlet of the front path.

Imogen's group were already racing ahead, knocking on the first door, holding their buckets and bags, plunging their hands into the offered bowl of sweets.

Then the kids moved on, disappearing into the shadows and Imogen quickly followed, trying to keep sight of a

Scream ghost mask and a clown amongst the dozens of other children that seemed to have swarmed down this end of the street. Then she saw them, hurrying up another path with a lit pumpkin outside the front door. She smiled. They were working their way methodically through every property that had a pumpkin outside. As long as she did the same she wouldn't lose them.

THIRTY-ONE

Saturday 31 October

'It's dark, isn't it,' said Beth as they left the house, peering into the blackness.

'Ta-da!' Nancy switched on the torch she'd put in her pocket and the driveway lit up.

'Get you. You're becoming quite the countryside expert.'

It was a surprise to Nancy just how dark it got up here. She had never even considered the need for a torch in London – or any other city for that matter – but here in the deepest countryside, especially where she lived, there were great stretches of road with very little lighting. Now the nights were drawing in, it was something new she was having to adjust to. It became properly dark, pitch black so you couldn't see your hand in front of your face.

'It goes with my other recent purchases of warm wellies, a decent waterproof coat and plenty of bread in the freezer,' she said. There was no late-night corner shop to nip to here, like there had been in London.

They walked up the lane, Lara holding the torch. They began to catch snippets of children's voices in the distance, the babble of excited chatter, screeching, then getting closer still, glimpses of figures moving in huddles, some running along the pavements. Nancy's mouth dropped as they came to the high street.

'It's like an attack of the zombies,' she said, looking at the crowds of children streaming up and down the front paths, whooping whenever they got sweets from the inhabitants inside.

'Good God,' said Beth. 'It's terrifying.'

Even Lara seemed to have been nudged out of her dolefulness. She looked around, trying to take it all in.

'OK,' said Nancy. 'You want to try the first house?' She pointed at a brick semi with a giant cauldron full of dry ice in the front garden.

Beth placed her hands on Lara's shoulders and pointed her in the direction of the house. 'A strawberry lolly for me, please.'

Lara set off with more enthusiasm than she'd shown all night, much to Nancy's relief. She watched as the front door was opened, Lara chatted to the woman inside who was dressed as the Grim Reaper and then came away with a lolly and a big smile on her face.

'Don't mind if I do,' said Beth, plucking the lolly from Lara's hand.

'Hey!'

'You'd better get on with it then,' said Beth, pointing at the next house. 'If you want anything for yourself.'

Lara knew she was beaten. She grinned, then set off determinedly for the next house along.

'Thanks, Beth,' said Nancy.

'What are surrogate aunties for, if not to steal their niece's sweets?'

They both waved back to Lara, who was up ahead delightedly brandishing a mini Mars bar, before swiftly moving to the next house.

'Any sign of the bunch that ostracized her?' asked Beth.

Nancy raised her hands, palms upwards. 'Who knows?' she said. And as they looked around, it was impossible to tell the identity of anyone.

'There's so many kids, we probably won't even bump into them,' said Beth.

'Look, Mum, a whole chocolate bar!' said Lara in amazement as she came running up to them.

'Give it to me!' yelled Beth, but Lara squealed and ran away again.

THIRTY-TWO

Saturday 31 October

Imogen stuffed her hands in her pockets. It was cold. She heard the church clock strike half past six, two mournful bongs, and her heart lifted. She only had to endure another fifteen minutes out here, then another fifteen to gather everyone to go home, and parents were picking up at seven. Thank God. It had been fun but she was ready to go back now and have a glass of wine on the sofa.

Seeing the girls come out of another driveway, she called over to them: 'Just to the end of the street, girls, then come back and meet me here and we'll head home.' They chorused a protest but she knew to smile and ignore it and they'd do as she asked.

She perched herself on the edge of a wall as she checked her phone. There was a message from James, asking if she was free the next day for a run. She messaged back saying she'd meet him as usual. She idly wondered if he was watching the football at home but knew he wasn't. He was probably at a concert with Carol or out to dinner somewhere. As much as she loved Dylan – and she did – sometimes she wished he was a little more into the finer things in life. She'd loved his earthy simplicity when they'd first met, his quiet intelligence and his strong sense of right and wrong. She'd even respected the way he liked to fight for the underdog, but it had got wearing recently. Still, her husband could be working in a new school soon, a whole new environment. She must remember to tell James that Dylan had an interview and see if there was anything she should know about that she could subtly pass on to improve his chances.

The clock bell rang again; three bongs, indicating it was a quarter to seven. Imogen stood up quickly, grateful to be able to go home. She looked around for Rosie and the other kids; they must be further down the road, she thought. But she couldn't see them as she walked along – not on the other side of the street either. There were still a few other kids about, but in twos or threes, not her big group. Imogen frowned, annoyed by the fact they hadn't followed her instructions. Of all the nights . . . She was cold and wanted to go home. There was nothing for it but to go and look for them.

THIRTY-THREE

Saturday 31 October

'Look who it is,' Tilly whispered in Rosie's ear.

Rosie turned to follow where her friend's finger was pointing. She saw a kid dressed in a black cape with a high collar, heading down a darkened front pathway.

'Girls,' she called urgently, holding out her arms so that they nestled in together, forming a circular pack, each with their arms on one another's shoulders. 'Group meeting,' she declared importantly. 'Lara's here, dressed as a vampire – *lame* – and I say we steal her sweets.'

She was met with nervous giggles. 'Are you all in?' she demanded. She could see their eyes buried in their masks and got a thrill from their apprehension as they looked at her Scream face.

They all responded in the affirmative, except for Mia.

'If you want to be in our group, you have to follow our rules,' said Rosie.

Mia looked at the ground. 'OK,' she said in a small voice.

Rosie cupped her ear. 'Can't hear you.'

'I said OK.'

'Good, cos otherwise I don't think you would have the right qualities to hang out with us.'

'Yeah,' said Tilly. 'Lara has to pay for trying to kill Rosie.'

'Dead right,' said Rosie.

'Wait, is her mum around?' asked Bella.

Tilly looked about, as did all the girls. 'Can't see her.'

'Come on then,' said Rosie, and she strode over to where Lara was coming back down the path and turning onto the pavement. Rosie stopped right in front of her.

Lara looked confused and tried to walk past but Rosie snatched away the bag in Lara's hand to a startled – 'Hey!' – then she turned and took off. She heard the thumping of footsteps behind her and looked back over her shoulder to be reassured that her friends were following, and they were – except there was one extra to their group. Lara was chasing and she was *fast*. Rosie was shocked – and thrilled. She kept up pace to the end of the street then headed for the park. No houses there so no trick-or-treaters, so no adults. She ran through the gates into the darkened grounds and stopped by the swings, her heart thumping. The other girls gathered too, most of them having realized on the chase that Lara had followed them. They eyed her warily then Rosie saw them look to her, waiting for her to tell them what to do.

She watched Lara for a moment; she could see Lara was breathing heavily and Rosie heard a wheezing sound coming from her mouth. Lara was looking at them all with an admirable attempt at bravery but there was something else in her expression – and then Rosie realized what it was.

She didn't know for certain who they were. They all had masks on except for Mia, remembered Rosie, but a glance around told her Mia hadn't come. She'd deal with that later.

For now Rosie held aloft the bag of sweets.

'Give them back,' said Lara.

'Come and get them.'

But Lara stayed where she was. Rosie knew she was aware she was outnumbered. She threw the bag to Tilly and a couple of sweets tumbled out. Lara's face fell.

'Is that you, Rosie?' she asked.

Rosie lifted her arms and waved them in Lara's face. 'No, it's your dad. I'm the ghost of your dad and I've come to kill you.'

'Shut up, Rosie,' said Lara, but Rosie could hear in her voice that she was upset. She added some more ghost sounds for effect and heard the other girls laugh. It made her feel good and important.

'This is your punishment for trying to drown Rosie,' she wailed in her ghost voice.

'You fell in and you know it,' said Lara.

'Liar,' said Rosie. 'Liar, liar, liar.' And then the other girls were joining in the chant, encircling Lara. Rosie got bored then and walked over to the roundabout. She stepped on, placing the sweets on the seat opposite, then she came off and stood nonchalantly to one side. And waited.

Lara looked at her, at them all, warily. For a minute Rosie thought she was going to walk away, too nervous to retrieve her stash, but then she had a sudden change of heart and leapt onto the roundabout, grabbing the bag. As she turned to get off, Rosie threw herself on the side of the roundabout and pushed with all her might. Lara wobbled and had to grab the seat to stay upright. The other girls cottoned on pretty quickly and they all took a rail on the outside and ran around, pushing the roundabout with all their strength. It went faster and faster. Lara clutched the seat with a new fear.

'Stop!' she yelled.

Rosie smiled behind her mask and pushed harder. It was going too fast for them to run around it now, they just had to stand there and watch as it spun Lara round and round, the other girls giving it an extra push whenever it lost a bit of momentum. Lara was half lying on the seat, the sweets crushed under her. She looked frightened, thought Rosie. *Good*.

And then she got a really good idea. She dug in her shroud, in the pocket. Earlier, back at the house, she thought her mum had seen her put something there but if she had, she didn't say anything, thank God, otherwise she would have taken it away. She didn't approve of the trick part of trick-or-treating. Bella had brought them all one, a small squirty pistol of fake blood that was so *cool*. She removed the cap and then held it up. She waited until the roundabout spun so that Lara was passing her and then aimed and fired. It made a very satisfying spattering pattern across her face. Lara screamed. *Baby*, thought Rosie. It's only fake blood. It reminded her of the art project they'd done in school last week, flicking paint onto canvas Jackson Pollock style. It had been fun.

The rest of them, one by one, copied her and taking out their blood pistols, they fired them at Lara while she screamed at them to stop, saying she felt sick and pleading with them to let her off. They just laughed and carried on until all the blood had run out.

Lara was *covered* in it, Rosie saw, surprised. It looked as if she had been really badly hurt, like she was bleeding everywhere. It seemed real all of a sudden, even though it wasn't.

Rosie felt cold. They'd been there for a while and she knew her mum would be looking for her.

She turned and ran out of the park, back towards the streets, her friends seconds behind her.

Lara lay on the roundabout seat feeling as if she was going to throw up. The seat was wooden and hard and it hurt her chin and her wrists. Her breath was ragged and she needed her asthma pump but it was with her mum. She tried to do what she'd been told: to relax, to take deep breaths. She could feel the roundabout losing momentum, slowing down, and with it came a sense of exhaustion.

Once it stopped she couldn't get off straight away; instead she clung to the seat and then great, racking sobs overtook her. Still crying, she put a hand up to her cheek, wiped away some of whatever they had thrown at her. It was in her hair too; she felt fear and nausea rising up in her again.

Then she heard a sound. Someone was there and she flinched, cowering with fright, desperately trying to get off the roundabout. She couldn't be on it again with them pushing her, she'd be so sick, but when she stood, her legs wouldn't walk in a straight line and she stumbled about, eventually falling off it, crying some more, shouting *no, no* and then she heard a voice.

'Lara, it's me.'

Lara backed away, losing her balance, and she hit her ankle on the edge of the equipment. She cried out, then she saw Mia in the dark, just in front of her, old toilet paper hanging off her clothes.

'Are you OK?' asked Mia.

Lara said nothing.

'I saw what they did to you. You look . . .' Mia was staring at her. 'They made a mess.'

'What is this stuff?' said Lara.

'Fake blood. Don't worry.' Mia pulled off some of the toilet roll from her costume, handed it to Lara.

'Thanks,' sniffed Lara, but the paper was ragged so it only cleaned up part of one leg and so she stopped. Mia took it from her and threw it in the bin.

'They said I'd used dirty toilet paper,' said Mia. Lara froze. 'I hadn't,' said Mia quickly. 'They were just saying that and holding their noses.'

Lara knew what they had been referring to – the smell that made you wrinkle your nose sometimes when Mia was around.

'I'm going to find my mum,' said Lara.

'What about your sweets?' asked Mia, looking quickly back at the strewn bag on the roundabout.

'I don't want them.'

She started to walk out of the park. Mia pulled her gaze from the sweets and followed after her. As they came onto the street, Lara saw her mother and Beth looking around anxiously.

Then Nancy turned and saw her daughter and let out a blood-curdling scream.

THIRTY-FOUR

Saturday 31 October

'Jesus, are you hurt? What's happened?' cried Nancy in a panic as she ran over to her child, her baby, desperately trying to find the source of all the blood. It was horrific; it was all over her, blood running down her neck, her arms, her legs, smeared across her face. The shock was stopping Nancy from thinking straight; but she needed to find out where Lara was bleeding. On some numbed level, Nancy was faintly aware that Lara didn't seem to be in any pain, but she couldn't make sense of it all.

'It's fake, Mum,' said Lara.

Nancy slowed, the information sinking in. 'What?'

'It's fake blood.'

Fake blood? How has Lara got covered in fake blood?

'Who did this to you?' asked Beth.

Lara looked at Mia.

'Her?' said Beth.

'No.'

'It was Rosie, wasn't it?' said Nancy, her voice dangerously low.

'They wore masks, so I wasn't completely sure . . .'

'*They?*' asked Nancy, incredulously. She turned to Mia, standing a distance away, reluctant to get too close. 'Were you there?'

'No . . .' she stammered. 'I mean, I wasn't throwing the blood.' She backed away a little, cut an anxious glance to Lara and then turned and ran.

'Mia helped me,' said Lara. 'Afterwards.'

'Did they hurt you?' asked Nancy, her rage growing. 'What did they do?'

She felt Beth place a calming hand on her arm.

Lara burst into tears.

THIRTY-FIVE

Saturday 31 October

Nancy lay in her empty king-size bed. Her heart raced faster than felt safe. She threw off the covers, unable to bear the heat. Her body was a raging furnace of fury. *Breathe, breathe*, she told herself as she tried to calm down, but the pictures kept on playing over and over in her head.

Lara on the roundabout.

Being spun.

Rosie laughing. All the girls laughing.

Jeering.

Throwing the blood at her.

Treating her like something subhuman.

Nancy was writhing in torment at the idea of it, of not being there, of not being able to stop it, of Rosie still laughing, even now.

She wanted to rip her fucking head off.

THIRTY-SIX

Sunday 1 November

Nancy had wanted to speak to Imogen the very next day, but Lara had begged her not to, fear in her eyes, and Nancy had reluctantly agreed. It was too raw at the moment anyway, and she was worried about how Lara would be after the attack. Halloween had fallen in half-term so there was no school. Time enough to consider what to do for the best, although Nancy was not going to let this go.

The rest of the holidays passed by in a calm bubble, just Nancy and Lara in the house. The pool was finished and although it wasn't summer temperatures, they had a day where it was warm enough to test it out. They swam, going from side to side in the clear water, racing, splashing each other, then lay on their backs, gazing up at the blue sky. As Nancy watched the clouds drifting over, she couldn't believe a whole year had passed since Sam's death. So much had happened since then and his comforting presence was becoming more ghostlike as the days floated away.

When the weather turned on the Thursday, Nancy and Lara retreated inside. They baked cakes, watched movies on TV. It was a peaceful few days, where everything seemed as it should be. It was only at night, when Lara was asleep, that Nancy would lie in bed and the huge black crow would land on her shoulder again and she could feel its weight, feel everything she wanted to say to Imogen, to sort this out once and for all.

On the first morning of the new half-term, it was cold and blustery. As Nancy was getting dressed she looked out of the large bedroom windows towards the reservoir and saw small waves, topped with white crests as the wind whipped across the water.

In the kitchen, Lara was subdued. Nancy tried to tempt her with a bacon sandwich, but she refused. She was sitting at the breakfast bar, picking at some toast.

'You need to eat something,' said Nancy.

'I don't want to go to school,' said Lara.

Nancy came over, sat next to her. 'It's going to be OK. They can't do anything to you. The teachers won't allow it.'

Lara wasn't convinced. 'You don't know that, Mum.'

'Miss Young already knows Rosie's caused trouble. I'm going to tell her about Halloween as well—'

'No, don't.'

'But—'

'Mum, it'll only make things worse. You don't understand.' Lara stood up abruptly.

'Hey,' soothed Nancy. 'She can't get away with this.'

'You can't tell the teacher,' insisted Lara.

Nancy took a breath. She could see Lara was getting

worked up, didn't want it to escalate. 'OK. I won't speak
to Miss Young.'

Lara looked visibly relieved. *When did my daughter get
put into such an awful position?* thought Nancy.

'You promise?' asked Lara.

'I promise,' said Nancy. And she wouldn't. But she was
going to speak to Imogen.

THIRTY-SEVEN

Monday 9 November

As they arrived at the playground, Nancy could feel Lara holding back, nervously scouting around for Rosie. There was the usual chaotic atmosphere: kids running around playing Tag, parents dodging them while still engrossed in energetic post-half-term-break conversation. She looked for Imogen among the parents, trying to spot her luminous blonde hair.

'How was your holiday?' asked Lorna, as she bounded up to them, a couple of school bags hanging off her arms.

'Fine,' said Nancy, burying her irritation. She wanted to be left alone to find Imogen so she could get rid of the weight from her shoulders that had been building all the previous week. Lorna was looking at her expectantly.

'How was yours?' Nancy parroted back.

'Oh, we had such a lovely time. It's so nice to spend time with the kids, you know? They grow up so fast – can't believe our two will be in secondary next year. Hopefully together – that is, if we're lucky enough to get a scholarship . . .'

Oh God, she couldn't deal with this today. Not today. Nancy felt her eyes glaze over. Why was Lorna so numb to everyone else's needs? Why was she so self-absorbed, so obsessed with her own desperate attempts to fit in, to reassure herself of her place in this little village world? Then Nancy saw a flash of blonde hair out of the corner of her eye.

She glanced over, saw Imogen was walking in with Erin. Both Rosie and Tilly were following behind, chatting non-stop. She looked down at Lara and saw Lara had clocked them. Lara moved slightly, placing herself behind Nancy so she couldn't be seen, and Nancy's heart twisted.

'. . . don't suppose your friend Beth has mentioned when they're sending out the letters, has she?'

Nancy turned back to Lorna. *What did she just say?* Lorna was looking at her in a way that made Nancy feel as if she'd pissed her off. She hadn't been listening. She hadn't behaved as if Lorna was important and that had offended her.

'Sorry, Lorna, I must . . .' Nancy stopped. Actually, she needed to talk to Imogen *after* the bell had gone. Once Lara was safely inside. She needed to keep her in her peripheral vision for the next few minutes and grab her before she left the playground.

'I didn't quite catch what you said.' Nancy smiled at Lorna wearily; the woman was still looking as if she'd been mortally injured. *Come on, where's this bell?* thought Nancy. Her heart was racing. A horse in a starting gate, skittish but raring to go at the sound of the gun crack.

Lara had spotted Mia and the two girls had gravitated towards each other a short distance away. Nancy was, cautiously relieved her daughter had someone, that Mia seemed to have seen Rosie in her true colours.

Rosie was drinking out of her water bottle, the plastic kind with the sports cap. She and Tilly were talking, their faces close to one another, their eyes glancing over to where Lara and Mia were walking. Then they headed in the same direction and Nancy frowned, sensing something was not right. She tried to look past the group of mums standing across her viewpoint, vaguely aware Lorna was awaiting a response on something she'd said about Beth. Nancy moved away from her to get a better view, ignoring Lorna's indignation, and then she saw Rosie walk past Lara and Mia, her water bottle held down low, so no one would notice and as she passed Lara she squeezed, striking Lara with a blast of water. She quickly went to drink again as if that was all she'd been doing in the first place and she and Tilly giggled, heads together as they turned the other way and hurried off.

A red mist came down in Nancy. She barrelled across the playground, her eyes fixed on Rosie like a heat-seeking missile. She came up to her and grabbed her arm, pulling her around to face her.

Rosie jumped in fright, looked down at the fierce grip Nancy had of her. Tilly stood by, dumbstruck.

'I saw what you just did,' hissed Nancy, 'and I know what you did at Halloween. You are a vicious little cow and if you ever touch Lara again, I swear to God, I'll make your life so miserable.'

'You're hurting me,' wailed Rosie and Nancy got a buzz of satisfaction. She could see her fingers were pressing deeply into Rosie's skin, but she wasn't going to relax them, not yet. She wanted to inflict something more on this child.

She squeezed harder.

Rosie cried out.

Good, thought Nancy. She was aware one or two of the other kids had clocked the altercation and were looking on, jaws dropped. It was only a matter of time before the ripples of interest reached the parents.

'Now you are going to come with me and we're going to talk to Miss Young and you will tell her exactly what just happened.'

She saw Rosie's eyes shift sideways – an expression of relief, a flash of glee – a second before a hand landed on her shoulder.

'Mrs Miller,' said the head, Mr Whitman. 'You will remove your hand from that child.'

His voice was chilling in its authority and Nancy got a glimpse of why he'd soared to such heights as a head teacher. It wasn't only the charm.

She dropped Rosie's arm and saw prints where her fingers had gripped. Rosie wailed and then rubbed her arm pitifully, squeezing out a few tears. It was all an act, any fool could see, designed to get Nancy into further trouble.

'What the hell do you think you're doing?' Imogen had stormed up to them, the shockwaves of the event having reached her. Nancy saw Erin on her tail, the two of them glaring at her in righteous fury. Behind them, dozens of other mums were looking, pretending to stay out of it, but in reality desperate to know what was going on. The kids were less surreptitious and had formed a wide circle, staring openly. There was an unusual silence.

'Mrs Wood, please . . .' said Mr Whitman, attempting to regain control of his playground. 'Rosie is fine,' he looked down and Rosie nodded bravely, 'and Mrs Miller and I are going to have a chat in my office.'

THIRTY-EIGHT

Monday 9 November

Mr Whitman had had the foresight to wait until the bell had rung and everyone had gone inside before he had taken Nancy into the school.

Now she was sitting in the chair in James Whitman's office, only this time he hadn't joined her opposite, instead he'd remained behind his desk.

'She's a nasty bully,' said Nancy. 'She has systematically bullied my child pretty much since Lara started here.'

'Is that why you laid your hands on her?' asked Mr Whitman.

What? He wasn't listening. He was focusing only on a single moment in time, not the campaign that had led her to snap. God, it wasn't as if she hadn't tried to alert them to this before.

She tried again. 'Mr Whitman, on Halloween night, Rosie and her friends ganged up on Lara and pushed her on the roundabout in the village park at such speed she could barely stand and then they squirted her with fake blood, while she was unable to defend herself.' She looked at him, confident of a reaction of disgust, horror, even alarm, but there was nothing. She pushed on. 'And then, just now in the playground, Rosie took her water bottle and squirted Lara again.'

'With water?'

'Of course water,' snapped Nancy. 'She's hardly going to have fake blood here at school, is she? The point is, she's reasserting her power over Lara. She's reminding her of what she did at Halloween – something that Lara found incredibly traumatizing.'

'I'm really sorry to hear that,' said Mr Whitman, 'and I sympathize with both you and Lara. As I've said to you before, we are aware of the friction between the two girls and we are managing it. Has anything else happened within the school grounds . . . ?' – he looked at her enquiringly and Nancy was forced to acknowledge a negative – 'Good,' he continued, 'so our processes are working—'

'They are *not*,' said Nancy, even while she was thinking: *what processes?*

'If Lara hasn't been the victim of bullying in the school, then something is working. Of course we can't be across everything the children get up to outside of school but we are open to hearing about things, and this Halloween situation is exactly the sort of event that I am glad you have brought to my attention. It's unacceptable,' he said firmly, making eye contact with her to reinforce his words.

Did she believe him? He sounded genuine enough. *He sounds like a politician, saying what you want to hear*, the devil inside her said.

'Mrs Miller, in our last Ofsted report – which I'm sure you've read – there is a particular mention of how effective our anti-bullying policy is. We all need to adhere to it. In no circumstances is it ever acceptable for a parent to lay hands on another child. If it happens again, I will have to escalate this. Do you understand?'

Later, she called Beth.

'The sneaky little bitch,' said Beth. 'You should have been equally sneaky, grabbed her somewhere no one could see.'

'Oh Beth,' said Nancy, exhausted. She sank into the chair and gazed out of the living room windows. The sky was grey and foreboding. A flurry of fallen leaves ran riot across the garden.

'I feel bad.'

'*You* feel bad?'

'She's a horrible child,' said Nancy, 'and I hate what she's doing to Lara, but you didn't see me there in that playground. I was . . . awful. So angry, so full of rage.' She paused. 'I didn't like myself.'

'You were protecting your child,' said Beth softly. 'You think a lioness bothers to be polite when her cubs are threatened? "Excuse me, Mr Hyena, but could you please leave my baby alone and not have her for your dinner?" No! She bares her teeth and sod the consequences.'

'But this is a civilized society, not the savannah.'

'Try telling that to Rosie.'

Nancy was silent for a moment. 'The other night . . .

after the whole Halloween thing, I couldn't sleep. I was thinking violent thoughts.'

'You and me both. Martin couldn't believe it when I got home and told him what had happened.'

Nancy sighed. She knew her friend was trying to help but she felt out of her depth.

'Look, it's only because you've been backed into a corner,' said Beth. 'It's natural. It's not like you're going to do anything for real.'

'I know.'

'OK, so let's look at our options,' said Beth. 'Move schools?'

'Again?' said Nancy, her heart sinking.

'Exactly. Lara has only just arrived.' Beth paused. 'Actually, I took the liberty . . . I called the next two closest schools to you, to check. They're both full.'

So there was no chance of moving anyway, thought Nancy.

'It's seven months until the end of the year. Five and a half, if you take off the holidays.'

Both a flash in the pan and an everlasting sentence, thought Nancy.

'Maybe, now you've spoken to Rosie – and whatever you say about your technique, I do think what you did is a good thing – maybe she'll lay off,' said Beth.

Would she? Had she been frightened into submission? Most bullies backed off if people stood up to them, this Nancy believed. Maybe there was a glimmer of hope.

THIRTY-NINE

9 November
RIPTON PRIMARY, YEAR 6

Imogen Wood, Rosie's mum
The woman's a total freak. Rosie has
bruises. Actual finger marks. 😣 10:19

> **Erin Mackie, Tilly's mum**
> That's assault! Who the hell does she think
> she is? 10:19

Sarah Ramsay, Noah's mum
Poor Rosie. I'm really sorry to hear about
this. It does sound as if Nancy is troubled.
10:20

> **Cheryl, Aisha's mum**
> If anyone ever laid hands on my Aisha, I
> don't know what I'd do. Go over and kill
> them probably. 10:20

Helen, Lottie's mum
You're amazing, Imogen, managing to stay
back and let the school handle it. 10:20

> **Lorna Fielding, Phoenix's mum**
> What did Mr Whitman say? 10:21

Imogen Wood, Rosie's mum
Read her the riot act. 10:21

> **Erin Mackie, Tilly's mum**
> Good! 10:22

Hannah Chapman, Jakob's mum
I heard something about Halloween night. A
horrible incident involving Lara. 10:24

> **Imogen Wood, Rosie's mum**
> What? 10:24

Hannah Chapman, Jakob's mum
Rosie and a few others squirting Lara with
fake blood. 10:25

> **Imogen Wood, Rosie's mum**
> Isn't that the sort of thing all kids do on
> Halloween night? Anyway, it wasn't Rosie,
> she didn't have any. 10:27

Nicole Wilson, Bella's mum
Actually, Bella might have given them all
some. At the party. I let her take some in
for the kids. 10:29

Imogen Wood, Rosie's mum
Thanks, Nicole. Not. 😣 Anyway, even if it was Rosie and all your lot too, I thought the point of Halloween was to scare each other. A bit of fun, isn't it? 10:30

Erin Mackie, Tilly's mum
It certainly doesn't justify physically harming another child in the playground. 10:31

Nicole Wilson, Bella's mum
Wasn't she a nurse before? 10:33

Lorna Fielding, Phoenix's mum
Yh. On a peediatric ward. Sorry for spelling, you know what I mean! 10:33

Cheryl, Aisha's mum
Wait, she worked with kids? 10:34

Erin Mackie, Tilly's mum
OMG, she's like one of those nutcases. You know, the nurses who actually go around harming the children in their care. 10:35

Hannah Chapman, Jakob's mum
Nancy did NOT harm the children in her care. 10:35

Erin Mackie, Tilly's mum
How do you know? She might have done.
10:36

> **Hannah Chapman, Jakob's mum**
> This thread is nothing but an underhand,
> cowardly bit of gossip. You should all be
> ashamed of yourselves. 10:37

FORTY

It was night. Dark. She rested her head on the window and looked up at the motorway lights, flashing past in a regular rhythm. It was quiet because it was so late.

When she saw the lorry move across the lane, she thought it was overtaking at first. But it kept on coming. Closer and closer. Getting bigger and bigger. And then its huge thundering bulk was towering over their small car and it was impossible to get away. Sandwiched between the lorry and the crash barrier, the lorry struck the passenger side of their car.

She'd never heard a sound like it. It was deafening, ripping at her ears. Buckling metal, crushed so that it filled the seat that was there, squeezing the occupant with it as it concertinaed inwards.

Then screaming.

She always asked herself the same questions. What had gone through his mind when the lorry hit them? Was he scared? Did he feel the impact? What was it like for him when he died?

FORTY-ONE

Wednesday 18 November

There was a splat of dried tomato sauce under the kitchen table. Lorna only noticed it when she'd gone to sit down opposite her mum, two coffees in hand. She'd tidied before Carol came over – a rapid shove of toys into boxes, a squirt of bleach down the toilet – but she'd missed the remnants of last night's tea on the floor. She hoped Carol wouldn't notice – for some reason it made Lorna feel substandard in her mother's eyes. Not that Carol was ever judgemental, not openly anyway. No, it was more that she wanted to prove she'd achieved some sort of level of success. One that was like the families depicted in the home and garden magazines Lorna bought, where children played prettily in bright, immaculate rooms and the mother, dressed impeccably in coordinated neutrals, held a mug of coffee and looked up smiling from a laptop on the kitchen counter having just closed another business deal worth several million. Or at least that was what Lorna always imagined was going on from the relaxed, satisfied expressions.

She had been in two minds about inviting her mother

over – especially after what happened the last time they'd met. She was still a bit wounded at her mother's incredulous response to the suggestion she help shape her own grand-children – it hadn't been *that* bad an idea. There were many grandparents who were kept at arm's length and would positively *jump* at the chance to be involved, and here she was offering an opportunity on a plate that had been quickly dismissed.

'I'd offer you cake, Mum, but all I've got are some very bright orange cupcakes from Halloween.' Lorna peered at the half-eaten pack dubiously. 'In fact . . . oh, they're out of date.'

'By how long?' asked Carol.

'Yesterday.'

'They'll still be OK.'

Lorna was secretly disgusted when her mum popped one in her mouth.

'Did the kids dress up?' asked Carol.

'Pepper went as a witch with her friend Amber, and Phoenix went out for the first time on his own with his friends and *no parents*. So I was at home for the first time in years.'

'Made a nice change?'

'Yes . . .' Actually, Lorna had been late to the party when it came to knowing about the incident in the park. She'd only heard about it when she'd taken Phoenix to football practice a few days later and one of the other mums had mentioned something. 'You heard what happened?' she asked Carol.

'No?'

Lorna regaled her mother with the story of the fake-blood incident and, more to the point, the way Nancy had man-handled Rosie in the playground. This part of the tale she was able to retell with great relish as she'd witnessed it first-hand.

'It was awful, Mum. She wouldn't let go and Rosie was *screaming*—'

'Screaming?' asked Carol.

'Well, crying out . . . or at least she would have been if Nancy wasn't so scary, you know. It obviously *hurt*. And then James had to come over and pull her away. Actually, physically, get her away from Rosie.'

'I'm not sure that's true.'

'Why not?' asked Lorna, put out.

'Well, maybe not quite as you say it.'

Lorna ignored the remark. 'I tell you, she's done herself no favours. The mums are outraged. You should see the messages on WhatsApp.'

'Like what?'

'Someone said something about her in her old job. Being one of those killer-nurse types, harming kids in their care.'

Carol was shocked. 'Good God, that's an awful thing to say.'

'I think they meant it as a joke.'

'A joke?'

'You know, nothing serious.'

'Lorna, there is no scenario where that sort of statement is not serious. Private chat groups are dangerous viper nests where things can quickly spiral out of control.'

Lorna gave her mother a dark, sidelong glance. She was irritated by the unspoken criticism, the notion that her mother disapproved of her, thought she was a gossip. Blunted by the snub, and sensing an atmosphere growing that she didn't have the energy for, Lorna decided to tone it down. 'It was mostly venting. No harm done.'

Her phone pinged – the announcement of a new email. She tapped on the screen and her eyes widened.

It was from Kingsgate School. She opened it and quickly read, her heart thudding in her chest.

'Is everything all right?' asked Carol.

Lorna frowned, her eyes skimming the email for the magic words, the key to the chest. She looked up in disbelief.

'Phoenix has got a scholarship!'

Carol's face broke into a smile. 'That's wonderful!'

He'd done it! Her amazing, clever, football-mad boy had got a 20 per cent reduction in fees. She had never felt so proud. She had never felt so *vindicated*. She clutched her phone and felt a mist form in her eyes.

The doorbell rang. Lorna sat up, surprised. Still on a high, she had a sense it was more good news. Another gift from the universe, just for her. She went into the hallway, opened the door to the visitor, then returned to the kitchen clutching a brown cardboard box.

'Amazon,' she said, placing the box casually on the table.

'Anything nice?'

Lorna didn't want to open it in front of her mother. 'Something for Pepper.'

Carol nodded. 'You're going to have to be more careful with money if you're going to have school fees to pay.'

Lorna said nothing.

Later, when Simon came back from work, she braced herself for the interrogation. He came into the kitchen, gave her a kiss and went over to where Pepper was playing at the kitchen table. He ruffled her hair, then saw what she was playing with and his face clouded over.

'Look, Daddy!' she cried in delight and held up the toy dog.

'Wow,' he said, but Lorna felt him look up to her.

'It's amazing, Dad. Look, you press this button and the bones come out of its bum.'

'I thought we said we weren't going to buy the pooing dog?' Simon said in Lorna's ear as he went to get a glass of water.

'We didn't,' she said lightly. 'Mum bought it.'

She looked up at him and smiled then picked up the empty can of tomatoes that she'd just poured onto the bolognaise sauce, rinsed it then took it outside to the recycling bin. As she placed it inside, she made sure the Amazon box was well and truly buried. He wouldn't ever know. No one would know. And Pepper had got her toy and wouldn't feel as if she was the poor kid, left out and shunned by her friends.

FORTY-TWO

Friday 20 November

RIPTON GAZETTE

THIRD DOG DEAD!

By Editor-in-Chief, Erin Mackie

In shocking news, it appears the Ripton Canine Killer has struck again. A dog was found dead in its garden in the centre of the village of Ripton late Sunday afternoon. It was discovered by its owner, 68-year-old Rita Townsend, who said: 'I'd gone to put some food out for the birds and I thought it was a badger at first. When I went closer, I saw it was Chequers. My heart broke, I've had him for ten years.'

Chequers, a border terrier, was taken to Ripton vet's where his death was established to be kidney failure – much like the recently deceased pets already reported in this paper. Mrs Townsend had no reason to think poor Chequers had ingested any poison at home, so has the Canine Killer struck again? Rita Townsend had this to say about her pet in the lead-up to his untimely death: 'We had gone for our usual walk along Heron Water and Chequers was fine. He slept perhaps a little more than usual in the afternoon, but it didn't seem anything to worry about. I let him out into the garden around teatime, as he likes to watch next door's cat in their window, and when I came out a bit later he was lying on the grass. It's impossible to believe he's gone.'

20 November

RIPTON PRIMARY, YEAR 6

Erin Mackie, Tilly's mum
You guys might have seen my article today
in the paper . . . Keep an eye on your pets.
14:02

> **Lorna Fielding, Phoenix's mum**
> So sad. 14:02

Erin Mackie, Tilly's mum
I've been thinking about this . . . Maybe it's
got something to do with the pool Nancy's
built. Has it interrupted the natural flow of
things? Added to the algae? 14:03

> **Lorna Fielding, Phoenix's mum**
> Oh wow, I had no idea that could happen.
> 14:04

Hannah Chapman, Jakob's mum
It can't. That's a load of nonsense. 14:05

> **Imogen Wood, Rosie's mum**
> Not necessarily. You see these climate
> change issues all the time from man-made
> changes to the landscape. 14:05

Lorna Fielding, Phoenix's mum
There's the water table, isn't there? Or at
least that's what I remember from my long-
ago school days!!! 😄 14:06

> **Erin Mackie, Tilly's mum**
> Yh, digging such a big hole, just for her
> own pool. Maybe that's done something to
> the flow in the reservoir. 14:06

Hannah Chapman, Jakob's mum
You're nuts. 14:07

> **Erin Mackie, Tilly's mum**
> Well it wasn't like that before. So explain
> that! 14:07

Lorna Fielding, Phoenix's mum
Hey guys, are we doing a Xmas collection
for Miss Young this year? 14:09

Nicole Wilson, Bella's mum
Sure. 14:10

Lorna Fielding, Phoenix's mum
I'm happy to organize. Shall we say ten
pounds per child, or whatever you would
like to give? 14:11

Erin Mackie, Tilly's mum
Thanks, Lorna. Appreciate you taking this
on. 14:11

Lorna Fielding, Phoenix's mum
No problem. ☺ 14:12

FORTY-THREE

Wednesday 25 November

Imogen watched as James appraised the interior at The Wood Oven pizzeria. He was assessing everything with his astute eye, checking the details of the interior design, the table layout and mentally calculating the income they would be generating. She'd done a good job; she knew it, and she knew he knew it too.

'Are bookings still strong?' he asked.

'Fully booked every weekend right up until Christmas,' she said. 'And over New Year, there's very little space left. Erin has given us some fantastic publicity and will be here opening night too.'

'That's good. Carol's looking forward to our first night.'

'She's got the best table in the house,' said Imogen, 'reserved for her and Lorna.'

'Thanks for that.' James kissed her appreciatively on the lips. She felt his hand reach up to her breast. 'Fancy a quickie?' he murmured into her ear.

She supposed it couldn't hurt. It was early – only 7.45 in the morning, so none of the staff or deliveries were here yet.

As he lifted her skirt, she wondered how much longer she might carry on with the affair. It had been good, and both had gained a lot from it. She knew James was eminently flattered by sleeping with a woman eighteen years his junior. She had a backer for her new business at a time when traditional financial help was impossible. She had no plans for their liaison to go on forever though, especially now life seemed to be turning a new corner.

She briefly wondered how things might have been different if she were married to James, the ambitious man, rather than Dylan, the worthy man. She'd certainly have been able to keep the house; James would have been able to buffer the financial fallout of her Covid-blighted restaurant. She would never have had to move, suffer the humiliation of the bank taking her home away. She brushed these thoughts aside. Thinking about what might have been was never a good idea. And anyway, there were other ways of changing one's destiny.

Imogen had been very interested in the last flurry of messages in the mums' WhatsApp group – all that talk about Nancy being responsible for the increase in algae. She wasn't sure how much truth there was in it, but it had set her thinking. What if there was a connection of sorts, no matter how tenuous? The council took these sorts of things very seriously indeed. What if some planning law had been broken? Or some environmental regulation? Then Nancy would have some very uncomfortable questions to answer. She would find herself even less accepted in this village – and if she was by some chance responsible for this spate of dog poisonings, my God, it would be impossible for her to stay.

Imogen allowed herself to fantasize for a moment, remembering to respond to James's thrusts. Imagine, she thought, imagine if Nancy decided to move out. If her house became available again. The thought was so exquisite, Imogen found herself coming to orgasm, much to James's delight.

The timing of their affair was currently fortuitous. There were other things too – small things he could do that would make a big difference to her life.

'James,' she said, kissing him softly on the lips as he leaned, panting against the bar. 'Dylan has his interview Friday.'

'Want me to put in a good word?' he asked.

She smiled gratefully. 'Only if it's not too awkward.'

'Not at all.' He bent down to retrieve his pants, which had gathered around his ankles.

She kissed him again. 'Thank you. And one last thing,' she said, taking over and buckling up his trousers for him. 'I had an email. From Rebecca Young. Asking me to come in for a chat. Something about Rosie not being very nice to Lara again. But I think she's forgetting what Lara did to Rosie back in September. Trying to drown her,' she reminded him. 'Plus there was that altercation with the mother,' she added darkly.

'If Rosie's out of line,' said James, 'then I can't ignore it. We have to deal correctly with inappropriate behaviour, or it will damage the school's reputation.'

You mean your reputation, thought Imogen. She looked up at him. 'I completely get that,' she said. 'And I know we all have to follow policy. And of course I'll have a word with Rosie. But there's no need to exacerbate this further by my coming into school. You know how the mums love to gossip. Rosie has been attacked twice, the second time very publicly by an adult who should absolutely know better. Rosie may have done some unkind things but there's always unkindness – they're children. The point is getting the balance right. It wouldn't look good if the heavy hand-edness came down on Rosie when it should so very clearly be on Nancy.'

He gathered up his things. 'Are you telling me how to run my school?' he asked, but it was said lightly and she knew she'd got through.

She smiled. 'Wouldn't dream of it.'

The day was long and exhausting with all the last-minute details needed at the restaurant, and Dylan had picked up Rosie from after-school club by the time Imogen got in.

'All set for Friday?' he asked, as she dumped her bag and coat on the kitchen table and went to get herself a glass of wine from the fridge.

'Pretty much. It's going to be good,' she said, and as the words left her lips she had a strong premonition that it would be. But not just opening night, dozens, hundreds of nights to come. This new restaurant – it was going to be a turning point in their fortunes, she could sense it.

'How about you?' she asked, topping up his glass for him. He was cooking something delicious and mushroomy for tea. Risotto, by the looks of it. 'How are you feeling about your interview?'

He wiped his hands on a cloth, exhaled a little. 'Nervous and . . .'

'Go on,' she said, knowing what was holding him back. *Out with it*, she thought, *say it once more and be done.*

'I can't help thinking I'm selling my soul.'

She buried the flicker of irritation. 'The kids at Kingsgate deserve an education just as much as those at Ripton High.'

'Yes, I suppose . . .'

'So don't take against them just because their parents are wealthier,' she said. 'That is also discrimination.'

He rolled his eyes but knew she had a point. 'I will keep the chip on my shoulder tucked firmly under my jacket. I realize you've been working your socks off for this family and I need to do my bit too.'

She felt a surge of relief.

'They probably won't want me anyway . . .'

Imogen kissed him. 'I don't know,' she said. 'I've got a good feeling about it.'

FORTY-FOUR

Thursday 26 November

Rebecca Young had received an email from her boss, head teacher James Whitman, government adviser, asking her to 'pop in' for a 'quick catch-up' during her free period at eleven that morning. It was the time that she usually allocated to her extracurricular work as Head of English.

She wondered what it was about. She didn't like unexpected summons. They rarely brought good news.

James's door was shut. She knocked.

'Come in,' he called.

She opened the door and stepped over the threshold. He indicated the door. 'Close it behind you.'

It was said pleasantly but she got the sense she was now caught in a trap. She went to sit down. He joined her, coming out from behind his desk.

'Everything OK?' he asked.

It was, but that's about to change, she mused. 'Fine,' she said.

'Good. I just wanted a quick chat with you. I know

you've had a particularly challenging set of friendship issues in your year.'

'You mean the ongoing bullying issues between Rosie Wood and Lara Miller?'

He looked mildly taken aback. She felt a small satisfaction – probably misjudged, but she liked the direct approach.

'Exactly,' he said. 'I understand you've asked Mrs Wood to come in and chat about Rosie's behaviour.'

So Mrs Wood must have spoken to him directly, thought Rebecca. 'That's right,' she said. 'Rosie has been making Lara's life miserable for some time. She's quite sneaky about it but I caught her knocking a paint pot over Lara's bag earlier this week.'

'An accident,' said James.

She got the strangest feeling he was telling her, not asking her. 'That's what she claimed.'

'But you think different.'

'Yes, I do,' she said, riled. 'Backed up by comments that are designed to be belittling and undermining.' Rebecca occasionally caught little phrases, or words and saw Lara's crestfallen face. 'Telling Lara a particular bench in the playground is only for kids who've been at the school a long time. Asking other children why they're talking to Lara. Making loud comments about being "ugly" that are designed for Lara to hear.'

'Hmm, I can see how that would be hurtful.'

Hurtful? It was positively destroying. Rebecca always pulled Rosie up on what she said but she couldn't monitor everything, and she had a suspicion Rosie kept most of her comments away from teachers' ears.

'The thing is,' said James, 'kids don't know the power of their words. They don't really understand what they're doing.'

'Oh, I think they do,' said Rebecca. 'They know *exactly* what they're doing. That's why they do it. They see how upset they can make someone.'

Rebecca knew the power of nasty comments, they chipped away at the recipient's confidence and happiness until they were reduced to a miserable shell. It had happened to her as a child too. By another girl. Amelia Keatley her name was. Rebecca would never forget it. She had made her life hell. Constant comments about her body. She was an underdeveloper and Amelia and her cronies called her 'Tortilla Tits'. Once, in PE, the other girls had taken her uniform, towel and PE kit when she was in the shower and hidden them in the boys' changing room. She had stood there, naked, hands covering herself, enduring their humiliating laughter until the teacher had come in and they had scarpered. The teacher had been more irritated that she herself had had to go and retrieve the clothing than anything else, and said Rebecca would do well to get out of the shower quicker in future to prevent something like this happening again. She'd hated swimming after that. *Still* hated swimming.

It was always the girls who carried out the bullying campaigns, Rebecca mused. Boys just punched each other. So much easier to manage when it was something tangible.

'Are you aware of the petition some of the mothers put together to get Lara ousted as Head of School?' she asked.

James looked surprised. 'Petition? Sent to you?'

'No . . .'

'Who did it go to then?'

'I don't know.'

'I didn't receive anything.'

'They definitely talked about it,' defended Rebecca.

He smiled. 'If I acted on every piece of gossip from parents, I would never get any work done.' He rested his clasped hands on his knees, leaned forward. 'In my experience, we should avoid over-involving the parents too soon. It's better to work on the girls' friendship in class. Get them to talk.'

You don't know what you're talking about, she thought. 'I've tried that,' she said.

'I think we should give it another go. We don't want to give up too easily, do we?'

Rebecca bristled. She wasn't giving up. She was taking decisive action. And it was perfectly clear from this conversation that Mrs Wood had gone over her head and asked James Whitman to interfere. Stop any kind of meeting. He'd agreed in order to keep things quiet, keep the impression of a smooth-running school. Presumably Mrs Wood hoped – or assumed – it would all be brushed under the carpet and Rosie would be allowed to continue with her devious destruction of another girl's confidence. It pissed Rebecca off. Pissed her off no end.

'I really don't think there's any love lost between these

two girls,' she said, trying again. 'No matter what I try, they are not destined to be friends.'

'They don't have to be friends. Just civil enough that we can all get on with our jobs.'

Oh great, thought Rebecca. Now it was down to her to fix it, but he'd completely taken away any power she had to do so.

'Think you can manage that?' he asked. 'Only it's parents' evening tonight and I'm aware it might come up. Be good to have your ducks in a row beforehand.'

She was speechless for a moment, not quite believing the position she was being put in.

'You know how these parents can collar you,' he added sympathetically, conspiratorially.

She stood, fuming, but was smart enough not to show it. She was learning how James operated. He was a political animal – that was how he had got so far. Only four years out of training college, she was ambitious herself and did not want her career unfairly curtailed by a powerful megalomaniac.

'Of course,' she said. She nodded and left his office, still livid. It was unfair what he was doing. He was putting himself and his career before some poor kid who was getting picked on. Well, Rebecca wasn't having that. Oh no. And she could find another way to address the unfairness, she thought, as she walked back down the corridor.

FORTY-FIVE

Thursday 26 November

Nancy sat outside Miss Young's classroom waiting for her allotted ten minutes to discuss anything and everything about her child. Lara was sitting beside her, playing a game on Nancy's phone.

Ten minutes for parents' evening, thought Nancy. It was laughable really. Ten minutes wasn't going to solve anything. For the bullying and the tormenting was still going on, Nancy was certain of it. Lara had stopped talking about it so much; she'd become more quiet and withdrawn, seemingly accepting of the fact she'd been selected to be Rosie's punchbag.

'Oh, hi, Nancy,' called a voice from down the corridor. It was Lorna, walking towards her with a large white envelope clutched in her hands.

'Teacher collection for Christmas,' Lorna whispered theatrically, even though Miss Young's door was closed and there was no way she could hear. Lorna shook the envelope and there was a jangle of coins and the muffled sound of several notes. 'Mums are putting in a tenner – no pressure, of course

211

– but I know I like to know what the going rate is!' She laughed.

Nancy got out her purse, pulled out a ten-pound note and posted it into the held-out envelope.

'What are you going to get her?' she asked.

'We usually do one of those voucher cards, you know, the ones you can spend in a number of shops.'

'Sounds great.'

'Christmas, eh. Can't believe it's coming so soon. And the fair's only two weeks away! Everything OK?' asked Lorna.

'Yes, fine.' In fact, it had been fairly straightforward. The Christmas fair happened every year and was a well-oiled machine. 'You're organizing the floats, right?'

'Yes. I'll get them from the treasurer and hand them around as we set up Saturday morning. I'll collect as we go too, take some of the notes and put them in the safe.'

'OK, great.'

Lorna hesitated, clearly wanting to say something else. 'Did you get a place? At Kingsgate?'

Nancy nodded. She knew it was a good school and liked the idea of Lara being near Beth. 'We did.'

Lorna squealed. 'Oh, how fantastic! Phoenix too. And he got a scholarship,' she said, faux casually and Nancy knew she was waiting for a suitable response to her boast.

'Congratulations.'

'Aw, thanks. Yeah, we're pleased,' she said, shrugging modestly, obviously beside herself with delight. 'We didn't put any pressure on him, you know, I think it's so awful when parents do that, always pushing their kids to achieve. It can be so damaging to their mental health, don't you think? Kids should be kids, no one should rob them of their childhood.'

Through the window of the classroom, Nancy saw Miss Young and the mother she was with stand up. She gathered her coat and bag. 'I think it's me,' she said to Lorna.

'Oh yes. Well, I won't keep you. Lovely to chat.' Lorna gave a little wave and went on her way.

'Mrs Miller,' said Miss Young, holding the door open. Nancy went into the classroom and took a seat on one of the undersized chairs. The room was bright and cheery, hung with Christmas paintings and decorations that the children had made.

Miss Young consulted the pile of flash cards in front of her, holding them upwards so Nancy couldn't see anyone else's notes. 'Lara is extremely bright and capable,' she said. 'She's working at the level we'd expect for her age in all three core subjects: reading, writing and maths.' Miss Young looked up and smiled, having delivered the good news.

Nancy focused on the teacher's face. 'Is she happy?'

It wasn't the response Miss Young was expecting. Her eyes sparked with alarm and, Nancy thought, a flash of guilt.

'Mostly, I'd say. There have been a few run-ins as you know—'

'I think it's a bit more than that,' said Nancy coolly. 'You are aware of what happened at Halloween? I'm assuming Mr Whitman told you?'

'He did.'

'And despite his assurances the school are dealing with it, I know Lara is not her usual upbeat self and I strongly suspect Rosie is still not being very nice. What's she like in class?'

'You mean Rosie?'

'Of course Rosie.'

'I can't really discuss another—'

Nancy leaned forward, an edge to her voice. 'I mean Rosie in relation to her behaviour around my daughter.'

'I try and pair them up with different people.'

'So she's still not being kind to Lara.'

'I didn't say that.'

'But if she was being kind, you wouldn't need to keep them apart.' Nancy could feel her patience wearing very thin. She was sick of the pussyfooting around, the careful, careful, touchy-feely, uber-PC approach to what was a very straightforward problem. A problem that was being danced around when it should have been resolved weeks ago.

'Miss Young, let me ask you something. Do you think it's OK for this girl to continue to bully Lara? And yes, I know the school doesn't like using that word because it pertains to all sort of seriousness and problems for your management and paperwork and records for Ofsted inspections, but as far as I can tell, it is *still happening*. You are the one person who spends more waking hours with my daughter than anyone else, even more than myself during the week. You must see things. You must know things. Tell me something else. Has Rosie's mother been spoken to? Is she *aware* of what her child is doing? Does she believe it? I'm asking you, as a worried mum, to please be honest with me and tell me what you think.'

She hadn't meant it to be such an emotional plea. The worry and pressure of the last few weeks must have got to her more than she realized.

Miss Young's face had changed. She'd dropped the mask, Nancy thought. She could read empathy and anger and frustration. A flare of hope rose up in her; finally, maybe she would have an ally where it really counted.

'I'm so sorry Lara's had a bad time of late,' said Miss Young and her voice had lost its cool, professional tone, the one designed to keep a distance between herself and parents, the one all teachers used for self-preservation, and Nancy was almost giddy with relief. Now Miss Young spoke genuinely and from the heart. 'It's completely unacceptable and I'm aware of a number of—'

A movement at the window made Miss Young look up. Nancy followed her gaze. Mr Whitman was passing the classroom. He gave a clear, courteous nod towards them.

Nancy saw Miss Young stiffen. Then she turned back and Nancy could see she had deflated.

'No unkind behaviour is acceptable,' she said. 'We always work to nip it in the bud as soon as it materializes, and we have a system of escalation if things continue.'

No, please don't spout generalities and policy at me again, thought Nancy. 'I'm not talking generally,' she said desperately. 'I'm talking about my child. Who is miserable.'

The door suddenly opened. 'Oh, sorry!' said a mother,

cheerfully apologetic. 'I didn't realize you were still going.' She backed out again.

Nancy's time was up. The ten minutes had ticked by. The interruption had broken any rapport or attempt at salvaging one.

'I am keeping an eye on them,' ventured Miss Young, but for Nancy it wasn't enough. Nowhere near enough. How many more times was she going to be fobbed off?

Rebecca let her next parent take a seat inside as she watched Nancy and Lara walk down the corridor. James had deliberately walked past the classroom at that moment, she was sure of it. He knew the parents' evening schedule, it was taped to her door.

It was a reminder. A warning. It had shocked her to see him, but then maybe he knew her better than she knew herself. Maybe he knew she'd respond to that poor woman's heartfelt plea.

It was wrong, she thought. It was all so fucking wrong.

FORTY-SIX

Friday 27 November

'Service!' Imogen hit the bell for the umpteenth time that evening – and it had only just gone six o'clock. One of the waiters came to take the plates of pizza and deliver them to another customer in the restaurant. It wasn't exactly the high-end fare she had been used to making but she still cared deeply enough about what she made for her diners to go the extra mile. If you put your mind to it, even pizza could surprise the taste buds. And it was that extra effort that – hopefully – would bring the customers back. She hadn't had any feedback yet though and it was making her nervous. The plates came back (mostly) empty, and they'd had dozens of orders for takeaway as well as the fully booked restaurant, but she wanted to hear what her customers thought.

She considered peering through the hatch into the restaurant itself but there was no time. The orders kept coming in. She'd asked the waiting staff if people were enjoying her food, and they said 'yes', but were too busy to elaborate.

The door to the kitchen opened and James came in, looking sombre.

Imogen looked up, concerned. 'What is it?'

'You need to come out here a moment,' said James. 'Customer complaint.'

Her heart sank. She handed over to her sous chef and wiped her hands on her apron. 'What's the problem?' she asked as she nervously walked into the restaurant. She thought: *Please don't let this be serious, please not after all this hard work, all these hopes*, everything she'd put in to make this place something, to improve her family's situation . . . and then she realized that everyone was cheering, clapping her, smiling, their faces full of admiration, and she had absolutely nothing to worry about.

'I suppose you think you're funny,' she murmured to James.

'Oh, I am. Hilarious,' he said, and she knew he enjoyed exerting control over her when he could. It was not to her liking.

The relief that there wasn't a problem was intoxicating and she went around the tables, humbly taking in the compliments, the good wishes, people telling her they'd missed her on the high street, missed her cooking, her ability to create magic in the kitchen. *They were on her side*, she realized, more than she'd ever thought possible.

'My husband got very lucky when you invited him to go into business with you,' said Carol, as Imogen stopped by her table. 'This is the best pizza I've ever eaten, and I've been to Italy many times.'

'Thank you,' said Imogen. She agreed with Carol, James was very lucky. In more ways than Carol knew. James was sleeping with *her*. Imogen just wasn't sure he appreciated how lucky.

'It's amazing,' gushed Lorna, who was sitting opposite her mum. 'You're going to be famous again. Our very own celebrity chef. And this place,' Lorna gazed around, wide-eyed, 'well, you must be making a killing! It's so full!'

Not yet, she wasn't, but Imogen was forecast to. Not that she was going to engage in any conversation with Lorna on the matter. Her crassness was irritating.

She smiled warmly. 'It's so nice to see such close friends here,' she said, placing a hand on each of Carol and Lorna's shoulders. 'And James is an excellent business partner,' she added, looking at Carol. 'So attentive, and he has a real personal touch.'

'He's spent so much time here on the run-up to opening. I can see why now,' said Carol.

No, you can't, thought Imogen. *He's been here for other reasons*. She shouldn't have said anything about James's *personal touch*. Her annoyance was with Carol's daughter, not Carol herself.

'Will you excuse me?' she asked. 'I hope you have a lovely night.' And she headed to another table.

'I think the whole village must be here,' said Lorna enviously.

'Not the whole village,' said Carol. 'That isn't possible.'

'Oh, look, there's Nicole!' said Lorna, calling out the other mum's name and waving enthusiastically. 'She's come in for a takeaway. Bloody hell, eight boxes! At ten to fifteen pounds a pop! And there must have been at least four other people come in to collect in the last ten minutes alone. Plus, once we're all gone,' she waved a hand over the diners, 'there's another seating at eight. *That* will cover the whole village,' she said jokingly, 'well, except perhaps Nancy.'

'Is that the woman who lives in Imogen's old house?' asked Carol.

Lorna nodded. 'She's not exactly Miss Popular around here.'

'Has something else happened?'

'Some of the mums think she's ruined the water down at the reservoir. Ever since she built her natural pool.'

Carol laughed at first. 'That's ridiculous.'

'Try telling them that.'

'But the whole of Heron Water? It doesn't make sense.'

'Not the whole of it. The bit near her house. At least that's what some people think.'

'What people?'

'Well, Nicole for starters,' said Lorna, waving gaily at Nicole as she left the restaurant, pizza boxes piled high. 'And quite a few of the others. It's the dogs,' she explained, 'they're getting poisoned, and people think it might be due to the unusually high levels of blue-green algae near her place.'

Carol was shocked into silence for a moment. 'And they genuinely believe this?'

'Yes. I mean, it's because the village has never had this problem before. With the algae. And the dogs. It's only since Nancy moved here. At least, that's what they're saying.'

'It's like a witch-hunt,' Carol said quietly.

Imogen was high on all the congratulations. Every table had stopped her, told her how much they loved her food, said they'd be recommending the restaurant – and even more importantly that they'd definitely be back. And she could tell in their eyes that they meant it. It was better than she'd ever imagined. She felt someone come up behind her, touch her gently on the lower back and for a brief second she thought it was James. Alarmed, she turned quickly.

It was Dylan. She felt a flush of relief. Her husband was looking buoyant.

'How was the interview?' she asked.

'Surprisingly good. I liked him. The head. And I think he liked me too.'

'Of course he did,' said Imogen, kissing him on the lips. Out of the corner of her eye she saw James watching them, giving a minuscule frown. He didn't like seeing her being affectionate with her husband. She turned her back.

'You think you got it?' she asked Dylan.

He hesitated and she could see he was seriously entertaining the idea, and for the first time with a sense of optimism.

'Who knows?'

'You want it?'

He looked at her and smiled. 'I do. I never thought I'd say that but I really do.'

He was going to get it, Imogen thought. She knew it. And in that moment she was filled with such a sense of euphoria she felt lighter than air. They were on the up. The tide had turned and she was going to get back everything she'd lost.

FORTY-SEVEN

Friday 27 November

Carol had been unusually quiet as she and James had walked Lorna home. She'd let her husband and daughter chat about the restaurant, the success of the evening. It wasn't far to Lorna's house, only ten minutes, and then she sensed her husband's relief that he no longer had to make polite conversation.

They said goodbye and James took Carol's hand as they continued down the road. She could tell he was pleased with the evening, pleased with himself.

'It was a good night,' she said.

'Wasn't it? And I sense there'll be many more like it.'

'Fingers crossed.'

He looked at her, perplexed by her cautiousness. As if he didn't understand it, understand her. And not for the first time she felt a growing distance between them. Not in a way that he might acknowledge. But she felt as if he didn't quite see her as an equal, as if she were merely one of the things he had acquired in his very successful life.

A reliable wife. Now she was pushing sixty, in his eyes

no longer glamorous or sexually attractive (their sex life had dwindled to once a month, if that). Instead she felt as if she was the respectable backdrop to his status and career. Someone in situ to reassure parents, governors, government civil servants, while he went about his very important business.

'Honestly?' he said, not quite believing what she'd said. 'Of course there's an element of risk in any new business but I think I made a very wise move investing in Imogen Wood. She knows exactly what she's doing. And she's hungry for success. In fact, I've never seen a woman so determined to make an enterprise work.' His eyes shone with some sort of private admiration.

'Well, that's terrific,' said Carol, half despising herself for pandering to her husband's ego. But she didn't want to challenge him, not tonight. There was something more pressing on her mind.

'James, are you aware of infighting between some of the mothers at the school?'

'You might as well ask if I'm aware the school contains children. There are always mothers falling out. It's part of the tapestry.'

'No, but this . . . it seems different somehow. Some of the things that are being said. It seems to be that group, you know from before. The mums involved in that incident at Heron Water, plus their friends. It feels as if it could spin out of control.'

He laughed and it irritated her, but she bit it down.

'How do you know this?' he asked.

'Lorna was telling me.'

He smiled, a dismissive smile that held no secret of what he thought. 'No offence, darling, but your daughter . . . well, let's just say she likes a bit of gossip. And she likes attention too. I would not be surprised if what she's told you is exaggerated.'

There was a truth to what he said but it still hurt. Carol knew she had to put aside the rudeness and open contempt for her daughter and remember what she needed to make her husband see.

'Honestly, I don't think it is. It feels . . . I don't know, like some sort of *Lord of the Flies* thing. The majority of them ganging up on one person. As if they're at war.'

'And there will be casualties?' he said in a light mocking tone. 'Darling, you make it sound so dramatic!'

She kept quiet after that. It wasn't getting through. And banging on about it wouldn't make him see either. Only a regrettable event would wake him up to the undercurrents she could sense building in this village. She hoped she was wrong but had a deeply disturbing sensation that she wasn't.

FORTY-EIGHT

Thursday 10 December

Walking helped clear Nancy's head. She would drop Lara at school, keeping a close eye on Rosie and making sure the other girl stayed clear. Mia was always waiting in the playground for Lara now, a solitary soul in need of Lara's friendship as much as the other way around. It pained Nancy to see them sometimes, the two outcasts, but then she reminded herself there were other children in the class as well. Children who may not be best friends with Lara and Mia but who rubbed along fine with them.

All this she would talk through in her head as she took off through the countryside that surrounded the village. Having time off in the day was a luxury Nancy was still getting used to. She'd never had time to do this sort of stuff before; she'd been working all hours. Somewhat self-consciously, she'd invested in a pair of proper walking shoes and an ordnance survey map. Then had tried to fathom out the orange topography lines, the blue streams, the dotted green markings that indicated the next footpath that she accessed over yet another stile.

Her walks had got longer as she'd gained confidence and experience. Today she would go seven miles without once seeing a car or a shop or barely a soul. She would bump into the occasional rambler, and they would wish each other a cheery good day, then would pass and after a few minutes, when she looked back across the hill trail, they would have vanished. Ahead of her she saw a dirty, dark cloud. It was dumping rain on the land, the grey sheet of hazy water visible. It looked as if the wind was blowing the cloud in the opposite direction. Or at least she thought so.

She was about three miles into her walk when her phone beeped. She retrieved it from her small backpack and saw she had three missed calls and a voicemail. All from the school.

Service could be patchy out in the hills. She stood exactly where she had been when the message had come through, telling herself not to panic. Dialling into her mailbox, she heard Esther, the woman from the office, asking her to call the school as soon as she could. She didn't give any other details. Nancy swore.

Fingers fumbling now, she quickly dialled the school's number. A drop of rain fell onto her face.

'Hello, it's Nancy Miller, Lara's mum,' she babbled as soon as she got through. 'I had a message to call as soon as possible. Is everything all right?'

'Ah, Mrs Miller. I'm afraid not. Lara asked to go to the toilet during lessons this morning and didn't return to the classroom.'

'What?' Nancy couldn't quite process what Esther was saying. 'Where is she?'

Esther cleared her throat. 'I'm afraid we don't know. We were wondering if she had come home to you?'

'I'm not there, not at home.' As she spoke, Nancy had instinctively started to walk back the way she'd come. She had to head home to find her child.

'Sorry? You're breaking up,' said Esther.

Shit. If she moved, she lost service. 'I said I'm not at home.' She looked back along the footpath. She was at least forty-five minutes from her house, maybe thirty if she ran. Too long, a nagging voice said in her head. 'But I'm going back now. I'll hurry.'

'OK, well, let's not panic. We've called the police and they're taking a drive around. Is there anywhere else you think she could have gone?'

'No. No . . . we don't really know anyone around here yet.' The rain was coming down heavier now.

'We will find her, Mrs Miller, rest assured. I'll call you again in another twent—'

She didn't hear the rest. Esther's voice fractured then disappeared.

Nancy broke into a run.

FORTY-NINE

Thursday 10 December

Nancy ran all the way home without stopping. She staggered back into her driveway, bedraggled and out of breath. She unlocked the front door, even knowing as she did that Lara couldn't be inside the house – she didn't have a key.

Standing dripping wet mud on the hall floor, she called out Lara's name but the house was silent. She ran out into the garden, searching by the chickens, the wooded area and near the pool, but Lara wasn't there either.

Her phone was ringing again. The school.

'Have you found her?' she barked.

'Not yet.' It was Mr Whitman this time. 'I know this is an incredibly worrying time for you, but we will find her. I wanted to let you know we've checked the CCTV and Lara is on camera leaving the side gate of the school at nine forty-five this morning.'

Nancy's heart skipped a beat. She looked at her watch. That was over an hour ago.

'How the hell did she get out? Surely these things are locked?'

'She used the code.'

'What?'

'Yes, the door code. I have no idea how she knew it. For obvious reasons, this kind of information is kept strictly confidential amongst the staff.'

She wasn't sure if she heard right but was there something about his tone that had an accusatory edge? Or was she imagining it? Nancy shook her head. She couldn't deal with that now. 'What about the police?'

'They're searching the village. Are you sure there's nowhere else she might have gone?'

'No,' she said desperately.

'OK. Please keep your phone with you and let us both get in touch as soon as we hear anything.'

They hung up.

Nancy gazed helplessly around. It suddenly hit her hard and a sob caught in her throat. Her ten-year-old daughter was out there somewhere alone.

FIFTY

Lorna seemed to spend a disproportionate amount of time in the broom cupboard, as she liked to call it. It was the tiny room the school allocated to the PTA to store items. Some of the remnants of the second-hand uniform sale were still there but now the space was shared with a mountain of bags placed haphazardly on shelves and the floor, spilling out with donated toys and games for the Christmas fair.

It was Lorna's job to sort them. She sighed, knowing it would take her a significant amount of time. First she'd treat herself to a cup of tea and a custard cream, she thought, and headed to the staffroom. She passed Lara on the way. She was going into the girls' toilets. Lorna would have said hi but Lara had her head down.

Refuelled with a tea and a chocolate digestive as well as a custard cream, Lorna went back to the broom cupboard. She set to work, splitting the games from the cuddly toys, the latter of which had their own stall, such was the sheer volume of them. In the past, the teachers manning the stall had been so desperate to get rid of them, they'd pretended every child's lucky dip ticket was a win, much to the dismay of the mums. Soon Lorna had a shelf stacked with bags of lurid-coloured soft toys. She appraised them, shuddering as she considered how much bacteria might be harboured in all that synthetic fluff.

It was then she heard footsteps outside and looked out the cupboard to see Miss Young walk past at pace, a worried expression on her face.

'Hi,' Lorna called, as ever alert to any kind of ripple on the vital signs monitor of life.

Miss Young nodded briefly but hurried on.

Interesting, thought Lorna, *I wonder what's going on?*

'Everything OK?' she called out.

Miss Young heard, Lorna knew she did, but she deliberately ignored her. *Charming*, thought Lorna.

She went back to the cupboard, this time pulling out all the jigsaws. She was still disgruntled. To think Lorna had spent the last couple of weeks collecting for Miss Young's Christmas present! Almost two hundred and fifty pounds, if you don't mind! It was extraordinary that so far, nearly every single child's parent had put in. Even Mia's mum had put in a fiver. Usually there were always one or two who abstained entirely, saying they didn't see why a Christmas gift should be something a teacher should expect and they'd quite like a present themselves from their place of work thank you very much. Lorna thought it was probably down to her powers of persuasion – all that effort she was putting into tracking down every parent individually – and look at the thanks she got. It made her feel less guilty about the fact that not the whole amount might find its way onto the voucher. After all, no one knew who had donated what. And it was only down to her own skills that there was that much in the pot anyway. Two hundred was still a very generous sum. Hell, even one hundred and fifty was a large amount! Anyone should be grateful to receive one hundred and fifty pounds.

Lorna could hear another pair of footsteps out in the corridor. She peered out: it was Mrs Fox, Miss Young's teaching assistant. She looked harassed.

'You haven't seen Lara Miller, have you?' she asked.

Lorna's antennae picked up. 'Why? Isn't she in class?'

Mrs Fox shook her head. 'Not for forty-five minutes. I've been sent to search the school premises for her.' She looked around worriedly. 'She left the class to use the toilet and never returned.'

Lorna felt a cold thrill run down her spine. 'I saw her. When she went to the bathroom.'

Mrs Fox lit up. 'You did?'

'Yes, but only for a few seconds. I saw her go in but not come out again.'

The TA's hopes were dashed.

'Oh, I feel bad now,' said Lorna. 'I should have stopped her. She looked . . . I don't know . . . worried. As if something was preying on her mind.' Lorna wasn't sure if that was entirely true, but it could have been.

'OK. I need to keep searching. Will you let someone on the senior leadership team know if you see her?'

'Of course.' Lorna pulled her most empathetic face. 'Poor you. And poor her,' she added quickly.

Mrs Fox went on her way. *Wow,* thought Lorna, *a child has absconded.* It wasn't often the school was the centre of such drama.

She was about to return to the cupboard – board games this time – when she heard the door buzz further down the corridor – the door that let people in from the outside. She saw Mr Whitman come out of his office and go to meet whoever was coming through.

Lorna gasped. It was the police! So this was serious. She watched for a moment and then, not wanting to be detected, scuttled back into the cupboard.

She got out her phone.

10 December

RIPTON PRIMARY, YEAR 6

Lorna Fielding, Phoenix's mum
Terrible news. Lara Miller's gone missing at
school. The police have been called. Can
everyone keep an eye out? Such a sad
thing. 10:05

She pressed send, then waited. There was something quite exciting about being the carrier of big news.

Already she could see various live notifications that people were typing a response.

FIFTY-ONE

Thursday 10 December

Lara crouched down, hunched over her knees, arms wrapped around herself. She'd found the perfect spot: a little clearing under some bushes that faced directly out over Heron Water. It was reasonably dry and when she'd walked along the reservoir path in the rain, the opening had seemed to beckon her: come inside and shelter! She'd nestled in, feeling safe and at peace from the constant nasty comments from Rosie.

—Did you see her on that roundabout? I thought she was dead there was so much blood!—

—Don't you have any friends, Lara? Only Mia doesn't count cos she doesn't have any friends either—

—She's a murderer. She tried to drown me. You know murderers go to jail. Forever—

Accompanying the constant digs were the sniggers from Rosie's friends: Bella and Tilly. Miss Young had sat them on the opposite side of the classroom, but it didn't matter. They all mixed in the playground anyway.

And then that morning in assembly, Lara had been called up for an award. 'For conquering her fractions.' She'd got up from the floor where they all sat squeezed together and had to walk through a sea of legs and feet to get to the end of the line in order to make it to the front of the hall where Mr Whitman was holding her certificate. In the middle of the line she'd had to pass Rosie.

Wary, Lara had stepped carefully so as not to catch Rosie's legs, but the other girl had lifted her knee at the last minute, making Lara stumble. She'd pitched forward, almost falling, her backside up in the air in front of the whole school. She'd gone crimson with embarrassment.

'Sorry,' Rosie had said loudly, contritely, which Lara knew was for the benefit of the teachers, and she'd got back up and continued to the front of the hall feeling sick with shame and misery. It had taken all her effort not to cry and she hadn't dared look at Rosie or her friends while she stood with the other kids, all receiving a round of applause.

When they were back in the classroom, in the melee of returning to their seats, Rosie had whispered in her ear, 'I think the whole school saw your knickers,' and Lara had felt utterly crushed again. Her chest was tight with anxiety and she hadn't been able to concentrate on the English assignment at all and had asked to go to the toilet so she could breathe.

It was on the way back she knew she couldn't go into the classroom again, she just couldn't. So she'd got her coat and gone along another corridor that led to the back of the school, and she'd punched in the code that she'd seen the teachers use. They never covered the keypad when they did it. They thought no one was looking or the kids were all too babyish not to watch and remember. As soon as the door opened, she stepped outside.

She ran down the pathway, past the teachers' cars and out onto the road. The bad weather meant there weren't many people about, which suited Lara; she avoided the high street and ran down towards the reservoir. After a few minutes she had to stop and walk; she could feel her asthma taking hold and she didn't have her inhaler. When she reached the cafe she turned left, in the opposite direction to her house, and walked along the path, glancing over at the grey, white-topped water, the rain lashing down. She saw the place where Rosie had fallen in all those months ago and wished Rosie had drowned so she wouldn't have to deal with her every single day. It was all so final, like switching someone off. Like what had happened to her dad. He'd been playing with her on the beach in the morning. By night-time he was dead. She'd found that hard to comprehend for a very long time.

After another five minutes of walking in the rain, Lara began to feel cold and the mud was getting more slippy away from the stony path. Then she saw the clearing and, relieved, ducked in for shelter.

She didn't know how long she'd been there but she'd already looked around at the branches and roots and found a place she could sleep and store food and was imagining a cosy den where she'd live and be safe when she heard the rustling of leaves.

She stiffened, not frightened, but cautious. Perhaps it was a badger, come to share her home. Or a fox. Since moving to Ripton, Lara had fallen in love with nature and at times half-imagined herself as a lone wolf, solitary and territorial.

There was a snuffling sound and the animal's movements got closer. Then all of a sudden, a nose burst through the bushes, followed by a head and two erect ears. It was a dog. Lara was delighted and put her hands out to it. It barked excitedly and she tried to shush it but then she saw its harness and knew it belonged to the police.

A moment later, a uniformed man poked his head into her clearing.

'Hello,' he said. 'Can you tell me your name?'

Then a woman officer appeared too. Lara's heart sank.

'Come on,' said the woman. 'You look cold. Fancy a hot chocolate?'

Lara looked at the woman's outstretched hand. She had no choice really. With one last glance back at her den, she allowed herself to be led away.

FIFTY-TWO

Thursday 10 December

Nancy paced the kitchen, constantly looking up at the window. The rain had eased. She'd had a call from Mr Whitman saying that Lara had been found, hiding out at the reservoir. She was safe and well. The police were bringing her straight home.

The relief had been immense. Nancy had sunk into a chair. Then Mr Whitman had gone on to say that as soon as Lara felt settled, they needed to both come in for a chat. It was part of the policy on absconding from school. He suggested the following day, if Lara was up to it. Nancy, who hadn't even seen her daughter yet and couldn't think straight until she did, had been non-committal and then hung up. She'd rested her head in her hands, suddenly overcome with exhaustion. It would be the post-adrenalin comedown, she knew; emotional, she burst into tears. She quickly blew her nose and got up. Now was not the time to fall apart. Lara would be back at any moment.

She was still looking out of the window when she saw the police car turn into her circular driveway. Nancy glanced anxiously and could see her daughter's small white face in the back seat. She rushed to the front door and pulled it open.

Lara was getting out of the car. She was clutching a paper cup, Nancy noticed, and it seemed bizarre, as if she'd been on an outing to a cafe with these two police officers. The female officer escorted Lara over.

'She's a little bit cold but otherwise right as rain,' said the female officer cheerfully.

Nancy put her arms gently around her daughter. 'Thank you,' she said, 'for looking after her.'

'Thank you,' called Lara, all grown-up, as the police officers made their way back to their car. They waved big, generous waves then got in and drove off.

'What's that?' asked Nancy, pointing at the cup.

'Hot chocolate,' said Lara. 'From the cafe. They got it for me.'

'That's nice,' said Nancy.

'Yes.'

'Are you OK?'

Lara looked up at her, her eyes fragile. 'Yes. I'm sorry, Mum, for running away from school.'

Nancy stroked her daughter's cheek. 'You want to tell me why?'

Lara shrugged. 'Rosie. Saying mean things. And then tripping me up in assembly.'

Nancy felt her blood boil. 'Didn't the teachers say anything?'

'They didn't think it was on purpose. Rosie made sure she apologized in front of them.'

'But surely they *know*,' said Nancy.

'She's too sneaky,' said Lara. 'They might suspect, but they don't have any real evidence.'

'Hmm,' said Nancy. She would be making sure Mr Whitman was aware of the deviousness of this child when they went in to talk to him. 'We'll make them see,' she said to Lara.

As she turned to lead Lara inside, she saw a disturbed patch of earth at the side of the house. She hadn't noticed it before. She took a step closer then started as she saw a few bedraggled feathers sticking up out of the ground. 'What's that?'

'Oh. It was the bird,' said Lara.

'What bird?'

'The one that flew into the window. On the day we moved in.'

Nancy thought back. The bird with the red patch on its head. 'But . . . what happened? Why's it in the ground?'

'It died. It flew into the window again, only this time it didn't get up.' Lara paused. 'I buried it so you didn't see. I didn't want you to be upset,' she added.

Nancy was taken aback. 'I wouldn't be upset.' She looked down at the feathers, could see now that it was the edge of a wing. Poor bird, she thought, dead in the ground. 'How do you know it's the same bird?' she asked.

Lara shrugged. 'It looked like it.'

'When did all this happen?'

'A few days ago,' said Lara. She walked away, back into the house.

Nancy watched as she left, then looked down again at the bird. It seemed wrong somehow that it wasn't fully covered. She knelt down, gathered up some wet soil and placed it over the protruding feathers. Then it seemed wrong that the creature was out of sight. As if it was too unsightly to be part of the world any more. She decided to leave it. She took one last look at where the bird was buried and followed Lara inside.

FIFTY-THREE

Friday 11 December

Nancy could feel Lara's nerves as they were buzzed into the school by Esther. Mr Whitman came out of his room to meet them. Inside his office, he directed them not to the armchair seating area but to the more formal table and chairs on the other side of the room. Then he closed the door.

'Is Miss Young not joining us?' asked Nancy, surprised.

'It's difficult to get cover for her this morning,' said Mr Whitman, not looking her in the eye.

This announcement put Nancy on the back foot. Although how much Miss Young would have helped was debatable. She'd shown signs of being supportive in the past, but equally, had clammed up in the presence of her boss. Perhaps it was better without her. In any event, Lara running out of school was a strong reaction to everything that had been going on. Nancy felt certain Mr Whitman would take the bullying far more seriously now. He had safeguarding issues to contend with. At long last, the situation had to be tackled.

'I'm very glad to see you safe and well,' Mr Whitman said to Lara.

Lara nodded nervously. She was sitting at the table, looking as if she'd rather be anywhere but the head teacher's office.

'Do you want to tell me a bit about what happened yesterday?' His voice was gentle, encouraging.

Lara shrugged and Nancy knew she was struggling. 'I needed some space,' she said.

'Space from what?' asked Mr Whitman.

There was a moment before Lara answered. 'Rosie,' she mumbled, so quietly she was barely audible.

'You haven't been getting on too well recently, have you?' asked Mr Whitman.

Lara shook her head.

Nancy frowned. That wasn't quite right. It was more than that. Much more. Rosie had been systematically tormenting her daughter.

'I know it's sometimes hard being around people you don't really like but that's not an excuse to run away from school. You do understand that what you did is very serious, don't you?'

Nancy couldn't believe what she was hearing. She saw tears gather in Lara's eyes.

'Hang on a minute,' said Nancy. 'Rosie has been *bullying* Lara. Constantly—'

Mr Whitman held up a hand. 'Please, Mrs Miller. I know things have been difficult for Lara and I sympathize' – he looked genuinely empathetic – 'but I don't need to tell you how important it is that your daughter remains in school for her own safety.' He turned to Lara and said kindly: 'We really can't have children wandering around Ripton by themselves. We need to know you're safe.'

Lara nodded mutely.

'If you ever feel like you need to get some space again, then you can come and see me.'

Lara nodded yet again and Nancy could tell there was no chance of that ever happening. Her daughter would rather die than go and knock on the head teacher's door.

Mr Whitman turned to Nancy. 'I know you have concerns about Rosie, and we have put a mechanism in place. Rosie and her friends will be spending two or three breaks a week with the class teaching assistant talking through friendships; how to be a good friend to others; and if you're not able to be their friend, then how to learn to walk away.'

Nancy's mouth dropped. 'Is that it?'

Mr Whitman looked surprised. 'What do you mean?'

'Well, is she not going to be punished?'

'For what exactly?'

'All the things she's said and done to Lara!'

'Mrs Miller, as I'm sure you appreciate, it's often very hard to ascertain exactly what has happened and when between children. As much as the teachers keep an eye, they can't watch every child twenty-four seven.'

'They don't have to watch every child. Just Rosie,' snapped Nancy. She could see Lara staring off into the distance.

'And they will. But we also want to take some proactive steps. Previous situations have shown us that talking to children who have issues with friendships and workshopping with them often has a very positive outcome.'

'Workshopping?' repeated Nancy, aghast. 'What is this, some kind of corporate "getting to know you" bullshit?'

Mr Whitman frowned at her use of language.

'And what exactly happens in these workshops?'

'The girls will be encouraged to articulate what they find difficult about certain friendships and how best to navigate them. Often they use role play.'

Role play? She resisted the urge to roll her eyes. She was trying to see his point of view, she really was. But she was highly dubious that a child as devious as Rosie would fall for such a pile of touchy-feely crap.

'Mr Whitman, with all due respect, I do not think for one minute this is going to change things.'

He frowned and glanced at Lara as if to remind Nancy that she should be remaining positive for her own daughter's sake. It riled.

'Mrs Miller, I think you need to have a little more faith. It has certainly worked in the past and I see no reason why it shouldn't work again. We need to at least give it a try.' He paused. 'We should also remember that Rosie has been through quite a tough year.'

Nancy was staggered. '*What?*'

Mr Whitman realized he'd been insensitive, attempted to cover. 'I know that's not an excuse and I know she's not the only child with big life-changing challenges to overcome' – here he glanced at Lara – 'but we need to look at the whole picture.' He took a breath and laid his hands flat on the table, brightening his tone. 'Right, well, I need to let you know that we will not be punishing Lara for leaving the school as she's already been through enough.'

Punishing *Lara?* Nancy was so shocked she didn't know what to say.

Mr Whitman smiled at Lara. 'Are you ready to go back to class now?'

Lara obediently stood, just as there was a knock on the door and Esther put her head round.

'Your next meeting's arrived,' said Esther.

'Great. I'll be there in a minute,' said Mr Whitman.

Nancy saw Lara give her a tiny wave as she slunk out of the door. Esther held it open wider and smiled at Nancy. The implication, whether deliberate or not, was clear. Her time was up.

Mr Whitman stood. 'I know it can seem unfair and all you want is to protect Lara but we would please urge you to trust us to make the right decisions. This kind of thing happens a lot in schools, and you'd be amazed at how in another few weeks or months it can all blow over.'

He sounded experienced, he looked confident, he seemed so *convinced*, it was hard not to be reassured by him. And part of Nancy desperately wanted to be reassured. But the only thing she knew for certain as she walked back across the playground was that she was stuck in a system. A system devised and managed by the school. A system that, as a parent, you had no power to change.

She headed home, wrapped up against the cold. When she got back, she felt as rudderless as ever.

Nancy took her coffee up to her room and stepped out onto the balcony. She took a few deep breaths, trying to work out what to do. But she had no answers. She realized she was just waiting to see what happened next.

As she gazed out across the grey water, she noticed with a shock that she could no longer see the chimney pots. And the church spire was almost swallowed up by the rising water. She'd become so used to seeing them and now they'd vanished beneath the reservoir.

She gulped for breath without really knowing why.

FIFTY-FOUR

Friday 11 December

Lorna loved Christmas. It was her favourite time of the year. And there was a day she always spent decorating the house while the children were at school. She loved seeing their faces when they ran up the front path ahead of her, eyes lit up with excitement as they took in the wreath on the front door. That was the signal that everything was different inside and they would rush in with impatience, squealing at the wooden nativity, the large Christmas elves at the fireplace, the gold stars strung from wall to wall and the musical model Christmas scenes, complete with snowy mountains and Swiss-style chalets. The best part was of course the tree, and although Lorna dug it out of the loft (she didn't go with the real ones, preferred instead to get something that required less hoovering), she let the kids decorate it themselves.

This year there was something new, something extra special that Amazon had delivered that morning. She looked out of the living room window and smiled. In the tiny front garden was a giant pop-up snowman, its LED lights currently unlit and unimpressive but come four thirty, when dark was setting in, it would come alive. Lorna couldn't wait – the kids were going to love it! She was still admiring it when she saw Simon open the front gate. She started – what was he doing home so early?

He stopped when he saw the snowman and frowned. Lorna braced herself and fixed on a smile. She waved to her husband from the window, but he pointed at the snowman and mouthed: *What the fuck?*

God, men could be such humbugs at times, thought Lorna. She went to the front door and opened it.

'Hi, darling,' she said.

'What's going on?' asked Simon, looking back at the snowman.

Nice to see you too, thought Lorna. 'It's our new decoration,' she said. 'Like it?'

'How much did it cost?'

'Why does everything have to be about money?'

'Er . . . because we haven't got any?'

'That's not true and you know it.' Lorna walked into the house, Simon following. He took off his jacket, put it on the kitchen table.

'Lorna, I'm serious,' said Simon, and he did actually look it. 'We don't have the spare cash to buy naff snowman decorations.'

Lorna bristled. It wasn't naff, it was cheerful and festive. It put a smile on her face.

'You do know how much I earn, don't you?' continued Simon. 'And while we're on the subject of money, we still haven't had a proper conversation about schools. I know it's great that Phoenix got a scholarship and all that, but there's no way we can pay the rest.'

'I'm going to contribute,' said Lorna. 'I've been applying for loads of jobs.' She hadn't really, not yet. Things were always so busy in the run-up to Christmas, she hadn't had time to look. 'And Mum is going to help too.'

'Is she? Has she actually said that?'

'Yes,' lied Lorna. 'She's going to help a lot. Who do you think bought the snowman?' It was another outright lie but better that Simon thought Carol was putting her hand in her pocket than the actual truth. And there would be more where that cash had come from – much more. Lorna planned on staying class rep and chair of the PTA for a very long time.

'I don't feel comfortable relying on your mum,' said Simon.

'She wants to be a part of her grandchildren's lives,' said Lorna, switching on the kettle. 'It would be unkind to stop her,' and she turned away to get a couple of mugs to make them both tea. Conversation over.

FIFTY-FIVE

Friday 11 December

The last of the receipts were tallied up and Imogen was once again very pleasantly surprised by how much they'd taken. She sat back in her chair. She was the only one in the restaurant as the lunch staff had finished and the evening staff didn't start for another hour. And they were fully booked for that night too. She gazed around, a feeling of contentment washing over her. She should have done this ages ago, she thought, then remembered that actually, it hadn't been possible – still wouldn't be without private financing. James had come good, but with his investment she'd noticed a growing sense of propriety about him. Or was that the fact they were sleeping together? Maybe the two things were so intertwined, it was hard to distinguish what was what. She felt a low sense of unease and knew it was something she had to be mindful of. She'd noticed him getting irate at the opening night and it had annoyed her. He did not own her.

She heard a rap on the window and frowned. The closed sign was clearly up. She turned to see who it was.

Talk of the devil. Imogen morphed her frown into a smile, even though she could really do without a visit from her business partner right now.

She got up and went to let him in. 'What are you doing here?'

'Do I need a reason to come and see my investment?'

He didn't but it riled how he was looking at her, as if *she* was the thing he'd invested in. Or maybe she was reading too much into it. She decided to defuse the situation and went to kiss him.

'Not at all,' she said. It was an unexpected surprise, that's all. A nice one,' she added. 'I don't usually see you on Friday afternoons, there's too much going on at school just before the weekend.'

She felt James place a hand on her backside and pull her closer. 'I managed to escape for a bit,' he said, 'seeing as we're neither of us going to get our Saturday run in tomorrow.'

No, thought Imogen, they weren't. The Christmas fair meant they'd both be at the school in the morning.

She wriggled away from him. 'Not now,' she said, of his desire for sex.

He looked disgruntled. Like a child who'd been told no more chocolate biscuits, she thought.

'Why not?' he asked.

'I'm busy.'

'I'm busy too but I've made the effort to come and see you.'

She sighed inside but put on a smile. 'We're going to take

an awful lot of money tonight but only if I make a large vat of tomato sauce.'

He put his arms around her waist from behind, pushed himself against her and murmured in her ear. 'We can do it while you're stirring stuff on the stove.'

'It might spill on you,' she said. 'Hot sauce on your cock. Painful.'

He winced and pulled away, defeated. 'By the way, Dylan's got the job.' His tone was petulant.

Imogen felt her heart inflate, as if she was being lifted off the ground. 'He did? Oh my God, that's amazing!'

'He'll be getting a call this afternoon.'

James was looking at her expectantly. She dutifully kissed him. 'Thank you. For all you did.' Inside she was ecstatic but careful not to show it too much. She remembered James's face when Dylan had come to opening night at the restaurant.

Her clever, clever husband, she thought. He had just changed the direction of all their futures. She wished she could congratulate him there and then but of course she had to wait for him to be told and then call *her* – and then she had to remember to react as if it was new news.

'I had Lara Miller's mother in my office this morning,' said James.

Imogen's euphoria instantly evaporated.

'Following Lara's absconding from school. I think it would serve Rosie well if she backed off a bit.'

'She's hurt,' said Imogen. 'And upset. Lara tried to drown her.'

He smiled, his brow furrowed with mild impatience. 'Did she? Really?'

'Yes,' said Imogen stubbornly.

'Rosie is fine. Whatever happened back in September has passed. Lara has displayed no violence towards Rosie that we have seen at the school. Look, I have to follow protocol, OK? I know it's all going to be fine, but maybe you could have a word with Rosie, nip this in the bud before it escalates.' He kissed her on the lips, long and sensual. 'I'll see you tomorrow,' he said, 'and I'll try not to think too much about what we should be doing at ten o'clock on a Saturday morning.'

She watched as he left, then let out a long, heavy sigh.

FIFTY-SIX

Saturday 12 December

Nancy lay in bed the morning of the Christmas fair wondering if she could pretend it didn't exist. Pretend Imogen and her cronies wouldn't be there on a stall, hell, pretend even that none of the last few months had even happened. This thought scared her because it tapped into the nagging doubt that was poking its head above the surface of something she was burying deep: *had she made a huge mistake in moving here?*

She quickly jumped out of bed; she was not going to delve below the surface and examine the size of the iceberg she feared she had created. There was the fresh air, she reminded herself, the air that was saving Lara's life. That was priceless.

Nancy opened the curtains and gasped with delight. Fat white flakes floated past the window and the garden was covered with a layer of fresh snow. Nancy ran out of her room and down the corridor to Lara's. She went in and saw her daughter rousing.

'Guess what?' said Nancy excitedly.

Lara yawned. 'What?'

'Come and look out the window.'

Lara got up, her hair tousled, and stuck her head behind the curtains. 'Snow!' she squealed.

The hall was decorated for Christmas, adorned with tinsel and bunting that the children had made. A large tree stood in the corner, covered in baubles, and music was blaring on the speakers: the festive pop songs that were wheeled out each year. Imogen was at her usual stall with Erin; she refused to do it without her friend. Being with Erin made it more fun, they got to chat.

Imogen looked around. It was already busy. The fair was the biggest event of the PTA calendar and nearly all the kids and their families came. The teachers were in full attendance too, forming a rota on the refreshment stand, and usually there was a real festive feel about it all. She could see Nancy milling around, checking each stall in turn. At some point she would come to them on the bottle stall.

Sarah approached. Today she was wearing a tie-dye tunic and a Christmassy bandana. Appalling really.

'Oh, go on, I'll have a go,' said Sarah and handed over ten pounds.

'How many tickets?' asked Imogen.

'Whatever I get for that,' said Sarah, pointing at the money. 'It's all for a good cause, isn't it.'

Imogen gave the tombola a twist and opened the flap. 'Pick ten,' she said. Sarah pulled them out and one by one opened them up with excruciating slowness. And one by one they failed to produce a number with a five or a zero on the end.

'Oh, what a shame,' said Imogen.

'Maybe God doesn't reward the righteous after all,' Erin whispered into her ear as Sarah wandered away and Imogen giggled.

'I wonder if our girls are having more luck,' said Imogen. 'I've sent them to the raffle stall, with strict instructions to get the winning ticket for the day pass for two at the spa.'

'Maybe we should run the raffle stall next year so we can rig it,' said Erin.

Imogen laughed. 'I have a feeling I'm going to be too busy to be on any PTA next year,' she said. 'I can only stay an hour today as it is.'

'Oh yes. The incredibly successful restaurant.'

Imogen thought she detected the tiniest hint of envy in her friend's voice. She looked at her.

'I'm so pleased for you,' added Erin quickly. Imogen nodded.

'What's Mr Whitman like as a business partner?' Erin looked across the hall where the head teacher was standing talking to the local councillor, a pair of felt antlers on his head.

'He lets me get on with it,' said Imogen.

'That's good. Is he, you know, looking at investing in any other opportunities? Only I'm thinking of expanding my PR business.'

Imogen didn't think her friend was serious, but it was best to shut this down straight away. She did not need any strain on her own investment during these crucial first few months of her restaurant. 'He's fully committed.'

'Shame,' said Erin. 'How did you get him and Carol to come on board anyway?'

'His wife?' asked Imogen.

'Yes. Surely she had a say in it?'

Imogen shook her head. 'It was nothing to do with Carol.'

'What was nothing to do with my mum?' asked Lorna as she came up to them, clutching a fabric money bag and a large white envelope. Pepper was trailing behind her.

'Imogen's restaurant,' said Erin. 'Apparently, Imogen has special persuasive tactics when it comes to our head teacher.'

'That's not what I said,' snapped Imogen.

Erin looked hurt. 'I was only joking.'

'My mum would've probably vetoed it,' said Lorna lightly. 'She's not one for putting her hands deep into her pockets.'

'Mum,' said Pepper, tugging on her skirt, 'can we go and see Father Christmas?'

'It's not her money,' said Imogen curtly. 'This is strictly between James and myself.'

Lorna looked at the tin on the stall. 'I'm here to clear away any surplus cash,' she said.

Imogen opened the tin and Lorna felt a surge of pleasure as she saw it was bursting with notes.

'Mum, I want to see Father Christmas!' repeated Pepper.

'Not yet,' said Lorna. She turned back to Imogen. 'Give me what you don't need,' said Lorna, 'and I'll go and put it in the safe.'

Imogen handed her a thick wodge of money and Lorna stuffed it into her bag. She would go and count it in a minute but could tell there was already a couple of hundred pounds there – and that was just one stall and only forty-five minutes since the fair had opened. She closed the bag safely then took the envelope she'd tucked under her arm and held it up. 'Erin, did you want to contribute to Miss Young's Christmas present? Last day to put in.'

'MUM!' yelled Pepper.

'Oh. Sure,' said Erin. She got out her purse. 'What's the going rate?'

'I put in a tenner,' said Imogen.

'A tenner? That seems a lot.' Erin cast around, saw Nicole and Helen. 'Hey, guys,' she said, 'how much did you put in for Miss Young's Christmas collection?'

'Ten pounds,' said Nicole.

'Yeah, me too,' said Helen.

'Right, well, I suppose I need to do the same then. That's forty quid just with us here,' said Erin, indicating their little group.

'Only put in what you would like,' said Lorna quickly. She didn't like Erin's calculations.

'MUUUUUMMMMMM,' said Pepper.

'It's fine,' said Erin. She put a ten-pound note into the envelope and handed it back. 'You will let us know how much you raise in the end, won't you?'

Lorna smiled. 'Course!'

'Only then we can see if some of us have been Christmas scrooges,' said Erin, laughing.

Lorna laughed with her but inside, her stomach was curdling. It was all getting a bit too specific for her liking. People focusing on exactly who was donating what. Adding it all up. Coming to a final figure. What if they started exchanging notes and compared how much had been raised to the amount actually given to Miss Young? Lorna felt a bead of sweat form on her upper lip. She'd already spent some of the money. The LED snowman in her front garden. She wanted to get away. Pepper was driving her mad, tapping her on her leg.

Lorna saw Nancy approaching and felt the animosity come off Imogen and Erin in waves. An idea sprang into her mind. Before she had really thought it through, she turned and smiled at Nancy. 'You've done such an amazing job,' she said, 'the fair is running like clockwork.'

'Thanks,' said Nancy, and glanced at Imogen and Erin. 'You have everything you need?'

'Yes. Been doing this several years now,' said Erin.

Even Lorna flinched – Erin could be so cutting! Imogen said nothing. Still, Lorna needed to grab Nancy before she moved on. 'Could you possibly hang on to this for a minute?' she said, thrusting the envelope for Miss Young into Nancy's hand. 'I want to take Pepper to see Father Christmas before the queue gets too long.'

'Oh yes. Course,' said Nancy.

'It's the collection for Miss Young,' said Lorna, reverently patting the envelope, then she walked away.

That was better, thought Lorna as she held hands with a

skipping Pepper beside her. They had both seen – Imogen and Erin. And now she wasn't the only person who'd had sole charge of the Christmas present money. It probably wouldn't be needed but it was good to have a bit of insurance.

12 December

RIPTON PRIMARY, YEAR 6

Lorna Fielding, Phoenix's mum
I wanted to say a big thank you to
everyone today for your hard work at the
Christmas fair. No total yet but we'll have
one by next week. I thought it was our best
fair yet! 19:14

> **Sarah Ramsay, Noah's mum**
> The kids LOVED the Baby Jesus biscuits. So
> glad we got to do them. It really gave the
> day some extra meaning, I thought. 19:14

Nicole Wilson, Bella's mum
Especially when the kids bit Baby Jesus's
head off. 19:15

> **Lorna Fielding, Phoenix's mum**
> In other news, we have raised £170 for Miss
> Young's Christmas present! See pic – it's
> one of those cards that you can spend in
> loads of different shops. Well done,
> everyone! 19:16

FIFTY-SEVEN

Saturday 19 December

The Christmas holidays were a welcome respite and Nancy and Lara took to the hills with a flask of hot chocolate, covering miles. On one of these walks, Nancy noticed something that filled her with an unexpected joy. Lara was happily chatting away to her as they climbed a hill. Six months ago she would have been wheezing and unable to breathe. Tears welled up in Nancy's eyes, which she quickly brushed away. But it was good. It was better than good, she thought, it was bloody miraculous.

When the weather was wet, they camped out in the new studio Nancy had put together in one of the empty rooms in the house. They played with clay, laughing as they threw it on the potter's wheel and attempted to make something resembling a pot.

Christmas Day dawned with pale pink and mauve skies that blended into a bright azure blue as the sun rose. Nancy and Lara walked along the edge of Heron Water, amongst the reeds and bullrushes, just the dark brown seed heads visible on tall, slender stems. Much of the bird population had migrated for the winter but the herons stayed, and Nancy and Lara watched as one took off from the bank, flying low over the water.

Back at the house, they opened presents and Lara squealed with delight at the new iPad Beth had bought her. It was her second-favourite present, she declared, as nothing could top the kitten Nancy had got for Lara a few days beforehand. Lara and Pebbles, a little tabby, were already inseparable.

They wished Beth a happy Christmas via video call and hid their giggles when Martin's mother, Angela, complained that the Brussel sprouts weren't up to last year's standard (when she had spent Christmas Day with her daughter).

It was a good day, quiet but happy. She and Lara had lit a paper lantern for Sam and reminisced, laughing, about how a few years ago he had insisted on his own chocolate advent calendar after he'd been caught red-handed pinching from Lara's.

After Lara had gone to bed, Nancy settled down in front of the deep red embers of the fire with a glass of wine and thought maybe she hadn't done so badly after all. It had been one of the hardest years of her life, holding everything together after Sam's death, and on the second Christmas anniversary, she had been dreading a return of the awful pain of the first. But Lara and she had done OK; they had even had fun. They'd remembered Sam with fondness and had started to make memories of a new type of Christmas, just the two of them.

January came around quickly and the new term beckoned.

On the first day back, Nancy approached the school gates with an element of trepidation. But it was fine. Lara settled back in and Rosie left her alone.

It wasn't until the end of the week that things started to go wrong.

FIFTY-EIGHT

Friday 8 January

Miss Young clapped her hands for quiet and the class settled. 'Now as you all know, there is a very big event happening in a couple of months' time. The Straw Bear Festival is going to need its Spring Queen, and as usual, it's a Year 6 girl who has the honour of wearing the crown.' She paused and took in the flurry of excited murmurs and darted looks. 'This year, the Queen will have the added honour of riding on a pony that one of you knows particularly well. Lupin, who used to belong to Rosie, is going to be very kindly lent to the festival for the occasion by his new owners.' Rebecca glanced at Rosie, but she was holding her head high, eyes strong. 'So . . . if you think there is a potential Spring Queen in this classroom, I need someone to nominate them. You cannot nominate yourself,' she added loudly over the growing buzz of excitement.

Lottie stuck her hand up at great speed.

'Yes, Lottie?'

'I nominate Aisha,' said Lottie.

'Happy with that, Aisha?' asked Miss Young.

Aisha blushed pink and nodded. Miss Young wrote her name down on the whiteboard.

'Who else?'

Tilly waved a hand.

'Tilly?'

'I nominate Rosie.'

It was inevitable, thought Miss Young, but it still rankled. Mostly because she knew Rosie would win. But she had to remain neutral. 'OK, Rosie?' she asked, then on Rosie's affirmation, wrote her name on the board.

Jakob put his hand up.

'Yes, Jakob?'

'I nominate Noah.'

Miss Young paused. 'It has to be a girl.'

'Why?'

Good question, she thought. 'Just the way it is,' she said, looking at the clock. It was almost time to get them all outside for PE. 'Any more, or are we closing the books?'

A shy hand went up.

'Mia? You have someone you want to nominate?'

'Yes. Lara.'

The entire class shifted their eyes to Lara, who was sitting at the table, her face fiery red.

'How about it, Lara?' asked Miss Young.

'I don't know . . .'

'Go on,' said Mia, nudging her arm.

'It's open to everyone,' said Miss Young pointedly. She ignored the indignation on Rosie's face, prayed that Lara would too.

'Not everyone,' grumbled Jakob.

'Please?' asked Mia.

The room held its breath.

'OK,' said Lara, barely audible.

'Brilliant!' said Rebecca quickly, before she changed her mind. She wrote Lara's name on the board, then clapped her hands again to get their attention. 'Voting will take place in a couple of weeks. Now get changed for PE!'

Lara ran out onto the field with Mia, checking over her shoulder for Rosie. 'I'm scared Rosie's going to be mad,' she said.

'Oh, who cares if she is,' said Mia. 'We all know she's going to get the most votes, so it doesn't really matter. I just thought you'd make a good queen.'

Lara gave her friend a grateful smile. The children were lining up at the start of the track on the cross-country field and they went to join them. Since moving to Ripton, Lara was thrilled to find she was not automatically excluded from PE and instead she'd gradually joined in. And she'd found she loved sport. Loved the way it made her feel after being the invalid for so long. She still needed her inhaler now and then, but she could take part. And that was really cool.

It was cold and the field, although not sodden, was muddy. In her ten-year-old eyes it was enormous and stretched for miles in all directions. Her last school had no green outdoor space at all, just the grey playground.

Miss Young was holding up her whistle. 'We're going to time you,' she said, and half the class groaned. 'Try and beat your personal best! Remember, three laps!' She gave the whistle one sharp blast and the children set off. Some of them – the boys especially – broke into a sprint immediately but Lara knew better than that. She'd been looking up blogs of famous runners on her new iPad that Auntie Beth had given her for Christmas and had learned about pacing and lactic acid. Sometimes she would foster a fragile dream of being on Team GB, running alongside her heroes. Something that, deep down, she knew would probably never happen – unless she got completely cured, but sometimes she would dream of that as well.

She set off at a pace that felt right and soon some kids began to fall behind. The field's perimeter was surrounded on most sides by farm fields. At the furthest point from the school, the field on the other side of the school fence was full of sheep. It was Lara's favourite part of the run. She loved seeing the sheep with their bulbous, knowing eyes staring at her as she ran past. Lara had fallen in love with them all with their woolly coats and expressive 'baas' and had refused to eat lamb from that point onwards. She smiled as she neared the field, seeing Daisy and Mr Chops, as she'd named them. She gave them a little wave and continued onwards. Soon she had finished the first lap and only two runners were ahead of her: Bea and Aiden, arguably the most sporty kids in the school. They had already lapped the slowcoaches right at the back and now she was nearing them too. One of them was Mia and she slapped hands with her as she passed.

'Go, Lara!' shouted Mia, and Lara gave a thumbs up.

She carried on at her steady pace, feeling her rhythm guide her, and soon she was passing Daisy and Mr Chops again. Up ahead she could see Rosie and Tilly and she felt herself automatically tense but then she checked herself. *Just keep running*, she thought. She still gave them a wide berth as she passed though. She heard sniggers from behind her and wasn't going to look back but couldn't help a quick glance. They were whispering to each other. *Nothing different there*, thought Lara and carried on, grateful to have passed them. She continued round, starting her third and final lap of the field.

Her legs were beginning to tire a bit now but nothing she hadn't handled before. In fact, it gave her pleasure to know she could push through it. After another minute the tiredness had become more of an ache, but she refused to slow down. She didn't want to be the kid who couldn't do it. Not any more.

She looked towards the finish line. It wasn't far, she thought, only another three quarters lap of the field. Bizarrely, she couldn't see Miss Young any more. She wasn't standing watching them all and Lara wondered where she'd gone. The ache in her legs took her mind away from her teacher. It's the lactic acid, she reminded herself. When she got to Mr Chops she had no choice but to slacken her pace, but it wasn't her legs letting her down, it was her lungs. She started to feel the age-old tightness in her chest, the breaths that didn't fill her lungs and the increasing lack of oxygen. She fell into a walk and reached in her pocket. Wheezing now, she took the cap off and gave it a shake. Then suddenly, it was plucked out of her hands.

Lara's eyes widened with shock. Rosie had caught up with her and had snatched the inhaler out of her reach. Tilly was beside her, the two of them laughing gleefully.

'Give it back,' said Lara.

'You want some drugs?' Rosie said to Tilly, and they pretended to puff on the inhaler.

Lara felt her chest tighten further. 'I need it,' she said, trying to pull more air into her lungs. 'Give it back!'

'Give what back?' mocked Rosie. 'You mean this?'

To Lara's horror, Rosie had her finger on the inhaler's button and was pushing it over and over; clouds of the medicine were being dispersed into the air. More and more of it. Lara looked back at the school in desperation. Miss Young still wasn't there.

'Please don't,' she pleaded. She held out her hands, tried to get closer to Rosie to get the inhaler back but she was too fast for her, dodging away, and Lara couldn't breathe, couldn't catch her.

'Maybe we should give it back to her,' said Tilly dubiously.

'No,' said Rosie. 'She's faking it.'

Lara shook her head desperately and wondered about what to say to make Rosie give the inhaler back, but she couldn't speak, then the breaths became more panicked and more shallow and she couldn't get enough air, she bent her head, utterly terrified, gasping, her chest in pain, and then suddenly she didn't have any other thoughts in her head and she collapsed on the muddy grass.

FIFTY-NINE

Friday 8 January

Why did Charlie's parents always give him such crap food? Rebecca had thought as he'd retched up the putrid mess of his lunch: a crust-less white bread sandwich with a square of processed cheese, a packet of cheesy crackers, a packet of salt and vinegar crisps, a large blueberry muffin and a full-size Mars bar. She couldn't of course tell what he'd eaten by the foul-smelling mush at her feet. She had seen it when she'd gone into the hall at lunchtime and overheard him claiming his fruit allowance was in his muffin.

Well, it wasn't any more, it was fertilizing the school field. Revoltingly, some of it had splashed onto her trainers.

She'd radioed the office, needing someone to come out and collect him, but there was no answer. She'd tried again, frowning when no one picked up. Charlie had looked so out of it, his fat cheeks devoid of any colour at all, as if he was going to faint or chunder again, that she couldn't entrust him to another child. Rebecca had looked around the field at the other kids who were still running. She didn't like leaving them, even though she knew they'd be OK, but

Charlie needed help. And if he fainted alone on the playground on the way back . . . no, it wasn't worth it. She'd only be three minutes, four at most.

She'd taken him by the shoulder and marched him back to the school building, and deposited him, sick stains on his shirt, with the office staff, who had been on the phone earlier, hence not picking up her call out. She'd glanced ruefully at her trainers but there was no time.

She'd run back across the playground towards the field. At first glance, it looked exactly as she'd left it, the kids still running around, sporadic gaps between them all, but then she'd seen Mia put on such a sprint, she'd made a note to give her an extra star on the board for effort. This lasted for all of a second because then she saw where Mia was headed and – my God – was that a *child* on the ground?

Rebecca broke into a run herself, reaching the child, who turned out to be Lara. She was ghostly white and unmoving. *Jesus*, thought Rebecca, *what's happened?* She dropped to her knees and put a hand on Lara's cheek and it felt cold, but it didn't really tell her anything and she was aware of Mia bleating in her ear, asking if Lara was all right. Rebecca didn't know, *she didn't know* and, hardly believing what she was doing, she put two fingers on Lara's wrist and felt for a pulse.

It was there. Weak, almost fluttering, she thought, but maybe that was because her own heart was thumping so hard and fast, it made it difficult to focus on Lara.

'Go and get someone from the office,' Rebecca said to Mia, who was still hovering.

'Who?' asked Mia, frozen to the spot.

'Anyone!' barked Rebecca. She took a breath. *Must remain calm. Don't frighten her.* 'Just go and get help. They need to call an ambulance. Tell them to bring a blanket. Tell them it's urgent.'

Mia ran off and Rebecca took off her tracksuit jacket and laid it over Lara as she radioed the office again, to reaffirm Mia's message.

By now the rest of the kids had stopped running and some were watching, confused and scared. A couple had run up to her and were asking if Lara was all right; a couple more were crying. Rebecca ignored them all and leaned her ear down to Lara's mouth, listening for breath. It was irregular; a few short, desperate wheezes in and then a gap, then another inhale that didn't seem to bring enough oxygen. The edges of Lara's lips were blue. Rebecca took her hand. 'Come on,' she muttered, trying not to panic. Then she heard a shout and looked up and saw a couple of other staff running towards her. Oh thank God, she thought.

'Oh my God,' said Mr Chappell, the Year 5 teacher, 'is she breathing?'

Esther was on the phone and Rebecca could tell it was to the emergency services and they were asking the same question.

Lara's breaths seemed to get more laboured, more pained.

'Lara?' said Rebecca, leaning over her, desperately looking for signs that she was coming back round, but Lara's eyes remained closed and Rebecca wasn't even sure the girl could hear her as she continued to gasp for breath. She held her hand and was vaguely aware of Mr Chappell rounding up the rest of her distraught class and taking them inside. Esther waited beside her, still giving a running commentary to whoever was on the other end of the phone, and then Rebecca heard the thwack thwack of a helicopter in the distance, which seemed to be upon them in seconds. She shielded Lara's body as it landed, not wanting the down-draught from the blades to extinguish this child's barely-there breath. By now Mr Whitman was also on the field and the paramedics were running up to them and taking over, and Rebecca felt an overwhelming sense of relief that Lara was in safe hands.

She answered some brief questions: yes, Lara was asth-matic, no, she didn't know how long she'd been lying there before she found her but no more than two or three minutes, and then the paramedics had parcelled Lara onto a stretcher. Mr Whitman told the paramedics that Rebecca was the right person to go with Lara, and she followed the crew as they ran with Lara back over to the air ambulance. She was helped up on board and within seconds the door was closed. As they rose into the air, Rebecca thought she saw something small and blue lying on the ground a short distance from where Lara had been found: her inhaler. But the helicopter moved so fast she couldn't be sure and then the field was barely a speck below them.

SIXTY

Friday 8 January

Nancy ran through the doors of Royal Derby Hospital. The Accident and Emergency department was busy: medical staff, kids, parents, carers filled the area. Some of the parents were sitting on rows of blue plastic seats, small children on their laps. She looked for the main desk and rushed over.

'My daughter was brought in, Lara Miller,' she blurted out to the receptionist.

A nurse in scrubs was heading past the desk and overheard. 'She's through here,' he said. 'You're mum?'

Nancy nodded and followed the nurse down a busy corridor. She'd been cleaning the house when her phone had rung, putting away the Christmas decorations and storing them in the cupboard in one of the spare rooms. Then she'd got out the hoover and was getting rid of the pine needles. She hadn't heard the first ring, or the second or the third. She turned the hoover off to rescue a felt reindeer who'd fallen under the sofa and had gone to put him on the mantelpiece ready to take upstairs with the rest of the decorations and that was when she saw her phone screen.

Three missed calls from the school.

Nancy's heart had started to beat rapidly. She tried to unlock her screen so she could ring back but the stupid thing decided at that moment not to recognize her face and she jabbed in the code, once, twice, both times missing a digit in her haste and then – thank God – the phone rang again.

'Hello!' she'd cried out.

Esther had told her that there had been an accident on the school playing field; that Lara had collapsed and had been taken to Royal Derby Hospital in the air ambulance and that Rebecca Young had gone with her. Esther had asked if Nancy was able to get there herself and was she feeling OK to drive?

Each word was like a bomb detonating in her head until her mind was full of dust and noise and terror and she could hardly think straight.

Not again, she felt herself plead – or did she say it out loud?

Nancy raced to the hall, threw on some boots, grabbed her keys and bag and with a coat hanging off one arm, she'd got into her car and sped off.

The journey had been excruciating. Every crossroads, every light was conspiring to keep her from her child. She kept telling herself Lara was in the best possible hands: doctors, consultants with decades of training and experience between them would be monitoring every second of her daughter's short precious life and making sure she got through, that she was all right.

The nurse stopped at a curtained off bay, pulled the

curtains aside and there she was, her darling daughter, sitting up in bed, an oxygen mask on the sheets, machines by her side. Miss Young was on a chair next to her.

'She's doing well,' said the nurse. 'Had rather a nasty asthma attack so she's a bit tired, aren't you, poppet?'

Lara looked up and, on seeing Nancy, dissolved into tears and held her arms out.

Nancy dropped her bag and coat on the floor and ran over to hold her daughter. She kept her close, feeling her warmth, her small but strong arms clinging tightly as if she never wanted to let go.

'It's OK,' she said, stroking her back, her voice choking. She saw Miss Young get off her chair and move a little further away to give them some space.

Nancy prised Lara off and smiled at her, wiping the tears from her cheeks with her thumbs.

'What happened?'

'It was PE. We were running.'

Nancy was aware of Miss Young listening in. She was disturbed by her expression – was it guilt? Upset? It rang a distant alarm bell, but she couldn't think about that at the moment, she needed to focus on Lara.

'But you had your inhaler with you, didn't you?' Nancy glanced at Miss Young as she spoke – maybe that was why the teacher was looking a little discomfited – had Lara not had access to her medicine?

'Sort of . . .' said Lara.

Nancy turned sharply to Miss Young, but she was looking at Lara, surprised.

'What do you mean, sort of?' asked Nancy. She turned to Miss Young. 'She had it, didn't she?'

'Yes, yes, of course. She carried it with her during PE.'

Lara cast her eyes down at the bed and silent tears started to run down her face again.

'What is it?' insisted Nancy, gently tilting Lara's face up towards her. 'You have to tell me what happened.'

SIXTY-ONE

Friday 8 January

It was shortly after lunch when Rebecca got back to the school. A taxi dropped her in the staff car park and she headed to the office entrance.

Esther pounced on her almost immediately. 'How is she?'

Rebecca took a moment to answer. 'She had a severe asthma attack but the doctors say she's much better now.'

'Oh, thank God for that,' said Esther. 'First time I've ever had to call 999. Hopefully it'll be the last. Is she still in hospital?'

Rebecca nodded. 'They're keeping her in for a few days. How's Charlie?'

'Gone home. His mum picked him up a couple of hours ago.'

'Good. Right, better get in,' said Rebecca, walking towards the door that led into the school.

'I'll buzz you in. No doubt Jenny will be delighted to see you.'

No doubt she would, thought Rebecca. But she wasn't

going to relieve her TA just yet. She pointed back towards the car park. 'There's a taxi outside. Needs paying.'

Esther looked at her, befuddled, but Rebecca didn't wait to explain further. She headed towards Mr Whitman's office, knocked, then pushed the door open. He was alone.

'Rebecca! You're back!' He quickly got up. 'Why didn't you call? Is everything OK with Lara?'

'I didn't have my phone,' said Rebecca. 'No time to get it, the air ambulance didn't wait around.'

'No, of course not. I did call the hospital. They couldn't give out any information . . .'

'She's fine,' said Rebecca. 'Luckily.'

'It was extremely unfortunate that she had her attack at the point you were away from the field,' said James. 'I understand you had another medical emergency at the same time.'

'Yes. Charlie Green was vomiting.'

'You mustn't feel guilty about not being there at that exact—' continued James.

'It's not me who should be feeling guilty,' said Rebecca. 'Pardon?'

'I said, it's not me who should be feeling guilty. That privilege belongs to Rosie Wood.'

James frowned. 'I don't follow.'

So Rebecca filled him in. Told him what Lara had said: she had been running, had needed her inhaler, and would most likely have been fine if she'd been able to use it, but Rosie had withheld it and Lara's attack had magnified into a full-blown emergency. When she finished, she waited for James to speak.

'You believe this tale?'

'Yes.'

'That's quite a shocking version of events.'

'It is.'

'We will have to bring Rosie's mother in. Have a talk with both of them. See what Rosie has to say about it all.'

'I would like to be there.'

'That's not necessary. Claire can join the meet.'

No, not your deputy, thought Rebecca, *who effectively does whatever suits you to secure a promotion.*

'It should be me,' she said. 'I'm the class teacher of both girls. It's going to be me,' she reiterated and even though she was shaking inside, she held firm until he capitulated with a terse nod.

SIXTY-TWO

The barista was flicking buttons on the coffee machine and filling steaming cups. Now that Lara had been moved onto the children's ward, the nurses had insisted Nancy take a quick break. Away from the immediate task of caring for Lara, Nancy found her mind wandering to what had happened to her daughter that morning.

She pictured Rosie on the field. Saw them all running. In her mind, she witnessed Rosie snatch away Lara's inhaler. Only this time, Nancy placed herself on the running track, saw her holding Rosie by the arm, her fingers gripping tightly, oh so very, very tightly. She leaned right into Rosie's face and the kid backed away, her expression a mixture of fear, cockiness and affront. Nancy gripped her arm tighter still. Rosie squealed. Nancy felt a frisson of satisfaction.

'You think you're clever?' spat Nancy. 'Funny? You enjoy upsetting other kids? Making them terrified that they can't breathe? You're a vicious, nasty little brat.'

Stop.

Nancy snapped out of her daydream. Her heart was

racing. She took some deep breaths. Her mind kept wandering back to the torture of what Lara must have endured, the complete and utter terror at not being able to breathe, and she felt devastated. And consumed with an anger that was primal in its intensity. It threatened to take over everything: her mind, her rational thought, her sanity.

Don't keep playing it over and over in your mind, she told herself. *It will send you mad. Lara doesn't need you mad, she needs you to fight for her.* She took her freshly made coffee from the countertop and headed back up to the ward.

SIXTY-THREE

Friday 8 January

It was January, for God's sake, thought Lorna. Christmas was over and done with – forgotten pretty much and, as for the end of last term, well, that felt like light years away.

So why the hell were people messaging each other about the end-of-year gift for Miss Young?

It had started that morning. One of the mums – Stacey – had put a message in the group saying she'd bumped into Miss Young in John Lewis in Derby over the holidays where she was buying a new toaster and kettle with her voucher. On the WhatsApp group Stacey had congratulated all the other mums on their generosity: 'Thirty of the best mums in Derbyshire!' she'd typed, and loads of them had responded with hearts, smiley faces and kisses – except for Hannah.

It was always Hannah who had to rock the bloody boat. She either said the opposite to everyone else – just to wind them up, Lorna sometimes thought – or she had to point out what everyone was politely avoiding or she deliberately challenged someone's views, when it was so obviously a *joke*. Whatever it was, she always had to spoil the party.

So Hannah, bloody Hannah, had only gone and written: 'Pretty special toaster and kettle for £300!'

Then Sally had pointed out that no, the total had been £170 and copied and reposted Lorna's message that she'd sent to everyone at the end of term saying how she'd bought a multi-store voucher for £170 and taken a photo of it.

And then Hannah had said: 'Oh, I forgot about that message. But didn't we all put in a tenner?'

At that point, Lorna had started to sweat and she'd sworn out loud. The poor dog had looked up in alarm. Lorna had had to stop her ironing. She couldn't focus and she was very, very nervous about what was going to happen next.

The thread went quiet for a bit then a couple of them felt compelled to declare what they had donated.

5 January

RIPTON PRIMARY, YEAR 6

Erin Mackie, Tilly's mum

Yes, I put in ten quid. 11:27

Helen, Lottie's mum

I did too. 11:27

Nicole Wilson, Bella's mum

Me too. 11:27

Cheryl, Aisha's mum

And me. 11:27

Harriet, Milo's mum
👍 11:28

         Anna, Seb's mum
         Me too! 11:28

Darcie, Oscar's mum
Ten pounds. 11:28

Oh my God, thought Lorna, they were gathering strength. The more of them who declared their amount, the more would follow. Any concerns about what this actually meant for her – Lorna – would fly out the window as the herd stampeded. If anyone else put a message on, she'd have to start thinking of a response. This was definitely one of those situations where silence smacked very heavily of guilt.

Lorna held her breath as she watched her phone screen anxiously. *Please let this go away*, she thought.

The doorbell rang. Lorna's head jerked up. Who the hell was that? She wasn't expecting anyone. She didn't want to see anyone – not right now. She had to keep an eye on this group.

She thought about ignoring whoever was at the door, but the doorbell rang again. She opened it.

And instantly regretted it.

'Mum,' she said.

'Hi.' Carol hesitated, no doubt having picked up on her less than enthusiastic welcome. 'Can I come in?'

What circumstances warranted a 'no'? Lorna couldn't think of one off the top of her head. Someone in the house was ill? Dying? No, the most extreme of situations would only have made her mother more likely to step over the threshold and help. Lorna was aware she was waiting a little too long with her response.

'Course,' she said, irritated beyond words that her mother had picked now for an impromptu visit. As soon as Carol slipped off her coat and shoes, Lorna realized that she should have said she was going out. So simple. She kicked herself but it was too late now.

'Would you like a cup of tea?' she asked.

'That would be lovely,' said Carol, and Lorna noticed for the first time that her mother looked drawn, maybe even a little upset. As she put the kettle on she took the opportunity to surreptitiously check her phone.

Sarah Ramsay, Noah's mum
I always tend to split my donation between
the teacher and the church, so I only gave
a fiver. 11:30

Oh, thank you, thank you, thought Lorna. *I will forever love you.* That's all she needed, one or two to say they hadn't donated the suggested amount and then this would all die a natural death and everyone would forget about it.

Lorna made two teas and joined her mum at the kitchen table. She placed her phone carefully next to her mug.

'Sorry to arrive unannounced,' said Carol.

'Oh, no problem,' said Lorna, on cue.

'I just needed a bit of company, I suppose.'

Oh God, was Lorna's first thought. Did this mean Carol was going to be here for a while? Didn't she have other friends she could call on? Ordinarily, she would've been fine about it but . . . her eyes slid to her phone, vibrating on the table. She pressed the button on the side and the green WhatsApp symbol appeared in a white bar teasing her with its notification: 1 new message. *Open me*, it was saying. *Come and see what someone else has said about this Christmas gift impending disaster*.

'What do you see when you look at me?' asked Carol suddenly.

Lorna looked back at her mother. 'What?'

Carol was self-conscious, awkward. 'Do you see a dowdy, late-middle-aged woman, or someone with a bit of pizzazz still about them?'

Why was her mother asking this? Another vibrating sound came from the table. Lorna quickly looked back at her phone. Another bloody message. Buzz, another. Buzz, buzz.

'Only sometimes . . . recently . . . I'm having a conversation with James and I feel as if his mind is elsewhere.'

'Is it?' asked Lorna.

'It seems that way.' Carol shook herself and put on a smile. 'Oh, I don't know, maybe I'm just being silly. Do you need to check that?'

Lorna looked up, saw her mum was pointing at the phone. She blushed. 'Sorry, yes, do you mind?' She didn't wait for an answer and quickly read the messages.

Megan, Chester's mum
I put in £10. 11:33

> **Imogen Wood, Rosie's mum**
> Me too. 11:33

Heather, Cleo's mum
Same. 11:33

> **Lynette, Jack's mum**
> I did too. 11:33

Sally, Maya's mum
Yep. 11:33

> **Prabh, Safia's mum**
> I put in ten! 11:33

Tina, Molly's mum
Also ten. 11:33

> **Rowan, Ben's mum**
> Ten from me as well. 11:33

Oh Jesus. Lorna's heart was racing. What should she do? This was gathering momentum and had the power to get out of control. Maybe she should just say the total had been £270, not £170, something like: *Meant to be a '2'. Me and my fat thumbs!* That would make the numbers stack up more. She remembered that the gift card hadn't actually stated the amount on it, so she *could* take this route. But what if someone actually went up to Miss Young and asked her what she had received? Lorna felt quite faint. There would be nowhere to hide if that happened. She wouldn't put it past Hannah to do such a thing, Lorna thought darkly. She wiped a film of sweat from her upper lip.

'Is everything OK?'

Lorna looked distractedly up at her mum. 'Yes, fine.' It was anything but. She had to think of something and fast.

Actually . . . there was that insurance, that idea she'd already seeded. But how to go about it?

Her phone buzzed again. She sensed her mother flinch. Lorna opened up the message. It was from Erin.

Erin Mackie, Tilly's mum
Listen, I think we have to be careful here.
Lorna is a good friend of ours and I'm sure
she can easily explain this. 11:36

It was an open invitation to step up to the witness box. Lorna felt the spotlight well and truly blind her. She had to message something.

Lorna Fielding, Phoenix's mum
I'm sure I counted it right. 11:37

Oh God, what did that mean? She hadn't done anything to close this down, she thought in panic.

Erin Mackie, Tilly's mum
But eighteen of the thirty mothers in the
class have said here they put in ten pounds.

Which makes a minimum of £180. Didn't you
say the card had a value of £170? 11:37

Breathe, breathe, thought Lorna. Her hands were shaking.
She was aware her mother was watching her and she tried
to make everything seem normal.

Lorna Fielding, Phoenix's mum
I don't understand. I had full responsibility
of the envelope at all times. 😕 11:37

Should she mention the Christmas fair? No, that might
be a little too obvious. Better wait and see if someone took
the bait. She pressed 'Send'. It didn't once occur to her
about the repercussions on Nancy. She was aware that no
one really knew her that well – they were such a tight-knit
group and with it being the last year of primary school, it
was almost as if Nancy was just passing through. No one
had paid her that much attention. The appetite of the
established mums to make new friends had waned.

And anyway, Lorna needed to get out of a hole. A massive,
deep, dark one.

A message came through from Erin. Lorna read it with
bated breath.

Erin Mackie, Tilly's mum
That's not true. You gave the envelope to
Nancy. When you took Pepper to see
Father Christmas. 11:37

Lorna was awash with relief. Thank God Erin had remembered.

She quickly typed:

> **Lorna Fielding, Phoenix's mum**
> OMG I did! 11:37

Nicole Wilson, Bella's mum
So what, we think some of the money went
missing when Nancy had the envelope? You
do know what that insinuates? 11:38

Lorna made sure she was the one to make the next point.

> **Lorna Fielding, Phoenix's mum**
> Can't be her. She doesn't need it, she's
> loaded! 11:38

Imogen Wood, Rosie's mum
People steal for more reasons than just
getting something extra in their pocket,
you know. 11:38

> **Erin Mackie, Tilly's mum**
> Yes, it's not always about the money. It's
> about the kick. 11:39

Lorna was suddenly aware of Carol standing in front of her. She looked up; for a moment she'd forgotten her mum was there.

'I've obviously caught you at a bad time,' said Carol.

'No, it's OK, Mum.' And it was now, Lorna thought. Even if someone confronted Nancy – and they wouldn't, she was sure of it – then Nancy would deny it and the local mums would remain suspicious. They'd badmouth her for a bit then something else would happen in the busy whirlwind of the school calendar and it would become just some anecdotal: *Remember when . . . ?*

'I think I'd rather go,' said Carol and Lorna caught the sadness in her mother's voice and felt bad.

'Sure I can't tempt you to stay with an out-of-date cake? Probably got one here somewhere.'

'Not today,' said Carol. She gathered up her things and left.

She would make it up to her sometime, thought Lorna. She tried to remember what her mum had been talking about – something to do with being despondent about the way she looked? Lorna thought her mother was supremely elegant – she was actually envious of her – but she hadn't had the time to say it.

No, she'd been doing something really urgent. She felt giddy with relief. What a close shave that had been. But she had got out of it. No one suspected a thing.

SIXTY-FOUR

Friday 8 January

'And then Lara started wheezing and me and Tilly, we went up to her and we asked her if she was OK,' said Rosie.

'And what did she say?' asked Mr Whitman.

Rebecca watched as Rosie looked down at her lap, her hands placed carefully in front of her, her head hung meekly, a loose blonde strand dangling down. Her mother was next to her, sitting right back in the chair, her elegant legs crossed. She oozed confidence and something else – gracious tolerance, Rebecca thought. As if she had generously taken time out of her very busy day to attend this meeting. Rebecca was still staggered that, despite the fact Mr Whitman had explained at the start of the meeting that they were here to discuss the circumstances leading to Lara's hospital admission, not once had Mrs Wood asked if the child was all right.

Right now it was very clear that Mrs Wood didn't think her daughter had done anything wrong at all.

Mr Whitman was sitting on a chair opposite her: teachers on one side, pupil and parent on the other. 'Rosie?' he prompted. 'What did Lara say when you asked her if she was OK?'

'She said she was fine,' said Rosie.

What? thought Rebecca angrily. Did Rosie really think they were going to believe this total nonsense?

'And then what happened?' asked Mr Whitman.

'We saw her get her inhaler out of her pocket and she took some puffs, so we ran on.' Rosie shrugged. 'She said she was fine,' she repeated.

'Is there anything else you want to tell us?' asked Mr Whitman.

Rebecca saw a frown appear on Mrs Wood's smooth forehead. 'She's just told you what happened,' she said.

'If you could let me ask the questions,' said Mr Whitman and Rebecca noticed Mrs Wood's eyes harden. She did not like being put in her place.

'There's nothing,' said Rosie.

'Do you know how Lara's inhaler ended up on the ground?' Rebecca asked.

She saw a flash of alarm in Rosie's eyes. So she did dump it there, thought Rebecca, right after she'd taken it from Lara.

'No,' said Rosie. 'Maybe Lara dropped it or something.'

'Lara or you?' said Rebecca. She was getting thoroughly fed up with this charade, of letting this child spout all sorts of rubbish with no one challenging her. Rebecca thought she would remember the moment she'd first seen Lara, lying on the ground, for the rest of her life. She had looked so fragile, so small. So still.

Mrs Wood sat up, the relaxed, slightly bored stance finally broken.

'Rosie has told you what happened,' she repeated.

'Except Lara's version of events is very different,' said Rebecca. 'She said that Rosie took the inhaler out of her hands so she couldn't use it – during an *attack*,' she added for emphasis, 'and then Rosie wouldn't give it back, even though Lara pleaded for it.'

'That's not true,' said Mrs Wood.

'It's Rosie who should be responding, not you,' said Rebecca.

Mrs Wood looked shocked and Mr Whitman placed a warning hand on the table, an indication Rebecca should rein it in.

'Is it true?' he asked Rosie. 'Did you take the inhaler out of Lara's hands?'

Her bottom lip wobbled a little, and her eyes filled with fear and uncertainty.

Finally, thought Rebecca, we're getting somewhere.

'Should we ask Tilly?' said Rebecca. She made to get out of her chair. 'Maybe I should go and get her from class right now . . .'

'This is outrageous,' said Mrs Wood.

Rosie glanced at her mother and kept quiet, much to Rebecca's irritation.

'Or we could look at the CCTV that's directed towards the field,' added Rebecca. 'That would save us all a lot of time and then we would know for sure which one of you is telling the truth.'

Rosie looked terrified then and before Mrs Wood could say any more, she burst into tears. 'It was only meant to be a joke,' she wailed. 'I didn't know she would go to hospital.'

Rebecca folded her arms. She considered Rosie with a mix of pity and anger.

'Right,' said Mr Whitman quietly. 'Rosie, you do know that what you did is very serious indeed.'

Rosie continued to cry.

'We're going to have to ask you to leave the school for the rest of the day.'

'You're *suspending* her?' said Mrs Wood. She quickly gathered herself, smiled. 'Oh, come on, James, I realize we need Rosie to understand what she did is completely wrong, but that's a little over the top, isn't it?'

Rebecca watched as Mr Whitman wrestled uncomfortably with the familiarity of her using his first name. 'I think, under the circumstances, it's the very least Rosie should expect.'

Mrs Wood didn't like that, not one bit. Rebecca got the sense she expected Mr Whitman to take some token action to let it be known it wasn't OK to take another child's vital medicine, then brush it all under the carpet and move on as if nothing had happened.

'Rosie, we will talk about this more on Monday. Over the next few days you need to think of a suitable apology for Lara,' continued Mr Whitman.

Mrs Wood stood. 'Was Lara suspended when she tried to drown Rosie?' she asked.

'Imogen, that wasn't—'

Mrs Wood put up a hand to silence him and walked towards the door. 'This questioning' – she waved a hand at Rebecca – 'is completely unethical. The way you've handled my daughter, it's bullying,' she spat, helping Rosie out of her chair, and they left the room.

All of a sudden it was silent. It was a moment before Mr Whitman spoke.

'It's lucky Imogen doesn't know there is no CCTV directed at the field,' he said.

Rebecca shrugged. 'No one ever knows where the CCTV is. And it got the confession, didn't it?'

SIXTY-FIVE

Friday 8 January

Nancy received a telephone call from Mr Whitman. He informed her that Rosie and her mother had attended a meeting with himself and Miss Young, and that Rosie had been suspended until Monday. She'd owned up, he'd said. When Nancy had asked: 'Willingly?' he hesitated long enough for Nancy to understand it was a 'no'. She briefly wondered how they'd prised it out of her, but that brought forth various imagined scenarios: Rosie denying it at first, squirming, showing absolutely zero regard for her daughter, and it angered her so much she had to stop thinking about it. Mr Whitman had gone on to say that Rosie would be apologizing to Lara once both girls were back at school. 'We will also be putting her on supervised play for a week. In case you're not aware of what this means, she will be staying inside the classroom for all breaks, accompanied by a teaching assistant.'

'And then what?' Nancy asked.

'I don't understand,' he said, sounding genuinely surprised at her question.

'What happens when she decides to bully Lara again?'

'Well, we don't know she will,' he stated firmly. 'Hopefully she will have understood that it's not something we tolerate here at Ripton Primary. Not under any circumstances.'

Except it had been going on for months, Nancy thought. Months of torment before any real attention had been paid to it, and that was only because Lara had ended up in hospital. And now Rosie had a mere week of sitting colouring in a classroom during breaks before she was let loose in the playground again to do whatever the hell she liked.

Nancy didn't believe for a minute Rosie understood they didn't tolerate bullying at Ripton Primary, because they turned a blind eye, or they followed some feeble process that was always weighted in favour of the bully. Rosie had proved to herself again and again that she could get away with it. She might have been caught this time but that was only going to make her a whole lot more sneaky in the future.

Nancy knew the school couldn't ignore it if it happened right in front of their noses but actually relying on them to stop it, to suitably punish the perpetrator, to put Lara first and be angry on her behalf – as angry as she felt now – well, that was never going to happen.

Which was why she was going to take matters into her own hands.

SIXTY-SIX

Friday 8 January

Nancy walked steadily down the high street, her breath blowing clouds in the cold air. Lara was still in hospital and Beth was visiting her, so Nancy had taken the opportunity to come home briefly and pack an overnight bag before she went back to stay in the put-up bed next to her daughter.

It was almost six and the street lights picked out the frost on the pavements. The shops were all closed and the only buildings that were lit were the pubs and eateries.

Even though it was early January, The Wood Oven still had quite a number of people sitting inside. Nancy opened the door and strode right in.

'A table for one?' asked a smiling waiter, stepping forward to meet her.

He was young, early twenties at most, and dressed in black trousers and a brand-new white shirt that still had the crease marks from the packet. His name badge read: Toby.

'No thanks,' said Nancy. 'I need to see Imogen Wood.'

This threw Toby. 'Oh, right. Is she expecting you?'

'She is not.'

'Oh . . . OK. Could I take a name?'

'Nancy Miller.'

He nodded and headed to the back of the restaurant and the door through to the kitchen. Nancy looked up, could see through the hatch to where the large stone pizza oven was glowing with red hot embers. She saw Imogen pull two pizzas out on a paddle and put them on plates. Then as she loaded up two more to go in, Nancy saw Toby come over to speak to her. He gestured towards the restaurant, said a few words.

Imogen stopped. Glanced up through the hatch. Then Nancy saw her shake her head and say something to Toby.

Toby came back. 'I'm very sorry but Imogen is busy at the moment,' he said as charmingly as he could.

'You can tell Imogen that I don't care if she is busy. I need to see her now.'

Toby paused. Thought of saying something but then changed his mind and headed back to the kitchen. Nancy watched: there was a more taut exchange between the two of them.

Then Toby reappeared, alone, more awkward now. 'I'm sorry, but Imogen really is very busy.' He took a small notepad from his pocket. 'Perhaps if I could take a number—'

'It's OK,' said Nancy. 'I'll just go and talk to her.' She marched off towards the kitchen, Toby frantically following, asking her to wait. A few of the customers had noticed now and were raising curious heads.

Nancy saw Imogen look through the hatch and all of a sudden she abandoned her post at the pizza oven and headed towards the kitchen door. She intercepted Nancy just as she made it to the back of the restaurant.

'You have no right to—' started Imogen.

'I have one thing to say to you,' said Nancy, all her pent-up fury rising to the surface. 'If Rosie touches Lara one more time, I swear to God, I will inflict the exact same injuries on you.'

The entire restaurant fell silent. Nancy turned on her heel and with everyone watching open-mouthed, she walked out.

8 January
RIPTON PRIMARY, YEAR 6

Erin Mackie, Tilly's mum
OMG, you guys, you have to be aware of the dreadful situation that happened at the restaurant tonight. Nancy Miller only went and stormed in, dealing out threats to Imogen. 21:01

> **Nicole Wilson, Bella's mum**
> OMG, WHAT? 21:01

Erin Mackie, Tilly's mum
Yeah, said she was going to inflict injuries on poor Imogen. 21:01

> **Hannah Chapman, Jakob's mum**
> No she didn't. 21:02

Erin Mackie, Tilly's mum
Yep, actually she did. There were several
witnesses too. Customers AND staff. I'd
write about it in the paper in the spirit of
public interest but Imogen doesn't want
any negative press. She's worked so hard
to get the restaurant up and running. 21:03

> **Nicole Wilson, Bella's mum**
> Poor you, Imogen. Are you OK? 😩 21:04

Imogen Wood, Rosie's mum
Thanks Nicole. 😩 Yes, it was a bit of a
shock but I'm fine. 21:05

> **Lorna Fielding, Phoenix's mum**
> Hold on, isn't that sort of thing ABH or
> something? And there's that missing money
> too . . . 21:05

Nicole Wilson, Bella's mum
OMG, yes. What is it with this woman?
Stealing from us, threatening us . . . 21:06

> **Hannah Chapman, Jakob's mum**
> Has this got anything to do with what
> happened in school earlier? Jakob said Lara
> had fallen ill and been airlifted to hospital
> and that Rosie had been sent to the head
> then suspended. 21:07

Erin Mackie, Tilly's mum
It doesn't matter what, if anything happened
at school. You can't go around threatening
innocent people. It's not right. 21:07

> **Lorna Fielding, Phoenix's mum**
> It is a bit crazy. Not the sort of thing we
> usually see in the village. 21:08

Nicole Wilson, Bella's mum
Imogen, gutted you ever had to sell your
house. Can't you buy it back? LOL 21:09

> **Sarah Ramsay, Noah's mum**
> What exactly did she say? 21:10

Imogen Wood, Rosie's mum
She said if anything bad happens to Lara
she would inflict the same injuries on me.
21:10

> **Stacey, Fred's mum**
> Wow. I mean, whatever else is going on,
> you don't say stuff like that. 21:11

Lorna Fielding, Phoenix's mum
Do you think she'd actually follow through
with it? 21:12

> **Erin Mackie, Tilly's mum**
> She probably would. Maybe she already
> has. Maybe she's a total psycho. 21:12

Lorna Fielding, Phoenix's mum
What do you mean? 21:12

> **Erin Mackie, Tilly's mum**
> Maybe she's the Canine Killer. Probably did
> her husband in as well. That's what they
> say, psychos progress from one to the
> other. 21:13

Hannah Chapman, Jakob's mum
FFS, her husband died in a car accident.
And anyway, it's not progression from
humans to animals, it's the other way
around. 21:14

> **Erin Mackie, Tilly's mum**
> Takes all sorts. 21:15

Hannah Chapman, Jakob's mum
This is bullshit. 21:15

Hannah Chapman, Jakob's mum left.

SIXTY-SEVEN

Saturday 9 January

If there was ever a morning Imogen needed to run, it was today. She was still fuming about the public dressing-down she'd received from Nancy the night before. In her restaurant! How dare Nancy waltz in like that, throw her weight around. Embarrass her like that. Imogen had had to smile and act as if it was no big deal. Had to apologize for the interruption to her diners' evening. It had been utterly humiliating.

And not once had Nancy ever acknowledged her own daughter's part in any of it. The whole thing was a joke and Imogen was not going to let it go.

The sex was more urgent today. Imogen pulled James upstairs and he was pleasantly surprised by her enthusiasm. Afterwards they lay spent on the bed.

'I'm still upset that you suspended Rosie,' said Imogen.

'What was I supposed to do?' said James. 'You need to let her know that what she did can never happen again.'

'She didn't mean it. You make it sound as if she's evil. She's not just stepped out of *The Omen*, you know. Kids can be kids and sometimes it goes wrong.'

'Imogen—'

'I've spoken to her, OK? She knows she made a mistake.'

Imogen rolled onto her side, caressed James's chest. 'I also wanted to speak to you about Miss Young.'

'What about her?'

'It's clear she dislikes Rosie intensely. It's highly unprofessional. And the way she questioned her. It was out of order.'

James grunted in a non-committal way.

'You know I'm right. I'm not sure she's the best teacher for your school.'

James lifted his head. Frowned. 'What are you saying?'

'Nothing. Just voicing an opinion.'

When she got home, Dylan and Rosie were tidying away the breakfast things.

'Good run?' asked Dylan.

Imogen went to get a glass of water. 'Great.'

'Rosie and I have been talking about her apology to Lara.'

She tensed. 'Oh yeah?'

'She's going to put it in a letter. I think it would mean more,' said Dylan, looking at Rosie, who was subdued.

'Fine,' said Imogen.

'You want to go and write it now?' Dylan prompted, and Rosie left the room. Dylan moved over to his wife, exhaled deeply. 'I've had to have a long talk with her. She seems to think it was all a joke gone wrong.'

'It was,' said Imogen.

'Jesus, Imogen, that girl could've died.'

Imogen pulled a face.

'Don't try playing this down. Making out it's no big deal,' said Dylan sharply.

Imogen took a calming breath. 'I'm not, Dylan. It *is* a big deal. And I, too, have spoken to Rosie, explained how she must never, ever withhold anyone's medicine. But what happened, none of that was part of Rosie's plan. She didn't *want* to harm Lara. She's mortified about it.'

'Is she?'

'Yes!' said Imogen, dismayed. 'You don't honestly think our daughter set out to . . . God, I don't even want to say it.'

Dylan was looking at her, somewhat mollified. He didn't believe it either, not deep down, she could see. Rosie wasn't capable of that sort of dark malevolence. No, never.

'She needs to know how serious it was,' he said quietly.

'She does,' said Imogen. 'As is Nancy's threat to me yesterday. Erin thinks she's the Canine Killer.'

Dylan scoffed. 'The Canine Killer is something dreamed up by Erin's paper. A load of sensationalist crap.'

Imogen didn't answer. On her run home, she'd thought long and hard about what to do about Nancy. She finished her water and left the room. She had a phone call to make.

SIXTY-EIGHT

Monday 18 January

'Everyone will find a ballot paper on their table,' said Miss Young. 'There are three candidates on there: Aisha, Rosie and Lara. You will secretly mark which candidate you want to be Spring Queen with an "X" in the box next to their name and then come and post your paper in here.' She indicated a large box with a slot cut out of the centre at the front of the classroom.

There was much rustling and arms wrapped around ballot papers so no one could see. Rebecca watched her class carefully. It was Lara's first day back after her spell in hospital and she was more subdued than usual. Rebecca had taken Lara and Rosie to Mr Whitman's office first thing, and Rosie had conjured up a contrite face and soberly delivered her apology. She read from a letter saying she was sorry for 'taking the asthma pump' and it was a 'very stupid thing to do' and she 'regretted it and the harm it had caused Lara'.

Rebecca thought it sounded like something a parent had scripted – Mrs Wood, most likely – and that Rosie had rehearsed, although she couldn't prove any of that, of course. Lara had listened, stiff with tension and her eyes downcast, then Rebecca had escorted them both back to class.

She got the kids to come up in small groups to post their vote even as she already knew what the result would be. She'd seen Rosie and Tilly canvassing in the playground that morning, knew without a doubt that they would have been persuading the kids to put an 'X' next to Rosie's name. It would work too, of that Rebecca was certain. The other two girls didn't stand a chance. Aisha was a nice kid but didn't have the dazzle that Rosie possessed. And Lara . . . well, it had been sweet of Mia to put her friend forward, but she wasn't going to get the votes. Not with Rosie's campaigning. The whole thing was a stitch-up.

It was funny, thought Rebecca, as she tipped the box of votes onto her desk, you weren't supposed to have favourites among the children in your class but every teacher knew that was a crock of shit. It was impossible not to, especially when some could be so vile. And Rebecca always thought it was grossly unfair how so many of the vile ones landed on their feet. It was kids like Lara who deserved a chance at being the Spring Queen. She consoled herself with the notion that, really, the whole Spring Queen thing was massively outdated and it offended her feminist sensibilities.

She told the children to read their English books then started to put the ballot papers into three piles. The first vote was for Rosie – of course it was – as was the next. Then, to Rebecca's surprise, there were a couple for Lara. One for Aisha. One ballot spoiled, the owner having scribbled on it, declaring it should be a Spring King. Then another three each for Lara and Rosie.

Once she'd counted them all up, she called the class to attention.

'We have the result,' she announced, pausing for dramatic tension. 'In third place is Aisha with five votes.' There was a smattering of applause and Aisha tried not to look downcast. 'In second place . . .' Miss Young looked around the class. The children were all holding their breath. '. . . with eleven votes . . . is Rosie.'

Gasps from the kids. Miss Young glanced at Rosie, but her expression was surprisingly calm resignation at her position.

'Which means in first place, and this year's Spring Queen with thirteen votes is Lara. Well done, Lara!'

More clapping. Lara's face was a picture of shock. For a moment it looked as if she didn't fully understand what her teacher had said, then as it dawned, she took the tiniest little intake of excited breath before closing down again, obviously fearing retaliation from Rosie. 'No,' she said, 'I don't want to be queen.'

But then, amazingly, Rosie turned to look at Lara. She shrugged. 'It's OK. It's only fair that it's you after what I did.'

Rebecca, stunned by this admission, watched carefully but Rosie appeared to be utterly genuine.

'Right,' she said, putting a sheet up on the overhead projector. 'We're going to do some comprehension questions on the text you've just been reading.' Rebecca scrutinized Rosie's face again but it was completely devoid of guile.

Rebecca had been right about Rosie canvassing in the playground that morning but what she hadn't realized was who Rosie was telling the kids to vote for.

'We're changing,' Rosie said to Tilly. 'Tell everyone to vote for Lara.'

'What?' said Tilly, astonished. 'Why would you do that? It's your *pony*!'

Rosie shrugged. 'I'm kind of bored with the whole Spring Queen thing. So Lara can do it.'

Tilly was still looking at her, gobsmacked, but Rosie walked away and, approaching the next child, began her campaign.

SIXTY-NINE

Monday 18 January

Nancy threw a slab of clay onto her pottery wheel and it landed with a satisfying thud. She dipped her hands in the water and started throwing her bowl. Carefully, gently, she pulled up the sides as she'd seen the guy do on the YouTube tutorial she'd watched. It was relaxing, soothing. She felt in control, a sensation that had been lacking in her life recently. Until she'd taken on Imogen in the restaurant. It had felt good to tell her exactly what she thought, to stand her ground for once instead of helplessly watching events unfold.

Not her finest moment perhaps, but necessary.

The bowl was almost at full height. A few more minutes and it would be finished. She focused carefully, making sure the sides didn't collapse, but then the doorbell rang.

Nancy frowned, her concentration interrupted. She couldn't go to the door right now, she'd lose everything she'd done. She decided to ignore it.

It rang again.

Ignore it.

Two more long rings followed, a finger left on the button for some time. Nancy flinched and the top of her bowl flopped over. Ruined. She sighed, looking at her clay disaster and then, wiping her hands on her apron, went to open the door.

Two police officers stood there.

Her heart lurched with fear.

'It's OK . . . Mrs Miller?' said the first officer quickly, on seeing her face. 'There's nothing to worry about. It is Mrs Miller, isn't it?'

Nancy nodded.

'May we please come in?'

She stepped to one side. 'Of course.'

The two officers followed her through to the kitchen, where she washed the clay off her hands and offered them a cup of tea. She pulled out some chocolate biscuits. One of the officers, a world-weary man in his late forties, took one with relish and Nancy got the feeling his day had just improved. The other officer, a younger man, politely declined. Once they were all sitting down at the kitchen table, he was the one who led the conversation, while the other proved himself a noisy tea drinker.

'I'm Police Constable Dawes,' said the younger officer, 'and this,' he said, indicating, 'is my colleague, Police Constable Hollie. We've had a complaint about an account of threatening behaviour. Ten days ago, at The Wood Oven in Ripton.'

Nancy placed her mug down on the table, confused. 'What?'

'From a Mrs Wood. She says that you went to her restaurant shortly after six p.m. on the eighth of January and threatened her. Do you know what I'm referring to?'

'This . . . this is ludicrous,' said Nancy. 'Imogen went to the *police*?'

'So you did threaten her?'

'I . . .' Nancy was at a loss as to what to say. 'You don't understand. My daughter has been bullied by hers for *months* and nothing is ever done about it. My God, my daughter even ended up in hospital, airlifted off the school field because of something her daughter did!'

'I'm sorry to hear that,' said PC Dawes. 'Is your daughter OK?'

'Yes. She is now.'

'Have you spoken to the school?' asked PC Dawes.

'Of course I have!'

'So they're handling it.'

'Yes . . . No! Not properly. Not in my opinion.'

'Mrs Miller, these things really are best resolved in school. I would suggest you go back and talk to the head. Is it still going on?'

'Well, yes, no, I mean Lara's only just gone back.'

'I understand these situations are hard, and it's a very emotional time, but you need to know that Section 4A makes it an offence to use threatening, abusive or insulting language with the intention of causing someone else harassment, alarm or distress.'

'Oh my God, are you *serious*?'

'It can lead to a fine of up to five thousand pounds, a

community service order, or potentially a prison sentence.'

'This is a joke, right? What about the bloody threatening and insulting language Rosie has been using on Lara, who has been *harassed*, *alarmed* and *extremely distressed*?'

'Mrs Miller—'

'No. You listen to me. What I don't understand is that if an adult hits you, calls you names, threatens you, then you guys, the cops, are called. When it happens to children, it's downgraded to "bullying", when actually there's your harassment right there, officer.'

PC Dawes waited for her to calm down, and in the silence, PC Hollie slurped his tea. PC Dawes then gave a small, sympathetic smile. 'Look, I've had this with my kid. Got it in the neck at school from another boy. I just told him to walk away. It's a good tactic.'

Nancy opened her mouth to explain how completely and utterly inadequate this suggestion was, but suddenly all her energy left her.

'I'll bear that in mind,' she said quietly.

'Stay away from that child and her parents,' said PC Dawes kindly. 'It won't do you any good to get involved.'

I am involved, thought Nancy. *How can I not be? I'm her mother*.

He got up. 'Thank you for your time. And the tea,' he added, as PC Hollie placed his empty mug on the table.

As Nancy closed the door behind them, she rested her forehead on the wood in despair.

SEVENTY

Monday 18 January

Lorna had half thought about going to a bank out of the village to do her business, but it was impossible as Simon used the car for work and the village bus only left every hour to the town and every hour back and she just didn't have that sort of time to spare.

She slowed as she neared the branch of HSBC then, checking no one she knew was around, she quickly tied up Cooper outside and slipped into the warmth of the building. A quick look around told her there was no one inside she knew and she also didn't recognize the two cashiers. There was only one other person in front of her in the queue and then it was her turn. She'd already made an appointment online and as soon as she gave her name, she was escorted into one of the tiny customer rooms by Ross; his name badge informing her he was an account manager.

'So you're here to open a new savings account with us today?' asked Ross once they were both sitting down.

'That's right,' said Laura. 'Easy access.' She held her bag close to her side.

'And you have all the relevant ID? We need two types: one photo, one with an address.'

'I have my passport and the council tax bill,' she said, taking them out of her bag and placing them on the desk Ross was sitting behind.

'Fantastic. And what sort of deposit would you like to make?'

Laura thought of the notes held carefully in an envelope in her bag. Not too many, not enough to make people think Christmas fair takings were lower than usual. In fact, she'd worked extra hard to make sure the fair had raised more than in previous years, so no one would notice if not all of it ended up in the school safe. So you could argue the extra cash was all down to her anyway.

Ross was still waiting for an answer. She reached into her bag, pulled out the envelope and placed it on the table next to the identification documents.

'Eight hundred and ninety-two pounds,' she said. She held her breath, waiting for some sort of response – she wasn't sure what. A raised eyebrow? A suspicious frown? But Ross didn't even bat an eyelid.

'Let's get started,' he said, and began to type into the pad on the desk, inserting her personal details.

Ten minutes later and it was all done. Ross reassured her that her bank card and PIN would arrive in the post in the next few days. Her stomach lurched as he said this until she reminded herself that Simon had a few days lined up in the office and so she could easily intercept the post before he ever had an inkling of what had gone on.

She said goodbye to Ross and left the bank. It was all done. She felt light and free, uplifted that it had all gone so smoothly.

Outside, Hazel was digging into her pocket, about to feed Cooper one of the treats from her tin.

'Oh no,' said Lorna. 'Much as he'd love it, he can't. He's putting on too much weight. The vet has told us to restrict treats.'

'Well, boo to the vet,' said Hazel. 'Ruining everyone's fun. But he's like me. On a health kick! You know, I've lost a stone and a half since the doctor told me to get out and walk more. And I miss Sukey still, of course I do, but I've met so many other dogs! And they've always got a waggy tail for me.'

Cooper obliged with an enthusiastic wag. Hazel laughed. 'And I know your wag especially well. It's one of my favourites; extra friendly.'

'That's because you're his second-favourite person in the whole wide world,' said Lorna, buoyed with goodwill after her fortuitous meeting.

'Oh no,' said Hazel, 'not before the family. Maybe fifth favourite person. You know, you shouldn't leave him tied up outside – someone could steal him.'

Hazel was right, thought Lorna. But he'd been fine. She'd been fine. The money had been fine and been deposited in a very fine manner. Everything was fine! Lorna felt as if she had just set up something very clever. Accomplished. She would keep adding to it and who knew how much she could accumulate. As long as she was careful (not like the Christmas gift – Lorna had since put this down to a 'run-through', she would not be making any mistakes like *that* again), she was onto a nice little income generator. Payment really, as she kept reminding herself, for all her efforts. And being Chair of the PTA did take a huge amount of effort.

'You're right, Hazel, but they won't let our furry friends into the bank, you know.'

'Pah,' said Hazel. 'Dogs should be allowed everywhere.'

'Couldn't agree more. Anyway, it's not theft we should be worried about around here, it's the Canine Killer.'

'I've read about him in the paper,' said Hazel, shuddering.

'Might not be a him.'

'Oh?'

'Some say it's happening because of the water quality down at Heron Water. One part in particular.'

'What part?'

Lorna lowered her voice. 'You know the woman who bought Imogen's place? Well, she's gone and dug beneath the water table or something. Upset the equilibrium.'

'How does that work?' asked Hazel, puzzled.

'I don't know. I'm not a scientist. It's calmed down a bit recently – but the algae always lessens in winter.'

'Yes, it does, thank goodness.' Hazel wagged a finger at Cooper. 'But still, don't go drinking from the reservoir if there's something up with the water there! Or at least keep away from that dangerous part!'

'He will, won't you, Cooper,' said Lorna. She said goodbye and went on her way, a new spring in her step.

SEVENTY-ONE

Monday 18 January

If she was honest, Imogen was a little tired of pizza. She placed the topping on the dough of a recipe she was creating for Valentine's Day. Red pepper, ham and strawberry. The saltiness of the ham should contrast well with the sweetness of the fruit. It was something a bit different, but every day was pizza. She got a wistful longing for the rarity of the dishes she used to invent when Luna's was a Michelin-starred restaurant. Also, she couldn't deny she'd loved the prestige Luna's had given her. It wasn't as if Nigel had been on the phone asking to come to The Wood Oven. But then she would remember that this was a means to an end. She was making so much money it didn't really matter whether she liked making pizza or not. It sold. And that was what counted.

Imogen glanced at the clock. Almost two. She wondered if the police had been to see Nancy yet. No one spoke to her the way that woman had. Once Nancy had had a warning from the cops, maybe she would think twice about ever approaching her again.

She quickly put the pizza into the oven. Imogen had an hour before she had to pick up Rosie. She wondered how the Spring Queen vote had gone. She hoped Rosie had won but suspected that Miss Young might do something to sway the kids in another direction. It was all so *unfair*.

Before Imogen had dropped Rosie at school that morning, she'd prepped her. Explained that if Lara won the vote and ended up as Spring Queen and riding Lupin, then Rosie shouldn't get too upset. Life had a way of rebalancing and there were other ways of getting back at someone. She didn't want to go into the full details of how she'd had a nasty visit from Nancy and so had called the police, but she'd tried her best to get her message across: Lara would get her comeuppance. Maybe not now, but at some point in the future.

Imogen thought she might have even got through to Rosie as her sadness had subsided and she'd gone very quiet in the way she always did when she was thinking things through. Pleased, Imogen had congratulated herself on some excellent parenting.

SEVENTY-TWO

Monday 18 January

After the police had left, Nancy returned to her wheel. She tried to put the police visit out of her mind. It was only Imogen throwing her weight around as usual. Wanted to remind everyone she was Queen Bee. She'd probably been spooked by the visit Nancy herself had made to the restaurant, was just flexing her muscles.

But the *police?* Warnings of prison sentences? Nancy knew it was very unlikely to come to that but what unsettled her, she realized, was the lengths Imogen was prepared to go to in order to make her point. Phoning the *goddamn police*!

She remoulded her slab of clay and threw it back on the wheel. Gently started shaping it back into the bowl she'd been making before she'd been interrupted.

Jesus, the audacity of that woman! She absolutely refused to acknowledge that her child had done anything wrong at all. Even though Rosie had put Lara in hospital!

Nancy tried her best to relax, to work the clay, to feel how it moved under her fingers.

But she was too tense, too stiff. Too angry, too upset.

Imogen had sent the police round to warn her off, when she was just trying to stop her child from being bullied.

So she wasn't even allowed to stick up for Lara, to protect her?

Nancy put a fist through the side of her bowl. She pummelled the clay again and again with her knuckles. Globules of clay splattered everywhere – all over the floor, her apron, wet droplets splattered across her face.

'Hi, Mum,' called a voice from the hallway as the wheel slowed to a stop.

Nancy jerked her head up, her furious trance broken. She looked at the mess of clay and was about to clear it up when Lara bundled into the room, closely followed by Beth.

'Wow, Mum, you've made a mess!' said Lara, both surprised and delighted. 'It's all over your face!'

'Is it?' said Nancy, trying to wipe it off.

'Guess who has some pretty special news?' said Beth.

Lara's face lit up. 'Oh yeah. Mum, I'm going to be the Spring Queen at the festival.'

'What?' Nancy was deeply confused.

'We had the vote. I won!'

'Wow. That's great.' Nancy paused. 'How does Rosie feel about all this?'

'This is the extraordinary part,' said Beth.

'She said it was cool,' said Lara.

'She did?' asked Nancy, astounded.

'Yes, even gave me a jelly bean at afternoon break to prove there were no hard feelings. Can I get a snack?'

Nancy was so dumbfounded she mumbled a 'yes' and Lara scooped up Pebbles, who was weaving his way around her ankles, then scarpered to the kitchen and no doubt the biscuit tin before Nancy could even process what she'd been told.

She looked up at Beth. 'Can you believe this?'

Beth shrugged. 'Maybe something's finally got through to her. Maybe Lara's near-miss actually frightened Rosie so now she's woken up to how seriously shitty her behaviour has been.'

Nancy wasn't sure. 'Maybe.'

Beth stared at Nancy's face. 'Do you always get this messy when you're doing your pottery? You look like you've been in a slasher movie – but with a zombie's grey blood.'

'I thought zombies had red blood like us.'

'Whatever. You're a mess.'

Nancy glanced ruefully down at her wheel. 'Had a bit of a fight with my bowl.' She took a breath. 'Police came round to see me today.'

'*What?*'

'Yeah . . . Turns out telling Imogen I'm personally going to make sure she gets whatever her daughter dishes out to Lara isn't such a good idea.'

Beth's mouth dropped. 'You said that?'

Nancy nodded.

'It's a *great* idea. Though maybe not a legal one.' Beth sighed. 'Maybe that family has switched target.'

'What, to me?'

'I don't know. Maybe.'

The notion settled on Nancy like a cold chill.

SEVENTY-THREE

Monday 1 February

It had been over three weeks since Lorna had seen or heard from Carol. She'd been upset, Lorna remembered, something about James not being around much although whether that was in body or spirit, she couldn't quite recall. Lorna sighed; Carol wasn't usually one to sulk, so perhaps she had genuinely hurt her mother's feelings.

She had to make amends. She still had to keep her on side.

By the time Lorna reached the house Carol shared with James, she was pretty fed up with the cold rain that had come at her sideways and soaked her right through, so when Carol answered the door and offered less than her usual generous welcome, Lorna was a bit put out.

She held her tongue though and remained polite as she hung up her coat and accepted the offer of tea.

As she came into the kitchen, she saw the partially constructed costumes for the Straw Bear Festival in the corner of the room. Carol had offered to make them for the last few years. The straw was sitting in bundles on the floor; a small amount was woven onto a metal frame that

still had a skeletal look to it. Lorna sat down at the breakfast bar and heard the sound of a female voice coming from
an iPad on the worktop.

'My daughter is here,' said Carol to whoever was on the
other end of the video call. 'I'm so sorry, Marian, we'll have
to continue this another time.'

Lorna noticed she was apologetic and warm to Marian,
whoever she was – a lot warmer than she'd been to *her*
when she'd knocked on the door.

'I'll bear in mind what you said, I promise,' continued
Carol. 'Give me one more peek at your view, won't you?'

'I'll just turn the camera around,' said Marian.

Carol gazed at the screen rapturously. 'That sea! The
sunshine! We'll catch up later.'

Amidst a flurry of goodbyes, they hung up.

It half crossed Lorna's mind she'd interrupted the call
and perhaps she'd come at a bad time but she was hardly
to know, was she? And she'd walked a mile through freezing
weather to get here, whereas Marian appeared to be somewhere quite warm and sunny without shifting a muscle on
the other end of a screen.

As soon as Marian had gone, Carol lost some of her zest
again. She put the kettle on, got out some mugs. 'To what
do I owe the pleasure?' she asked.

Lorna smiled winsomely. 'I haven't seen you in a while,
Mum, so I thought I'd drop by.'

Carol cut her a glance, as if waiting for more.

'And . . . I owe you an apology. For the last time we
met. I was distracted. I'm sorry.'

Lorna thought she saw a flicker of tenderness from her mother. She was relieved. She needed this relationship back on an even keel. Her new funds were going to help with her project, but it wouldn't be enough.

'Apology accepted,' said Carol, and Lorna received her first genuine smile.

Carol put two mugs of tea on the worktop.

'So how have you been?' asked Lorna. 'How's James?'

Carol hesitated. 'Fine.'

They weren't, Lorna could tell. 'Has something happened?'

Carol appraised her. 'You're not about to rush off, are you?'

The implication was that Lorna didn't have enough time to listen. Lorna was offended but buried it. 'I've got all day,' she lied.

Now she had her attention, Carol seemed to slump. 'Oh, I don't know. Maybe it's nothing.'

'What's nothing?'

'James. Never around. And when he is – he's not "here", if you know what I mean. His mind is on something – or someone – else.' She paused, as if debating whether to say any more. 'And the other day, I went into the front spare room. The sheets were different.'

'Sorry?'

'When I last changed them, I used the blue ones. But the sheets on the bed were white.'

'So maybe you changed them again without remembering?'

'I'd remember.'

'Maybe James changed them.'

Carol looked her straight in the eye. 'And why would he do that?'

Lorna's jaw dropped. 'What, you think he's having an *affair*?'

Carol shrugged, the pain obvious in her eyes.

'Who with?'

'I don't know. I don't even know that he is.' Carol sighed heavily. 'Maybe I should just get away for a bit. Go on a world cruise.'

Lorna's first reaction was one of alarm. 'What? No!'

'Why not?' asked Carol, taken aback.

'Well, I mean, it sounds lovely,' said Lorna, hurriedly backtracking, 'but I'd miss you – the kids would miss you.'

'I'd come back. Eventually. Marian – my friend on the call just now – she's living in Bermuda. Perhaps I should spend the rest of the winter out there with her. She's thinking of chartering a yacht around the Caribbean.'

'Sounds expensive.'

'She has the funds. Her divorce payout was substantial.'

'But you don't. Have the funds, I mean.' What Lorna really meant was that her mother's rental income was not supposed to be frittered on a luxurious trip lasting months. It would cost thousands! No, that wasn't what she had in mind *at all*.

'Don't I?' said Carol.

Lorna was starting to panic. 'Well, I mean, you might. But it wouldn't be wise to spend so much money. All in one go.'

'Why not? It's my money.'

Lorna could feel the situation slipping away from her. A sense of desperation made her agitated and she spoke without thinking: 'But I was hoping you'd come round. About the school fees. For your grandchildren.'

Carol placed her mug on the worktop. 'No, Lorna,' she said calmly. 'I will not "come round". I've always made it perfectly clear what I think.' She paused. 'Is this the real reason for your visit?'

Lorna blushed. 'Course not.'

Carol raised an eyebrow. She looked sad. Worse, disappointed.

SEVENTY-FOUR

Wednesday 17 February

Nancy had been living in a state of low-level anxiety since the visit from the police. Looking over her shoulder. Wondering. Waiting.

She stiffened at every knock on the door, braced herself as she walked across the playground, hiding her uneasiness from Lara.

But there had been no further police visits. No cruelty in the classroom. In the playground, no one really paid her much attention at all. On the rare occasion she saw Hannah dropping Jakob, Hannah would make a point of saying hello and asking after the chickens (all fine, still laying, albeit a lot less frequently now it was winter), but everyone else seemed busy, dashing back to the warmth of their cars, houses and offices as soon as they'd delivered their children safely to school.

She'd seen Imogen only once, from a distance. Imogen had given Rosie a hug near the entrance and then left. Nancy had stayed back, watching Imogen as she departed. She'd been dressed in Narnia witch white: a long, pale woollen coat with large collar, blonde hair falling over shoulders, cream fur-lined boots.

As February came in, so the snow returned. And this time it fell thick and hard. Heron Water froze at the shoreline, opaque, jagged and cracked where the water had moved under the ice. Frost clung to the bulrushes, a frozen, speckled casing entombing their brown stems.

Nancy's own pool froze solid – even at its deepest point – or at least it *seemed* that enough ice had formed to make it walkable on. She smashed a hole to check. It was lucky she hadn't stepped on it. An inch wouldn't take her weight.

The garden had a stillness to it, a sense of everything on hold. Life held in frozen limbo. But under the surface a beat ticked on silently. *Tick, tock. Tick, tock.* Waiting. She felt the same beat within herself thanks to the ever-present unease that had settled inside her. When would the explosion come? *Would* it come?

The wintry countryside was beautiful. After taking Lara to school, Nancy would go for a walk around the reservoir, even if the snow was driving hard in her face. The soft flakes absorbed all sound, muffling the splash of a duck landing on the water, or the flap of the wings of a buzzard as it pulled back up into the air after diving down to catch some unsuspecting prey.

One day, the snow stopped. The clouds cleared and the sky was lit a pristine blue. The snow and frost sparkled with the intensity of a fine cut diamond.

Nancy was excited to get out in the winter wonderland on her doorstep. She got back from school after dropping

Lara and headed straight out again, through the garden. The grass was a white blanket and Nancy smiled as she caught sight of Lara's wild dance of footsteps from that morning. There was something so satisfying about stepping in pristine snow. She went down the steps, through the wooded area with the bare-limbed trees and out through her gate, then it was just a short walk onto the reservoir path.

There were a few more footprints here, of both the two and four-legged variety. Nancy headed east, away from the direction of the cafe. The further she went from civilization, the quieter it would be, and she wanted to immerse herself in as much untouched nature as possible. She had an idea for a new decorative glaze she wanted to try, inspired by the patterns the frost made on the leaves and the icicles hanging from the dark branches. She took photo after photo, mesmerized by the beauty of the cold, the way nature held the land in its grip. An hour passed, then two, without her even realizing. It was only when she was aware of her fingers feeling numb that she checked her watch. She had enough pictures to use for her project and suddenly the prospect of a hot coffee and a heated house was all that she wanted so she turned and headed back.

Her feet were like blocks of ice by the time she got to the path that led up to her gate and when she got to the gate itself, she could hardly open it, her fingers were so frozen. As she manoeuvred the latch, she noticed a disturbance in the snow by the fence. The fence was made of open vertical slats – Nancy relied on the bushes and brambles to keep out intruders, along with the fact her gate was a way off the main path. Under the bottom rung the snow had been flattened, indented, as if something or someone had crawled underneath. She stopped and peered into the wooded area at the bottom of her garden but could see nothing.

Nancy shut the gate slowly behind her. She walked through the trees and up the steps to where her lawn began – the large white expanse where the slanting sun, low in the winter sky, was casting gold shards as it shone through the trees.

Then up ahead, lying in the snowy lawn near the pool, she saw a darkened shape. Something inert.

She stiffened then made herself walk closer. She saw animal prints in the snow and followed them to whatever was lying on the cold ground.

It was a dog. Nancy gasped and moved towards it, tentative at first in case it was nervous around her. The black retriever lifted its head, briefly and only a short distance off the ground.

Nancy could see it was ill or injured. It was trembling. She spoke softly to it while she carefully put her fingers in its fur around its neck, searching for its collar and tag. She exhaled in relief when she found it. She'd call the owner and often, the tag had a vet number on it too. She'd call them both, get the dog the help it so clearly needed.

She flipped the tag over to see who it belonged to and read the engraved name on the gold disc.

Imogen Wood.

SEVENTY-FIVE

Wednesday 17 February

Nancy's heart plummeted. Jesus, why did it have to be *Imogen's* pet? In *her* garden.

Shit. *Shit, shit, shit!* What should she do? The poor dog looked weak. It could barely lift its head and would gaze at her imploringly, she thought, before closing its eyes every now and then. Nancy hurriedly called the vet number on the tag – they asked if she could bring the animal in immediately as it sounded as if it needed urgent treatment. She readily agreed and, hanging up, went to scoop Arthur, as she now knew he was called, into her arms.

He was a dead weight. The more she tried to lift him, the more impossible it was. She looked helplessly at the expanse of garden she needed to cross to get to the front of her house and her car. There was no way she could do it. She looked at Arthur, her mind spinning. Maybe it was her imagination, but he seemed more lethargic still. She had to get help and quickly.

Getting her phone back out, she dialled the other number on the tag.

SEVENTY-SIX

Wednesday 17 February

Imogen shivered as she turned off the path from the high street down towards the reservoir. You could feel the cold wind blowing off the flat expanse of water even from this distance. She'd walk Arthur then get back to the warmth of her kitchen. Working next to a pizza oven was a real bonus on a day like today.

As she passed the cafe, she was half-tempted to go in for a coffee, especially when she saw Hazel come out with a steaming cup. Imogen sniffed the air quizzically.

Hazel flushed with guilt. 'You caught me,' she said dolefully, lifting the cardboard cup. 'It's so cold I got myself a hot chocolate.'

'You're going to need the extra sugar being outside in this weather,' said Imogen.

'You think so?'

'Without a doubt.'

'Oh, you're a love,' said Hazel. She dived into her pocket and retrieved her tin. 'Because you have such a kind mummy, I think you deserve two of these today,' she said to the excited retriever. 'Sit!' she commanded and as the dog obeyed, she gave him the treats.

Imogen was getting cold standing still. 'Well, we'd better get going,' she said, forgoing the idea of coffee. If she was honest, she didn't have time anyway. Better to get Arthur walked and get back to the restaurant.

'Nice to see you,' said Hazel, patting Arthur's head. 'Oh, and you too, Imogen,' she added quickly.

Imogen smiled and walked on. Reaching the reservoir path, she decided to turn right, towards her old house. She wasn't going to go as far as Willow Barn, but the view of the water from this side of the reservoir was particularly beautiful.

Arthur ran on ahead and Imogen followed, pulling her scarf up around her nose and tucking her hands in her pockets. The wind was icy today, cutting into any exposed skin.

Up ahead she thought she saw Arthur stagger but then he seemed fine so she reasoned she must have imagined it. She looked at the ice at the water's edge – it was rare the reservoir itself froze. She went down to the shoreline, saw the ice crystallizing around the rocks and was reminded of a time when Dylan had taught Rosie how to skim stones across the water. After a few minutes she realized she hadn't seen Arthur in a while, so she called out his name. He didn't come running. She shouted again, louder this time as she thought her voice was getting lost in the wind, but still he didn't appear.

She groaned. She could do without an errant dog on a

day like today. It was too damn cold to go traipsing through all this snow in these freezing temperatures and she had to get to work. She called a third time but again, his lithe body, tail wagging, didn't come running up to her. Something exciting must have distracted him. A pheasant or another dog.

She had no other choice than to go on.

Five minutes later she was starting to worry. Arthur was pretty good at recall, so where the hell was he? She stopped and gazed around, sharpening her eyes for any sign of movement in the frost-blackened ferns. But it was silent and empty.

It was then that her phone rang.

SEVENTY-SEVEN

Wednesday 17 February

'Imogen, it's Nancy Miller here. Your dog is in my garden. He's ill. I've called the vet and he needs to get to the surgery as soon as possible. He can't walk but he's too heavy for me to lift to my car. Are you nearby?'

Five minutes later, Imogen was racing up the steps to her old garden. She ran towards her pet and dropped to her knees, her face stricken. Then she looked at Nancy.

'What have you done?'

'I haven't done anything . . .' stammered Nancy. 'I found him here – on the ground in the snow . . .'

Imogen's eyes darted around. She saw the swimming pond, a hole smashed in the ice. Had Arthur drunk from it?

'Help me,' she demanded, and Nancy bent down. Together they lifted the dog.

'The car's up here,' said Nancy, indicating with her head.

'I know where the drive is,' snapped Imogen.

Nancy remained silent after that. Together they laid Arthur onto the back seat, then Nancy drove to the vet's as quickly as she could.

A nurse in scrubs came out braced against the cold as they pulled up in the car park.

'How long has he been like this?' asked the nurse as she and Imogen eased the dog onto a stretcher.

Imogen flashed an accusatory look at Nancy.

'I don't know,' said Nancy. 'I found him in my garden and he was already collapsed on the ground.'

The nurse nodded and she and Imogen, the dog between them, disappeared into the surgery.

'You're welcome,' Nancy said ruefully under her breath as the door slammed shut.

SEVENTY-EIGHT

Friday 19 February

RIPTON GAZETTE

CANINE KILLER STRIKES AGAIN!

By Editor-in-Chief, Erin Mackie

A dog was rescued, just hours from death, by its owner in what is believed to be another strike by the Canine Killer. Imogen Wood, owner of The Wood Oven in Ripton, found her dog severely ill and managed to transport him to the local veterinary practice. The vet, Stephanie Prosser, said the dog was suffering from liver failure as a result of being poisoned, much like the other animals found in the area.

The dog – Arthur – was discovered on land belonging to the individual believed to be the Canine Killer. This person cannot be named for legal reasons. The dog is currently undergoing treatment.

19 February
RIPTON PRIMARY, YEAR 6

Erin Mackie, Tilly's mum
I can't believe it – caught in her own
garden! 10:08

> **Lorna Fielding, Phoenix's mum**
> Maybe she'll get that pool filled in now.
> 10:10

Nicole Wilson, Bella's mum
Was she there when you found him? What
did she do? Deny everything, I suppose?
Wash her hands of him? 10:11

> **Imogen, Rosie's mum.**
> She drove Arthur to the vet's actually. 10:13

Cheryl, Aisha's mum
What, she *helped*? Don't tell me it's out of
some sort of guilt complex. 10:13

> **Stacey, Fred's mum**
> This gets sicker and sicker. 10:14

SEVENTY-NINE

Friday 19 February

There was no name in the article. Nancy scanned it for the third time but Erin Mackie, Editor-in-Chief, had not actually printed 'Nancy Miller' in the newspaper text.

It didn't matter a damn.

Everyone would know whose land Imogen's dog had been found on. In a place like Ripton, Imogen only needed to tell one person and it would be all over the village by nightfall.

Everyone would be saying that she, Nancy, was the Canine Killer.

It was a joke. A cruel, humourless joke played on her.

Her phone rang. It was Beth.

'Um . . . I've just had a notification on my phone of a news article . . .'

Nancy explained.

'The bitch!' said Beth. 'How *dare* she! You need to do something.'

'Do what? There's nothing I can do. She's been very careful not to break the law.'

'Except meanwhile the jungle drums will be thrumming constantly.'

'Until I'm tomorrow's fish-and-chip paper.'

The two women lapsed into silence.

'This is so not fair,' said Beth. 'You want me to come over?'

'Don't be daft. It's eight o'clock at night and the weather's awful.'

'Honestly, I don't mind. I can hear in your voice – you're upset.'

She was – she was devastated, but she didn't want to let on to Beth. 'It's fine. I'm a big girl, I can look after myself.'

After she'd hung up, Nancy wasn't so sure if she could look after herself. When exactly had things got so bad? She'd come here in good faith, with a desire for herself and Lara to start a new life. She'd wanted to make friends, be a part of the community. And yet she was somehow implicated in a heartless crime and had made enemies with the most powerful woman in the village who was intent on making her life hell.

Nancy could hear the hum of the shower pump upstairs – Lara was getting ready for bed. At pick-up, Lara had come out of school, looking concerned.

'Mum,' she'd said quietly when they'd left the playground and were walking home. 'I heard two girls talking about you today. In break. But when I got closer to them, they stopped and ran away.'

'What were they saying?' asked Nancy carefully.

'I don't know. Something about a dog. We're not getting a dog, are we?' she asked hopefully.

'Afraid not,' said Nancy.

'So what was it about?'

Nancy had considered. Should she tell Lara so she was pre-warned? It would upset her so much. She'd decided against it. 'I've no idea,' she'd said, smiling brightly. 'Probably best to ignore it.'

Nancy got up from the sofa and drew the curtains back to look out of the living room window. It was pitch black and her own reflection stared back at her. She could still make out the snow drifting past the glass; flakes in their millions.

She suddenly felt incredibly exposed and vulnerable. Framed in the light for anyone to see.

She yanked the curtains shut again and, realizing her heart was going like the clappers, took in some long, deep breaths. An instinct made her go and check all the doors were locked; satisfied they were, she went upstairs to say goodnight to Lara.

EIGHTY

Saturday 20 February

The next day, as Nancy trudged through the snow into the village, everywhere she went people seemed to be whispering. Hushed voices hidden behind hands, heads turned away so she couldn't see, but she *knew*. She knew they were talking about her. Other people made their feelings known in subtle ways. The woman in the deli was cold when she served Nancy, uttering only the most basic of sentences. Hazel, the older lady who adored the entire village population of dogs, made a point of crossing the road when she saw her coming.

Tomorrow's fish and chips, Nancy reminded herself, but it still hurt. She hurried home with Lara and stayed inside the house. The sky was grey and foreboding, the snow still falling steadily. There was a dismal quality to the day, as if the sun had barely risen. It was claustrophobic.

She had a sudden urge to get out of the village. Go somewhere where there was more life, more light. Somewhere bigger. A city.

She bundled Lara into the car. 'We're going on a surprise visit to Auntie Beth's,' she announced.

Lara cheered.

The weather had worsened since they'd been out that morning, the snow more persistent as they left their circular driveway. Nancy felt her wheels skid in the lane but she held her nerve and they kept going.

The high street was now eerily quiet. Some of the shops had closed early, no doubt due to the heavy snowfall. Snow covered everything, making it impossible to make out where the road became the pavement. Nancy kept going, her wipers fast against the snow that fell relentlessly. She peered through the windscreen. Visibility was down to about fifteen metres. The snow swirled in the cone of light in front of each headlight. Not long and she'd be at Beth's. They'd have a cup of coffee and it would be warm and friendly.

Nancy headed onto the country lane that led out of the village. The snow piled up in drifts on either side of the road. It was always narrow but now it seemed less of a road, more a passageway.

She stopped the car and looked out the windscreen at the thick snow in front of her. Should she go for it? Nancy edged forward at a snail's pace and felt the car slide. This was madness. Even if she did manage to make it all the way down the road to meet the main junction, it would take about an hour. And she would still be several miles from Beth's house.

But there was more than one way out of this village. Some of the smaller lanes would be impassable but there was another road. It was a longer journey to Beth's, but it was wider, more often used. Other cars would have gone the same way, made a pathway she could follow.

She reversed slowly until the road was wide enough to turn around and then drove back down the high street. The street lights were barely penetrating the gloom. Nancy put her head down, determined to keep going. The junction loomed. She went to turn. Her car slid from under her and she spun one hundred and eighty degrees. She fought to regain control and skidded to a stop. It was silent; the only sound being the hum of the car, the sweep of the wipers still gamely pushing away the relentless snow.

'Is everything OK, Mum?' asked Lara, looking up at her nervously.

Then Nancy knew she couldn't do it. Not after what had happened to them all. She must be mad, thinking of driving on a day like today. What if they had an accident? What if Lara lost another parent? What if she lost Lara?

'I think we should go back,' said Nancy.

She gingerly drove the car back along the lane to their house. She parked up; the hollow in the snow where the car had been earlier was already filling up.

They pulled their coats close then opened the car doors and ran.

After they came into the house, Nancy dumped her stuff and put Lara in front of the TV. She wanted to call Beth. Tell her about their plan, even if they hadn't been able to make it.

She listened to the ringing in her ear. *Please answer*, she thought. *I could really do with your friendly voice.*

'Hello?'

Nancy frowned. That wasn't Beth speaking.

'Is that Nancy? It's Martin.'

'Martin?' She thought she heard a catch in his breath. 'Is everything OK?'

'I'm so sorry,' he said, his voice cracking, 'but I have some bad news. Beth has been in an accident.'

EIGHTY-ONE

Saturday 20 February

Lorna had been up since six after another sleepless night. Despite her recent financial successes, her grand plan just wasn't possible without her mother's help. She'd been counting on it, but Carol wouldn't budge. After everything Lorna had sacrificed, the risks she had taken!

She had lain awake, her mind going round and round. Desperately trying to find a way to forge her children's future. Railing against the unfairness of it all. Why should people with money have access to a better education for their children? They got to send their kids to schools where supply teachers were non-existent, where small classes meant that every attention was paid to their child, where they mixed with other children whose parents had equally en- titled views on what opportunities their offspring should be offered.

And after that? With the contacts they had made and the school on their CV they got the best places at university, which led to the best jobs – often offered by a friend or a family member of a school 'chum'. Jobs that paid the most money, so when those children were grown up and decided to have kids of their own, they could afford to send them to the best schools where they would get the best education.

It was a closed circle. One that was guarded by the few, and Lorna was finding it impossible to break into.

She was enraged with it all. Enraged with Carol, who could change their destinies but refused to.

As she poured herself a third coffee, she heard Phoenix and Pepper thunder down the stairs. It was only seven thirty but she knew why they were up early – it was a Saturday morning and there was fresh snow. She could already tell by the shouts that they were beside themselves with excitement.

She smiled as they burst into the kitchen and she insisted on hot Ready Brek before they went out to the garden in the freezing cold. As she spooned it into their bowls, she wondered how she was going to break it to Phoenix that he couldn't go to Kingsgate. Her heart cracked at the wasted opportunity – he was such a talented sportsman, he *deserved* to go.

Simon came into the kitchen, yawning and still in his pyjamas.

'You're up early,' he said.

Lorna gave a half smile. He didn't know the half of it. Sometimes his obliviousness irritated her so much. Now she had to tell him too, about the change of plan with their children's schooling. Make up something about how Carol had decided not to contribute after all. He wouldn't outright say, 'I told you so', but he'd say that was how it was for people like them. He would simply accept their lot and forget about it. 'Don't get upset about the things you can't control,' he would say, but that was exactly what the elite wanted. To take away your control. They wanted to reserve the cherry-picked parts of life for themselves and quietly look down their noses at the rest of the population who were so browbeaten they no longer rose up against what they had no control over.

God, she was fuming this morning. Probably because she was tired. Being tired made her extremely tetchy.

Maybe she should tell Simon first. The kids had finished their breakfast at record speed (why did they never eat this fast when she was rushing to get them ready for school?) and were already dragging on coats, wellies and gloves. Better to let them go outside and have some fun. She opened the back door and they bolted, barely giving her a second to pull Pepper's hat down over her ears. She smiled as she heard their shrieks of joy and as she looked out of the kitchen window, saw them running around in utter delight, lifting up great swathes of snow and throwing it at each other.

She loved them so much. She'd do anything for them. Yet she felt as if she was failing her children, standing by and watching as they fell further and further behind in society, in life. What was the saying? *Give me a child until he is seven and I will show you the man.* Well, Phoenix was eleven – did that mean his blueprint for prosperity in life was already set? She felt a cold sweep of panic wash over her.

'Maybe we could . . . you know,' said Simon, putting his arms around her from behind and nuzzling her ear. 'While the kids are occupied.'

She didn't want to. She was tired and frazzled and her mind was far too occupied with the epically proportioned disappointment she had yet to fully accept. If only Simon cared a bit more about these things, if only he could *see* what destiny they were setting for their children by not breaking the cycle.

If only she could think of a way to raise more money.

A crowd-funding page? She dismissed it with a silent sigh. It was unlikely that total strangers would fork out for private school fees for a child unknown. No, these kinds of things were generally only successful if the kid was sick or needed urgent medical treatment abroad – usually somewhere diabolically expensive like America. She'd heard in the past of mothers faking children's illnesses just to get the cash and the stories made her skin crawl. She didn't understand the cruelty of inflicting an illness, fake or otherwise, on a perfectly healthy child.

If only Simon earned more, she thought. If only he were one of those wealthy investment banker types, a trader or something. Or even a doctor who owned his own practice. Or anything more than a data analyst who loved to play football.

'Did I tell you I have to meet up with the rest of the Ripton Rhinos at lunchtime to talk over the arrangements for the Straw Bear Festival?' said Simon, still with his face buried in her neck.

Lorna pulled away and turned to face him. *No, you did not.* 'You know you didn't.'

'I'm sure I did.'

'How long for?'

'A couple of hours.'

'*What?*' Last time the all-male charity group, the Ripton Rhinos, met 'for a couple of hours', Simon didn't come back until late afternoon and he was stinking of beer. Why did men never seem to carry the weight of family worries? Why was it always up to the women to sort and organize, make plans and change things for the better? Only she wasn't doing too well at that at the moment. She could do with a shoulder to lean on. Lorna felt completely abandoned.

'It's the meeting we do every year,' said Simon. 'Same as always. And you know what a big deal the festival is for everyone. We raise a load too – don't forget some of it goes back to the school.'

Lorna ignored the irritation she felt at Simon trying to cajole her into letting him go to the pub with his mates, in order to benefit her PTA, because she had just had a realization. A significant one.

The Straw Bear Festival raised an enormous amount of money. Simon had been on the committee for three years now and he always told her what they had taken. It ran into several thousand. They didn't charge for tickets, just had people out with donation buckets throughout the village on the night itself. And seeing as almost the whole village turned out and there was a sense of pride about this ancient festival that marked them out from all the other villages, they liked to show their appreciation through their wallets.

Even better, Simon was the treasurer. He took the money home with him at the end of the night and got it ready for banking.

Could she?

A plan was worming its way into her head. It was so simple it was almost irresistible. She tried to fight it off, knowing it wasn't right. But the more she thought it through, the more she realized it was easy and foolproof and really quite low risk.

There were no ticket sales, no records of anything. It was just cash in a bucket.

Lots and lots of it.

EIGHTY-TWO

Wednesday 24 February

Nancy came off the phone to the hospital. Beth was still in ICU. There was no change to her unresponsive state, but she was what the staff were calling 'stable'.

Martin had told her that Beth had decided to drive over to Ripton to see her in all the snow – the same time Nancy had been trying to get out. Beth had made it to the road into the village when she'd lost control of her car and smashed into a tree. The paramedics thought it had been almost an hour before another car had driven past and called for help. Beth had suffered a brain injury and was in a coma. The doctors were hopeful – she could breathe on her own – but she was showing no signs of awareness.

When Nancy had asked Martin why Beth was driving over on such a precarious day, he'd become evasive. Said something about how she had wanted to see if Nancy was OK. He didn't need to spell it out – Nancy knew her friend had made the effort because of their last phone call, when she'd been so upset about the newspaper article. Martin didn't say that because he didn't want her to feel guilty.

Nancy knew how physically close they'd been to each other as they tried to get to one another. The place where Beth had had her accident was only half a mile from the point where Nancy had had to turn back. She knew the bend in the road, knew the tree. They'd been minutes from each other.

Nancy gazed out of the window feeling trapped. She was desperate to go and visit Beth, but the snow was still too deep to get out of the village – and who would look after Lara? It was the half-term holidays and so there was no school. She'd told Lara about the accident but had played it down. Then prayed to a greater being that Beth would recover soon. She didn't dare think about an alternative. It would break her, break Lara. She called in to check on Beth daily, only to be told there was no change, and the fear and isolation grew.

After a few days playing in the snow in the garden and watching movies at home, Nancy needed to go out to get some groceries. She wasn't looking forward to it but if she wanted to eat, she had no choice. They both put on their warmest coats and boots and set off down the lane, crumping through the snow. It reached two or three feet in the drifts and Lara ran up and down, getting more than her fair share of snow in her wellies.

As they walked along the high street one of the shop doors opened just ahead of them. Nancy looked up, too late to avoid the person who came out. Her stomach tightened; she couldn't deal with Imogen, not at the moment.

Imogen didn't notice Nancy at first. She had her dog on

a lead by her side and was too engrossed in expressing her gratitude to the vet, who was standing next to her.

So the dog had made a recovery, thought Nancy, relieved. For the dog, especially. Whatever was going on in this village, it had managed to escape the fate of some of its fellow pups.

She was just wondering how she could get past without being noticed when a voice cried out behind her.

'Oh, thank goodness!'

Nancy turned to see Hazel trudging up the pavement, making a beeline for Imogen and Arthur. At the same time, Imogen's face darkened as soon as she clocked Nancy.

'You poor thing, are you OK?' said Hazel, bending down to stroke the retriever.

'He's fine, thanks to this amazing lady's intervention,' said Imogen, smiling at the vet. 'Thanks again, Stephanie.'

'What was it?' asked Hazel, all concern.

'Some sort of poison. Same as the other dogs.'

Nancy could hear everything – as she suspected they knew.

'What crazy monster would do such a thing?' asked Hazel.

Nancy bristled. She was torn between wanting to get as far away as possible and being rooted to the ground, waiting to hear if they damned her in public.

'Can I give him a treat?' continued Hazel, digging into her pocket for her tin.

'Sure,' said Imogen.

'He deserves it, after his ordeal,' said Hazel, and Nancy wasn't sure if she was imagining it but thought Hazel's voice had raised in volume – for her benefit, perhaps. She was considering going over to them, challenging them both when she heard Stephanie speak.

'What's that?'

'Treats,' said Hazel, opening the tin. 'Organic chicken flavour.'

'No,' said Stephanie. 'I mean the white stuff.'

Nancy saw Stephanie had taken the tin from Hazel and was examining a treat she'd plucked out.

Hazel looked bemused for a moment, then realized. 'I spilled my sweetener,' she said. 'You know, cutting down on the sugar. Doctor's orders.'

'Sweetener?'

'You can't tell the difference, you know. And I can drink as many teas as I like.'

'What's it called?'

'Xylitol. I only remember because it sounds like xylophone.'

'Stop,' instructed Stephanie urgently as Hazel went to post a treat into the dog's ready mouth.

Hazel stood up straight. 'Pardon?'

'It's poisonous to dogs. Xylitol.'

'It is?' said Hazel, her face slack.

'Very. The tiniest amount can be fatal. Did you . . . sorry to ask this, Hazel, but did you by any chance give Arthur a treat last Wednesday?'

Hazel was floundering, her mouth opening and closing like a shored fish. She looked from Stephanie to Imogen in desperation.

'I think you did,' said Imogen carefully. 'Two. By Heron Water Cafe.'

'Oh my goodness, I think you're right.' Hazel visibly crumpled.

'And have you been feeding treats to other dogs around the village?' Stephanie asked gravely.

Nancy didn't hear Hazel's answer, but she didn't need to. Imogen told her everything when she looked up at her.

Nancy returned her gaze, eyes steady. Then, head held high, she took Lara's hand and crossed the road.

EIGHTY-THREE

Friday 26 February

RIPTON GAZETTE

Correction: In an article about the Canine Killer, the author incorrectly stated that the land where an injured dog was found belonged to an individual suspected to be the so-called 'Canine Killer'. It has since been disproven that the owner of that land harmed any dogs. We apologize for any distress caused. (**Canine Killer Strikes Again!** 19 February, page 1)

EIGHTY-FOUR

Monday 1 March

Nancy closed down her phone and quickly put it in her pocket as Lara came downstairs.

'Ready?' asked Nancy, putting on a smile. She'd been talking to Martin and was planning on going to the hospital to visit Beth later. There was no change. Beth was still unresponsive. Nancy waited for Lara to tie her shoelaces then they walked to school. In the village high street, someone had put posters up for the Straw Bear Festival.

'Will Auntie Beth be better for the festival?' asked Lara.

'Let's hope so,' said Nancy brightly. She still hadn't told Lara the extent of Beth's injuries, but the hope she was pinning everything on – that Beth would make a full recovery – seemed to get more fragile by the day. Nancy was doing her best to hold it all together, despite the spectre of loss descending upon her in the night, causing her to lie tossing and turning, her mind playing over the worst. She would wake feeling hollow and wrung out, steeling herself to act positive for Lara.

The snow had melted and Lara was full of talk about the new lambs that had appeared on the other side of the fence to the school's playing field. Dozens of them, by all accounts, but she had still managed to fall in love with and name them all: Lambie, Twizzles, Curls, Fluffy, Butternut Squash, Tiptoe, Munchie.

When they reached the playground, Lara ran off to chat to Mia and Nancy was left on her own. She thought she clocked one of the other mothers looking over – a glance of . . . was it chagrin? Compassion?

Imogen and Erin were standing together a short distance away. They were with Nicole and a couple of other mums in their clique. Nancy looked over and felt sure they knew she was there but none of them turned and looked her way. Imogen was speaking loudly: 'It was a misunderstanding. Unfortunate, but when you look at the facts, everything seemed to point to that logical conclusion. And you have to remember, Arthur was *there*, on that land.'

A hand tapped Nancy on the shoulder. She turned to see Hannah.

'It's the closest thing you'll get to an apology,' said Hannah, looking over at Imogen and her gang. 'That and the half-arsed three lines in the paper.'

Nancy smiled. So she wasn't the only one who thought Erin's 'correction' in the *Ripton Gazette* was insulting and inadequate. 'No real harm done,' she said.

'Really?' asked Hannah, giving her a searching look. 'I've

got to say, you're very forgiving. If it's any consolation, at one point they insinuated it was me.'

'What?'

'Uh huh. Revenge for the sheep attacks up at the farm, apparently.'

'You've had more?' said Nancy, worried.

'No. Police caught the culprit. They were tipped off about a dog that was escaping from a house a mile away.' She looked over at Imogen and the others. 'It's amazing what poisonous drivel can be contrived from a combination of self-righteous folk and a group chat. Hey, Jakob says Lara likes the lambs near the school field.'

'She's mad about them.'

'Would she like to come up and feed some orphans we have on the farm?'

Nancy smiled. 'She'd love that.'

'Great. Let's do it this weekend, if that suits. I'll message you. Better get back.' Hannah waved goodbye to Jakob then headed off.

As the bell rang, Nancy gave Lara a hug, quickly telling her about the invitation. As she had anticipated, Lara was ecstatic.

Nancy decided to take the long route home, down towards the reservoir and along the water's edge path. No one else was around and she felt adrift as she walked along the water. She thought about her trip to the hospital, later that day. Why wasn't Beth coming out of her coma? *Please,* she pleaded silently to whoever might be listening, *please don't let Beth die.* Nancy felt herself well up, had to stop and compose herself. Then, as she was blowing her nose and trying to hold back the tears, she saw her first daffodils of the year. Bright yellow nodding bursts of cheer.

She decided to take it as a good omen.

EIGHTY-FIVE

Saturday 6 March

Imogen zipped up her run vest and kissed Dylan goodbye. 'It's going to be a shorter one today,' she said. 'Probably only an hour.'

'Don't rush back on our account,' said Dylan as he whipped up batter mix for Rosie.

As soon as Imogen stepped out of the door, she felt a sensation of relief knowing the next hour was hers and hers alone. A time where the only thing she had to think about was putting one foot in front of the other. She headed towards the high street then took the usual lane out of the village. She hadn't texted James this time – in fact, not for the last couple of Saturdays. It had been too cold and today she'd been so pleased the snow had gone so she could get out, she'd simply forgotten. He'd been in touch with her though, persistently. Wanting to know when they were meeting again.

Imogen was feeling frustrated as she ran today. All that irritating stuff about the Canine Killer. She wondered if things would have been different if Nancy *had* been behind

Arthur's illness. If she had been the one accidentally going out with contaminated dog treats. Would she have stayed? Would she be able to? Hazel, as a long-standing resident, would be forgiven her awful mistake. Especially as it was so obvious she was completely cut up about it. But Nancy? As a newcomer, it would have been miserable for her for months. Possibly years. Who could endure living in that sort of climate? She would surely have had to move.

That wasn't the way events had panned out. But there would be another way. There always was.

Spring was in the air. The catkins were hanging from the trees, their buds as soft as kitten's ears. The green shoots of the bluebells were coming up in force. In a few weeks the ground would be awash with blue. As Imogen ran on, her problems seemed to take on some perspective. She felt as if there would be solutions for them all. The problem of Nancy. The problem of Nancy's daughter, Lara. What those solutions were, she didn't know yet, but she felt alive, energized and full of a sense she could achieve anything. She felt as if her body and mind were god-like, a higher being, so when she saw James running towards her, she realized she was pleased.

'You didn't say you were going out this morning,' he said, piqued, as he stopped, panting slightly in front of her.

'Last-minute decision,' she said. She looked behind him where his large, detached house stood on the hill. 'Carol at the gym?'

He smiled.

*

She lay on the sheets in the bed in the spare room and her mind turned back to the problem that was always there, festering away in the background. She had a suspicion she wanted to run past James.

'What do you think of the Spring Queen vote?'

'What?'

'Lara winning.'

'I've no idea. Does it matter?'

'Of course it matters!'

He smiled and kissed her. 'It's just a silly little village thing.'

'Not silly if you're eleven years old.' She looked at him. 'I think Miss Young rigged the vote.'

He laughed out loud.

'Seriously. She dislikes Rosie. Deny it.'

He hesitated a millisecond and she knew she was right.

'She doesn't,' he said unconvincingly.

'You need to work on your poker face,' said Imogen. 'I really think you could find better teachers.'

'She's fine.'

'*Fine?* I should imagine she's a bit of a pain to you too. Challenging? Punk attitude? Doesn't always know how to work the politics?' She knew by the irked expression on his face that she was right. She got out of bed and started to get dressed. 'I won't be able to make the next few Saturdays.'

He sat up, taken aback. 'What?'

'In fact . . . I hate to say it, but I'm worried Carol might find out.'

He scoffed. 'Why would she?'

'It's obvious. The longer we continue, the greater the risk. Maybe we should cool off.'

'You're kidding, right?'

She made sure she looked pained. 'No. And anyway, I need to spend more time with the family. With Rosie. Especially now she's so upset over being unfairly shunted to the back of the queue.'

'I see. That's what this is about. I won't be blackmailed, you know.'

She went over to the bed and kissed him. 'I'm thinking of you as well. You and I both know Miss Young stirs up trouble. And although I hate to admit that Rosie has been a little . . . out of line, shall we say, Miss Young doesn't like the way it's all been handled.' She paused. 'Aren't you due an Ofsted inspection in the next couple of months? You want a whistle blower in your school?'

'She wouldn't do that.' But James looked concerned.

'Oh no? Didn't she say in the last governors' meeting that the school should be reviewing its bullying policy?' Imogen knew this because Erin, as Chair of Governors, had been there and passed it on. Said that Miss Young had used the words 'failing their children'. 'She's an idealist,' continued Imogen. 'A foolish one. And didn't she have other job offers before she came to Ripton Primary? She'll be OK. I wouldn't put it past her to sink your ship and then abandon it.'

Imogen put on her trainers then stood. 'Wouldn't it be nice to get all of our worries out of the way? It would give us more time to spend together.'

She kissed him goodbye and then left.

EIGHTY-SIX

Saturday 6 March

Imogen let herself into the house. She could hear Rosie in the garden with Dylan. She quickly undid her running shoes and thought she'd slip upstairs for a shower before anyone noticed she'd been more than an hour.

'Hi,' said Dylan, coming into the hallway.

Imogen turned from the bottom step where she'd been about to escape. *Dammit.*

'Hi,' she said.

'Turn into a longer run?'

'Yeah, that's right.' It came out sharper than she'd intended.

Dylan was taken aback. 'I'm not saying it's a problem.'

'No, I know you're not,' said Imogen quickly.

Dylan frowned. 'Is everything OK?'

'Yes, fine!'

'Only you seem . . .'

'What?'

'Agitated. Something happen on the run?'

Imogen forced a smile. 'No, just lost track of time, that's all.'

It was a moment before Dylan nodded. 'Want to come outside and help build the bug hotel?'

'Might just take a shower first.'

'OK.'

She smiled and then turned and went upstairs, feeling his eyes watching her. Her heart was racing but she thought she'd got away with it. It had been a mistake to snap. She had to remember to keep her cool.

EIGHTY-SEVEN

Saturday 6 March

The kids had started to ask Lorna why they hadn't seen Grandma recently. It wasn't fair to keep them from their grandmother, so Lorna had invited Carol and James over for lunch.

It had been a little strained. Forced politeness between herself and Carol. Every now and then Lorna would think of her mum lying on the deck of the floating palace of a cruise ship and get incredibly wound up. She shook the image of coconut cocktails from her head and reminded herself she had a plan B.

James was picking at his food and had hardly said a word. Lorna felt another frisson of annoyance. She'd always had the vague sensation that he only tolerated her company because of his wife. Except recently Carol had hinted that their relationship was on the rocks. Was that why he was letting his guard down? She gave him a sidelong glance. *Was* he having an affair? Who on earth with?

'Everyone going to the Straw Bear Festival this year?' asked Simon.

'James isn't,' said Carol.

'I've done the last three,' said James. 'And as much as I love it, I've got quite a bit going on at the school. The call from Ofsted could come any day and I have preparation to do.'

'Costumes going OK, Mum?' asked Lorna.

'Nearly done,' said Carol. 'You still want me to take the children on the night?'

'Yes please.' In fact, it was essential. She was going to be helping Simon collect the donations.

'We'll have fun, won't we, children?' said Carol.

They chorused back their agreement.

Simon started to clear the empty dishes and Pepper slipped from the table, got her toy dog from the box in the corner of the room.

'Look, Grandma,' she said, pressing the buttons on its plastic lead. 'It poops!'

'Oh wow. All over the nice wooden floors,' said Carol, smiling.

'It's not *real*,' said Pepper, shaking her head.

'Thanks for getting it for her, Carol,' said Simon. 'She plays with nothing else.'

Carol looked confused. 'Getting it?'

'Yes, you bought it as a gift.' Simon looked from Lorna to Carol. 'Didn't you?'

Lorna was holding her breath. Jesus, why hadn't she put the toy dog away in Pepper's room? She gave a tight smile, desperately tried to think of a way out of what was about to come crashing down around her ears.

'You're right, I did,' said Carol brightly. 'I'd forgotten. I'm very pleased that she likes it so much.'

What had her mother just said? Lorna glanced at Carol, but she'd stood up.

'Right, kids, who wants to kick a ball around the garden?' She led them out amid loud cheers.

Lorna watched them go. Her mum had lied for her. But she knew that wouldn't be the end of it.

EIGHTY-EIGHT

Monday 8 March

Rebecca Young had prepared a few questions for her annual review. She wanted to suggest a couple of new clubs for the children, also wanted to put herself forward as head of Key Stage Two, as the current teacher holding that role was retiring. Rebecca would've been at the school a year by then – had learned the ropes and was ready for more responsibility.

She knocked on James Whitman's door and he called her in. He sat down in the armchair opposite her with a notepad and pen.

'Hi, Rebecca, good to see you. As you know, this is your official annual review where we will go through your performance for the year and what happens next.'

She nodded. 'Where's Claire?' she asked. The assistant head always came into these meetings as well.

'I'm afraid she was called away for something urgent.'

'Oh?'

He didn't elaborate. Just smiled and held his hands up, asking for her permission. 'Are you happy to continue?'

'I guess . . .'

'OK. That's good to hear.' James took a breath. 'I'm afraid I've decided I'm not going to be renewing your contract at the end of this academic year.'

Rebecca was completely blindsided. She thought she hadn't heard right. 'Sorry?'

'I know it's going to be a disappointment but there have been a few issues that unfortunately I can't overlook.'

She was still reeling. 'Issues? What issues?'

He looked at her sombrely. 'Safeguarding. It's of the utmost importance that we follow this to the letter.'

'I don't know what you're talking about.'

'Back on . . .' – James looked down at his notepad – '. . . Friday the eighth of January, you left your class alone on the school field during a PE lesson and a child had a severe asthma attack.'

'It wasn't like that. I had another sick child I had to attend to. You know this.'

'What I know is that the asthmatic child ended up in hospital.'

'Yes . . . I know. I went to the hospital with her. We spoke about this before. You said I had done the right thing.'

'I said no such thing.'

'No way,' started Rebecca, 'no way are you doing this to me.'

'I am simply following the correct protocol.'

'Bullshit!' said Rebecca. 'What's going on? Why is this coming up now?'

'It's your review.'

'I'm not having this. I'm taking this to the union.'

James looked hard at her. 'If you resign, I won't mention it on your reference.'

Rebecca was stunned. 'What?'

He shrugged.

'This is blackmail. I'll contest it.'

'Who are they going to believe? You? Or me, a long-standing head and government adviser? At the end of the day, this is just going to be one person's word against the other.'

EIGHTY-NINE

Monday 8 March

It was personal. It had to be. There was no other reason to sack her, thought Rebecca, still devastated. That bullshit excuse about safeguarding was obviously a cover. What she couldn't work out was what she'd done to offend him so much. There had been no clues before now. Yes, she'd challenged him on occasion, but he wasn't threatened by her. He was too successful and too powerful.

So why get rid of her?

Mondays were her days on lunch patrol. She walked around the playground, the kids high on the scent of spring. As ever, she kept an eye on friendships – looking out for any sort of unkindness. She rounded the corner – an area part-hidden from view. Lara and Mia were there and Rebecca saw Rosie and Tilly standing next to them. She narrowed her eyes and went over.

'Everything OK here, girls?'

'Yeah, fine,' said Rosie.

Rebecca bristled at her cockiness. She looked at Lara. 'What's going on?'

'Rosie was offering to help me at the Straw Bear Festival. She's going to help with Lupin at the start of the procession.'

'Is that right?' Rebecca watched Rosie carefully for signs of duplicitousness. But Rosie gazed up with wide, innocent eyes.

'Yes, miss.'

'OK. Well, that's a nice thing to do.' And as there was nothing left to assess, she reluctantly moved on.

NINETY

Monday 8 March

Lorna was making herself some lunch when her phone rang. She stopped buttering her sandwich and looked at the screen – it was her mum. She knew what the call was going to be about, knew it would be better to confront it sooner rather than later.

'Hi, Mum.'

'Thanks for a lovely lunch on Saturday,' said Carol.

'A pleasure.'

'Yes, it was good to see you all again. And Pepper is as mad about animals as ever.' She paused. 'Why did you tell Simon I'd bought that dog for her?'

Laura pretended not to remember at first. 'Dog? Oh! I didn't.'

Carol was taken aback. 'So why did he think I had?'

'You know men. Never pay attention. Think he got it mixed up with the cuddly toy you got her for Christmas. You know, the Dalmatian puppy? One toy dog is the same as another in his eyes.'

Lorna held her breath, could almost see her mother

processing this, wondering whether to believe her daughter or not.

'That's strange,' said Carol. 'They look quite different to me.'

Lorna swallowed. 'Yes, well, me too. But honestly, I have a haircut and Simon doesn't notice.' She gave a forced laugh. 'What can you do?'

NINETY-ONE

Friday 19 March

Rosie was allowed to walk home by herself now it was getting lighter after school. Her parents had agreed it was good for her to get a little independence, especially as there were only a few months left of primary school. She loved it and she and Tilly, who'd also been granted the same privilege, would be the first to walk out of school, heads held high, while the collected kids had to wait for the teacher to identify each of their parents in turn before they were released.

The freedom was intoxicating. They felt years older than they were, and were heady with the knowledge that for the first time in their lives they were completely unsupervised.

It was Friday. The day before the Straw Bear Festival. As usual, Rosie and Tilly marched out of the school without a backwards glance at Miss Young or their classmates and headed towards the high street. Friday was extra special as their mums would give them some money to buy a milkshake from the village cafe on the way home. Rosie loved going in and ordering, sitting with Tilly and sucking all the chocolatey cold milk from the bottom of the glass, not wasting a drop.

Except today she didn't want to.

'I've forgotten my money,' she said to Tilly, whose face dropped in horror. Rosie pretended to be devastated too. 'Trauma,' she added.

'Maybe I've got enough for both of us,' said Tilly, peering into her little zip-up purse with a ladybird on it.

'No, you should save your money,' said Rosie quickly.

Tilly didn't have enough anyway. There was only five pounds. Milkshakes cost four pounds each.

'I'm such an idiot,' said Rosie.

'We could share one?' suggested Tilly, hope in her eyes.

'That might be a bit weird.'

Tilly looked affronted.

'I mean with the lady behind the till. Us only buying one drink.'

'Yeah. S'pose.'

They shrugged at each other then continued on their way. As usual, they came to Tilly's house first.

'See you at the festival tomorrow,' said Rosie.

'Yeah. I'll ask my mum to ask your mum what time you're going so we can meet up.'

'Great,' said Rosie. 'See you there.' She hesitated. Part of her was desperate to get away, to get on with what she wanted to do. But she had a very strong feeling she might need some help. She questioned whether she could trust Tilly. She questioned whether she had any choice.

'Maybe we could meet earlier. Before the festival.'

'OK.'

'It's for something important.'

Tilly looked interested. 'What?'

'You have to promise to keep it a secret.'

'Course,' said Tilly blithely. Greedily. Wanting to know.

'No, I mean it,' said Rosie. 'Or I might have to kill you.'

Tilly started. 'Okaaaay . . .'

'I'll tell you tomorrow. When I come to your house. About two o'clock, OK?'

'Can't you tell me today?'

'No.'

Tilly accepted the rebuff and they gave each other a little lightweight hug, a sort of resting of the hands on each other's shoulders and then Tilly went up her front path.

Rosie didn't hang about. She walked swiftly away and when she was out of view of the house, she broke into a run. But instead of going home, she headed back up to the high street, crossed over the road then made her way down the lane that led towards the woods.

After a couple of minutes, she came to a large house that had a stable block off to one side.

Rosie didn't bother with the house, instead she went straight towards the yard. Over the other side of the gate was a woman. Rosie stopped and the woman looked up.

'Rosie?' the woman said.

It was Olivia. The lady who had bought her pony for her own daughter.

'Hi,' said Rosie.

'Nice to see you. It's been a while.'

Rosie nodded. Last time she'd seen this lady and her daughter was the day they'd come to take Lupin away from her at her old house. Olivia had said that Rosie could come and visit Lupin at any time but she hadn't wanted to. She would have been too upset, she knew. She would have wanted to jump on Lupin's back and ride him across the fields, over the fences and hedges until they were free forever.

'Is it OK if I say hello to Lupin?'

Olivia's face broke into a smile. 'Of course. He's just come out of the field. You want to give him a carrot?'

Rosie opened the gate and went into the yard, taking the carrot Olivia had picked out from a bucket in a small shed off to one side.

'Izzy loves him,' said Olivia.

Rosie nodded. She knew Izzy wouldn't be home for another hour as she went to a private primary school.

'I just need to get our other horse down from the field,' said Olivia. 'You OK if I leave you for a minute?'

'Yes.'

'You know, you're welcome to come and say hello any time.' Olivia stroked Lupin's nose.

'Tomorrow?' asked Rosie.

'Afraid we're out at horse trials tomorrow. Not Lupin as he needs to keep his energy for the festival.'

Rosie took this information in as Olivia headed off to the fields. She went over to where her pony was in his stable, his head over the door watching her, smelling her – welcoming her. She scratched his ears, stroked his nose and he whickered softly.

'It's your big day tomorrow, Lupin,' she said. 'I'm sorry I won't be riding you.' Her voice caught in her throat. It wasn't fair that Lara had been given the role of Spring Queen. Rosie was sickened by the idea, hated the fact she'd had to engineer it so Lara won the vote. She remembered what her mother had said: *Life has a way of rebalancing. There are other ways to get back at someone.*

She kissed Lupin's nose and whispered to him.

'You mustn't be scared, OK?'

She checked that he understood what she was saying, searching his eyes for understanding. He seemed to look right back at her and she hugged his neck. 'I knew you'd be on my side,' she said. 'Just remember, nothing bad is going to happen to *you*.'

NINETY-TWO

October, the previous year

It was night. Dark.

There was still screaming.

Her body was shaking from the impact. She was winded, confused. There was a pain in her neck from where it had whipped forward. Now everything had stopped. The lorry seemed to have become a part of their car. Fused itself to the front passenger section. Then she saw something in the footwell. A dark liquid pooling. With a shock she realized it was blood. She could smell it now. She reeled and felt herself gag. She was going to be sick.

Then she heard the sirens.

Later, she always asked herself the same questions. What had gone through his mind when the lorry hit them? Was he scared? Did he feel the impact? What was it like for him when he died?

NINETY-THREE

Saturday 20 March

The sun rose at 6.11 a.m. Having already warmed the start of the day in Europe, the earth had rotated that little bit more and it was the turn of the lands and waters of the United Kingdom. It crept across the North Sea, then over Lincolnshire with its flat plains, then through Robin Hood country and was now brightening the horizon in Derbyshire. It appeared over the hills of Ripton and lit up the edge of Heron Water.

Today was the spring solstice, when the land would enjoy exactly the same amount of day as night. After the long, frozen winter, the sun had a warmth to it and it brought energy, awakening the perpetual circle of life.

Nancy stood in her garden, eyes closed, face tilted towards the sun. It felt so good to feel its warmth on her skin. Spring was her favourite season; she loved how it held an abundance of promise. All those months of good weather and growth ahead, each day becoming steadily longer towards midsummer, filled with light and heat.

Lara had been up since seven. She was full of nervous

energy and Nancy had sent her to retrieve the eggs from the chickens. She could hear her making her way back up the garden.

'Three eggs, Mum,' said Lara.

Nancy looked up. 'Great!'

Lara came up and showed her spoils. 'Mum, what if I get lost?'

'You mean tonight?'

'Yes.'

'You won't. The horse is part of the procession, you just follow the band in front of you.'

'But what if Lupin decides to go another way?'

'He won't. He's on a lead rein, remember.' Nancy squeezed Lara's shoulder. 'It's going to be fine.'

Lara sighed. 'Yeah.'

'What?'

'I wish Dad was here.'

Nancy felt her heart pinch. 'I wish he was here too.'

Lara was quiet for a moment. 'And Auntie Beth,' she said tentatively.

'I know.' Nancy had to work hard to keep her voice from cracking. 'It's a shame she's still in hospital.'

'But it's been ages,' said Lara. 'Mum?'

'Yes?'

'Is she OK? I mean, she's not going to die or anything, is she?'

Heart in mouth, Nancy looked at Lara, her daughter's face fearful and desperate for reassurance.

She didn't know. The doctors were saying the same things;

a person could come out of a coma at any point. Nancy had visited on a number of occasions and every time her friend had lain in the bed, still and unresponsive. It was difficult to witness. Beth was always so animated, so resilient.

'She's just very ill,' she said carefully. 'After the car accident. Some people take months to get better.'

'But she will?'

'I really hope so,' said Nancy fervently.

She looked at Lara and saw a flash of fear in her eyes as she processed this. She also saw her daughter was grateful for the honesty. There was a silent understanding between them about the severity of Beth's illness. Lara suddenly threw her arms around Nancy and Nancy had to bite back the tears.

'Can you French-plait my hair?' asked Lara, her voice muffled against her mother's jumper.

'We're not going till later on this afternoon.'

'I know, but I want to get ready.'

Nancy smiled. 'Breakfast first!'

NINETY-FOUR

Saturday 20 March

Imogen swiftly tied her trainer laces. She was feeling agitated today. Silly really, as it was just a village festival but every time she thought of what was going to happen later – her husband being part of a procession through the village accompanied by a young girl on a pony – she got a tight feeling in her chest. It should be Rosie on Lupin next to her dad.

She called out her goodbyes, leaving Rosie and Dylan to their pancakes, and set off. The thoughts consumed her brain as she ran, going round and round in circles. Nancy. Lara. Her beloved house. Her daughter's rightful place. So much taken from them. She ran harder, knowing the pounding would help to settle her.

Imogen heard another pair of footsteps fall in beside her and turned to see James. They exchanged a look. At least one thing was going her way, she thought. James had mentioned about Miss Young leaving them at the end of the academic year. *Good*. It served her right for the way she'd treated Rosie.

She let him go on ahead a safe distance, then once he'd turned up the driveway to his house, she checked behind her. No one was about and she followed him up the path and through the door he'd left open.

Later, in the shower, Imogen didn't know that Dylan had picked up the running watch she'd left on the kitchen table. He guiltily listened out, heard the water running and clicked on the buttons at the side of the watch face, telling himself there was nothing odd, nothing to explain. It was just his imagination running wild. Everything was fine.

A map came up on the screen and Dylan looked at it. A line marked out the route Imogen had taken that morning. She'd run down Cuckoo Lane then through the outskirts of the village in a circular route back to their place. He felt bad about looking and was about to put the watch down when he noticed something that landed a sucker punch to his stomach.

The line was all reds and oranges. He knew the colours indicated Imogen's pace. She was fast, consistently so.

So why was there a very tiny section of the line that was blue?

It meant she'd gone slow, very slow indeed. Or she'd stopped.

He looked at the map again, wondering what had made her stop running. Had she injured herself? Of course not, she hadn't mentioned anything and had been absolutely fine when she'd come back. He suddenly realized that at the point at which she'd stopped, there was a house. A house he knew. So she must have gone in.

He needed to know more. He clicked again, frustrated at not knowing how the watch worked but managing to navigate his way around by pressing various buttons. Gradually more of the watch's intel revealed itself to him. He saw Imogen had taken the same route the previous Saturday too. And the one before that. Each time she'd stopped at the house.

Two weeks ago she'd gone in for twenty-five minutes. He thought back – that was the day she said she was only going to be an hour but had ended up staying out for ninety minutes. He delved further. More Saturdays. More stopping at the house for twenty, forty-five, even fifty minutes. He looked at the map. Pictured the house, its shiny black front door. James and Carol Whitman's house.

Why was Imogen going to their house every Saturday morning? Maybe it had been to talk about the restaurant, go over various business issues? But why keep it a secret from him?

He heard footsteps on the stairs and hurriedly reset the watch to how it had been and put it back where he'd picked it up off the table.

Imogen came into the kitchen, her hair still damp from the shower. She picked up her watch and put it on.

'I'll grab some breakfast at the restaurant,' she said. She gave him a kiss. 'See you in all your finery later. I'll try and escape as soon as I can, even if it's only to see the finale down at Heron Water.'

He nodded his agreement then heard her dash into the living room to say goodbye to Rosie. Two minutes later he heard the front door shut.

NINETY-FIVE

Saturday 20 March

Twelve red buckets, each with a label sellotaped on the front: 'Ripton Rhinos Straw Bear collection.' Lorna put the roll of tape away in the kitchen drawer and surveyed her handiwork. Each of these money-collecting tubs would be held by a member of the Ripton Rhinos at various points on the straw bear route through the village. Once the procession had passed and the villagers had followed on behind, the custodian of the bucket would bring it, full of cash, down to Heron Water, where Lorna would be waiting in her car. They would hand it over and Lorna would wait until all twelve buckets were safely with her before taking them home, where she would count the donations then later hand them to Simon for banking.

After she had proposed her idea to Simon, also suggesting that he and the rest of the Rhinos could go for a well-earned pint after the festival if she took the money home, he had put her completely in charge of looking after the buckets. Carol was supervising the children at the parade. All Lorna had to do was wait for the cash to be brought to her.

It was easy. Too easy. For a moment, Lorna had a stab of conscience. She shouldn't really be taking from the people she lived and worked with, the parents whose children went to school with hers.

But no one would know.

A part of her felt scornful of the system. At the way so much money was allowed to be handled by just one person. Even the bucket holders themselves, standing in the street in the dark; they had plenty of opportunity to relieve the weight of their load by several pounds. She sighed. It was a massive oversight really. Maybe in the future she'd point it out to someone.

For now, she picked up the stack of buckets and took them out to her car. When she next saw them, they'd be full.

NINETY-SIX

Saturday 20 March

All day, Dylan thought of Imogen. While he was tidying away the breakfast things, he thought of her running down that lane then going into that house. Again and again he pictured that shiny black front door opening and her slipping inside. Did she *slip*? He immediately felt guilty about his choice of words. Perhaps his imagination was going into overdrive. Maybe she was innocent and the door didn't close quietly and secretly behind her. But the image wouldn't go out of his head.

He took Rosie to the movies but he didn't see what was on the screen. His internal projector was running a continuous loop in his mind. That shiny black door opening. Imogen slipping in. It closing quietly behind her. Then his mind took him inside. Inside the house with his wife and James. Just the two of them. That was the version he imagined.

Suddenly he laughed, shook his head. Surely Imogen wasn't fucking that old, pompous bastard. It was madness, insane. She wouldn't look at him. She had standards.

He attempted to release his mind from the torturous

thoughts, tried to look for evidence to disprove what was plaguing him. If he could find nothing, the impending catastrophic disaster that was nudging at the edge of his consciousness would evaporate in a blessed relief. He thought back to the time James and Carol had come to their house for dinner after Rosie's birthday. Had there been any sign of anything between James and Imogen? He didn't think so. If there had been, he'd *remember*, right? He would have noticed something. Or he would have picked up on a distance between James and Carol. But there was nothing he could recall. Other than James being his usual supercilious self – all that crap about teaching at a decent school. Working in the private sector.

Dylan felt another landslide plunge into his world. The new job – the one he felt he'd got on his own merit. Had Imogen and James talked about it? Had they laid in bed together and discussed how to 'help' him, how to improve his lot? A fury washed over him as he made Rosie a sandwich for lunch. *You don't know that happened*, he reminded himself.

'Dad, can I go and see Tilly for a bit?'

Dylan turned, distracted. Rosie was asking to go and see her friend. He agreed, handing her the sandwich, and telling her to be back by four so they could go and get ready for the festival.

Once she left, he made a decision. He would see Imogen later. He'd ask her outright: was she having an affair with James Whitman?

What he didn't know was what he'd do if her face said 'yes'.

NINETY-SEVEN

Saturday 20 March

'Where did you tell your mum we were going?' Rosie asked Tilly as they walked away from Tilly's house.

'Just the cafe or something. She gave me some money. Shall we get a milkshake?'

'We don't have time,' said Rosie, leading Tilly across the high street to the lane that led to the woods.

'Where are we going?' asked Tilly.

'Wait and see.' Rosie hurried on, so Tilly had to run to catch up.

'What's with all the secrecy?' she asked, disgruntled.

Olivia's house was up ahead. No one was there because she and her family were out at horse trials until later that afternoon. Rosie opened the wide wooden gate and gestured to Tilly to follow her into the yard.

'Whose house is this?' asked Tilly, wide-eyed at them letting themselves in.

'The people who bought Lupin,' said Rosie. 'Don't worry, I'm allowed to come here all the time.'

It wasn't untrue but she made it sound as if she had permission to be there right now, which she didn't.

'Oh, OK. So are we here to see Lupin?' asked Tilly, confused.

'Kind of.' Rosie gave Tilly a hard stare. 'This is the secret,' she said. 'You have to promise . . .'

'On my heart,' said Tilly solemnly.

Rosie nodded, satisfied she meant it. 'We're going to organize a little surprise for Lara. At the festival. And I need your help.'

'What kind of surprise?'

Rosie heard Lupin whinnying behind her, knew he'd seen her come into the yard. She went to get two carrots from the shed, along with a ball of strong twine she'd seen on the shelf last time she was there. She put one of the carrots in her pocket and took the other to Lupin, stroking his head as he leaned over the stable door.

'He's such a nice horse,' said Tilly. 'It's so sad your mum had to sell him.'

'I know,' said Rosie, scratching Lupin's ears.

'It should be you riding him later too. You should be the Spring Queen.'

Rosie turned to Tilly. 'How are you with mucking out?'

Tilly pulled a face. 'You mean . . . poo?'

Rosie got a bucket from the yard and a shovel. She handed the shovel to Tilly. 'We need a couple of scoops.'

Tilly stared at Rosie then something twigged. 'Is this part of the surprise?'

Rosie smiled.

*

402

The two girls walked back up the lane, Rosie carrying the bucket. As they neared the high street, she stopped.

'We need something to cover it,' she said, indicating the bucket's contents. It wouldn't do for them to be seen carrying horse manure around. She didn't want anyone to see them carrying a bucket either, but the high street was quite empty, so she was planning on hurrying down towards the road that led to Heron Water as fast as possible in the hope they weren't spotted.

Tilly pulled at some bushes and offered up a handful of leaves. 'Will these do?'

Rosie nodded, pleased. They filled the bucket with the green cover, then checking there was no one close by, headed into the high street, staying as invisible as possible. There was only one other person on the other side of the road, who paid them no attention at all. Then they were in the road that went to the reservoir. Rosie kept a look out but not many people were around. A dog walker in the far distance but that was all.

'We need some water,' she said, and Tilly nodded. They went down to the shoreline and removed the leaves from the bucket. Then, careful not to tip out the rest of the contents, they tilted the edge of the bucket against the water so some washed in. A stick provided something to mix it all together.

It was heavier now. Rosie had to be careful as they walked back up towards the ancient yew tree. Behind it were some bushes and the two girls crept inside.

'Check no one's coming,' said Rosie, and Tilly peered

through the leaves while Rosie set to work. She threaded the string through the same holes where the handle was attached and tied a strong knot, leaving one end of the string very long. Then she got the second carrot she'd put in her pocket earlier and tied it to the long end of the string.

'What about Lupin?' asked Tilly. 'Won't he get . . . ?'

'I've made the string really long,' said Rosie. 'He'll be far enough away.'

Tilly peered outside again. 'No one's here.'

The two girls carefully made their way out from under the bushes. It had been decided that Rosie would climb the tree and Tilly would hand the bucket up to her.

Rosie wasted no time in grabbing the lower branches and, like a monkey, she was up in the tree in seconds. Now was the most difficult part. One hand clinging to the tree, she reached down with the other as Tilly held up the bucket, her arms stretched as high as she could. Rosie made a grab for it and managed to catch the handle. She tightened her grip, then lifted the bucket up onto the branch beside her.

'It stinks,' said Tilly.

'Only cos you're close up,' said Rosie. 'You won't be able to smell it when it's in the tree.'

Rosie edged up another layer in the tree's branch system, hidden now amongst the evergreen leaves. She carefully manoeuvred the bucket along a branch that had broken off in a storm a few years ago and, lying flat on the branch, her legs wrapped around it for dear life, she hooked the bucket over the stump of the broken limb. It swung for a few seconds and she saw Tilly jump out of the way down below. Then the bucket settled.

Rosie edged backwards towards the main trunk, then climbed down.

She dusted off her hands and looked up. You couldn't see the bucket from the ground – the leaves covered it. And it would be dark when everyone was here, so you *definitely* wouldn't be able to see it, nor would you see the carrot that hung down from the string just below the leaves.

Rosie looked back again at the ground underneath. This was where the Spring Queen's throne would be, where she would be crowned.

The bucket was positioned perfectly.

NINETY-EIGHT

Saturday 20 March

'Give us a twirl,' said Nancy, and Lara slowly turned around. Her green dress floated around her legs, the dozens of sewn-on fabric leaves lifting as she spun.

Carol clasped her hands together in delight. 'It looks wonderful on you.' She had also made a crown of yellow daffodils and attached more daffodils and white narcissi to Lara's shoulders. They tumbled down the front of the dress to her waist.

'I'm in awe,' said Nancy. 'How did you make such a thing?' Lara looked like some sort of wood nymph and she glowed with excitement.

The community hall was bustling with activity. Lorna was giving out red buckets and high-vis vests to all the collection volunteers. In another corner, Dylan was getting changed into the straw bear costume. Rosie was by his side. Nancy was aware of her glancing over as Lara got changed. Then suddenly, she walked over.

'You look really cool,' she said.

Nancy watched Rosie carefully, looking for signs of trouble, but she seemed genuine.

'Thanks,' said Lara.

'Lupin's outside,' said Rosie. 'Olivia's just tacking him up.' She produced a bunch of daffodils from behind her back. 'I brought some flowers to go on his bridle.'

Lara's eyes lit up. 'Wow, thanks.'

'He's really nice. Not scary at all.'

Unlike what was coming towards them. An enormous creature was lumbering ominously across the hall. Seven feet tall and faceless, its entire being was covered in dense, bristly straw. Tufts of it gathered at the knees, a thickened waist and somewhere a neck might exist. Two straw-clad arms lifted upwards and Nancy felt herself draw back.

'What do you think?' asked a voice from inside the straw.

Rosie's eyes were wide with alarm. 'Dad, you look terrifying.'

Nancy had to agree. The straw bear was monstrous. It was looking at her but she could see no face, no eyes, just a huge cone-shaped straw 'head' turned in her direction.

'How can you see?' she asked tentatively as she gazed upwards.

'Small gap. Here,' said Dylan, pointing with straw hands at some fronds somewhere on the front of the costume. Then he lifted the headpiece off and Nancy got a sense of relief as she saw his face.

'That is very creepy,' she said.

'Isn't it? I guess the villagers' idea of fun was different two hundred years ago.'

'I should think all the kids had nightmares.'

'For weeks probably.'

Nancy smiled. She knew this to be Dylan, Imogen's husband. She hadn't met him before. He seemed nice, not at all what she might have expected, even while knowing someone's wife didn't determine their own personality.

'Are you nervous?' Dylan asked Lara.

'Bit.'

'Don't be. It'll be fine. You follow the band and I'll be right behind you. And don't worry about the end. I take off the costume long before they set fire to it. And so concludes the ritual expulsion of winter and the Spring Queen reigns again. Have you ridden before?'

'Only once. On holiday.'

'Lupin's a great pony. Really steady.'

Nancy looked around, frowned. 'Where's Rosie?'

Dylan couldn't see her either. 'Probably gone to see Lupin. Trust me, he's really gentle.'

Outside, the light was fading. Rosie watched as Olivia finished tacking up Lupin in the courtyard of the community hall.

'Can I put a flower in his headband?' she asked.

'Course you can,' said Olivia.

Rosie tucked the small posy of daffodils into the browband. She took her time, waiting until Olivia turned away to put up the gangplank of the horse trailer. Then she whispered in Lupin's ear.

'Just eat the carrot. Like every day. OK?'

NINETY-NINE

Saturday 20 March

James pulled the cork out of the wine bottle with a satisfying pop. He breathed in the scent of the Chilean Malbec. Then he poured himself a glass, the rippling sound of the wine leaving the bottle putting him in a good place. Carol had taken her grandchildren to the Straw Bear Festival and the rest of the evening was his alone. He intended to drink his wine in front of the television, and watch the rugby.

He eased himself into the leather armchair and pointed the remote control at the TV. It burst into life and the lead-up to the match was on. The timing couldn't be more perfect. He lifted his glass, ready to savour the first sip of ruby liquid when his phone rang. The glass paused halfway to his lips. He looked at the screen of his phone. It was Esther, from the school office. On a Saturday. He frowned.

'Hello, Esther,' he answered, already knowing he wasn't going to like what she had to say.

'Sorry to disturb you at the weekend,' said Esther. 'I wasn't sure whether to call or not but then I thought I had better, just in case.'

'Go on.'

'I'm at the school. The caretaker rang me because the alarms had gone off.'

'Everything all right?' asked James.

'Oh yes, everything's fine. That is, there was no break-in.'

'Did you check the CCTV?'

'Now you know I'm not the most technical—'

'Esther, you really need to get yourself on a course or some—'

'If you'll let me finish,' said Esther. 'I eventually found the footage for today. There was nothing untoward. But while I was working it out, I found something else.' She paused meaningfully.

James put aside his mild frustration. 'What?'

'I think you'd better come and see for yourself,' said Esther.

James wasn't in the best of moods as he walked into the school office. His evening had been interrupted and he didn't much like Esther's insistence on mystery. But she had refused to explain what had made her ask him to come in.

She was sitting in front of the computer and when he arrived, she got up and indicated he should take her place. Then she clicked a button on the keyboard. In front of him, CCTV footage began to play out.

He didn't understand at first. There was Lorna Fielding – his wife's daughter – sitting at a table in the staffroom. Alone.

'We were scrolling through the footage to get to this evening,' said Esther. 'And we saw this.'

'What's she doing?' asked James impatiently. Then his jaw dropped as he realized.

ONE HUNDRED

Saturday 20 March

Nancy came out into the courtyard and immediately saw Rosie next to her horse. Not *her* horse, she mentally corrected. Someone else's horse now. Rosie stepped away when Nancy came out. Lara and Dylan were now also in the courtyard. The village brass band was gathered near the road, warming up. A small crowd was watching the start of the procession.

Nancy looked at the horse: Lupin. A woman called Olivia came to introduce herself to Lara and shook Nancy's hand too. She helped Lara mount Lupin and showed her how to hold the reins. She reassured Lara she would have hold of Lupin at all times – even though there was nothing to worry about as he was the calmest pony.

The line-up got into place. The band was at the front, followed by Lara and Lupin. Alongside them were a number of torchbearers, then behind them, it was the turn of the straw bear. Someone came round and lit the torches one by one, the wax bursting into life, lighting up the darkening evening.

Nancy looked up at Lara, sitting on the pony. Her daughter flashed her an excited smile and Nancy's heart swelled. Sam would have loved to have seen this, she thought, Beth too. She suddenly felt an overwhelming sense of loneliness that was physically painful. *Not tonight*, she told herself quickly, *don't go falling apart now. Not on Lara's special evening.*

'I'll see you down by the water,' she said with a smile, and Lara nodded. Nancy was going on ahead to get a good spot right near the yew tree, where Lara would finish this odd, ancient ritual.

The band started up and the procession set off. Nancy gave Lara one last wave as she rode down the high street. The deep orange flames of the torches rippled skywards, dense black smoke reeling off them into the air. The straw bear, from a safe distance, brought up the rear. Soon everyone had left.

Nancy had forgotten all about Rosie and it was a surprise to turn and see her still there. Rosie stared at her, her expression bordering on insolence. Nancy was taken aback. She was about to say something but then Rosie walked off.

ONE HUNDRED AND ONE

Saturday 20 March

From the kitchen in The Wood Oven, Imogen could hear the faint sounds of the band at the top of the high street. She was going to open an hour later tonight – most of the villagers would be down by the water until the solstice celebrations were over anyway. She only had a small amount of prep to complete before she could go and join them.

She started at a sound – someone had come into the restaurant. But she'd locked the door. She tentatively moved so she could see through the kitchen hatch.

It was James.

'What are you doing here?' she asked, coming round into the dining room.

'Saw the light was on – came to say hello.'

He looked distracted, thought Imogen. 'Everything OK?'

'Yes, fine.' He kissed her hard on the lips.

'Don't,' she said, pulling away. The procession's coming past soon.'

James pulled out a chair, rubbed his hands through his hair. 'Mind if I wait here until it's gone?'

His voice had a sense of purpose about it, thought Imogen. 'Before what?'

'Just got something to sort out.'

She was going to ask more but the band were coming into view outside the window. The players' brass instruments gleamed in the light from the procession torches. The drummers' beat thumped through her. Next to pass by was the Spring Queen. Imogen watched, tight-lipped as the imposter child sat atop the pony she'd once bought for Rosie. Then it was the turn of the straw bear. Imogen looked out at what she knew was her husband in the eerie costume. She smiled and waved. He didn't wave back. She frowned – she was sure his head was turned in the direction of the restaurant window, although it was hard to tell as there were no eyes.

She watched him continue down the high street. Felt James step up close to her, but she moved away. There were still people walking past outside.

James understood. 'I'll see you down at the water later,' he said.

Imogen nodded. 'Maybe.' She didn't like him being there, she realized, and thought perhaps it was time to bring an end to their affair. Dylan had done an amazing thing getting that job and she still loved him. Things were on the up for them. She watched as James left the restaurant. She didn't feel guilty; they'd both got something out of the relationship. She'd have to let him down gently, didn't want him making a scene, but she'd manage that somehow.

Imogen turned and went back into the kitchen.

ONE HUNDRED AND TWO

Saturday 20 March

They were together. Right now. He'd seen them in the restaurant. Imogen waving to him as if he was an absolute fool. As if he didn't know what they did together. James sitting near her, leaning back in his chair, arrogant as you like.

A new thought punctured Dylan in the gut. *They shagged in the restaurant too.* All those hours together, going over the plans for the new business. Just the two of them in the building. For weeks.

His throat felt thick with hurt and anger. He'd been such an idiot. He'd blithely gone on with his life without even noticing what was taking place right under his nose. *What is probably taking place right now*, he suddenly realized with a sickening lurch. The restaurant wasn't yet open. They were the only two in there. He'd almost let them get away with it again.

He stopped suddenly and took a few furious breaths. In that moment, the procession moved on. He felt a detachment from them. He had a physical pull to go back to the restaurant. To stop it, break it, before it completely broke him. For his own sanity, his own dignity, he had to confront them.

The procession was now even further away. A few people glanced up, bemused at why he wasn't following.

Dylan didn't notice any of them as he turned and strode back up the high street.

ONE HUNDRED AND THREE

Saturday 20 March

Imogen placed the last of the chopped vegetables into the fridge then took off her apron and left the kitchen. She got her coat and pulled it on as she crossed the restaurant. Grabbing her keys, she switched off the lights.

Then screamed.

At the window was a large lumbering monster covered in straw. Staring right at her.

She laughed with relief; it was only Dylan.

But why was he here? On his own? She looked out at him, bemused, and lifted her hand in a tentative wave.

He didn't respond. Imogen didn't understand. She went to the door and let herself out but as she came onto the pavement, Dylan had gone.

ONE HUNDRED AND FOUR

Saturday 20 March

'I can hear the band,' said Tilly, clutching Rosie, her voice high with nervous excitement.

Rosie pulled her friend's hands off her. 'Shush,' she said. They were watching from the shadows, away from the gathering crowd. Down a small bank, behind some trees. Up at the festival area the cafe was open, spilling light from its windows and selling hot drinks that sent steam into the cold evening air.

Underneath the yew tree, the Spring Queen's throne was now in place. A grand wicker chair, woven with ivy, daffodils and sweet-smelling daphne. Beside it lay the sword, a willow twig that also had ivy twisted around it, interspersed with pale yellow primroses.

No one had noticed the carrot in the dark.

ONE HUNDRED AND FIVE

Saturday 20 March

Dylan was walking at speed down the road that led to Heron Water. He reached the car park; his costume was cumbersome and he stopped. Looked around. The procession was ahead of him but he wasn't interested in that.

Christ, the bear thing was impossible to move in. Dylan pulled at the headpiece, then took off the wire frame body.

He dumped it next to a tree in the car park then strode onwards to the reservoir.

ONE HUNDRED AND SIX

Saturday 20 March

Lorna took the bucket from the collector, thanking him. She kept the light in her eyes dampened down – it wouldn't do to let him see her excitement, for this bucket was the fullest so far and there were plenty of notes sticking out from underneath the coins.

She got into her car that she'd parked a short distance from the cafe. Once the interior light had gone off and it was dark again inside, she held the bucket on her lap, shook it around a bit. Good God, was that a *fifty* in there? She pulled out the pink-coloured note and stared at it. Someone had been especially generous. Looking back in the bucket, she also picked out some other notes. Then quickly took out the daisy print purse she had tucked at the bottom of her bag and went to put the money inside.

Just as the passenger door opened, flicking the light on.

Lorna gasped in fright.

James got into the car and closed the door. He looked across at her, his eyes suddenly resting on the fistful of notes in her hand.

'What are you doing?' he asked.

'Just putting some of the money in a safe place,' said Lorna quickly. She ventured a smile. 'I like to take out the bigger notes from the buckets, keep them together. I think it's safer, you know, good practice. Seems less chance of anything going missing.' *Not missing, Jesus, that sounded so dodgy. And I'm talking far too much.*

Lorna swallowed, tried to calm her racing heart, and changed the subject. 'I didn't know you were coming to the festival this year? Mum said you were staying in and watching the rugby.'

James looked around the car, including over to the back seat where the other buckets were stacked. 'Those all full of money?'

'Well, not full, exactly but—'

'And you're responsible for collecting it all?'

'Yes.' Lorna was beginning to get irritated by his interrogatory tone.

'Is anyone supervising you?' asked James.

Supervising? Who did he think she was, one of his pupils? 'No!' said Lorna. She didn't like the way he was looking at her, as if he could read her mind. 'I'm actually rather busy, so if you don't mind—'

'I've just come from the school,' said James, talking right over her. 'I had a call from our office manager – you know, Esther. We had a little incident earlier so she had a look at the CCTV footage. Saw something that she needed to tell me about.'

Lorna's first reaction was one of tentative relief. This

seemed to be about something else entirely – certainly nothing to do with her.

'The footage was recorded in the staffroom.'

Lorna shook her head. 'And? Why are you telling me this?'

'It wasn't from tonight.' James's gaze turned steely. 'It was from the day of the second-hand uniform sale.'

The feeling of relief was swiftly replaced by one of ominous dread.

James continued. 'You, counting the takings.' He glanced down at her hands again, at what was in them. 'Putting some of them into a daisy-patterned purse.'

Lorna's stomach plummeted off the edge of a cliff.

ONE HUNDRED AND SEVEN

Saturday 20 March

The band was closer now, the drums puncturing the growing darkness, sending goosebumps running up Nancy's skin. The players, resplendent in their uniform, continued their march towards the water and the ancient yew tree. They stopped by the cafe and let the rest of the procession continue ahead of them. Nancy stood on tiptoes to peer over the crowds, her eyes hungry for Lara. She glimpsed Hannah and waved. There were a few of the other mums she recognized too. Then she saw Lara, a vision in nature's green and yellow, smiling as if she was having the time of her life, looking as if she'd been riding for years. Nancy was suddenly swamped with that most precious of emotions: maternal love.

The crowd lifted phones, flashes went off and the torch-bearers' flaming candles left a path of acrid smoke as they crackled in the dark. Lara and Lupin slowed, caught in the crowd, and Nancy briefly lost sight of them. She looked for the straw bear but couldn't see him either. Perhaps Dylan was also hidden amongst the horde, although with his height, Nancy thought she'd be able to spot him.

It's said that the one thing the human eye notices most is movement amongst stillness. Nancy was distracted by a sudden motion a short distance away from the festival, where it was empty and dark. Two faces, lower down, among some trees. Children. Hiding. On some subconscious level, she felt a frisson of uneasiness. Unexplainable but distinctly threatening.

She looked over. Then she saw them again, pressed close. Two girls. One of them, Rosie.

And she was staring gleefully, right into the crowd near the yew tree.

Nancy immediately turned her gaze back to the tree to try and ascertain what Rosie was staring at. But everything seemed to be fine. The throne was in place, waiting. She caught another glimpse of Lara on the horse.

Nancy looked back at the girls. *You're tired*, she thought. *All those sleepless nights. Maybe you're imagining things.* But it was clear they were beside themselves with anticipation and excitement. But for *what*? It panicked Nancy that she couldn't work it out.

Suddenly people were around her, blocking her view. She couldn't see the girls, couldn't see Lara.

ONE HUNDRED AND EIGHT

Saturday 20 March

Rebecca had decided to come down to the festival. She thought it was important that teachers were seen by the children to be a part of the community – especially something that brought out the crowds like the solstice celebrations did in Ripton. And the Spring Queen was selected from her class after all. She wasn't going to stay for long, she would say hello to a few faces and see Lara in her costume and then she had plans to meet friends for a drink.

She'd got a coffee from the cafe and was walking around, trying to find the best spot to get a view of the procession. It was busier than she'd thought and the place was packed. She decided to slip behind the crowd, over to where there was a cluster of trees at the bottom of a small bank. As she made her way, she thought she saw somebody – two children – hiding in the shadows of one of the trees. She narrowed her eyes; Rebecca knew mischief when she saw it. And then she clocked who it was.

'Girls?' she said, swooping down, making Rosie and Tilly jump out of their skin. 'Want to tell me what's going on?'

426

They couldn't have looked more guilty, but Rosie recovered quickly, lifted her chin.

'Nothing,' said Rosie.

'Something tells me that's not the case,' said Rebecca. She looked up at where the girls had been staring, over by the yew tree and the crowds. 'What's so interesting over there?'

'Nothing's interesting, miss,' said Rosie. 'We're just watching the festival.'

Rebecca raised an eyebrow. 'From back here?' She looked over again. Then she got it. In amongst the crowd was Lara on the pony.

'Have you two done something?'

'No,' said Rosie, incredulous at the slur.

Rebecca tried Tilly, who looked terrified. 'Is Lara going to be OK?'

'Why wouldn't she be?' said Rosie, answering for her friend. 'And it's not school, so we don't have to tell you anything.'

Rebecca had a sense of great unease. Part of her wanted to take Rosie to task for her attitude, but she had a feeling she should go over to the yew tree and quickly. See what was going on. With a last glance at Rosie, she headed back up to the crowd.

Rebecca pushed her way through until she could see Lara. Everything seemed as it should be. She stalled for a moment. Was she upsetting the whole evening by stepping in?

She saw a woman who was holding the pony help Lara dismount, then the woman tethered the pony to the yew tree. She took Lara's riding hat and handed her a crown made of flowers, which Lara placed on her head.

What is it? thought Rebecca. *What am I missing?*

She couldn't see anything. A space cleared for Lara to walk towards the throne under the tree and Rebecca suddenly stepped up.

'Just a minute,' she said, taking Lara's arm and smiling brightly. She had to speak loudly over the sound of the band. 'If I could have a very quick word with Lara.'

Lara looked up at her, surprised, but Rebecca guided her away.

'What's wrong?' said Lara.

Rebecca bit her lip. She didn't know.

ONE HUNDRED AND NINE

Saturday 20 March

'Please,' said Lorna, trying and failing to keep the desperation from her voice. 'It's not what it looks like.'

'I think it's exactly what it looks like,' said James. 'You've been stealing from the PTA funds, just as you're stealing now. Jesus, Lorna, what on earth are you thinking? How am I supposed to explain this to Carol?'

'Don't tell Mum,' begged Lorna. 'I'll pay it back, I'll—'

She was stopped as the passenger door opened a second time and a large, brutal arm reached in and grabbed James, yanking him from the seat.

Lorna heard a sickening crunch and blood splattered on the car window. She scrambled out and saw James lying on the ground clutching his nose, Dylan standing over him, his fist rising for another strike.

'Stop!' yelled Lorna, frantically looking around for help. She saw Simon approaching with another of the buckets. He clocked her stricken face and ran over, dropping the bucket of money and throwing himself at Dylan, attempting to pin his arms to his side and pull him away.

Dylan struggled against him, still a ball of fury.

'What's going on, man?' said Simon. 'Whatever it is, it's not worth it.'

'He's been screwing my wife,' said Dylan, his eyes blazing.

James hauled himself to his feet and staggered a few steps away from the car.

The fight had caught the attention of some of the crowd and people were heading their way. A couple of torchbearers, some of the men sensing a need to calm the situation.

'You what?' said Simon.

'Him and Imogen. For months.'

Simon looked at James in disgust, at the blood running from his nose. 'Are you serious?'

'Don't be so quick to judge,' said James, wiping his face.

Lorna shrank back as James's eyes rested on her. 'You want to tell him, or shall I?' he said.

ONE HUNDRED AND TEN

Saturday 20 March

Nancy tried to get closer to the front of the crowd. *Dammit, is the whole village out tonight?* She eventually pushed her way through and saw Lupin tied to the yew tree, nibbling at a carrot that Nancy supposed someone had left for him, hanging from the branches.

Lara wasn't there. The throne was empty.

Confused, Nancy looked around but she couldn't see her daughter anywhere. She edged through the dense crowd with a growing anxiety, looking for her, but the darkness swallowed everything up. The smoke from the torches that were placed around the yew tree was making her cough. The band seemed deafening, the crowds claustrophobic.

Suddenly a deluge of brown sludge fell from the tree in a loud splash and clattering of metal. It covered the throne, splattering beyond the platform. The crowd looked on, not understanding what was happening. Nancy opened her mouth in shock.

Brown mess dripped off the wicker chair. A strong, disgusting smell permeated the air.

People pulled faces, wrinkled their noses. Nancy covered her mouth and nose with her hand. The identity of the smell was indisputable.

Shit.

Nancy reeled. Horror and disgust engulfed her. Was that meant for Lara?

She spun around, appalled. Where the hell was she? She looked again, getting more frantic. People were trying to get away from the mess and were pushing past her. She stumbled, tried to get some space. *Where was her daughter?*

Then Nancy caught sight of Rosie still hiding by the trees. She was alone now. Rosie was staring at the throne with a mixture of awe and disappointment.

Nancy moved away from the crowd, propelled by a terrible rage that was primal in its power.

Rosie was so fixated on her failure she didn't see her coming, had no time to get away.

'What have you done with her?' demanded Nancy.

'What?' said Rosie.

'Lara! Tell me where she is.'

Rosie held her gaze. 'I don't know. Isn't she sitting on her throne?'

'Was that you? You rigged that up?'

'Don't know what you're talking about.'

Nancy tried to hold it together. She knew this child had done something to her daughter. Knew it in the very essence of her being. Where had she taken her? What had she done to her?

Nancy's voice was dangerously low. 'You tell me where she is,' she growled, 'or so help me God . . .'

ONE HUNDRED AND ELEVEN

Saturday 20 March

As Imogen came down to Heron Water, she could tell almost immediately that something was off. People were moving away in droves from the yew tree, their faces appalled, their conversations seemingly full of disbelief and confusion. The band were still gamely playing, the leader holding his baton aloft and conducting, even though it was clear to him that there was a disturbance of some kind.

Imogen moved closer, about to go and see what was going on, but it was then she heard shouts coming from the opposite direction. She peered through the darkness. There seemed to be some sort of scuffle over by a car. Was it a *fight*?

Oh my God, was it *Dylan* in the fight?

Imogen ran over just in time to see her husband's knuckles land on James's face. Her mouth opened in horror. And it wasn't the first punch he'd thrown, judging by the state of James.

'Stop!' she yelled, trying to get past the small crowd, some of whom were attempting to pull Dylan away, some forming a barrier around James.

In the dark, no one saw the straw bear – smaller, almost child height – stumbling slightly, perhaps unable to see through a costume designed for a taller man. The bear almost appeared to be disorientated as it headed up towards the fight.

Imogen shouted again. 'Stop! Both of you!' As she forced her way through the onlookers, a torchbearer was shoved aside.

In the chaos, no one saw the flame ignite the bear's costume.

ONE HUNDRED AND TWELVE

Saturday 20 March

'Maybe she's turned into the bear,' said Rosie.

'What?' said Nancy, confused.

'Yeah. Maybe she's gonna be slain.'

Nancy grabbed Rosie by the throat, pushed her up against the tree. 'Where is she?'

She was maddened with rage and fear. How dare this child keep her from her daughter? A black fog descended, blocking out all sane thoughts. The shutters slammed down on her soul. All she wanted was to wipe the smirk off Rosie's face, make her tell the truth.

She had been pushed too far, silenced for too long, a wild animal that had been tricked again and again into submissiveness.

She wasn't moved by Rosie choking, her eyes bulging in terror. She thought the girl was exaggerating, trying to trick her.

Then, a light out of the corner of her eye. Something moving. Flames.

Nancy looked up, confused at first. Then her world stopped.

The straw bear danced a petrified dance, unable to get free of the flames.

Nancy was engulfed with terror. Stricken, she flashed a look back at Rosie, finally understanding. *Jesus, no . . .*

She dropped Rosie, who crumpled to the ground, clutching her neck and crying big, snot-laden sobs. Nancy ran, scrambling up the bank to the figure on fire.

Flames burst from straw arms that waved frantically. Nancy screamed. She tripped, her fingernails full of dirt as she clawed her way back up. Even as she ran, the flames grew with a terrifying speed. She knew she couldn't get there in time and let out a desperate moan.

Then small hands tugged on her arm, pulling her back. She tried to bat them off, despairing as she struggled to get to her daughter.

'Mum!'

Nancy turned and wailed in relief at the sight of Lara, here with her. She threw herself down beside her, holding her, pressing her face against Lara's hair.

'I saw you earlier,' said Lara. 'With Rosie. It doesn't mean anything. It's not worth it. You don't find out.'

In the distance there were screams. People running. Jackets thrown and patting out the flames. The band abruptly stopped playing. Then the silence was punctured by the sound of sirens.

EPILOGUE

Carol had watched Dylan turn away from the procession with a note of concern. Where was he going? What was to become of the procession? She hesitated a moment – should she go after him and see what was going on? With a small sigh, she gathered her grandchildren and together they headed in the same direction as Dylan. She got as far as The Wood Oven, then saw him coming back at them. She was about to call out but he marched past, ignoring her. A figure further up the street came out onto the pavement. It was Imogen. Carol looked back in the direction where Dylan had vanished and shrugged. Something was going on between them, but she hadn't a clue what.

'Come on, let's go down to the reservoir,' said Carol. 'Maybe the bear's gone that way too.'

As they came into the car park for Heron Water, they all stopped, seeing something lying against one of the trees.

'It's the costume,' said Phoenix.

'We don't have a straw bear,' said Pepper sadly.

'No,' said Carol. She looked around for Dylan. Why had he dumped the costume?

'You could do it, Grandma,' said Phoenix.

She laughed. 'I don't think so.'

'Yes, you could. You *made* him. You can be him!' said Pepper.

She really didn't want to. It was heavy, that much she knew. But the kids were looking at her as if she might be SuperGran and save the day. And it would only be for a few minutes, while the ceremony took place.

'What about you two?' she asked.

'We'll be OK,' said Phoenix. 'Can we have some money for the cafe?'

Carol laughed. Gave him ten pounds. He hugged her delightedly then took Pepper's hand.

'Look after each other!' called Carol as they ran off.

That's decided then, thought Carol. She put on the costume and headed towards the water.

A few people saw her coming and smiled and waved. Parents leaned down to small children, pointing out the straw bear. The little ones looked on, wide-eyed, and gave half-hearted waves; part wanting to join in the fun, part terrified at the cone-headed, faceless straw creature.

Carol couldn't wait to take the costume off. It was more difficult to move in than she had anticipated. She was about to head over to the yew tree and let the Spring Queen slay the bear so she could find her grandchildren and join in the festivities when she heard a shout from the other direction. It was a voice she recognized: James's.

She glanced over, moving her head under the costume to try and get a better view. It was awkward – the slot in the straw for the eyes was not designed for her height, but she caught a glimpse of several men in what looked like an argument of sorts. Lorna was there too.

Something was wrong. Carol looked back at the tree. Maybe they could wait two minutes. She headed over to her husband and daughter, stumbling as she went.

As she got closer, she saw James had a bloodied face. She reeled, tried to move faster. Dylan was also there, she realized, and Imogen. What the hell was going on? Dylan was being held back by some of the other men. Was it he who had inflicted those injuries on her husband? Whatever for?

She was almost upon them when she felt a warmth on her arm.

Strange.

She tried to tilt her head, see through the slot. The warmth was getting uncomfortable now. Hot. Burning.

Then she smelled something. Smoke.

A rising sense of panic ran through her.

Carol's death hit Lorna hard. It wasn't until she lost her mother that she realized just how much she had taken her for granted in life. When the will was read, she learned she had been left everything. She was grateful that the two-timing bastard James hadn't got a penny. Lorna thought carefully about how she would use her inheritance and perhaps always knew in the back of her mind that it would pay for her children's schooling. She reconciled the thought that Carol hadn't approved with the argument that her mother's disapproval was only because she had planned to spend it on herself. Something that wasn't now possible. That cruise Carol had been thinking of. Other cruises to follow, no doubt. Lorna booked one for herself and her family in memory of her mother, and they enjoyed three weeks in the Caribbean that Easter. It helped her grieve, she said, to do something her mother was passionate about.

Thankfully her mother had never known about the theft and Lorna used a bit of her inheritance to return the monies she'd taken from the PTA. Secretly, of course, no one needed to know it had been 'borrowed', and James agreed to keep it quiet. He had enough to deal with regarding his guilt over the affair. Another blessing: her mother had never known for sure that James had been cheating on her. Worse, that it was with a woman the same age as her daughter. Lorna vowed never to go to Imogen's restaurant ever again.

At first, Imogen had wanted to involve the police. Rosie had been almost strangled, for God's sake. It was a terrible event in a night of terrible events, but when she brought it up with Dylan, he shut her down. Their daughter also had her hands dirty, he said. He didn't believe that Nancy would have done anything fatal and wouldn't entertain a conversation that she might. For once, Imogen had no choice but to go along with what he said. Their own relationship was also under scrutiny and, after many painful late-night discussions, they both decided it was better to part. Imogen moved to the next village and Dylan, for now, took a small flat there too, so he could stay close to Rosie. She needed close parenting, he said, still unable to believe the way their daughter had attempted to humiliate Lara the night of the festival.

Nancy had expected to hear from the police after her attack on Rosie. But the days ticked by and nothing happened. Rosie wasn't at school the following Monday and the restaurant was closed. James Whitman had taken indefinite compassionate leave and in fact never returned to Ripton Primary, instead accepting a new, more senior post some months later as an executive head in charge of a dozen schools in the next county. On the first day of school after the festival, Miss Young had had a talk with the class and Nancy was relieved at how she handled everything with care and sensitivity. Nancy had heard rumours that Miss Young was going to leave at the end of the year but a new head teacher was appointed and the gossip around the playground became that Miss Young had been asked to stay on.

Once, Nancy asked Lara what she meant on the night of the festival, that strange thing she'd said: 'You don't find out', but Lara looked at her puzzled and said she didn't remember. Nancy let it go.

Two days after the Straw Bear Festival, Nancy got a phone call from Martin that made her burst into tears with relief. Beth had come round. She was disorientated at first but every day she became stronger. The doctors expected her, in time, to make a full recovery.

October, the previous year

It was night. Dark. Lara rested her head on the window and looked up at the motorway lights, flashing past in a regular rhythm. It was comforting, added to the content, fulfilled feeling she had after a week's half-term holiday. They'd been to Cornwall and even though it was October, it had been unseasonably warm; the sun had shone every day.

It was quiet because it was so late. Only a few other cars passed them. And lorries, there were quite a few lorries, getting their goods to their final destination. Lara liked to look at the number plate country codes. Think of holidays in European lands: Holland, Spain, France. She remembered a trip to Brittany on the ferry a couple of years ago. They had eaten lots of crepes. Played as a family on the beach.

When she saw the lorry move across the lane, she thought it was overtaking at first. But it kept on coming. Closer and closer. Getting bigger and bigger. And then its huge thundering bulk was towering over their small car and it was impossible to get away. They were between the lorry and the crash barrier, and the lorry struck the passenger side of their car.

She'd never heard a sound like it. It was deafening, ripping at her ears. Buckling metal, crushed so that it filled the seat that was there, squeezing her dad with it as it concertinaed inwards.

Then screaming.

Lara's body was shaking from the impact. She was winded, confused. There was a pain in her neck from where it had whipped forward. Now everything had stopped. The lorry seemed to have become a part of their car. Fused itself to the front passenger section. Then she saw something in the footwell. A dark liquid pooling. With a shock she realized it was blood. She could smell it now. She reeled and felt herself gag. She was going to be sick.

Then she heard the sirens.

Later, Lara always asked herself the same questions. What had gone through his mind when the lorry hit them? Was he scared? Did he feel the impact? What was it like for him when he died?

When Rosie had teased her about drowned straw bears on the water, that day of her birthday party when they were all paddleboarding, Lara tried to ignore her at first. Paddled away so she didn't have to hear Rosie's words stinging her ears, but Rosie followed, taunting her again and again.

In Rosie's attempt to catch up with Lara, she threw her oar across, lost her balance and fell in. Lara watched her plummet beneath the surface in fascination. Such a violent sinking. When Rosie tried to come up, Lara lay across her board, reached out a hand and held it on the top of Rosie's head. She watched the bubbles escape frantically, bursting on the surface, watched Rosie's arms flail in panic. What was going through her mind? What was it like to die?

She stared, wondering.

Then Rosie's struggle seemed to weaken. She wasn't thrashing her arms about so much.

Lara was suddenly frightened. Jolted by a memory: the shock of loss. The awful reality of it.

She removed her hand. Raised it upwards and shouted for help.

ACKNOWLEDGEMENTS

Francesca Pathak, Jayne Osborne and everyone at Pan Macmillan who has worked so hard to get this book out there into the world.

Gaia Banks, Lucy Fawcett, Alba Arnau, Dave Taylor and all at Sheil Land Associates for being eternally brilliant.

Viki Hill, for her amazing medical advice. Any inaccuracies are entirely down to me.

My family for their continued support. Big love to Jonny and the girls.

A huge thank you to all the fabulous readers, your support means everything to me.

To anyone who has been bullied, or who has a child who has been bullied. Keep fighting back.

THE
BOY
FRIEND

He loves you.
He loves you not.

Amy is fiercely independent, with a high-powered career, a flat of her own and tight-knit friendships. But as she approaches her thirtieth birthday, she can't help but rue the one thing she doesn't have – a relationship.

Following a serious fall, Amy can't remember anything from the last six months. Not even the upcoming skiing holiday at a luxurious chalet in Val d'Isère to celebrate her birthday. And she certainly doesn't remember being swept off her feet by the handsome Dr Jack Stewart . . .

Jack is the full package – charming, caring and devoted to Amy. Everyone is smitten with him, but as the holiday in Val d'Isère goes on, Amy begins to find Jack's presence chilling. Is her broken mind playing tricks? Or is the perfect boyfriend really too good to be true?

THE
GIRL
FRIEND

A girl. A boy. His mother.
And the lie she'll wish she'd never told.

The number one bestselling psychological thriller

Laura has it all. A successful career, a long marriage to a rich husband, and a twenty-three-year-old son, Daniel, who is kind, handsome and talented.

Then Daniel meets Cherry. Cherry is young, beautiful and smart, but she hasn't had the same opportunities as Daniel. And she wants Laura's life.

Cherry comes to the family wide-eyed and wants to be welcomed with open arms, but Laura suspects she's not all she seems.

When tragedy strikes, one of them tells an unforgiveable lie – probably the worst lie anyone could tell. It is an act of desperation, but the fallout will change their lives forever.

THE
TEMP

**No one was going to replace her.
Were they?**

Carrie is a successful TV producer in a high-pressure job. She's talented, liked and well-respected. She and her husband, Adrian, an award-winning screenwriter, decided years before that they didn't want children. But now, just as they're both at the pinnacle of their careers, she has discovered she is pregnant, and is shocked to find that she wants to keep the baby. But in a competitive industry where time off is seen as a sign of weakness, Carrie looks on the prospect of maternity leave with trepidation.

Enter Emma, the temp, who is everything she could wish for as her cover: smart, willing and charming. Carrie fears that Emma is manoeuvring her way into Carrie's life, causing turmoil in both her marriage and her work as she does so. The problem is, everyone else adores her . . .

Increasingly isolated from Adrian and her colleagues, Carrie begins to believe Emma has an agenda. Does Emma want her job? Or is she after even more?